SANCTUARY

FIRST COLONY - BOOK 4

KEN LOZITO

ACOUSTICAL BOOKS LLC

Published by Acoustical Books, LLC

KenLozito.com

Cover design by Jeff Brown

Editor: Myra Shelley

Proofreader: Victoria Flickinger

IF YOU WOULD LIKE TO BE NOTIFIED WHEN MY NEXT BOOK IS RELEASED VISIT WWW.KENLOZITO.COM

ISBN: 978-1-945223-18-1

1

DURING THE YEAR since the Vemus attack, Sanctuary had become a community in its own right. Connor had lived there for the last eight months and it was peaceful without being dull, a bit on the edge, rustic, but most importantly, it didn't have so many reminders of everyone he'd lost. Perhaps this was because of the foreign nature of the alien ruins, which were constructed of a bronze-colored alloy with long ramps that spiraled through most of the city. For some reason, the aliens that built Sanctuary hadn't constructed anything like stairs, which led some scientists to speculate they must have had very short legs. The rounded architecture was tall enough for Connor to walk through, and some places were large enough to drive through, so Connor wasn't sure about the whole "short-legged aliens" theory. Those short legs would have had to carry a large body, which led other scientists to believe the aliens were some type of highly-evolved insectoid, but he didn't put much faith in that theory either. There were plenty of insects on New Earth, just not highly evolved ones. There was, however, an abundance of mammalian life-forms and an ecosystem of carbon-based life that Connor equated as a close cousin of Earth.

Connor spent most of his days in the ruins helping Lenora with her research and had begun to formulate his own theories about the intelligent alien race that had been native to New Earth. But his research duties had always been part-time at best, and he'd slowly transitioned into a point man for exploratory field-ops-type tasks. He'd also become an intermediary for the people living there. Dealing with other people's problems wasn't something he relished, but when it came to keeping Sanctuary's residents safe, he'd rather they came to him.

After the war, he'd had to distance himself from Sierra—and the Colonial Defense Force, in particular—which left him feeling conflicted about walking away from something he'd worked so hard to build. Some days he felt like he'd abandoned the CDF despite knowing that, due to having been exposed to the Vemus Alpha, he'd been unfit for duty when he'd first awakened. The risk of contamination had been much too high, and after the danger had passed, he found it was better if he didn't return to the CDF for his own sake. Despite Ashley's assertions that he was okay, there were people in the colonial government who knew of Connor's exposure and still wondered if there was something latent going on inside him related to the Vemus. It didn't matter that Ashley, the former Chief of Medicine at Sierra, and interim colonial governor had cleared him. He couldn't blame them since he'd spent quite a few nights dreading the same thing himself.

Connor had proposed the promotion of Nathan Hayes to General of the CDF based on his military career and Nathan's own actions on Lunar Base that had greatly contributed to the colony's survival. The colonial government had accepted Connor's recommendation and Nathan was a fine officer who had done an excellent job with the CDF.

Nathan understood why Connor needed to distance himself, but they'd kept in touch when time allowed. Nathan was a father now and had married Colonel Savannah Cross shortly after the war with the Vemus. It had taken awhile for Savannah to forgive Connor for relieving her of duty, but when their daughter Olivia was born, Savannah let go of her anger toward Connor. In the end, Savannah's presence during the defense of Sanctuary had been a deciding factor in the survival of a large portion of the colony's population, and while Connor didn't believe much in fate, he was still happy with the way things had worked out.

Connor's wandering thoughts were interrupted as the door to the ATV he was driving opened and Ian Malone climbed in.

"The seismic monitors are fine," Ian said.

"Matches with the quakes quieting down," Connor replied, but Ian didn't look convinced. "What is it?" Connor asked.

"Seismic activity doesn't usually just stop. It should take some time to settle down first," Ian said as he slipped into his seat in the ATV.

Connor hated it when Ian did that. Ian was known for speaking only half of what he was thinking, leaving Connor the task of pulling the rest of it out of him.

"Spit it out. How bad could it be? Is Sanctuary at risk?" Connor asked.

As if he'd been pulled from his thoughts, Ian blinked several times and shook his head. "I don't think so. I mean, it's possible that pressure could be building, but we'd see evidence of that. The aliens built a geothermal power-tap here because of its proximity to the fault line. Millions of years ago this was likely a supervolcano, or at least had the potential to be one."

Connor frowned. "Somehow this doesn't make me feel any better."

Ian snorted. "Remember Yellowstone National Park?"

Connor nodded.

"Like that."

"Yeah, but if I recall correctly, Yellowstone was much more active, what with Old Faithful and the hot springs," Connor said.

Ian glanced at him. "You're really wound up today. Let me be clear. We're not going to blow up in a supervolcano—at least not today or in the next hundred years ... probably."

"Thanks," Connor said. He glanced at the controls on the dashboard before setting off again and noted that the engine batteries were down to a thirty-percent charge—not ideal for a supply run to the remote caches but far from dangerously low.

In the eight years since he'd lived on New Earth, he'd taken so many things for granted about the sheer raw beauty of their home —humanity's home now since there was no one left back on Earth. Some scientists held out hope that there could still be people who had successfully stayed hidden from the Vemus on Earth, but Connor didn't believe it. The Vemus had been a ruthless, efficient weapon that had grown beyond its creator's control.

Though he kept his distance from the rebuilding of Sierra, he'd still been apprised of the latest theories for how the Vemus had survived the journey to reach New Earth—a combination of suspended animation and consumption of biological resources for the long voyage, which was science-speak for the Vemus cannibalizing themselves in order to survive. Connor had been around enough scientists to know they couldn't help their curiosity, but he'd rather forget one of mankind's darkest chapters.

Connor set the ATV at a comfortable pace as they drove down the path to the next supply cache. They were fifty kilometers from Sanctuary and heading farther afield for this supply run. Supply caches had been set up for remote teams to use when fieldwork prevented them from returning to Sanctuary, and routine checks were required since some of the local fauna had taken to raiding the caches on occasion. These small, rodent-sized, nocturnal raiders were highly adept at sniffing out improperly secured caches. Connor had seen images of the pesky critters. They were brown, furry creatures with large rounded eyes and hands that were similar to humans but with only four fingers plus the claws. Most wild creatures on New Earth had claws that were incredibly tough.

Ian settled back and pulled his wide-brimmed hat over his face in order to nap. Connor could have engaged the auto-drive function of the ATV but preferred to drive it himself, and he liked the quiet.

For the past eight years he'd been consumed with the Vemus threat, and now that he finally had a moment's peace he couldn't understand why the hell he was so restless. These past months living with Lenora were among the happiest of his life. Since being reunited, they had connected on a much deeper level than he'd ever anticipated. So why was he still haunted by nightmares? Sometimes he dreamed he was stuck in a sea of Vemus sludge while Wayne's combat suit stared at him, lifeless and intimidating, like the Flying Dutchman emerging from the gloom. Dark shapes of Vemus soldiers surrounded him and he was alone, suffocating. Just when he felt he couldn't take it anymore, he'd wake up with a gasp, shocked and sweaty. He had scars—the ones you couldn't see. He wouldn't have been able to face what he'd faced and walk away unscathed.

Lenora had her share of nightmares, but she tackled things a bit differently than he did. She had her research to focus on and Connor helped her with that. The work they were doing at Sanctuary—learning all they could about the intelligent indigenous species that had mysteriously disappeared—was more than enough to stimulate their imaginations. Lenora had been right. What they were doing here suited him, but at the same time he felt a growing frustration in the back of his mind.

A large group of people had elected to stay at Sanctuary after they could have returned to the main colonial encampments. Even so, Sanctuary wasn't a huge community, but it was close-knit. Most of the people who stayed just wanted to live on the fringes. Connor thought that some of them, like himself, didn't want to be reminded of what they'd lost, and he couldn't blame them. He'd committed himself to making sure those who lived in their community were as safe as possible, which sometimes led to him stepping on a few toes.

There was a lot of rebuilding and resurgence going on in the colonial cities, and cleanup efforts near the Lunar Base were almost complete. The derelict Vemus ships and large pieces of wreckage had been put on a course to intercept the sun. That way, nature would take over and none of the Vemus would survive to threaten humanity ever again.

Sometimes he thought about the billions of lives that had been lost back on Earth. Was it an accident of fate that those on New Earth had survived? Connor didn't think so. They'd stood upon the shoulders of giants and were able to claw a victory from certain death. When he stopped and thought about it, which he often did, it was a miracle they *were* still alive despite all they'd endured. He supposed the fact that they'd come here to New Earth and found something to help with their fight against the Vemus would be construed as providence by some, but Connor didn't necessarily agree with that. They'd put the pieces together and then done the work. Regardless, it had been a close thing, and no one would ever forget it.

He'd seen the rebuilding efforts going on at Sierra. Ashley was an excellent governor, though her term would be up within a few months and they would elect a new colonial governor. Ashley often complained about serving as governor, and her tenure had been intended as a temporary solution, but the fact of the matter was that if she chose to put her hat in the pot, she'd garner a lot of support from the colonists. She claimed that she wasn't Tobias, who'd been excellent at his job, but perhaps her long-term marriage to Tobias including during his two terms as governor had rubbed off on her. But Connor didn't think Ashley, whose first love was her career as a physician, would run a campaign to hold onto the governor's office, so there would be a few new candidates for the coming election. Connor had even received a small number of messages suggesting that he put his candidacy forward which he refused to even consider. He didn't want to run things. He'd served his time, both here at the colony and before he came to New Earth. This was his time now, his new beginning to make his life what he wanted it to be. And what he wanted was to live quietly, or as quietly as he could with an archaeologist who loved to discover and explore.

FOR THE NEXT FORTY MINUTES, Connor kept the ATV on course following the winding pathway to the supply cache. Ian snored next to him, completely oblivious. This far from Sanctuary the lands were heavily forested. Occasionally, he heard sharp blasts of air from the landrunners that sometimes made their paths through the forests instead of sticking to the wide-open plains. He glanced to the side and saw their thick, muscular bodies covered in long shaggy brown hair. The biggest of the group swung its head toward the ATV. The short tentacles along its mouth gave it a bearded look. The landrunner blew out a blast of air and several more came from around the trees to look at the ATV while Connor drove past. He didn't worry about them attacking. The landrunners' greatest strength was the high speed they were capable of due to their exceptionally long legs.

Connor left them behind and checked the recon drones on patrol. They would note whether any local predators were in the area and provide data updates to Field Ops. An occasional pack of berwolfs would move through the area, but they rarely came close to Sanctuary—with one notable exception. Lenora had cared for a berwolf cub she'd named Bull. Bull was now fully grown and moved with the agility of a wolf but was the size of a grizzly bear. The drones had shown Bull traveling with his own pack and his visits to Sanctuary were becoming less frequent.

Incredibly, the berwolves had actually attacked the Vemus during the assault on Sanctuary. Connor guessed they were natural enemies of sorts, or it could have been because of Bull's loyalty to Lenora; either way, Connor was thankful for the animals' actions. According to his friend Noah, it had been a very close thing.

The recon drones' status updates showed that there were no ryklars in the area. After their initial brush with the ryklars when they'd first pulled Connor out of stasis all those years ago, the colony had only needed deterrence systems to keep them away from the settlements. Once the ultrahigh-frequency signals that had drawn them to Sanctuary were suppressed, the ryklars had migrated away from colonial settlements, following the herds and essentially acting like normal predators.

An alert appeared on the ATV's heads-up display indicating they were approaching the beacon for the supply cache and rousing Ian from his slumber. A comlink call chimed on the ATV's HUD.

"Connor here."

"Hey, Connor," Chloe said. "I hate to bother you, but we've got an overdue survey team that's not far from you and I was hoping you could check it out."

Field Ops maintained a small squad at Sanctuary, but they were short-staffed and Connor had been called on more than one occasion to help with these sorts of requests.

"I thought Ramsey was on duty in the area. Can he check it out?" Connor replied.

"He was, but he's escorting another team and they're pretty far away. We received a distress beacon with a vehicle tracking ID of AC-217," Chloe said, then paused.

The tracking ID indicated it was an ATV assigned to Lenora's team, but Connor knew Lenora was working in the alien archives back at Sanctuary.

"It's Dash DeWitt's ID tag in the distress call," Chloe continued.

Connor blew out a breath. *Dash*, he thought and groaned. "I get it, Chloe. Send me the coordinates and we'll go check it out."

"Thanks. I really appreciate it. Normally I'd hate to bother you with this, but you did say you wanted to know if Dash gets into trouble again," Chloe said with a hint of amusement.

Connor massaged his forehead. "I know, and we'll see what's going on."

He closed the comlink and Ian rubbed his eyes.

"Well, I take it we're not going to stop at the supply cache, then," Ian said.

"No, we can stop there," Connor said and looked at the report Chloe had sent over. It was just an automated distress signal and any number of things could have happened to trip it off. Dash knew better than to not call it in though, which made Connor wonder if there was just a problem with the ATV's comms system.

"That kid always seems to find trouble," Ian said.

"Don't I know it," Connor agreed.

Dash DeWitt was a student archaeologist eager to make a name for himself.

"I wonder what he's up to now," Ian said and took a sip of water from his canteen. "Last time, he thought they'd found another site of undiscovered buildings."

"He's eager to prove himself, which would be fine if he wasn't so reckless," Connor said.

"So says every father, and I'm sure Dash's father said the same thing on more than one occasion," Ian said.

Dash's father had died during the war with the Vemus. There were a lot of orphaned children whose ages ranged from the very young to those on the cusp of adulthood. Some were students who rotated through various colony locations, including forward operating research bases called FORBs as well as the encampments. One thing Ashley safeguarded was the education of their youngest colonists. This was all in service of moving forward, and it gave the youngest colonists something to focus on other than rebuilding. All senior research scientists, like Lenora, were required to educate the next crop of young scientists. Because they hadn't gotten to fight in the war, and given that such a short time ago they'd almost died, some of the colonists on the cusp of adulthood had a burning desire to prove themselves.

Dash DeWitt had just turned eighteen. He was smart, competent, and contending with the loss of his parents. Coupled with a healthy dose of youthful vigor and a significant propensity for recklessness, these traits threatened to lead Dash into an early grave. Connor was familiar with the type and had been one of those eager young men himself a long time ago. Dash had come to Sanctuary six months earlier, and by now he should understand some of the dangers they had to deal with, such as the fact that help wasn't readily available due to the remoteness of their location.

Connor used his implants to send a signal to the recon drone so it would scout ahead toward the distress beacon.

Ian pulled up his own holoscreen and then brought up the supply cache's status. "The cache looks intact so I don't think we need to stop and do a full inspection. We should probably just head on over to the distress beacon."

Connor glanced at the status update and agreed. He was getting tired of babysitting Dash. What was it going to take for that kid to learn not to get in over his head?

Connor plugged in the new coordinates and increased their velocity. He hoped it was just a mechanical problem with the ATV, but with Dash's history, it really could be anything.

Connor suppressed a sigh and told himself to stop gritting his teeth. Lenora was always getting on him about that.

"Probably best to make sure our CAR-74's are fully charged," Connor said.

Ian glanced at him and then shrugged. He twisted around and opened the field case behind them.

They were remote from Sanctuary, so everyone had to be armed. At least Connor wasn't carrying the ordinary civilian version of the assault rifle. He'd modified his so it was a bit more powerful—not as powerful as his old AR-71, but it would get the job done and had enough stopping power to put even a berwolf in its place.

"They're fully charged," Ian said and turned back around.

Going faster made the ride much more uncomfortable, which irked Connor even more. He didn't want anything to be really wrong, but he hoped Dash had a damn good excuse for his latest mishap.

2

LIKING the almost prickly feel of his recent haircut on his fingertips, Dash rubbed the back of his head. He felt a bit of dampness from the sweat he'd worked up as they hiked through a canyon to reach this location. A quick glance at Jim showed him checking his CAR-74 hunting rifle for the umpteenth time.

Jim saw him looking. "We should head back to the ATV."

Dash suppressed a sigh and glanced at his friend. "We're just about to the other side and you want to turn back around? Seriously, Jim?"

Jim smiled guiltily and shrugged the narrow shoulders of his tall, lanky frame. Dash knew Jim wasn't tired at all. He could easily keep up with Dash on long hikes, but remote field surveys left him a bit nervous. Dash expected Jim's jitters at remote fieldwork would go away after a few more months; otherwise, why would anyone stay at Sanctuary, which was as far removed from the main colonial settlements as one could get these days?

Dash swung his gaze toward the other half of the impromptu survey team. "Do you guys want to turn back now?"

Selena Wilson looked up from the path and frowned. She glanced over at Merissa, who'd stopped next to her. "We haven't even reached the target location yet," Selena said.

Selena was in the middle of an educational track toward field biology in hopes of gaining approval to continue in the advanced colonial education program, and Dash knew there would be no lack of enthusiasm from her. She was almost as eager as he was about discovering something new.

Merissa gave Jim a sympathetic look. "We're fine, Jim."

Merissa was already in the advanced colonial education system for planetary scientific studies, and her rotation to Sanctuary was highly sought after because it was a competitive program. In the colony, the individual education programs were customized to play to a person's strengths, but it was the fieldwork that would allow a student to be awarded top-tier selections for their designated fields of study. This was the primary reason Dash had pushed so hard to come to Sanctuary and study under Dr. Lenora Bishop.

Dash's aptitude scores showed a strong inclination toward engineering. He loved figuring stuff out, unraveling the mysteries of the world around them, and there were no shortages of unknowns on New Earth. He had been highly sought after by the colonial rebuilding efforts, but he'd chosen archaeology. The intelligent species of aliens that had built a civilization here on New Earth and then disappeared was the ultimate mystery. This appealed to him much more than rebuilding what they'd lost during the war with the Vemus. He was more than just another engineer.

Selena and Merissa walked on ahead of them and Dash gave Jim a playful swat on the shoulder.

"I was just checking," Jim said.

Dash leaned over so only Jim could hear. "She noticed, buddy.

Your concern was . . . well received."

Jim jabbed his elbow into Dash's side, catching him off-guard. Dash laughed.

Jim had only been living at Sanctuary for a month and volunteered in the Field Ops office there, which didn't qualify him for fieldwork yet, but Dash thought Jim could use some fresh air and a break from his internship.

Dash took out his PDA and checked the information he'd copied from the alien archives discovered at Sanctuary.

"The map says there should be something at the end of the canyon," Dash said.

"There better be; otherwise, this field trip is a bust. As it is, we'll not get back before nightfall," Merissa said with a hint of annoyance.

They'd left before sunrise and it had taken most of the morning to reach this location. They were over a hundred kilometers from Sanctuary, which didn't sound very far except that there were no roads or marked paths they could follow to get out here. When they'd come upon the canyon, they realized that going around might have added days to the survey, which they weren't equipped to deal with, and carried the extra bonus for Dash of incurring the wrath of Connor Gates. Connor would likely be angry with him for this little field trip, but Connor was always irritated by something these days, so Dash considered it a breakeven proposition.

After a steady descent into the canyon the path narrowed considerably, which had instigated the discussion of heading back, but Dash wasn't too serious about that. Going through the canyon would be the quickest way. Their ATV couldn't fit through and the path hadn't widened as he'd hoped it would. They'd decided to take their field kits and hunting rifles and push on by foot. He'd set an hourly check-in beacon for the ATV so they could easily find their way back once they'd finished scouting the area. This whole effort would have been much easier if they could've flown one of the C-cat transports.

"Okay, let's go over this again," Merissa said as they walked along the path.

"It's the same as before," Dash said.

Merissa arched a dark eyebrow, but her smooth, golden features remained impassive as always. She was a poker player; there was no doubt about that.

"As if you don't want to talk about what you found again," Merissa chided.

Dash snorted. "You got me," he said and stuck his PDA into his backpack. "In the archives, I found a reference to the layout of Sanctuary, like a city schematic, but on it were structures beyond the city borders. The locations were marked, but there was no other mention of what they were or how they were used. A few of the locations have been scouted, but nothing was found. Dr. Kabbot thought they might have been marked as future sites for where the NEIIS intended to expand the city."

Merissa shook her head and rolled her hazel-colored eyes. "I never liked that name for them."

"New Earth Indigenous Intelligent Species is more of a mouthful," Dash replied.

"I know. Believe me, I know," Merissa said.

"We can call them Bobs if you want," Dash offered.

"Or Janes," Selena offered gleefully.

"So much for creativity," Merissa said.

"You can call them whatever you want, but it doesn't change anything," Dash said.

Merissa shrugged.

"The reason this site is important—"

"Uh, the reason you *think* it's important," Jim chimed in.

"Thanks, appreciate that, buddy," Dash said dryly. "—is that it's the most remote and it heads away from any other settlement we've found to date. Since we don't know what's beyond, it's incredibly interesting. Worth checking, in my estimation."

"I thought you said the reference was obscure," Merissa said.

"It is, but why would they put something all the way out here if it didn't lead anywhere?"

This drew silent stares from the others.

"Think about it. Why do we place something in a remote location? It could be something used for safekeeping, another storage facility, or a backup site. The possibilities are endless," Dash said.

"Or it could be as Dr. Kabbot already said—it was marked as a future site for something else and they never did anything with it," Merissa replied.

Dash shook his head. He'd seen the data and had been around the NEIIS architecture enough to know they didn't do anything without a reason. "Either way, we'll find out shortly."

"What did Dr. Bishop think of all this?" Merissa asked.

Dash's brow wrinkled as he glanced up at the canyon ridge.

Merissa repeated herself and Dash cursed inwardly. He should have known she wouldn't let up.

Dash looked back at them. "I didn't tell her about it."

Merissa frowned in consternation. "What!"

Selena gasped. "You didn't say anything to her? I thought Dr. Bishop knew about the site."

"She knows about the site. At least I think she does," Dash said quickly. "No, she does; I'm sure of it."

"Does she know we're out here?" Merissa asked.

Jim gave Dash a helpless look. Jim already knew that no one had given Dash actual permission for this field survey mission.

"Not exactly," Dash admitted and quickened his pace.

"Let me get this straight," Merissa said as she caught up with him. "The archaeological team of which you're a part falls under Dr. Bishop's domain, but you think that if you make this new discovery you'll get some credit for the contribution?"

Dash shook his head. "No, it's not like that at all. Technically, any discoveries made in the vicinity of Sanctuary would be associated with Dr. Bishop."

Merissa twisted her lips into an unconvinced frown. "So what's the rush then?"

"I'm not rushing," Dash replied, and glanced at the others. "The field is where the real work is done. They've had plenty of people devoting all their time to Sanctuary and the archives. With the constraints on Field Ops escorts, it would have been months before anyone would even consider coming out here. So I figured, why not gather some of the top people here for a little field trip and perhaps we'll find something interesting—something that will get the attention this new site deserves."

Merissa seemed to consider this for a moment and some of her ire appeared to dissipate.

"See, you agree with me," Dash said.

Merissa sighed. "I wouldn't go that far," she said and glanced at Selena.

"Dash isn't wrong about the timeframe for Field Ops," Jim said. "I hear Captain Ramsey talk about it a lot. Personnel available for field missions are restricted because of the colonial rebuilding efforts going on at the main city sites."

Selena nodded. "Dr. Wilson talks about it too. We had to wait almost three weeks for escorts for a standard field biological excursion."

"See?" Dash said. "We're all being kept under lock and key, doing busy work. The Vemus are gone. I understand that we need to rebuild and that safety is a number-one priority. You can't be around Connor Gates and not get that message, but still, there comes a time when we just need to get back out there and explore our new home."

Merissa gave him a long look and then smiled. "Do you feel better now that you've gotten that off your chest?"

Dash's eyebrows drew upward in surprise. "You knew?"

"Of course I knew, and I also knew you'd go anyway," Merissa said.

"And you're curious, too," Dash said.

Merissa cocked her head to the side. "I wouldn't have come all the way out here if I wasn't. You're not as clever as you think you are."

Jim frowned at them. "Curious about what?"

Merissa didn't answer but instead met Dash's challenging gaze.

"Merissa's research track in planetary sciences includes a specialization in ecosystems," Dash replied.

"I'm not following," Jim said.

"It means that since we're restricted to the colonial city sites or Sanctuary, there's been a shortage of people willing to put resources toward FORBs. Sanctuary is as close as we can get to research bases out in the field for the foreseeable future," Dash said.

"You're remarkably well informed," Merissa said.

"Not really, just cleverer than I look it seems," Dash said with a smile. "It's the same reason I busted my butt to get out here. The reason I came to all of you is because I knew you'd be interested and it could really help us all in the long run."

Merissa laughed. "Stop acting as if you put this together for everyone else's benefit. You wanted to come out here to make a name for yourself. You simply needed our help to do it."

Dash shook his head. "That's part of it. If that's how you want to see it, then by all means. Regardless, we're here. Might as well see what we've found."

Dash walked ahead and the others followed, noting that the canyon had been opening up as they approached the end of it. Dash used his implants to check his PDA again and the coordinates appeared on his internal heads-up display. The marker highlighted a point just over the trees beyond the area where they stood. He tried to peer through the forest but couldn't see any structures, so he sent a signal to the recon drone he had scouting the area. After a few seconds, he saw the small drone fly overhead. Dash took his rifle from its sling and the others did the same. He kept the safety on, but it didn't hurt to be prepared. All field teams were armed with at least some kind of weapon; New Earth wasn't safe enough without them, with the exception of the cities and encampments.

The recon drone sent back a video feed and Dash shared it with the others. The four of them stood in place while they watched, since walking while watching a video feed wasn't recommended. The drone was in survey mode, which made for smoother flying at slower speeds. The targeting systems cataloged anomalies until they could be identified. Dash studied the video feed, taking in all the details, and saw an area ahead of the drone that looked like a nest of long, thick vines.

"That's it," Dash said.

"How can you tell?" Merissa asked.

Dash took a snapshot of the image and set the drone to survey the area. "Because vines like those grow over and around existing structures. That formation isn't natural. See the curvature?"

Dash highlighted the area on the image on his heads-up display and shared it with the others.

Jim blew out a breath. "Good eye, Dash," he said, sounding impressed.

Merissa regarded him for a moment before giving him a nod.

"Let's go see what we've found," Dash said.

3

THEY LEFT the rocky remnants of the canyon, which quickly became more forested. Swollen reddish gourds grew along the vines that stretched along the woodland path. Some of the vines windmilled around, forming giant spindles. Dash kept a careful watch on the tree canopy. Some of New Earth's creatures spent the bulk of their lives among the highest branches, but after a few moments he suspected those creatures were deeper in the forest. Being so close to the canyon, the trees in the area weren't quite as tall as they would be several kilometers away.

Jim stopped walking and Selena almost walked right into him. "A little warning next time," she scolded.

Jim muttered an apology while frowning at his PDA.

"What is it?" Dash asked.

"The ATV beacon failed to check in. I hadn't noticed until now, but it's overdue by thirty minutes," Jim said.

Dash pressed his lips together in thought while he glanced back at the canyon. "We're about five or six kilometers away, but maybe the signal just has trouble getting through."

Jim glanced back at the canyon in thought. "Yeah, maybe."

Dash waited a moment. "Come on, it's nothing. Let's keep going. It's not like someone stole it."

Jim jutted his chin for them to keep going. Dash took point and they continued. Ten minutes later they reached the tangle of vines and Dash couldn't keep from grinning. His heart was thumping in his chest. They'd found something. He saw the aged bronze metallic alloy the NEIIS used between the thick tawny vines. He was so excited that he grabbed the person closest to him, which happened to be Merissa. She was startled for a moment but then pushed him away, and Selena grinned.

The NEIIS building had a dome-shaped roof which matched the rounded architecture they'd seen the NEIIS use for aboveground construction.

"It doesn't look like their subterranean buildings at Sanctuary," Jim said.

"No, they build them differently above the ground. Most archaeologists believe it's because they were built in two different eras. The aboveground buildings appear to be older; then, something drove the NEIIS to build subterranean dwellings or in difficult-to-reach places," Dash said.

Selena nodded. "We still don't know what happened to them. We haven't found any fossils, only what they've built and indications that they manipulated the genetics of some of the species found here."

"So, I guess them all climbing aboard a spaceship and leaving is out of the question?" Jim asked.

Dash shrugged. "They haven't found anything that indicates the NEIIS had the technology to do that—at least not yet. There are still huge portions of this continent that have never been visited, let alone studied. Who knows what we'll find?"

They circled the old building, looking for a way in. Dash pulled at the vines, searching for a door, but they couldn't find anything. The tracker in his internal heads-up display showed that the building was seventeen meters across and six meters tall.

"Okay, where's the door?" Merissa asked.

She looked pointedly at Dash and he frowned. "It's not like they built this thing and wouldn't have a way to get inside," he said.

"There are too many vines. We need to come back with something to cut through them," Selena said.

Merissa agreed and Jim looked conflicted as he held up his hands from the side.

"We *did* find it," Jim said.

Dash turned away from them and kept searching. There had to be a way to get inside. They couldn't come all this way and not get in. He turned toward the others and smiled. "Well, if we can't find the door, there might be a way to get inside from the roof," Dash said.

Merissa frowned and Dash sent the latest drone image of the roof to them. There was a large opening that looked like it had surrendered to the crushing pressure of the weight of the vines. Dash shrugged off his backpack and pulled out a small grappling hook and rope he'd been carrying. He had more than enough to reach the rooftop of a structure three times the size of this one. He took a few steps back and unfurled the rope in elongated sections as far as his arms could stretch, then swung the end with the grappling hook around, using its weight to build up the momentum he needed. He then released the hook and hurled it well over the rooftop. The drone feed showed that it had landed in the hole on the roof.

"Two points!" Jim shouted.

Dash grinned and quickly pulled out the slack until the rope was taut. He gave the rope a few powerful pulls to test that it would hold and was secured in place.

Dash glanced at Merissa. "Ladies first?" he asked.

"And rob you of this moment? I wouldn't dream of it," Merissa replied.

"Okay, I'll go first," Dash said.

Holding the rope, he quickly climbed up the wall of vines. A few minutes later he was at the top, hardly having broken a sweat. He stood up and looked back down at the others.

"I'll look for a door from inside," Dash said.

He used the vines to climb down into the building and dropped the last few feet, then pulled out a headlamp and strapped it to his head. Perhaps he'd request upgrades to his implants so he could see better in the dim light next time he was at Sierra.

"Find the door yet?" Jim shouted.

Dash glanced around. The forest had done its utmost to reclaim this small bit from the NEIIS.

Jim shouted again.

"Give me a minute, will ya?" Dash shouted back.

The vines weren't as thick inside, but they did litter the floor and he had to watch his step. He went over to the wall and looked for a control panel. The walls were covered with moss and dirt from prolonged exposure. Dash used his fingers to claw away the dirt to get at the actual wall, and after a few minutes of searching, he found a rounded control panel similar to what they had in Sanctuary. At least this had been built near the same time. He brushed away the dirt and saw that the panel had a faint red glow. Dash's eyes lit up. This place still had power! He pressed the panel and heard a mechanical whirl as the gears inside the walls strained to open the door. The sound became louder and a curved door pulled inside the wall and then stopped. The opening was just shy of a full meter, which was enough for the others to easily squeeze through.

The air inside the NEIIS building was moist, carrying an odor of mold. Merissa kept running her hands through her thick brown hair as if she feared something was crawling in it. Selena did the same. Dash and Jim both had short, cropped haircuts so there wasn't much to inspect.

"I'm surprised there's still power in this place," Jim said.

"In Sanctuary, the doors to the major structures ran on redundant power supplies, but I don't think this one's going to work again," Dash said. The control panel was dark now, but at least they were inside.

Now that the others were there, Dash took a good look around. There were a few NEIIS workstations that had been completely destroyed by exposure. As they walked away from the door, each of them put on their own headlamps, and shafts of light lit up the inside. Dash caught a glimpse of an intact workstation and hastened toward it. The NEIIS didn't use wallscreens, but they did project their computer interfaces onto a tightly knitted mesh.

The console looked dead and Dash squatted down at the base. He pulled open the panel and scooped out some dirt and leaves that had somehow made their way inside, blowing to clear away the rest. The internal components all looked intact. He closed the console and stood up, then carefully guided his fingertips across the mesh surface of the console. After a few moments, the console began to glow. Dash looked at the others excitedly.

"Make sure you're recording this," Merissa said.

Dash brought out his PDA and set it to record.

"Give it here. I'll hold it," Jim offered.

Dash handed the PDA to Jim and then waited for the console to finish running through its automated checks. The others pressed in close so they could see what was showing on the screen, but the NEIIS computer interface was heavily damaged and kept showing interference.

"Are you able to clean this up?" Merissa asked.

"It's old and has been exposed to the elements. I'm afraid anything I'd try would just make it worse or break it all together," Dash said.

The image cleared for a moment before becoming fuzzy again. Dash frowned as he tried to focus on the image behind the interference. There were NEIIS symbols that ran across the top from right to left. Then a map came to prominence on the screen. There were more symbols on the map, except the layout of the land didn't match up with any area Dash had ever seen.

"Do you guys recognize this at all?" Dash asked.

The others shook their heads.

"Make sure you get a good shot of this," Dash said to Jim.

One of the symbols on the map began to pulse, and Dash reached out and gently pressed his fingers down on it. Just after he did, there was a loud screech from outside the building. Dash jumped and his fingers plunged through the fragile mesh of the NEIIS interface. It went dark and Dash cursed, but then there was another screech. This one sounded much closer to them.

"What the heck is that?" Selena asked, her voice rising.

None of them moved as they waited for whatever had made the noise to do it again. Dash leaned forward and strained his ears while he tried not to think about the NEIIS console he'd just broken. He heard the echo of another screech and then subsequent answering calls.

His stomach tightened. He'd only ever heard recorded sounds

of those cries. He glanced at Jim and his friend's mouth hung open in shock.

"What is it?" Merissa asked.

Dash brought his finger to his lips, gesturing for silence, and then waved them closer.

"Ryklars!" Dash whispered.

4

THE ATV's amber-colored heads-up display had a miniaturized map in the upper right corner that had a glowing marker for vehicle ID AC-217. The designation AC stood for the team or research department that owned the vehicle. In this case, it was the archaeological research group. The number was a callback to the FORB designation for the site. FORB 217 was more commonly known as Sanctuary. Connor remembered first coming all the way out here at Frank Mallory's request because of Lenora's major find —an NEIIS city. The NEIIS had used geothermal energy to power the city, which was something they hadn't encountered before in any of the other alien ruins on New Earth. At the time, Connor was too preoccupied with the Vemus threat to give it more than a passing thought, but since coming to live at Sanctuary, he'd realized that the alien power station was unique. The geothermal taps had been destroyed while powering the colossus cannon and they'd switched over to a smaller, more efficient fusion-power core that would suit the needs of the growing community for years to come.

"So what is it about this kid that gets you so wound up?" Ian asked.

"He's reckless and always in a rush," Connor replied.

Ian snorted. "Sounds like every other kid I know."

"He's eighteen, so he should smarten up sometime in the next twenty to thirty years," Connor said dryly.

Ian arched an eyebrow. "Lenora likes him."

Connor nodded. "She says he's got all the skills and energy to excel in any field he chooses. I've worked with him. He's enthusiastic and has good instincts when it comes to figuring things out, especially about the NEIIS, but he's untempered and lacks almost all caution or careful planning," Connor said.

Ian grinned and shook his head. "God, Connor, do you hear yourself?"

Connor frowned and glanced at Ian. "What?"

"Dash is young and eager to prove himself. Most people who were selected to be part of the colony were picked because they had a proclivity for taking chances. They didn't want people who were lazy. They wanted smart and active people. Only people who embrace the pioneering spirit come to a place like New Earth," Ian said.

"'Pioneers' is one way to put it. Do you have any idea how many of them died because they were completely unprepared for what they had to contend with?" Connor asked.

Ian tilted his head to the side, considering. "No, do you?"

Connor frowned. "No idea, but I bet it's a lot."

"So, are you really going to sit there and tell me that you've never broken the rules, rushing off and getting into trouble? I don't believe that for a second," Ian replied.

Connor shrugged. "Of course I did, but it wasn't like this. He's over a hundred kilometers out in uncharted territory. There are rules in place for a reason," Connor said.

"Which I'm sure someone tried to explain to you when you were his age," Ian replied.

Connor didn't reply. Ian was right; Connor had gotten into more than a little bit of trouble growing up, which had landed him in the military. He was a military brat, born and raised—moving around a lot, never calling one place home for very long. His father had been killed in action when Connor was fifteen years old. Admiral Mitch Wilkinson had been his father's friend and had tried to provide Connor with some much-needed guidance while growing up. He wondered if the old admiral would have found Connor's current attitude amusing, with a certain amount of irony.

Dash must have disabled the vehicle's transponder for the trip, they couldn't be sure of the exact path he'd taken. All they had was the distress beacon's signal to go by. The path they were on smoothed out so the ride wasn't as rough as it had initially been, much to Ian's profound relief. They'd left the thick forests behind and Connor brought up a topographical map of the area ahead.

Mapping New Earth in its entirety had been a low priority when compared with their survival. They had data from the seed ship *Galileo,* which had arrived at New Earth years before the *Ark,* but that data was becoming a bit dated. Connor knew colonial efforts would eventually return to studying their home at a much higher priority than it had been in the past few years, but he hadn't anticipated that the lack of work in those necessary fields would be hindering their daily lives now. He supposed it made sense, though. There was only so much they could accomplish at any given time, and this was just one of those times when they'd have to stumble a bit to catch up. At least now they *had* the time.

"Looks like he took the ATV into the canyon," Ian said.

Connor studied the map and guessed that whatever Dash had been after was either inside the canyon or just beyond it. He didn't think even Dash was bold enough to go on a multi-day field survey excursion, and they were nearing the limits of how far they could travel and return to Sanctuary in a day.

Connor brought up the recon drone interface and deployed three drones to scout ahead. They couldn't tell from the map why Dash's ATV was at its current location. If this had been a CDF operation, he'd have had one of their satellites focus in on the area so they'd at least have an idea of what they were going to find, but he wasn't part of the CDF anymore so that option wasn't available. He supposed that if he were to request assistance, he'd get it rather quickly, but the CDF had their own things to worry about and didn't need to be involved with this.

"Looks like this way is the path they most likely took," Connor said.

He tried to open a comlink to the ATV, but there was no response. He strengthened the signal in an attempt to capture personal comlink channels, but he couldn't reach anyone that way either. Connor pressed on the accelerator and took them into the canyon.

Thirty minutes later they were closing in on the location of the ATV's distress beacon. The two recon drones he'd sent ahead hovered in the air above the vehicle and the live video feed showed on the heads-up display. The ATV was nestled before a narrow pathway with rocky canyon walls towering all around it. The only heat signal on IR was from the main battery. The rest of the ATV's outline appeared in cool blues. The bright headlights from Connor's ATV flashed on the video feed. There was still plenty of daylight but the area they were at happened to be pretty dark in comparison.

"Doesn't look like they stuck around," Ian said.

Connor stopped the ATV and peered ahead. The rear of the

Polaris ATV Dash had used was parked in front of them, dark and abandoned.

Ian made as if to open the door. "I guess we should go see if it's operational."

Connor continued to stare ahead, using his military-grade implants to see the Polaris in stunning detail.

"Wait a second," Connor said.

Ian stopped. "What is it?"

Connor took control of the recon drones and flew them over the vehicle. Their ATVs didn't come in that many different colors. The ones Lenora had managed to acquire for her use had been in service to Field Operations, so they were a traditional forest-green in color. And there were jagged tears along the roof of this one. Connor had the drone circle the ATV and saw similar scratches along the side.

One thing could be said for New Earth's native inhabitants: most had sharp teeth and exceptionally powerful claws, but there were only a select few that could penetrate the armored walls of a Polaris ATV.

"I don't see any berwolf tracks, so this narrows it down a bit," Connor said.

Ian's mouth became a grim line. "Oh, crap. Ryklars," he said.

Connor used the recon drone's control interface and switched on the sonic wave detector. The recon drone slowly panned across the area in front of the ATV, but there were no ryklars in the area. Connor hadn't seen New Earth's famous spotted predator in years. They'd migrated away, and knowing how sensitive they were to sound and ultrahigh-frequency waves, they could be deterred from going into the more fortified encampments and certainly any cities. But out along the frontier was another matter entirely.

"This just became a rescue mission," Connor said.

Ian nodded. "Shouldn't we call this in to Field Ops?"

Connor knew Ian was right. They had to get help, but if they took the time to backtrack, the ryklars would be getting closer to Dash and the others. He raised the signal strength of the ATV's comms systems to maximum and tried to reach the Field Ops Command Center, but no joy. They couldn't even reach the comms satellites orbiting the planet, most of which were tasked with communications near the central populated areas.

"How'd they even get the distress beacon then?" Ian asked.

"The report shows it was intermittent and provided just enough data to give us a location. Probably was picked up by one of the comms satellites that's long gone by now," Connor said and rubbed his chin. "I know what we can do. We'll send one of the drones into the upper atmosphere toward Ramsey's team. Perhaps they'll pick up the signal and relay it to Fields Ops back at Sanctuary."

"Sounds like a good idea. I'll go check the other vehicle. We'll need it if we're going to get those kids out alive," Ian said.

Connor quickly coded a message into one of the drones and sent it off. He then had his remaining two drones scout ahead, running in whisper mode. It would be slow going, but he didn't want to startle the ryklars if he could avoid it. Ryklars always traveled in packs of anywhere from a few dozen to a large alpha pride of over a hundred. It wasn't until the NEIIS ultrahigh-frequency sound waves were added to the mix that ryklars gathered in much higher numbers.

Connor opened the door and stepped out of the ATV. His boots crunched on the pebbled ground of the dried-out river bed as he went around to the rear door and opened it. He reached into the storage compartment and pulled out an SD-15 Sonic Hand Blaster—not that effective against a ryklar, but it had other uses. Connor walked over to the other ATV where Ian was checking the vehicle's systems.

"There's still plenty of juice in the battery, but I'm not sure how we're going to make it through that," Ian said and gestured in front of them.

Connor saw where the canyon walls narrowed, making driving through it almost impossible, even with things like a double-jointed axle assembly that allowed the wheels of the ATV to function at steep angles. Perhaps he should consider submitting a request to have the Field Ops development team build an ATV that could also fly short distances. He glanced upward and noted the jagged walls of the narrow canyon. Maneuverability would still be a problem in these close quarters.

"Have a little faith," Connor said.

He walked ahead and ran his fingers along the canyon wall. As he expected, it was mostly comprised of dry rock to match the season they were in. If they'd had some explosives with them, they could have blasted enough away to widen the path.

Ian powered on the ATV and turned on the headlights, then stepped out from the vehicle and came over behind him. He glanced at the SD-15 in Connor's hand. "I'm not sure that's going to do anything for us," he said.

"Not with the default setting, but we can modify it. Do you have yours handy?" Connor asked.

Ian shook his head and went back to the ATV. "At least they had the foresight to come stocked for a survey mission," he said.

Connor had a small side panel open on the SD-15. "I said Dash was reckless, not stupid."

Ian snorted. "Alright, what are you doing with that thing?"

"Modifying the threshold for the sonic-field emitter so it directs a more powerful blast, but it only has an effective range of about one meter. I figure it should be enough to make this path just a bit wider," Connor said.

Ian watched for a moment. "And you say you didn't get into trouble as a kid."

Connor smiled. "You'd be surprised by some of the skills you can acquire by getting into some trouble," he said and closed the side panel. "Let's try this one first, and if it works the way I think it will, we'll modify yours."

Ian frowned. "What happens if it doesn't work?"

Connor frowned, feigning ignorance. "Not sure," he said in a careless tone and squatted down by the wall. He glanced up at Ian. "It could take my hand off, so be ready with a tourniquet, and be sure to grab whatever's left of my hand."

"Maybe we should wait a minute and test this thing out first," Ian said, sounding genuinely alarmed.

"Nah, it'll be okay. Or it could just fizzle out, but if I'm right, it should do something like this," Connor said and placed the end of the SD-15 close to the canyon wall, then squeezed the trigger. An ear-piercing blast shot from the weapon and gouged a three-meter section of the canyon wall into dust. Connor felt the powerful blast press back against his chest, and Ian jumped nearly a full meter away.

Connor grinned and then coughed. "I think that should work."

Ian's eyes were wide as he looked at the pathway. "I didn't know these things could pack that kind of punch."

Connor smiled. "They can if you override the safeties, but it'll only get three shots like that one before the power needs to recharge."

Connor fired his remaining two shots and then modified Ian's SD-15. Though Ian was twenty years Connor's senior, he grinned as he was about to take his first shot.

"Just make sure you hold it firmly," Connor warned.

Ian nodded and squeezed the trigger. Connor kept an eye on the upper canyon walls in case they'd inadvertently started a landslide while Ian finished firing his salvo, and Connor thought it looked like they could squeeze the ATVs through.

Suddenly, they heard the sound of shifting rocks along the wall and Ian glanced at Connor in alarm.

"We've got to move! Get in the ATV, now!" Connor said.

Connor ran back to their ATV while Ian leaped inside the one Dash had borrowed and darted ahead. Connor slammed his foot down on the accelerator and the tires spit out rocks and dirt behind him in a long stream until they managed to bite into the ground. Then the ATV lurched forward. Connor glanced up at the canyon walls as a rocky cloud of debris began to slide down over him. Rocks and pebbles pelted the armored roof of the Polaris ATV.

"Come on, baby. Just a little farther," Connor urged.

The ATV was struck by a small boulder and Connor bounced around in the cab. He kept his foot on the accelerator and steered the ATV away from the landslide, but he could hardly see in front of him. The ATV was slowing down, succumbing to the weight of the rockslide.

Connor growled and the electric motor let out a high-pitched squeal as he engaged the high gear. After a heavy moment, the ATV slowly started to move and Connor extended the suspension kit, forcing the tires into the ground. The ATV burst forward, throwing dirt and rock out in front of it like a dark wave, and then he was clear.

Connor blew out a breath and caught up with Ian.

"That was too close," Ian said.

"It was," Connor agreed.

He heard Ian sigh. "I thought I was either going to have to dig you out of there or explain to Lenora how I had to leave you buried alive."

Connor watched as Ian began driving forward.

"Glad to save you from Lenora's wrath. Now, come on. We need to get caught up," Connor replied.

Connor sent the drones ahead. He doubted the ryklars would be running along the canyon floor. They could quickly scale the walls with those claws of theirs and have the high ground.

"Damn it, Dash," Connor said, gritting his teeth.

No one else was going to die on his watch. Enough people had already done so and he'd be damned if Dash and the others he'd convinced to come with him on this foolish trip would fall victim to the whims of the young.

5

Dash glanced toward the door, which was covered with thick, tan vines, but that wouldn't offer much protection if the ryklars outside discovered they were in there. He heard Jim trying to calm Selena down.

"What are we going to do?" Merissa whispered.

Dash had no idea. He'd never encountered ryklars before. He was aware of them, of course. All the colonists knew about one of New Earth's apex predators. He'd read reports, but he'd never had a firsthand encounter with them. Their cries made his skin crawl. He tried to block out the sound and gestured for the others to come closer. "We sit tight and remain as quiet as possible. Maybe they'll just move on," Dash whispered.

The ryklars communicated with each other through a series of harsh grunts and screeches. Dash knew they were susceptible to sound, particularly at the ultrahigh frequencies. A loud cry echoed from outside, much closer than the others had been before. Selena jumped and then immediately clamped her hand over her mouth to stifle a yelp. Jim put his arm around her shoulder. Merissa glanced up at the roof and Dash followed her gaze to the hole he'd descended through. For the last five minutes, the ryklars had been running around outside, scouting the area, searching for them. The more Dash thought about it, the more he started to believe the ryklars had tracked them there from the canyon. He didn't want to think about what would have happened if the ryklars had caught them out in the open.

Merissa came over to his side and leaned in. "What if they don't go away?" she asked.

Dash tried to think of something they could do, and for a moment his mind went blank. They still had drones in the area, so he opened the comlink to one of them and a video feed appeared on his internal heads-up display. The drone was in wide-area-patrol mode high above them and he angled the camera feed to point down toward the NEIIS building. The ryklars had leopard-like spots with a gray hide on their backs. They had two sets of arms and thick, muscular legs. When they stood up straight, they were over two meters tall, with rippling muscles. They were immensely strong and their claws could rend through the hardened alloys used on armored ATVs. The ammunition they used for the CAR-74 hunting rifles could penetrate even the toughened ryklar skin, but the rule was to avoid a confrontation. Ryklars were cunning hunters and it seemed that they had somehow stumbled onto the research party's scent.

"How many of them are out there?" Jim asked.

Dash engaged the drone's recognition software so it would identify individual ryklars and a count appeared on his heads-up display. Dash shared a map of the immediate area with the others, and as the drone identified ryklars, markers began to appear on the map for the creature's locations. The drone made a wide arc of the area and the count went up to over forty, but only twenty of them were near the NEIIS building.

"There's so many!" Selena said with a gasp, looking at Jim in alarm, her eyes wide with terror.

"Hey," Dash said calmly. "We need to keep it together. If we panic, they'll find us. We just need to wait them out."

Selena nodded her agreement, but as she did so, they heard loud footfalls on the roof. The four of them instantly froze, hardly daring to breathe. Another ryklar reached the roof. They couldn't see them through the hole, but they heard them shuffling around. Loud blasts of air came from the ryklars' mouths.

Dash gestured for the others to move toward the wall. He brought his rifle up and Jim did the same. Merissa had hers ready, but Selena's hands were shaking so badly that Dash just wanted her to keep still. Dash watched the gaping hole until his vision blurred and he slowly switched the safety off his rifle.

Don't come in here. Don't find us. We're not here.

Dash kept silently urging them to just move on, but he saw a shadow move across the opening in the roof and his heart sank. This wasn't going to work. The ryklars were going to find them in here. If they left the shelter, the ryklars would pounce on them, so they had to stay in here as long as they could. Dash frowned, trying to think of something he could do to buy them some time, and his eyes widened as an idea popped into his head. He opened the drone's control interface and engaged the comms systems, then put his hand over his mouth to muffle the sound he was about to make. As he started making growling noises, the ryklars heard him through the drone outside the building. He had the drone fly by the ryklars in a sweeping arc, snatching their attention. The ryklars on the roof padded off and leaped to the ground. Dash continued to make noises, doing everything he could think of so the ryklars would stay focused on the drone and not the building they were in.

He glanced at the others and they were watching his actions in surprise. Then Merissa nodded encouragingly. Dash wasn't sure how long he could keep this up, but it seemed to be working for now.

"I'm going to check the door," Jim whispered.

Dash nodded.

Merissa went over to Selena's side and Jim quietly went to the door. He took a deep breath and peered around the corner, trying to see through the vines, but his foot slipped on the mossy ground and he stumbled forward. As his shoulder slammed into the doorframe, his finger involuntarily reacted on the trigger and a single shot burst from his CAR-74 hunting rifle. Dash was so startled that he stopped making noises and everything went quiet for a heart-stopping moment. Then the ryklars screeched in alarm and Dash watched the video feed in horror as they converged on the building.

Dash looked over at Merissa. "I need you to cover the roof with your rifle. Got it?" he said

Merissa brought her rifle up and aimed it at the roof. After a moment, Selena did the same. Dash hastened over to Jim, who was muttering an apology. Dash waved it off; there was nothing they could do about that now. He hovered in the edge of the doorway and peered through the vines. The heavy footfalls of a ryklar charged right up to the wall of vines and stopped. He could only glimpse the creature, though it was less than two meters away. Dash aimed his rifle where he thought the creature's head was and waited.

The creature blasted an ear-piercing screech—a hunting tactic ryklars used to startle their prey—but Dash had been expecting it. For a fleeting moment, Dash's eyes locked with the ryklar's feral gaze. Then, with sickening clarity, Dash saw the ryklar charge forward and he fired his weapon. The slug tore through the vines and into the ryklar's head, silencing it, and he heard the dull thump as the ryklar stumbled backward. There was a moment of heavy silence and then the other ryklars started charging toward them, shrieking.

Jim took a position on the other side of the doorway, but they could hardly see through the tangled vines. They had to wait until the ryklars were directly in front of the doorway before they could shoot, so the ryklars quickly adapted and began to avoid the direct route.

Jim kept blindly firing his weapon and missing.

"Conserve your ammo," Dash warned. "We need to make each shot count."

The ryklar count had jumped to forty-eight. Dash encoded a distress beacon into the drone and sent it high into the sky. The distress beacon would broadcast at the strongest possible signal within the drone's capabilities. Hopefully, somebody would receive it and send help.

Dash kept a careful watch on the doorway, but the ryklars were regrouping.

"Dash," Jim hissed. "I've got a signal for the ATV—*our* ATV!" he said, his voice rising in surprise.

Dash frowned and brought up the PDA interface on his HUD. Sure enough, there was a return ping from their ATV. *How the hell did it get here?*

Merissa glanced over at them and then back up at the hole in the roof. "What's happening?" she asked.

"Help is on the way. We just have to hold out," Dash said.

Just then, several ryklars climbed onto the roof and the team heard more scaling the sides of the wall.

Oh crap, Dash thought.

He glanced at Jim. "Cover that door. We have to be ready!" Dash said.

He moved away from the doorway and positioned himself midway between Merissa and Jim so he could assist both of them since he was a much better shot than Jim. He tried opening a comlink to the ATV, but just as he engaged the link, a ryklar dropped through the hole in the roof. Then the screaming began.

6

THEY'D BEEN MAKING steady progress through the canyon, going as quickly as they could, knowing that the ryklars were closing in on Dash and the others. Connor hoped they'd found shelter. As foolish as Dash was, he could also think on his feet and Connor hoped it was enough.

The path had widened and Connor moved his ATV into the lead. Ian was driving the damaged one and Connor didn't want to risk it any more than necessary. He hoped the ryklars would concentrate on his vehicle when they caught up to them.

The ryklars were cunning hunters. He had little doubt that they had picked up Dash's trail and were tracking them wherever they were. Field biologists often reported that the ryklars would only relent if there was an overwhelming show of force. This behavior was also influenced by whether the ryklar pack had recently consumed a meal. Unless the ryklars were under the influence of the NEIIS and their ultrahigh-frequency devices, they would rarely kill for sport. They hunted to survive but were also territorial. The colonists hadn't tracked ryklar activities beyond colonial encampments, something else they would have to rectify now that they were making a permanent home here on New Earth.

Connor sent his two recon drones to scout the area ahead. As they reached the end of the canyon, he detected the signal of a third drone—the drone that was registered to the ATV Dash had used. At least he'd had the forethought to take a recon drone with them. If their drone was still active, there was a good chance they were still alive.

Connor tasked one of the drones to scan ahead with infrared while the other one scanned with sonic wave detectors because it was hard to predict whether the ryklars would try to conceal their presence. They could hide their body heat at will and then the only way to detect them was through the sounds of their heartbeats. The infrared tactical display appeared on his HUD and he noted the drone had detected over forty ryklars in the area, and their numbers kept rising. They seemed to be gathering around a structure that was almost entirely covered with thick vines. Connor had seen these vines before. They were quite common throughout New Earth and were incredibly durable. He'd made use of such vines while training early Search and Rescue teams to build a hoist or any number of things.

Connor noted that there were several dead ryklars just outside a particular area of the NEIIS building, so he assumed there must be a doorway hidden nearby. He broadcast a comlink and it was immediately answered.

"Connor, thank god you're here! We've got ryklars attacking us in here! Please help!" Dash said.

Connor heard the sound of CAR-74 hunter rifles being fired and saw ryklars storming the roof.

"Those kids don't have much time. Whatever we're gonna do, we need to do it fast," Ian said.

Their ATVs didn't have any weapons, so the only thing they could do was try to bait the ryklars into chasing them.

"I'm going to try to draw them away," Connor said and glanced at the other ATV. "I want you to hang back and see what they do. If you see an opportunity to get near that building, go for it."

Connor had kept the comlink open so Dash would know what they were planning even if he couldn't answer them.

Ian pulled his ATV over to the side and opened the door. He kept his foot on the door while he stood up so he could get a high vantage point of the building the kids were trapped in, then brought his rifle up and began firing on the ryklars.

Connor slammed his foot on the accelerator and the ATV darted forward. He drove straight toward a cluster of ryklars and slammed his palm down on the horn, startling them. Connor plowed into the nearest ones and the creatures screeched in pain as over twenty-five hundred kilograms of hardened metallic alloy crushed three ryklars before they could scramble out of the way. The ryklars regrouped and turned away from the building, jumping off the roof and barreling toward the ATV. Connor jerked the steering wheel and pressed down on the accelerator. Multiple ryklars slammed themselves right into his vehicle, which rocked violently with each impact. Connor heard several animals stomping on the roof. The ryklars snarled as they tried to claw their way inside and Connor yanked the steering wheel from side to side, trying to throw them off. Then he jammed on the brakes and the ryklars were flung forward. Connor pressed down the accelerator to run them over and one of the ryklars pulled its companion out of the way.

"Dash, can you and the others reach Ian? He's in the other ATV," Connor said.

Dash's reply came through so garbled that Connor couldn't

make sense of it, but the ryklars were gathering around his ATV, building up for another charge. He couldn't stay there.

"Dash," Ian said, "stay inside. There're still too many out here. Only half of the pack followed you, Connor, and the recon drones are showing more on the way."

Connor cursed. This was a big alpha pack with over fifty ryklars, but there could be many more spread throughout a five-kilometer zone. He'd seen ryklar packs form a temporary alliance before, and if fifty were already there, then more could be coming. The only thing Connor could think to do was to keep driving around, hoping Dash and the others would get a chance to reach Ian in the other ATV. Since only half the ryklars had followed Connor, he'd have to go back and try to get more to follow him. But the ryklars were too smart and would soon divide their efforts, coordinating their attacks.

Connor glanced around and saw Ian driving around the building, attempting to draw off the ryklars as well, but the ryklars stayed in formation, one group tracking Ian in the ATV while others watched the building. Connor shook his head. They were in trouble. They needed help, and for the first time in a long while he wished he had the CDF at his disposal.

Connor raced back toward the building, kicked his ATV door open, stuck out his hunting rifle, and shot blindly as he made a pass while being careful not to hit the NEIIS building. He made a second pass, but the ryklars wouldn't chase him very far.

"How many of you are in there?" Connor asked.

"There are four of us in here, sir," Dash said.

Connor flinched. They had to get them out of there.

"Sir," Dash said, "we're running low on ammo and they keep coming through the roof. There's a doorway through the vines on the south side that we can get through. We're gonna have to make a run for it."

Connor glanced at the NEIIS building and saw where the ryklars had fallen on the south side of the building. They knew about the entrance, which was why they seemed to be sticking to that spot.

"Wait! That's where they're gathered. Give me a chance to force them out of there," Connor said.

"We're dead if we stay here," Dash said, his voice sounding thick.

Connor heard the sound of someone else screaming over the comlink, but there was nothing he could do. They'd have to take the chance. Connor swung the vehicle around and barreled toward the southern entrance, seeing Ian do the same. The ryklars formed a line and only got out of the way at the last second as he came to a stop right outside the hidden entrance. The ryklars swarmed the vehicle, rocking it back and forth. Connor tried to peer out the window and could only see the thick protrusions of the creatures' cheekbones, ending in stubby tentacles.

"You kids stay there!" Ian shouted.

"We can't!" Dash screamed.

Connor put the ATV in reverse and slammed on the accelerator. The ATV lurched backward and crashed into a tree. Next, he threw the gear shifter into drive and went forward, rocking back and forth, using his ATV as a weapon as much as he could.

Connor heard Dash scream and he glanced at the entrance but couldn't see anything. Ryklars were scrambling up the wall again.

Without warning, a high-pitched squeal sounded overhead as a CDF Hellcat came to a hover right over their position. A heavy, 180 gauss cannon unleashed its fury as the soldiers targeted the ryklars all around them, tearing through the creatures as if they were nothing but fleshy sacks of meat. Within seconds, a dozen ryklars were down. The remaining ryklars scrambled to avoid the Hellcat's weapons.

A comlink opened to Connor's ATV.

"Vehicle ID AC-218, this is Captain Jack Fletcher of the Colonial Defense Force. We have you covered. If you can head away from the building, we'll continue to take out those vermin."

Connor released his white-knuckled grip on the steering wheel, blew out a breath, and slammed his foot on the accelerator. He glanced at a drone video feed and saw a soldier sitting in a gun nest on the Hellcat, mowing the ryklars down.

The ryklars weren't foolish; they knew when they were overmatched. With so many of their numbers dead or dying, they quickly abandoned the NEIIS building. Connor saw the spotted predators running off deeper into the forest with the Hellcat in pursuit and watched as several ryklars attempted to shield others from the Hellcat's fire. The soldier in the gun nest didn't stop firing the heavy gauss cannon despite the fact that the ryklars were fleeing.

"Captain, they're in full retreat. There's no need to wipe them out," Connor said and brought the ATV to a stop.

There was no response and Connor gritted his teeth as he heard the heavy gauss cannon firing in controlled bursts, followed by a hearty roar from the soldier. Connor felt bile creep to the back of his throat and shook his head, then turned the ATV around and drove back to the NEIIS building. He didn't have far to go and arrived just as Dash and the others were pushing their way through the vines. They looked badly shaken. Two of them were wounded and being helped by CDF mobile infantry. Connor checked both the IR and sonic wave detector on the recon drone feeds, which confirmed that the ryklars had fled the area.

Ian stepped out of his ATV, first aid kit in hand. Connor climbed out of the vehicle and did a quick assessment of the four-person survey team. Dash wouldn't meet his eyes. They were all young, hardly more than students.

"Are you guys alright?" Connor asked.

They were in shock. Connor looked at the other young man, who had a long gash down his arm. "What's your name?" Connor asked.

The young man looked at him as Ian checked his wound. "Jim Tucker, sir," he said and then winced as Ian began cleaning the gash. "Field Ops," he said after a moment, as if he needed to validate why he was standing out there over a hundred kilometers from the nearest colonial location.

Connor looked at him with flinty eyes. "You want to try that again, son?"

"I'm interning at Field Ops," Jim said quickly.

Connor glanced at the two girls. One of them had ryklar blood splattered on her jacket, with multiple scratches on her hands and arms. There was gray medipaste on her wounds, which had staunched the bleeding.

The young woman met Connor's gaze. "Merissa Sabine, and this is Selena Wilson, sir," Merissa said.

Connor nodded. "Just sit tight. A medic will be here in a minute," he said and swung his gaze toward Dash, waiting for the young man to look at him. After a few moments, Dash glared at Connor.

"What are you doing way out here?" Connor asked.

"We were doing a survey. This is one of the locations we'd seen in the NEIIS data we found at Sanctuary," Dash said.

Connor didn't reply right away, preferring to let Dash's flimsy reply sink in for a few seconds. "And you thought you'd come out here, just the four of you?" Connor said and looked over at the other three kids. "Hardly a survey team equipped to be a hundred and twenty kilometers from

Sanctuary. And you left your ATV in the middle of the canyon."

Dash narrowed his gaze. "It's not like we knew the ryklars were in the area."

Connor drew in a breath to reply, but Ian gave him a warning glance. Even in the face of almost dying, Dash wouldn't take responsibility for his actions.

The CDF Hellcat flew back over and landed nearby, deploying the mobile infantry squad inside, all armed to the teeth in their CDF green uniforms representing the ground forces. The high-pitched sound of the Hellcat's engines powered down as the captain walked down the loading ramp. He was a pale man with reddish hair. The captain's gaze swept the area, doing a quick assessment, but when his line of sight came around to where Connor was standing, his eyes widened.

"I'll be damned. General Gates, I had no idea you'd be here. I'm Captain Fletcher, CDF Mobile Infantry, sir," Captain Fletcher said and extended his hand.

Connor shook the man's hand. "Captain, your timing is pretty damn good."

"We received a distress beacon from one of the recon drones and hightailed it over here. Coupled with the earlier ATV distress signal report we received from Fields Ops, it was enough to know there was real trouble in this area. I'm glad we were able to make it here in time," Captain Fletcher said.

At the mention of Connor's name, one of the soldiers' heads jerked in his direction. He had dark hair and sported several days of stubble on his face. Connor met his gaze, but the soldier quickly looked away and went off to check the area.

A CDF medic came over and began checking the others. When the medic glanced questioningly over at Connor, he gestured back toward the two injured kids. He had no injuries other than bouncing around in the ATV. With that thought, he glanced back at the ATV and noted that the ryklars had really done a number on it. The vehicle looked beat-up, with puncture holes in the armored plating that made it look like Swiss cheese.

"Your ATVs look the worse for wear. I'll radio in for a transport to get you guys back to Sanctuary," Captain Fletcher said.

Connor looked back at the CDF captain. "I appreciate that, Captain. I really do. You guys just happen to be patrolling way out here?" Connor asked.

Captain Fletcher was about to reply when one of the soldiers fired his weapon at a ryklar that had been struggling to rise from the ground. There were several more shots as the CDF soldiers made a sweep of the area and systematically made sure the ryklars were all dead.

Connor heard another ryklar snarl as it tried to crawl away. One of the creature's legs had been blown off by the gauss cannon and Connor couldn't imagine the pain the ryklar must have been in. He saw that the ryklar was trying to reach a dead companion that had fallen near the NEIIS building, but a CDF soldier brought his weapon up and took it out with ruthless efficiency. The ryklar collapsed to the ground with one of its arms stretched longingly toward another of its kind. Connor had never seen such an outward show of loyalty between ryklars before. The shooter sneered down at the creature and kicked it, hard.

"This one isn't getting up again," the soldier said.

Captain Fletcher gave him a grim nod. "Lieutenant Maddox, make a quick sweep of the area, then report back to me."

Lieutenant Maddox acknowledged the order, but his gaze lingered on Connor for a moment. The lieutenant looked as if he wanted to say something, but instead he turned away and started giving orders to the rest of the squad.

Connor glanced at Captain Fletcher and pressed his lips

together. "I appreciate the help, but the use of force here was a bit excessive. Once the ryklars realized they couldn't get these kids, they were in full retreat. Why did you continue to pursue them?"

Captain Fletcher was about to reply when he was cut off.

"We just saved your ass and you want to question our methods?" Lieutenant Maddox said with exasperation. "A little show of appreciation would go a long way."

Silence took hold of everyone. Even the medic who was tending to the kids' injuries stopped what he'd been doing. Dash's eyes rounded as he glanced at the CDF soldier.

Connor's brows pushed forward and he glared at the lieutenant as he reminded himself that he was no longer in the CDF, but there was still a decorum to be followed when addressing former generals of any army.

"I didn't say I didn't appreciate what you did, but the way you go about executing your duties is a clear statement about how this unit is run," Connor said.

Lieutenant Maddox sneered and his eyes glinted dangerously. "Perhaps we should've just left you for the ryklars. Tell me, how was the 'driving around in circles' plan working for you?"

Captain Fletcher stepped in front of Connor. "You secure that shit, Lieutenant," Captain Fletcher scolded. "You're addressing General Connor Gates, founder of the CDF!"

Lieutenant Maddox's eyes became chips of ice. "My apologies . . . General," Maddox said. "I'll continue my sweep of the area, sir."

Maddox stomped off and Connor noticed that Ian was keeping a careful eye on him as he walked by. The field geologist's hand inched toward his rifle.

"Sorry about that," Captain Fletcher said quietly.

"He seems wound up pretty tight," Connor said.

Captain Fletcher gave him a long look. "He's a good man. He just lost a lot of people in the war with the Vemus."

Connor nodded. "I understand, Captain. The war is over, but not for all of us."

Captain Fletcher regarded Connor for a moment. "And not all of us got to retire," he replied.

Connor's shoulders stiffened. He almost couldn't believe the stones on this guy and his subordinate. "I'm afraid I didn't have much choice, Captain. The circumstances around my retirement are a bit more complex than what people were led to believe," Connor said. He wasn't about to discuss those circumstances with just anyone, and certainly not a captain in the mobile infantry. That information was classified, but the reactions of both the CDF captain and lieutenant made Connor wonder what other CDF soldiers had really thought of his retirement.

Captain Fletcher nodded. "I figured there was more to it than simple retirement, but still, it was tough on the mobile infantry units when you stepped down. Meaning no disrespect, General, but you were the figurehead of the CDF. And sir, I'd be remiss in my duty if I didn't tell you that more than a few of us feel as if you abandoned us."

Connor glanced away and noticed Dash and the others watching them. Abandoned the CDF?

"The CDF is more than just one man—even if that man is its founder. It has to be. The CDF is all of us," Connor said.

Captain Fletcher regarded Connor for a moment, considering what he'd said, and then nodded.

"How is the mobile infantry these days?" Connor asked. He didn't like where the conversation had been heading and thought it best to redirect it to more common ground.

"Well, this is a good squad made up of select soldiers who're having trouble coping with the end of the war. We do largely remote reconnaissance and support work, sir. These men have been through a lot."

"I understand and I really do appreciate the help from you and your squad. We wouldn't be alive right now if it weren't for you, but there's a fine line that needs to be walked by people like us. You go through what we've gone through and you think you're fine, but you're really not. Some days end up being worse than others," Connor said.

Captain Fletcher nodded. "Normally these survey missions are a walk in the park, but we've had a couple of reports of ryklars moving south again. We were part of a larger mission tasked with reclaiming materials from abandoned forward operating research bases. That's really why we were in the area—at least, within a few hundred kilometers."

Connor frowned. "Must be a recent thing. We didn't have any ryklar alerts from Field Ops this morning."

"It's pretty new, but we didn't know they were in this area, and a ryklar pack of fifty or more is definitely a force to contend with, though perhaps not with CAR-74s. I'm sure a request by you to the weapons depot in Sierra would give you something with more stopping power, as well as something to throw on top of those ATVs," Captain Fletcher said and then frowned. "What were you guys doing way out here? This is pretty remote, even for Sanctuary."

Connor glanced at Dash and the captain followed his gaze.

Dash walked over.

"Captain Fletcher was wondering what brought us all the way out here. Care to shed some light on that, Dash?" Connor asked.

"We found a working NEIIS console inside the building. There's a map in there that has new locations we haven't seen before. We were able to film it with my PDA, but during the attack the console became damaged so we're not sure what other information is on it."

"A map?" Captain Fletcher said and rubbed his chin, considering. "Seems a far-off place for a random map."

Dash licked his lips for a second. "Well, it doesn't match up with what we have so far. This is a NEIIS map, but the land looks like it was in a different position from when the map was created, meaning the landmarks didn't match up. We'll need to study it further to be sure. We didn't get a chance to see it for long, but there were other locations out there beyond where we've ever surveyed before. Some of the locations had NEIIS symbols that are akin to the identification we've found at Sanctuary. So there could be other major cities. The possibilities are really promising," Dash said.

Connor noted the excitement building in Dash's voice. "This is hardly something to be celebrated. You and the others almost died. Do you really think it was worth it?"

Dash looked away, embarrassed.

Captain Fletcher cleared his throat. "I can have my engineers remove the console and bring it back to Sanctuary so you can study it," he offered.

Dash's eyes lit up and he looked at Connor with a hopeful glint.

Connor frowned. He almost wanted to refuse the request, but that would have been foolish. He wanted to find a way to drive the point home that what Dash had done was wrong, but at the same time, if they returned to Sanctuary without the console, Lenora would read him the riot act—at least in private. Then he'd be back out here to retrieve the console in a few days' time. "I think that would be good, Captain. I'm sure Dr. Bishop would like a closer look at this console."

Captain Fletcher nodded and began issuing orders for his engineers to go inside and retrieve the console and any other NEIIS tech they could find in the small building.

Connor walked back over to Ian, who handed him a canteen filled with water. They leaned against the ATV.

"This bunch is a bit uptight. I wasn't sure what that lieutenant was going to do," Ian said quietly.

Connor nodded. "Yeah, they're a bit more intense than I expected."

"At least it's good they showed up when they did. Otherwise, I don't know how many of us would've gotten out alive," Ian said.

Connor glanced off to the side and caught Lieutenant Maddox watching him. The lieutenant boldly met his gaze and then went about his duties. "Intense" was one word for it, but these soldiers were really on edge. Connor decided he'd be making a call to Sierra about this squad of soldiers. Sean Quinn would get this sorted out.

"I'll reach out to Sean when we get back," Connor said and thought about how the squad had mowed down the ryklars even after they were retreating. He understood securing the area, but if this was how they operated in front of civilians, what were the soldiers doing when there was no one else around? He looked at Captain Fletcher. The man seemed calm now but there had been times during their conversation when Connor could see the razor-sharp edge he tried to hide. How many CDF soldiers were just like this? Connor had no idea, and that thought made him shiver. He knew there was a colonial effort to reintegrate soldiers who had fought in the Vemus war, but sending them on remote missions away from normalcy might not be the best approach for these soldiers. He made a mental note to speak with Nathan as well.

Within thirty minutes, a troop-carrier transport showed up. They loaded the damaged ATVs onto them and Connor and the others climbed aboard. The flight back to Sanctuary was quiet. Something about that squad didn't sit right with him, but he wasn't sure how best to handle the problem. He resolved to make a few calls when he got back to Sanctuary, right after he decided what they were going to do about Dash.

The young man in question had started heading for the seat next to him.

Connor glared at him and Dash rolled his eyes and turned back around, muttering about talking later.

Connor shook his head, not trusting himself to reply. That boy had put all their lives in danger and he still didn't realize how close to dying he'd come. All Dash could think about was the discovery they'd made. He needed to have a serious talk with Lenora when he got back. Dash was becoming too dangerous to keep under control. Connor didn't know whether they should try to keep a tighter rein on him or kick him out and send him back to Sierra with the other misplaced youths. Connor chewed on the inside of his lip while he considered what to do next.

7

CONNOR SAT at his kitchen table, sipping a cup of coffee he'd freshly ground that morning. The coffee beans had been grown in one of the greenhouses a few hundred kilometers outside Sierra that had miraculously escaped the Vemus bombardment. He glanced at the skull-and-crossbones packaging that bore the name Colonial Death Wish. It was a dark roast blend, bitter and potent. Just the way he liked it.

Lenora entered the kitchen and sniffed the air, then looked at him in exasperation. "You make the coffee so strong I don't even need to drink it to taste it. You do realize that the instructions are more of a guideline than a recipe you need to follow to the letter," Lenora said and grabbed a metal coffee mug off the top shelf. Connor took a moment to admire her shapely legs. She wore tan shorts and had on her rugged brown boots. Her green, long-sleeved mesh shirt hugged her athletic figure and her freshly washed auburn hair hung down her back. Did she even realize how beautiful she was or what seeing her like this did to him?

Lenora poured a half-cup of coffee, then added cream and

sugar. She brought the cup to her lips but at the last second set it back down on the counter. She glanced at him and Connor lifted his gaze to meet hers.

Lenora eyed him suspiciously. "What are you looking at?"

Connor stood up and took a step toward her. "Nothing. I was just waiting for you to taste some of that Colonial Death Wish coffee."

Lenora arched one eyebrow and then lifted the mug to her lips and took a sip. She sneered and spat it out in the sink. "Oh my god, this is awful! How can you drink this stuff? It's not like you need the caffeine."

She poured out the coffee and quickly filled the mug with water to wash the taste from her mouth.

"It's not *that* bad," Connor protested.

He pulled her in for a hug and moved to kiss her, but Lenora deftly avoided his lips.

"No way, not with that nasty coffee on your breath," she said and slipped from his arms.

Connor laughed and retrieved his mug. Then, in open rebellion, he took a hearty swallow.

Lenora shook her head and made a tsk-tsk noise with her tongue. "You're really not playing your cards right this morning," she said and used the insta-boil setting on their water reclaimer to make some tea.

Connor shrugged. "I was already going down. Might as well go down in flames," he said and finished his coffee while polishing off what was left of his breakfast. Nothing like a three-egg omelet to start the day off right.

Lenora preferred a quick instant breakfast comprised of some kind of protein paste and dried vegetables akin to field rations. Sanctuary was their permanent home address, but Lenora spent most of her time moving from place to place for her research and food had become more of a necessary evil than something to be enjoyed. Connor, however, relished real food. He'd lived off enough field rations and ready-made foodstuffs to last a lifetime. If there was some actual homegrown food to be had, he'd gladly take the time to prepare a proper meal. Lenora had come to appreciate it, but most mornings she was just eager to get the day started.

Lenora sat down at the table and opened the holoscreen for her PDA. After reading some of the messages, she glanced at Connor forlornly. "We need to talk," she said.

"I thought we already were," Connor said, feigning ignorance.

He'd been expecting this. It had been two days since the ryklar attack. Meanwhile, the NEIIS console and other artifacts had been sitting untouched in Lenora's lab.

"How long do you intend to make him wait?" Lenora asked.

Connor pressed his lips together, considering. "Oh, I don't know. Maybe a month."

"A month!"

"Two at the most," Connor replied quickly, only half-joking.

"You're incorrigible," Lenora admonished and leveled her gaze at him. "You're just being spiteful."

Connor shrugged and smiled. "You just want to look at what he found."

"You're right; I do. I admit it. The find is intriguing, and regardless of how it was discovered, we need to study it," Lenora said.

Connor had been expecting this and knew he could stall Lenora's curiosity for only so long. His curiosity was piqued, too, now that he'd calmed down a bit.

"Fine, let's study it, but I'm not sure we should allow Dash to be involved anymore. This would just reaffirm his reckless behavior," Connor said.

Lenora watched him intently for a moment. "Connor," she said in a patient tone. It was amazing how much Lenora could convey with such a singular utterance—anywhere from thoughtful indulgence mixed with a bit of warning all the way to "here it comes."

"This isn't the military and the students here aren't soldiers. They're here because they're passionate about learning, research, and discovery," Lenora said.

"I know that, but their efforts have to be guided so they remain safe to do all those things you value so highly," Connor said.

Lenora's cheeks reddened in frustration. "*I* value so highly?" she said severely.

Connor sighed. Now he'd stepped in it. "You know what I meant. What Dash did was—"

"What he thought he had to do given the confines we put on him," Lenora said.

"So this is our fault? That's what you're saying?" Connor said and shook his head. "We put rules in place with the expectation that they'll be followed, and when some of these curiosities become too much for them and they do something stupid, it becomes our fault?" Connor said, feeling the heat rise in his face.

Lenora shook her head. "At some point, the limitations on survey missions requiring Field Ops escorts are going to have to be lifted. You can't isolate people and only allow them to go outside with armed escorts. That's no way to live."

Connor couldn't believe what he was hearing. "If Ian and I hadn't shown up, they would have died!"

"I thought the CDF squad that showed up helped with that," Lenora said, with a hint of sarcasm.

Connor frowned at her. "Now who's being spiteful?" he replied evenly.

Lenora held up her hands. "I'm sorry, but Dash's actions are a symptom of a much bigger problem."

"Yes, the fact that he's on the fast track to getting himself and anyone around him hurt or killed. We don't live in a petting zoo, and if the ryklars are becoming more active, we need to be even more cautious than before," Connor said.

"Waiting for Field Ops escorts is unsustainable. They don't have the manpower to meet the needs. These are the facts," Lenora said.

Connor rolled his shoulders and stretched his neck. "What's so hard about waiting? So what if people have to wait a few extra weeks before they can go do their field research," Connor said.

"That's fine for a short while, but those delays become longer and longer as time goes on. Sierra isn't going to send more Field Ops personnel to Sanctuary. Just to be clear, I'm not condoning what Dash did. He made mistakes. All I'm saying is that he did what he did because he felt he couldn't come to us—me—with his frustrations at not being able to pursue an academic lead. And part of that is because of you," Lenora said.

Connor was silent for a minute while he thought about it. He glanced at the empty coffee mug. What really rubbed him the wrong way was that Lenora had this uncanny way of making a lot of sense. Sometimes it left him twisting in the wind.

"There have to be consequences for what he did," Connor said.

"What do you propose then? Give me some options to consider," Lenora said.

"Send him back to Sierra for six months," Connor replied.

Lenora shook her head. "I'm not going to do that to him," Lenora said in a matter-of-fact tone that meant she was unlikely to change her mind.

"Why not?" Connor asked.

A thoughtful frown came across Lenora's face while she considered her answer. "You've had a lifetime training soldiers. They follow orders and are sometimes called upon to take the initiative to achieve an objective. What Dash did was take the initiative to achieve an objective. Did he make mistakes? Yes, but I don't want to be among those who squash initiative. He needs guidance but not expulsion, which is what you're proposing," Lenora said.

They'd had similar conversations in the past. Connor's military training was as natural to him as breathing. His first instincts were to correct the problem quickly and efficiently, but civilians didn't work like that and scientists were in a field all their own when it came to the reasons for their actions. If he was honest, he'd found over the last year that sometimes those reasons were just as valid a concern as his own. Was he making this too personal?

"Sending Dash away now is the worst thing we can do for him," Lenora continued. "He needs guidance, and he isn't going to find that in Sierra."

"What's wrong with Sierra?" Connor asked.

"Nothing, if you want to be part of the rebuilding effort. People come to Sanctuary to get away from that. They want a new beginning, but they need time away from the reminders of everything they've lost. Dash is part of that." Lenora leaned forward and rested her elbows on the table, bridging her fingers in front of her mouth. "You may not want to hear this, but Dash needs someone like you in his life."

"I don't think he'd agree with you," Connor replied.

Lenora smiled. "Maybe not this second because he's angry, but he's not stupid and he knows what he did. He also knows you don't approve of his methods and that frustrates him as well. I think sometimes you're a little too hard on him."

"It's for his own good—" Connor began.

"Believe me, I know where you're coming from, but sometimes you don't have to be so severe," Lenora said.

Connor sighed and decided to try a different approach. "Okay, so we don't send him back to Sierra, but there have to be consequences for his actions. He's not to lead any more expeditions. I'll have him locked out of all vehicle systems. He can study everything he wants right here, but that's all for the foreseeable future."

Lenora pressed her lips together, hard, but Connor knew she couldn't overrule him in this. As the lead archaeologist for the Sanctuary site, she had authority over those who worked at the site, but Connor was also within his rights to make the recommendation to Field Ops that they restrict Dash's movements. And they would listen to him.

"Alright, we'll ground him," Lenora said at last.

Connor stepped toward her and placed his hand on her shoulder, rubbing it gently. "I'll try not to be so severe about it in the future," he said.

Lenora placed her hand on top of his and gripped it gently. "Your heart is in the right place, love. But sometimes you need to give people a break."

They left their housing unit, which was located at one of the permanent residency neighborhoods established at Sanctuary. New housing structures were being built to fulfill the burgeoning needs of the colonists choosing to relocate there. What had started off as a Forward Operating Research Base of a few dozen research scientists had grown to be home to over a thousand colonists. They had a surplus of building materials as a result of Sanctuary being designated a safe zone during the Vemus war, and Sanctuary was well on its way to becoming a full-fledged frontier city. Instead of camps of easily constructed mobile labs and command centers, they were outfitted with more permanent structures using refined building techniques and materials from New Earth. There were even architectural projects devoted to reproducing NEIIS architecture. Those projects had started off as purely academic pursuits, but one thing Connor could safely assume about Sanctuary's residents and all colonists of New Earth in general was their propensity to experiment and try new things rather than just recreate the Earth of old.

The growth of Sanctuary did put pressure on the colonial government to provide Field Ops resources in an already constrained and recovering government services sector. Almost everything Sanctuary needed regarding vehicles and supplies had to be imported, but there were groups devoted to changing that as well. Connor knew it would be a long time before Sanctuary became a bustling metropolis, and that was the direction they were heading, but for right now it was purely a frontier-type settlement with an active research community, of which Connor was now a part.

One of the things Lenora had pushed for after the Vemus war was the construction of state-of-the-art laboratories to support all the scientific research being conducted in their small corner of New Earth. Lenora had gotten other lead scientists from different research fields involved when they'd put forth their proposal. Connor had reviewed the proposal and was able to leverage his own experience with wrangling support from sometimes reluctant government officials. But negotiating these waters of acquiring resources for field research was where Lenora shined. For Lenora it wasn't a matter of give-and-take, which was where most egotistical research scientists and government planners bumped heads. For her, it was a matter of finding a win-win where everyone benefited. In this case, Sanctuary's first Colonial Research Institute, or CRI as it was becoming more commonly referred to by some of the students, was akin to the universities of Earth.

One of the things the late governor, Tobias Quinn, had worked to establish in the colony was the fostering and sharing of knowledge, especially when it came to the next generation. The colonial education system required that students were exposed to different fields of study through practical application while providing a service to the colony.

Commerce didn't exist here as it had on Earth, or at least it was measured differently. There was no magic green paper or universal credits that people coveted. Colony worth was measured in the time and efficiency with which a given task could be achieved. With the advent of fabricators, which had its roots in the three-dimensional printers that had begun to show up in the latter twentieth century on Earth, there really wasn't a need for factories to create multitudes of products that people might not need or want and reduced the psychological impact of convincing a populace that they needed these excess things to have a fulfilling life. Colonial life was an active thing and the world was infinitely more fascinating. Connor found it refreshing and a much-needed reset for the human race as a whole.

They walked through the settlement, heading for the Colonial Research Institute, which was only a short distance from Field Operations Command. Connor had to stop at the command center later that day for a meeting.

After the ryklar attack, he'd spoken to Sean Quinn about Captain Fletcher's CDF squad, and his conversation had been enlightening. Colonial Department psychologists were working with CDF soldiers on the various issues they were facing, but some cases were more difficult than others. Sean had promised Connor that he would look into it and recall Captain Fletcher's squad for immediate evaluation. Connor had advocated that he didn't want the soldiers punished in any way; he just wanted them to get the help they needed. Sean understood. The young colonel had his own ghosts to wrestle with on occasion.

They reached the entrance to the Colonial Research Institute and the automatic doors opened for them. Connor gestured for Lenora to lead the way.

"How very traditional of you, Connor. I do appreciate it," Lenora said with a grin.

"Who says chivalry has to be dead?" Connor replied.

The archaeological labs were off to the right and Lenora had almost an entire wing dedicated to her research. It was there that they'd stored the recovered NEIIS equipment from the remote site. Connor used his implants to authenticate the storage room and noticed that the lights were already on inside. Someone was working. He arched one eyebrow at Lenora.

"I had Malone begin the analysis to date the NEIIS equipment," Lenora said.

Connor should have known that regardless of what they decided, Lenora was determined to get a crack at this new piece of NEIIS technology.

8

THEY WENT INSIDE and Ian Malone waved them over, his eyes alight with excitement. "It's older than we thought it was," he said while holding a tablet computer and gesturing with a flick of his wrist toward the nearest wallscreen, which sent the report onto it.

"Dash did say the architecture favored the older or more traditional style than what we encountered with their subterranean cities," Connor said. He quickly skimmed through the report, as did Lenora.

"Is this accurate? This report says it's over three hundred years old," Lenora said.

Connor frowned in thought. He knew the NEIIS had disappeared sometime within the last one to two hundred years—or at least that was the current theory. As far as Connor knew, the only evidence the NEIIS had been here was the cities they'd found and the fact that they had genetically modified the local wildlife—the foremost of which was the ryklars, which were an apex predator sometimes rivaled by the berwolves. Both predators were highly lethal, but overall, the berwolves would generally leave colonists alone whereas ryklars were more unpredictable and should be avoided. They knew the NEIIS had used the ryklars for some purpose—be it protection, an attack force, or something else they simply hadn't thought of yet. Colonial geneticists had been studying the ryklars since they'd arrived on New Earth. There was evidence to support that the ryklars had even been manipulated to their current form.

"So, what does it matter if this new remote site is older than we thought it was?" Connor asked.

Lenora was watching the pallet of equipment sitting in the middle of the room that Captain Fletcher's team had recovered from the NEIIS building. It was covered in a protective shell, but Connor knew that wouldn't last long, especially not now.

"Well, it throws off the timeline we've been piecing together and supports some of the newer theories that the NEIIS had come to this part of the continent later—much later—in their development," Lenora said.

"New theory . . . " Ian said. "But I thought it was—"

"That's not important right now," Lenora said quickly.

Connor found himself wondering what she was up to now. A soft knock came at the door and Lenora called out for the person to come inside.

The door opened and Dash walked in. His gaze darted first to Connor for a moment before smiling a greeting at Lenora.

"Good morning, Dr. Bishop, Dr. Malone." Dash looked pointedly at Connor. "Sir," he said in a controlled, neutral tone.

"I thought you'd like to be the first to know that one of your theories is proving to be correct," Lenora said.

Dash's eyes became bright with excitement and he glanced at the pallet of covered equipment in hungry anticipation. "Which one? No, don't tell me. That remote site is older than we thought it was. That has to be it. The architecture matches the older style. Is that right?"

Lenora nodded. "Ian ran the numbers this morning. The date puts it at three hundred years old."

Dash's eyes took on a sudden intensity as he considered the implications. There was no doubt in Connor's mind that he was putting pieces together.

"We need to access the console and see if we can get more data from that map I found," Dash said.

"I think there are some things we need to discuss first," Connor said, drawing everyone else's attention.

"That can wait until later in the day. We have some work to do first," Lenora replied.

Connor considered pushing it, but Lenora had been clear. She wasn't about to send Dash back to Sierra. Dash would be reprimanded, but Lenora was not about to cast him aside. Connor was only slightly annoyed by this. He knew what it was like to have someone with real potential working with them. Most of the time, they were worth the effort. Sean Quinn came foremost to his mind. They'd had a rocky beginning, but he'd taken Sean's youthful potential and energy and honed him into an outstanding CDF officer. Perhaps Dash DeWitt was to Lenora what Sean Quinn had been to Connor. He was just worried that Dash's recklessness would be overlooked, which could lead to a barrelful of regrets.

Dash looked at Connor, considering. "I'm sorry for what happened. I did check the general Field Ops daily bulletin before we set off that day and there was no ryklar activity reported in that area."

Connor drew in a patient breath. "You're right. There was no ryklar activity reported when you left in the morning. The issue is that field survey teams need to be put on the schedule so they can be monitored in case something goes wrong. It was dumb luck that Ian and I were checking the supply caches within sixty klicks of where you were. There were no other Field Ops teams in the area. Do you understand that?"

"I do, but I'm just not sure it changes anything," Dash replied.

Connor felt his brows push forward in consternation. "It changes everything, Dash. We schedule field missions so there's support readily available if something goes wrong. But what you did is how lives are lost. What happened the other day would have resulted in the loss of the lives of the people with you and, possibly, Ian and me as well. But you don't see that, and that's the real problem. All you see is the discovery," Connor said and jerked his thumb toward the covered pallet behind them. "Whatever we find on that pallet isn't worth the lives of the people who were with you. It's certainly not worth my life or Ian's. Did you ever think about that?"

Dash's cheeks reddened and his mouth hung open for a moment before he clamped it shut, forming a stubborn line. "Of course I thought about it. What do you want me to say? It happened. I can't change it."

Connor shook his head. The kid just wouldn't get it. He glanced at Lenora and knew she understood. "I know you can't change anything. What I'm looking for are assurances that something like this will never happen again. We can do field missions, but they must be done the right way."

Dash looked away from Connor for a moment. "Is that all you want? A promise? I think you want more than that. You want me to admit that I shouldn't have gone in the first place and I won't do it. I don't regret going. Neither do the others. You can't keep us here under lock and key."

"That's just the thing. You're not being held here against your will. Right now you believe that because you made this discovery it wipes the slate clean and justifies the method that got you there in the first place. You're wrong. This time you were lucky. Next time you might not be," Connor said, and Dash rolled his eyes. "You can throw your life away," Connor continued, his voice rising. "You can walk right out that door, go off into the forest, and no one will stop you. But you put other people's lives at risk. I know your friends didn't want to die out in the field so you could pin your name to a discovery. I don't know why you don't understand that."

Dash narrowed his gaze and then tried to look at Lenora and Ian for support, but there wasn't any to be had. "We can't afford to wait for Field Ops to hold our hands every time we want to go out and do a survey. You think I haven't thought about what happened? I have. We should not have left the ATV where it was. We should have communicated back to Field Ops where we were and what we were doing. I get that now."

"Then why didn't you? The only reason there was a distress beacon at all was because the ryklars were trying to get into that ATV, which tripped the vehicle's automated systems, which overrode your lockout for the transponder," Connor said.

Dash glared at him and didn't reply.

"This is what comes from lying and trying to hide what you're doing," Connor pressed.

"No, this is what happens when you try to control everything and everyone around you. I've got news for you. I don't need your approval. I don't need your permission to do my work. I did the research and found a lead worth chasing, something the other research scientists either missed or thought they'd get to at a later date. You're making this place into a prison camp. We have the right to risk our own lives and you don't get to dictate that for me or anyone else!" Dash said coldly.

"Dash," Lenora said sharply. "That's not fair. Connor is looking out for you. And as far as who has a say in what work you get to do here, that's entirely up to me," she warned.

Dash looked at Lenora and his gaze softened. "I'm sorry, Dr. Bishop. None of this is directed at you," he said and paused for a moment, considering. "But I'm surprised to hear you say it because it's well known that you take matters into your own hands in pursuit of your research."

Connor's eyes darted toward Lenora, who was at a rare loss for words. The kid was right in that regard, at least. Dash idolized Lenora as a member of the scientific community, and the way he'd just called her out for her dynamic pursuits was shocking for her.

"You want a promise from me," Dash said, looking at Connor. "I won't hide the fact that at some point in the future I will be going on another field survey mission. It's part of what I want to do. We won't disable the vehicle's transponder like we did the other day. Is that what you're looking for?"

Connor pursed his lips in thought. "Not good enough. Field missions must be registered with Field Ops and the department head accountable for you."

Lenora recovered from Dash's audacious comment about her reputation. "I've been known to take matters into my own hands from time to time. I freely admit it. I do not, however, hide what I'm doing. There *is* a difference."

Dash nodded. "I understand," he said finally.

Connor wasn't sure if he believed it, but he had to admit it was a rare occurrence indeed when Lenora was at a loss for words. He was slightly amused, even in the midst of being annoyed with Dash, but Connor was careful not to let that show.

Ian cleared his throat and gave everyone a sunny smile. "What do you say we crack open that pallet and see what we found?" he suggested lightly.

Connor glanced at Lenora and shrugged while pursing his lips noncommittally. He wanted to know what was on that console, too. "Alright, let's table this discussion for another time and see what we can learn from this thing," Connor said.

They went over to the pallet and began removing the protective coverings that kept the NEIIS equipment safe. Lenora had them tag and catalog each item, which was then uploaded to their data repositories. Those repositories were backed up nightly to the main colonial library in Sierra. It took them several hours to go through everything collected. The CDF squad had been thorough in what they were able to retrieve from the NEIIS building. Connor looked at the items they'd tagged and arranged on the extended workbench of the lab and was a bit surprised by how much they'd been able to recover.

They settled into a quiet routine, which drained away some of the tension that had been building between them. Though Connor felt that Dash was still angry with him, there was an unspoken agreement to set their differences aside and learn all they could about the discovery Dash had made.

The NEIIS console had been damaged during the ryklar attack, but they were able to reproduce the woven mesh console the NEIIS used in their computer interfaces. It took them several more hours to connect the new mesh screen to the old console. They cleaned out the base so they could connect a power supply to the console.

Dash was lying on the floor, looking inside the base. He frowned as he cleared away some of the dirt and debris inside. "It looks like their data storage is in pretty bad shape from being exposed to the elements for so long," he said and let out a frustrated sigh.

Connor squatted down and looked where Dash was pointing. The rusty area showed signs of oxidation and calcium buildup from years of being exposed to moisture. "Well, we have your recording to fall back on. We could try throttling down the power so we don't burn the console out. Copying the data carries the same risk because we'd have to power it on in order to copy the data anyway."

Dash nodded and glanced at Lenora. "What do you think, Dr. Bishop?"

Lenora had been standing by the wallscreen, reviewing some of the data recovery methods they'd developed during their time researching the computer systems found at Sanctuary. She closed down her session and walked over to them. "It's a crapshoot. Either we'll get some usable data from it or it's gonna burn out. I think we should move forward and get as much as we can from it," she said.

Dash closed up the control panel and stood up, offering his tablet computer to Lenora. "Would you like to do the honors, Dr. Bishop?"

Lenora's gaze softened. "Go for it," she replied.

Dash's eyes widened in anticipation as he brought the tablet back in front of him. He glanced at the others. "Here goes nothing," he said and took one last look at the NEIIS console. Then he pressed the execute button for the power startup sequence.

They'd made great strides in adapting their colonial power generators to existing NEIIS technology. Connor knew there had been a lot of trial and error in those efforts. Most of the great strides they'd made had occurred within the past year, which were the result of Noah Barker's work on the colossus cannon that had been used to defend Sanctuary from the Vemus. The power startup sequence was monitored for feedback from the NEIIS device so it reduced the risk of overload but couldn't eliminate it altogether, something that had plagued Lenora's archaeological team across multiple dig sites. The software slowly ratcheted up the power output, and for the first full minute the NEIIS console remained a defeated, darkened shell. Then a faint light slowly began to glow on the mesh screen.

"Initiating recording and data retrieval," Dash said.

Connor watched as NEIIS symbols began to scroll across the screen from right to left. He'd seen them before, but he had no idea what they meant. There were linguists who were still working on deciphering the NEIIS language, but they hadn't fully cracked it. They could read some of the text, but to Connor it seemed like there was a lot of conjecture on just how much they understood about the NEIIS language. Until they had some kind of credible proof that the symbols meant what they thought they meant, he'd just assume that the margin for error was still much too high. They could do basic things, like figure out the protocol to initiate the ultrahigh-frequency sound waves that were used to trigger the ryklar protection or guard instinct for NEIIS sites, but this wasn't truly deciphering the language. It was just signal observance and regurgitation without a true understanding of what they were doing.

Dash approached the mesh screen. "Alright, let's try this again," he said.

One of the NEIIS symbols was more prominent than all others. Connor thought it resembled an inkblot with dark wavy lines running underneath. Dash lightly tapped the symbol. The other symbols faded away and a topographical map appeared on the screen. The much larger wallscreen nearby became active and showed the same information. They all watched the screen silently for a few moments.

"This is what we found before. These areas over here represent the part of the continent that we haven't fully explored," Dash said and brought up their current map of the area on the adjacent wallscreen. "This is from the *Galileo* seed ship that mapped the surface of the planet before the *Ark* arrived. If this is the same area we're looking at on the NEIIS console, the landscape doesn't match up. There are more lakes and hills now, and even that canyon wasn't there before."

Connor peered at the screen and rubbed the stubble on his chin with his thumb and forefingers, making circular motions while he thought. "Let's assume you're right. What could change the landscape so severely?"

"I'm not really sure. It could be anything—some kind of major catastrophe or—" Dash began.

"Not so fast," Lenora said. "Major catastrophes would affect the continent as a whole. We don't have enough data to support that based on this image alone. So we should start small and work our way up."

Dash nodded. "Agreed. This is why I had Merissa Sabine with us when we went to the site."

Connor frowned as he remembered the two young ladies. "What's her field of expertise?"

Dash smiled. "Planetary science with a specialization in ecosystems. Can we call her and share this info? Maybe she'd have something to contribute."

Connor suppressed a grin. He was sure Merissa was quite capable, but Dash's eagerness made him think there was more to it than that.

"Let's do that. Give her a call," Lenora said.

Dash opened a comlink and stepped off to the side, speaking quietly. A few minutes later he returned to them. "Merissa is on her way here and Selena was with her so she's coming, too."

Connor arched one eyebrow. "Perhaps we should get Jim Tucker here and the whole gang will be back together," he said dryly.

Dash's face blanched for a moment and Connor knew why. Jim

Tucker had gotten in trouble for his participation in Dash's survey mission. Technically, Jim wasn't part of Field Ops. He was just doing a work-study program; however, there were strict guidelines Jim was expected to follow while he was serving in any capacity at Field Operations. Connor knew Captain Ramsey wouldn't tolerate any such behavior, even from an intern at Field Ops.

"Jim isn't available," Dash said.

While they waited for the others to arrive, they ran some data-extract routines and analysis on the backup they'd made of the NEIIS storage device. As they suspected, it was severely damaged and only limited data retrieval was possible.

There was a soft knock at the door and Dash went over to open it. Two young ladies entered and nodded a greeting toward Dash before looking at Connor and the others.

"Ladies, please come inside. We're in need of your expertise," Lenora said in a friendly tone.

Connor knew Lenora loved this. She liked working with students almost as much as she enjoyed recruiting people into her field of study.

Lenora gestured toward the wallscreen. "I'm assuming you recognize the map. We were able to retrieve this from the NEIIS console."

Both Merissa and Selena nodded.

"Good. We hoped you would be able to help shed some light on why the landscape appears to have changed when compared with the *Galileo* survey data," Lenora said.

Merissa's mouth opened in surprise. "I'm sure there's someone else who might be able to give a better answer than what we could come up with, Dr. Bishop."

Lenora shook her head. "Nonsense. You're here and I want your opinion. Dash speaks highly of you both. He would never have recruited you for his. . ." Lenora paused and gave Dash a sidelong glance, ". . . rogue field survey mission if he wasn't confident in your abilities."

Merissa glanced at the screen and then walked toward it. She had her arms crossed in front of her while she studied the map for a few moments.

"So, the question is what could cause the landscape to change to the degree we're seeing here," Connor said and gestured to a part of the map that was highlighted with potential NEIIS locations. "We know the symbols mean there could be something at these locations, but we can't be sure where these places are in relation to the map."

"We think it's in the area north of where we are now," Dash said quickly.

"Yeah, but we can't know for sure. So let's focus on what could have happened to change the landscape like this, then try to pinpoint the current location for it," Connor said.

Connor watched as Merissa studied the *Galileo* topographical map and compared it with what they'd found.

"Typically, when you see widespread changes across the landscape like this, it's the result of some type of external stimulus," Merissa said.

Dash nodded enthusiastically. "I keep thinking of something big, like a supervolcano or something like that."

Merissa shook her head, not convinced. "A supervolcano would cause more damage, possibly even an extinction-level event, but there's no evidence to support it."

"Are you sure? Maybe we just haven't explored enough of the continent to find the evidence you need. We'd need a geological survey to determine volcanic activity," Dash said.

"Yes, I'm sure," Merissa said, sounding slightly irritated. "Supervolcanoes are massively destructive in force. What we see on the map is the result of subtle variations over time. We've seen this back on Earth during the last Ice Age. It requires further analysis, but I would put forth the theory that these changes are the results of glaciation."

"Are you saying glaciers caused all this change?" Connor asked.

Merissa nodded. "That would be my hypothesis."

Connor had worked with enough scientists over the past year to know that was as close to a "yes" as he was going to get.

"What would you need to do to know for sure?" Lenora asked.

Merissa thought about it for a moment. "I'd have to collaborate with other experts. One of the things I'd want to look for is whether the migration pattern had changed for the local fauna."

"Why would the migration pattern matter at all?" Connor asked.

Selena cleared her throat and Connor looked at her, nodding for her to speak.

"If there was an Ice Age, it would mean that food had become scarce and forced the local wildlife to scavenge farther south where it's warmer. The predators would follow and everything would just move south for a while. Then, after the Ice Age was over, they would eventually migrate back north," Selena said.

Dash nodded. "So we'd need to know the current migration patterns, but we wouldn't need to study all wildlife. We could base it on a sampling and then look for evidence of migratory behavior so we could match it at some of these other locations," he said, looking at Merissa and Selena. "Does that sound about right?"

Merissa pursed her lips in thought, her eyes still studying the map on the screen. Then she nodded. "Beyond the migration patterns, we would need to look for evidence that lakes and rivers had changed. Remember the Great Lakes of North America? They were formed by glaciers. They represent a more extreme kind of evidence, but we could start off with the most obvious pieces and then work our way down to the smaller ones. Then we'd have a picture of just how far the glaciers had come south."

Lenora nodded enthusiastically, apparently pleased with the discussion. "Outstanding, ladies and gentlemen. Scientific research is based on collaboration among our peers. None of us can do this alone. I'm glad to see that each of you had the instinct to immediately bring in your peers to work the problem. The other thing we need to consider is the timeline."

Connor frowned. He had no idea where Lenora was going with this, and by the looks of the others, neither did they. In this, she was one step ahead of them, and for once, Connor was glad it wasn't just him.

Merissa's eyes widened first as she finally understood. "We would need to understand whether this Ice Age and the disappearance of the NEIIS are correlated and possibly contributed to their disappearance," she said and looked at Lenora. "May I, Dr. Bishop?" Merissa asked, pointing at the wallscreen with the *Galileo* data on it.

"Go ahead," Lenora said.

Merissa walked over to the wallscreen and brought up the holo-interface. Connor watched as she brought up a couple of data models in reference to what they knew about the Ice Age that had occurred on Earth.

Once Merissa had what she was looking for, she took a step back. "I had to look it up just to be sure. Glaciers can form very slowly—less than a meter per day, for example—or quite quickly, forming upwards of thirty meters per day. In order for the glaciers to reach a few hundred kilometers north of here, they would've taken four hundred and sixty years just to get to that point and perhaps another four hundred and sixty years to retreat back to their normal area." Merissa frowned for a moment. "Actually, it's less than that. I was assuming the glaciers started at the North

Pole, which isn't right. So, if we assume this area here where the glaciers currently are is normal," she said, using her hand to draw on the holo-interface, which showed a thick line on the screen, "it would still take over two hundred years for a glacier to reach this far south."

"You don't sound very convinced," Connor said.

"I'm just not sure if it's right because the theory is that the NEIIS disappeared less than a hundred years ago. What do you guys think?" Merissa asked.

"I think you're on the right track," Lenora said. "But you're right about the timeline. It doesn't quite match up, which can mean a couple of things. One, we're wrong about when the NEIIS actually disappeared. Two, the glaciers could have formed faster than what we've observed back on Earth. This is a new planet and it has different systems at work. And we're not sure what would've triggered such a rapid Ice Age. The most recent Ice Age on Earth lasted about ten thousand years before conditions changed and it ended."

"I think the two are related. Let's assume for a second that the glaciers formed quicker than we thought. So if we just double the distance per day, that would mean that the glaciers reached here in less than a hundred years," Connor said.

"What could cause that?" Dash asked. "Was it something the NEIIS did, or was it something that occurred naturally?"

"Let's take a step back," Lenora said. "What causes an Ice Age?"

They all looked at Merissa, who seemed startled by the sudden attention.

"Oh, you want me to answer that. Okay," Merissa said and thought about it for a moment. "Causes for the planet to rapidly cool could be anything from the variation of sunlight, the distance of New Earth from the sun, ocean circulation changes, and composition of the atmosphere, just to name a few. The NEIIS had an industrialized society so that could have contributed to the rapid climate change."

Dash snorted, drawing their attention. "I just had a thought, but it's probably too far-fetched."

"Well, let's list everything we can and then we can start crossing stuff off the list," Lenora said.

Dash shrugged as if to say: okay, you asked for it. "How about a celestial body that moved through the star system and temporarily pulled planets out of alignment? It doesn't take much. It could be anything, like a gentle giant of a black hole whose mass is similar to our star so it wouldn't cause wanton destruction but would just be enough to temporarily alter the orbiting planets it passed closest to. All it would take would be a few degrees away from its current orbit to have a massive effect on the temperatures of the planet. Then, when it was gone, the star would re-assert control and the orbits would settle back to their normal position."

Connor arched an eyebrow at Dash. "Just a thought, you say?"

Dash smiled and then seemed surprised for a moment that he'd done so. "Well, we *are* brainstorming here and I thought, what the heck? It could happen."

Connor glanced at Lenora. "He's got a point. I remember Dr. Zabat speaking about anomalies in space—rogue planetary bodies that were ejected from their own systems, going about their business on a trajectory that could pass through a star system and impact it."

"An astrophysicist's point of view, but we can't rule it out. I'm not sure how we can prove it, but we can certainly ask him to look into it for us," Lenora said.

"That might be a tall order, given how much our war with the Vemus has impacted the star system. But you're right, we can ask," Connor said.

The comlink chimed on the wallscreen nearby and the header

information indicated that it was for Connor. He walked over to the wallscreen and acknowledged the incoming call.

Captain Ramsey's tanned, weather-worn face appeared on the screen. "Connor. Good, you're available," he said with a smile.

"I might be, but it depends on what you're going to ask me," Connor quipped.

Captain Ramsey chuckled. "You have a visitor at Field Ops who's been waiting for a couple of hours to meet with you. Are you able to swing by?"

Connor glanced at Lenora. He did have a meeting at Field Ops, but it wasn't for another hour. "Who is it?"

"His name is Bernard Duncan. He's from the Housing and Urban Development Committee at Sierra. He says he needs to talk to you specifically. So if you can make your way down here, I would certainly appreciate it," Captain Ramsey said.

Connor recognized the undertone of Captain Ramsey's statement, which was "please come here and get this guy out of my hair." Connor smiled. "Understood. I'll be there in a few minutes."

Lenora walked over to his side. "What's going on?" she asked.

Connor shrugged. "I'm not sure, but I'll go see what this Bernard Duncan wants and let you know. Then I'll meet up with you guys later. Can you stand to be without me for that long?"

Lenora gave him a playful swat on his arm. "Go on, then. We've got it covered here. Unless you'd rather stay and continue discussing how an impromptu Ice Age changed the landscape, which I know you wouldn't want to miss," Lenora said, her tone sounding almost accusatory.

Connor grinned and leaned in so only Lenora could hear. "I didn't arrange for this. I was actually enjoying the discussion for a change. Much better than arguing."

This seemed to mollify Lenora.

"Alright, students I think we're on the right track here so let's keep it going," Lenora said as Connor left the room.

Ian Malone followed him out. "Call me if you need backup," he said with a grin.

Connor turned around. "You can come if you want," he offered.

Ian shook his head. "I think I'd rather help mold young minds here. I'll see you later," he said and walked back into the laboratory.

9

CONNOR LEFT the Colonial Research Institute building and walked over to Field Ops Headquarters, which was essentially one permanent building and a nearby landing field. Officially, it was called Field Ops Headquarters, but Connor had to admit it was a small operation. Field Ops and Security employed around forty people who were tasked with protecting the thousand-odd residents of Sanctuary, the same number of people in their employ when Sanctuary had just a few hundred residents.

Connor walked toward the single-story prefabricated building that served as Field Ops Headquarters. Multiple thick antennas jutted above the roof which kept them connected to the main colony at Sierra. As Connor walked through the double doors, he saw that Jim Tucker was sitting behind the reception desk. Jim was focused on the holoscreen in front of him but glanced up as Connor approached. His eyes widened when he saw who was walking toward him.

"Hi, Jim. How are you feeling?" Connor asked.

Jim rubbed his arm where he'd been wounded by the ryklars.

The kid was lucky. Ryklars didn't usually deliver so shallow a cut, and thanks to the medipaste Ian had applied, there would be hardly any scarring.

"I'm fine, sir. Thank you for asking," Jim said, his cheeks going slightly pink.

"Good, I'm glad to hear it. I'm here to see Captain Ramsey. Can you tell him I'm here?" Connor said.

Connor was sure Ramsey wouldn't mind if he just headed on back, but Connor preferred to adhere to established protocol, and he was a civilian, after all.

"Right away, sir," Jim said.

Connor walked over to the sidewall to peruse a bulletin board hanging there while Jim contacted Captain Ramsey. Despite being retired from the Colonial Defense Force for nearly a year, people still referred to him as "sir." At first, he would kindly remind them that he was no longer in the military, but that didn't dissuade anyone, especially the younger generation. He supposed there could be worse things than a show of respect.

"Excuse me, Mr. Gates," Jim said, and Connor turned toward him. "Captain Ramsey is ready for you. He said you could just go on back."

Connor thanked him, but as he walked by, Jim looked as if he wanted to speak. Connor stopped and waited. "Is there something else?" he asked.

Jim sucked in a nervous breath and gathered his courage. "I just wanted to thank you for your help the other day. I didn't get the chance at the time and they've been keeping me busy here."

Connor regarded the young man for a moment. At least he still looked a little bit shaken by the whole ordeal. "You're welcome. I hope it doesn't happen again," Connor replied.

Jim met his gaze, then nodded.

Connor walked toward the back where Captain Ramsey's office

was. The office door was open and Ramsey waved him inside. He had his hand on his ear and was speaking to someone via comlink. Connor found it amusing that people still pretended to use an earpiece even though a comlink channel was handled through standard implants. He understood the unconscious gesture was so others would know they weren't talking to themselves, but it was also one of the quirks people used to convey information when they couldn't speak. He'd used that behavior himself in some of the covert operations he'd led for the NA Alliance military back in his Ghost days.

"What were they concentrating their search on?" Captain Ramsey asked. After a few moments, he continued. "That's still pretty far from any encampment or settlement or even any FORBs. No, I can't send a team to go look. We're already short-staffed as it is. If you'd like to send me more people, I could do a more thorough sweep of the area . . . No, I know we're all short-staffed . . . Fine, how about a shipment of recon drones that are capable of the range of patrol you're asking me to do . . . Well, you're not leaving me with a lot of options. Are we in danger or not?" Captain Ramsey asked crisply. "No, the ryklar attack the other day was ruled coincidental. The alpha pack was following the landrunners' migration patterns when they came across one of our remote field survey teams . . . I didn't say it wasn't a priority. Well, an additional Hellcat or even a couple of C-cats would make my job a little bit easier and give you the data you need." Captain Ramsey glanced at Connor and shook his head. "Great, you'll work on it. I appreciate it. Let me know what you can do and call me back."

Captain Ramsey finished his conversation and sighed heavily. He glanced at Connor and shook his head again. "You know you could have my job if you want it. Seriously, say the word and the job is yours."

Connor chuckled and shook his head. "No thanks. Sounds like they were giving you a bit of a runaround."

"I sympathize with what they're trying to do at the main Field Ops Headquarters in Sierra. Everyone is resource-constrained because of the rebuilding efforts. I think it's only a matter of time before we feel the pinch somewhere we don't want to feel it," Captain Ramsey said.

"What do they want you to do?" Connor asked.

"They've reopened some of the forward operating research bases and the Field Ops recon teams have been reporting increased ryklar activity moving through the area. I think it's catching them a bit off guard because they hadn't been in the area for so long," Captain Ramsey said.

"Have there been other attacks?" Connor asked.

Captain Ramsey shook his head. "No, not yet, at least. Well, there shouldn't be as long as they follow standard protocols and recon the area like they're supposed to. And set up the sonic wave emitters as a deterrent. That should deter mishaps like what we had the other day. Speaking of which, what are you going to do about Mr. DeWitt?"

Connor drew in a breath and raised his eyebrows. "Lenora and I have talked about it. We've spoken to Dash . . ."

Captain Ramsey snorted. "Let me guess. He's a promising young student and she's reluctant to let him go. That sound about right?"

Connor liked Captain Ramsey. They'd gotten along ever since Connor first arrived at Sanctuary. He was a good fit for the job he had to do, but the stress of being short-staffed was starting to take its toll.

"Something along those lines. The kid *is* smart and I think deep down he knows what he did was wrong, but his reasoning for going in the first place hasn't changed. He thinks they should just go whenever they want and be able to accept the risk."

"He's not the only one. That attitude appears to be a growing trend among the scientists and researchers who work here. Hell, even some of the residents feel the same way. And honestly, I'm not sure we can keep up with the demand," Captain Ramsey said and sighed.

That gave Connor pause. "Has it been that bad? Maybe I can make a few calls for you," Connor offered.

Captain Ramsey shrugged. "You could try. Maybe you'll have more luck than I've been having."

"What about a voluntary Field Ops squad? Something part-time that the people here could participate in," Connor said.

Captain Ramsey's brows furrowed and a half-smile adorned his tanned face. "That's a good idea. I don't know why I didn't think of it in the first place. A volunteer squad could handle the run-of-the-mill-type requests."

"You've had a lot on your mind and I only just thought of it right now," Connor said.

"Good. So you're in then. You can train up this volunteer squad?" Captain Ramsey asked, smiling widely.

"I could help," Connor said.

Ramsey's eyes widened. He'd been half-joking and was taken aback by Connor's offer. "Are you sure? I know you're retired and all that, but honestly we could really use the help."

"I said I would, so yeah. Just let me check my schedule and we can talk more about it," Connor promised.

"Excellent. Perhaps my luck is finally changing. Speaking of luck . . ." Captain Ramsey said and frowned, ". . . or perhaps not, but Bernard Duncan is here from the Colonial Housing and Urban Development Committee. Do you know him?"

"Name doesn't sound familiar. I'll make a few calls to Sierra after we're through meeting with Bernard Duncan. If it's a matter of equipment you need, perhaps the CDF could help out. At the very least, they might have a few C-cats they can give us on permanent loan. But you mentioned something about recon drones. What's wrong with the ones you currently have?" Connor asked.

"The recon drones we have are fine if we're patrolling within a hundred-kilometer radius, but that's pushing it. Field Operations HQ wants us to make a patrol of the area north of here in excess of five hundred kilometers from Sanctuary. That's a tall order when I can only field three or four small teams at a time," Captain Ramsey said.

Connor frowned and thought for a moment. "The ryklars spotted near the other FORBs—how many are we talking about?" he asked.

"That information is forthcoming, which means they're still counting. Nothing like a warning that says, 'Hey, watch out for this over here,' but more like, 'We're not going to tell you exactly how bad it could be, just that there's danger right around the corner. Have fun,'" Captain Ramsey said in a half-joking tone. Then he glanced at Connor as if he'd said too much.

"Don't worry about it. It's frustrating, I know," Connor said.

Captain Ramsey's lips formed a thin line and he shook his head. "No, it's not. I hate that crap. I hate being this frustrated, and if I heard any of my agents speaking that way, I'd chew them out."

"Nothing wrong with a little bit of a rant between friends. If I can get you more help, I will. I promise," Connor said.

Captain Ramsey smiled. "I appreciate it, Connor. I really do. And if you'd like to bring out your old Search and Rescue uniform, I'd be fine with that, too."

"You're relentless," Connor said mildly. "So where's Bernard Duncan?"

Captain Ramsey gestured toward the door. "Alright, I can take a hint. I will, of course, keep asking. Now, if you'll follow me, I'll lead you to Mr. Duncan."

Connor followed Captain Ramsey out of his office. It wasn't the first time Ramsey had asked him to moonlight at Field Ops and Security; it was more like the one hundred and fiftieth time, and each time Connor declined the request. If he was already out in the field, that was one thing, but he knew if he put on that uniform again it would be a slippery slope right back to where he was before, and he wouldn't do that to Lenora. What he *would* do was follow up on his promise and try to get them some more help out there, as well as offer a few suggestions about organizing a voluntary Field Ops squad.

They walked the length of the Field Ops Headquarters and came to the first of two small conference rooms. Inside sat a short man with thin, dark hair and brown eyes. He looked up in surprise and gave a friendly smile as they walked in.

"Mr. Gates," Bernard said and stood up. "So nice to finally meet you. Bernard Duncan of the Colonial Housing and Urban Development Committee," Bernard said and extended his hand toward Connor.

Connor shook the proffered hand. "You've certainly come a long way to meet me. I would've spoken to you via comlink or video call if I'd known you were looking for me."

Despite his short stature, Bernard Duncan had broad shoulders and a bit of a stocky build. He sat down at the conference table and gestured for Connor to do the same.

"I'll leave you guys to it. Please let me know if you need anything," Captain Ramsey said cordially.

"Actually, Captain, I'd love it if you could stick around. What I have to speak about concerns you as well, but I understand if you're busy and I'd be willing to send you a summary of today's meeting if that helps," Bernard offered.

Connor glanced at Ramsey, who looked a bit surprised that Bernard was willing to accommodate and include the Field Ops captain.

Captain Ramsey glanced out of the conference room and into the bullpen where his Field Ops agents were manning the command center. After a few moments' consideration, he walked over and closed the door, then turned toward them.

"Thanks. I could use a break," Captain Ramsey said and sat down.

Bernard smiled knowingly. "I'm sure you could, and it's part of the reason I'm here. We've received a lot of requests from colonists who wish to relocate to Sanctuary."

Bernard glanced at Connor.

"Does this have anything to do with my being here?" Connor asked in surprise.

"Honestly, we're not sure. When colonists started petitioning us for relocation assistance, they didn't specifically mention you. However, you *are* a war hero and there is some notoriety that comes with that. But I think it has to do with these people being temporarily relocated here during the war and liking the area. It's as simple as that," Bernard said.

"How many colonists are we talking about?" Captain Ramsey asked.

"We've received over five thousand requests. Some are individuals and some are families. There are obviously scientists, of course, who are trying to leverage their research at the Institute here as a way to expedite their requests," Bernard said.

Connor blew out a long breath. Sanctuary was already bursting at the seams as far as a permanent settlement went. They didn't have the resources to support so many coming so quickly.

He glanced at Ramsey and saw the same concern mirrored in his eyes.

"I see you understand the potential impact," Bernard said and raised his hands in a placating gesture. "Let me be clear, we're not going to suddenly dump five thousand colonists on you here without any support."

"That's good because we can't accommodate them . . . not without a lot of support from Sierra," Captain Ramsey replied.

"He's right," Connor said. "Field Ops and other services are extremely short-staffed here."

Bernard nodded in empathy. "It's part of the reason I'm here and why I wanted to speak with both of you, really. Officially, Sanctuary is a frontier-class settlement, or a glorified FORB if you will, but with so many people requesting to come here and the fact that you've already sustained a high rate of growth, indications are that this place is well on its way to becoming an actual city. However, there has been no official charter for Sanctuary to become a colonial settlement."

Connor took a moment to consider what Bernard was saying. "What does a charter give us?"

Bernard smiled. It was a friendly smile of the type one used when about to give good news. "This is a good thing. You're short-staffed now, but an official charter entitles you to the support you need in terms of expanding Field Ops and increased support for services to facilitate the expected growth here. This includes priority access to fabrication units and an even more robust tech base here so you can create the things you need concerning vehicles and equipment."

Connor thought it was almost too good to be true and said so. "What's the catch?"

Bernard chuckled. "Well, I'm here to do an assessment of the current situation. The *catch* is that in order to fulfill the requirements of the charter you need a working government, even in its most basic form. At the very least, you need a mayor."

Captain Ramsey glanced at Connor and started laughing. "I think you just got another job offer," he said with so much glee that Connor shifted uncomfortably.

Connor looked at Bernard and saw that was precisely what the Housing and Urban Development Committee member was angling for. "You can't mean me? We need to have an election, at the very least."

"Of course, but since this is a new settlement, we can appoint a mayor to get it up and running, then hold formal elections after the first term is served. The appointment would be on a trial basis, obviously, but I suspect even if we had elections, someone here would nominate you, Mr. Gates." Bernard said and leaned forward in his chair.

"I don't want to be mayor," Connor said firmly.

Bernard looked nonplussed at Connor's firm tone. "Your behavior says otherwise. I've asked around about you to many of the colonists who live here and you have a very active role in the community, Mr. Gates. One would say you already have half a foot in the door—meaning you're already doing the job. People bring their concerns and disputes to you and you provide sound counsel to those who request it. That's all being a mayor is. Your qualifications would clearly put you at the top of the list. I understand that a year ago there was an initial push for you to take over as colonial governor, which you refused."

"That's right," Connor replied. He hadn't wanted to be governor, and given his exposure to the Vemus, it hadn't been appropriate. However, being a town mayor was something altogether different. Connor narrowed his gaze suspiciously at Bernard. "Did Ashley put you up to this?"

Bernard's eyes almost shined with innocence. "I've met with

Governor Quinn on multiple occasions, if that's what you're asking."

Connor snorted and it came out in a half-chuckle as his lips lifted into a smile. He should've known Ashley would never let him go so easily. This was her way of telling him to put up or shut up. Perhaps he shouldn't have made so many requests on Sanctuary's behalf.

"Alright, let's say I consider this. What exactly do you need from me?" Connor asked and then held up his index finger. "And I'm not saying I've agreed to anything. I just want to know what it is you have in mind."

Bernard looked both amused and happy that Connor was at least willing to listen to him. "Thanks for hearing me out. Ashley bet me that you'd just walk out when I broached the subject. I didn't think so. You've raised a number of requests on Sanctuary's behalf. Clearly you care about this place and I think you'd be a perfect candidate for this job. And you wouldn't be alone in it. You'd have plenty of help."

"Like who?" Connor asked and then followed up. "Are you offering your services?"

Bernard laughed and there was an infectious quality to it as Captain Ramsey joined in. "Of course, I'd be willing to help. In fact, I'd be honored if you would make use of my services when the time comes. This is what I'll do. I'll lay out everything I have in mind. Then, I'll take a few days to do my assessment here and you can think it over, talk it over with your significant other, and what not. How does that sound?"

Connor drew in a deep breath. He liked Bernard. He usually had a good bead on a person, and from this brief encounter, he thought Bernard was actually a good man who was here to do some good by trying to fix a problem that needed to be addressed. That alone was enough to get Connor to listen to what the man had to say. What surprised him was that he was seriously considering stepping up and doing the job. He wasn't sure how Lenora would react. The way Bernard had put it, he was kind of doing the job anyway, even if it was only on a part-time basis.

He wouldn't make any decisions now. He glanced at Captain Ramsey, who was completely engaged with what Bernard was saying and, he noted, looked a bit relieved to at last be getting some help.

10

FOR THE PAST FEW DAYS, Dash had spent almost every waking moment in the laboratory. Dr. Bishop had even found him asleep on the couch in her office one morning. Dash, Merissa, and Selena had been putting together a joint academic research paper to support their theory about a recent Ice Age changing the landscape, having decided not to use the "foreign celestial-body flyby" theory Dash had hastily offered at the beginning. Dash had even managed to bring Jim in as a research assistant. At first, Jim had been reluctant to join them, but Dash couldn't stand seeing his friend languishing away at Field Ops any longer. So Jim was on part-time loan to Dr. Bishop. That was the official version, anyway.

Dash walked down the hall at the Research Institute, heading toward Dr. Bishop's laboratory where they had the NEIIS console set up. Jim was leaning against the wall outside the lab and glanced up at his approach.

Dash frowned. "I thought we got you clearance to go into the lab anytime."

Jim rubbed the back of his neck and nodded. "You did. I was just waiting for you."

Dash narrowed his gaze, his interest piqued. "Is Selena inside?" he asked.

"She and Merissa are inside. I accidentally heard them talking," Jim said.

Dash glanced at the door and then waved Jim over to create some distance so they wouldn't be overheard. "You heard something juicy, and by the look on your face, it's something they didn't want overheard. Well, now you have to tell me," he said with a smirk.

Jim glanced uncertainly at the door, taking a step toward it. "I don't know if that would be right," he muttered.

"Oh, come on, Jim. How bad could it be?" Dash asked. He heard the muffled tones of Merissa's laughter and Selena joining in from inside the room. Dash gave Jim an exasperated look and waited.

"It's not that big of a deal. They were just talking about the two tech engineers who arrived last week and who are working in the archives," Jim said.

Dash tried to think of who they were talking about but couldn't come up with anyone. "The NEIIS archives?" he asked.

Jim shrugged. "I guess. Anyway that's all I really heard."

"I wouldn't worry about it. You've got the inside track with Selena now that you're working with us more and away from that dreary desk at Field Ops," Dash said.

"It wasn't that bad. I wouldn't have had so much desk duty if we hadn't had the run-in with the ryklars," Jim said.

Dash pressed his lips together. "I just thought maybe you'd find what we're doing here more interesting. If you don't want to be here, you don't have to be. It's fine with me."

Jim shook his head. "No, I like it. It's something different, but I feel so unqualified. The three of you guys have the aptitude scores that qualify you to be here, whereas I don't. I'm just not sure I can contribute what you guys can."

"Don't give me that aptitude-score crap. Sometimes those tests are way off, and anyway, Dr. Bishop wouldn't have approved your appointment based solely on my request. She's giving you a shot. I think if you stay here for a while, you might find a place somewhere in the Research Institute. It doesn't necessarily have to be in archaeology. There's lots to do," Dash said.

"I know and I'm grateful, honestly. But I have no idea what the heck I want to do. I've always been like that," Jim said.

Dash put his hand on Jim's shoulder and gave a companionable squeeze. "I'll tell you something: it's not every day that we get to work with two pretty girls like those in there, so if you don't mind, I'd like to go inside."

Jim grinned and then nodded.

Merissa and Selena looked over as they walked in. "Did you sleep in or something? Why are you so late?" Merissa asked.

Dash gave her a level look with just a bit of mock severity. "I'm sorry, Mom. I won't let it happen again," he said and grinned.

Merissa rolled her beautiful dark eyes. Dash had to admit he was a bit smitten with the raven-haired future planetary scientist. Now, if she'd only give him a break.

"So where are we with our paper? When I left last night . . . err . . . early this morning, I'd added a few parts to the proposal section at the end," Dash said.

Selena nodded and swiped her hand toward the wallscreen, which had gone into standby mode. Multiple documents from their compiled research appeared. She quickly navigated through the interface and brought up the sections for proposed next steps to prove their theory. "We were just looking at that and . . ." Selena's voice trailed off and she glanced at Merissa.

"I don't think they're going to approve the proposal. You on another field survey mission, that is, and this one is pretty far away," Merissa said.

Dash sucked in his bottom lip, letting it slide under his teeth for a moment while he considered his reply. "You think the distance is too far? We might be able to select a closer area, but then we might just end up with another small outpost."

Merissa frowned in thought. "No, I agree with what you're saying. The higher the risk, the greater the reward. It's just that given the circumstances, I'm not sure whether they'll approve sending us on another . . ." Merissa paused and arched an eyebrow, ". . . registered field survey mission with Field Ops support. The other thing that might be a problem is we're not sure of the state of any of these sites. I wonder if it would be better to request some satellite time to photograph some of the areas before we request resources for a field trip."

For the first few seconds after Merissa had said she agreed with him, Dash hadn't quite heard what she'd said. But his brain slowly caught up with it and she was actually making a lot of sense. "I guess I was putting the cart before the horse," Dash said and glanced at Jim. "You think they'll give us satellite time?"

Jim shook his head. "Not anytime soon. Both Field Ops and the Colonial Defense Force have been devoting a lot of resources toward tracking ryklars because of increased reported activity in the northern areas."

Selena's eyes widened at the mention of ryklars. "Where have they been spotted? Is it anywhere near where we think there are NEIIS locations?"

"No, it's more northwest of here, but I've heard Captain Ramsey and Connor speaking about the lack of planetary survey capabilities because Sierra has been so focused on rebuilding the city. The Vemus decimated our satellites and the ones we have . . . well, you get the picture," Jim said.

"Perhaps we should add an addendum that states something about how the limited availability of Sat resources necessitates the need for our own survey mission. We can focus our efforts away from the riskier areas. I'm not keen to run into any more ryklars," Dash said.

Merissa glanced at him, seeming a bit surprised by the admission. "And here I thought you'd be trying to convince us to go anyway."

Dash smiled. "I still want to go, but I want to be smart about it. Being trapped in another outpost is not my idea of fun and is certainly something I don't wish to repeat. I'm sorry I dragged you guys into that."

Merissa's gaze softened and Dash felt his chest tighten. "You couldn't have known, and we didn't have to go."

Jim and Selena repeated the sentiment and Dash felt a small weight lift off his shoulders.

"Thanks," Dash said.

"So how do we convince Dr. Bishop and the Research Institute to support a field survey mission to one of the locations on the NEIIS map?" Jim asked.

They were silent while they all considered it. Dash had been thinking about it since they'd first started working on the console. Then, as they were drafting their peer review research paper, he'd begun to get a bit restless to be back out in the field. They should be able to just go if they wanted to. Before the ryklars had attacked them he'd been in his element, and couldn't wait to go back out there and explore. He didn't want to be cooped up anymore, and he had the feeling that at least to some degree the others felt the same way.

Dash glanced down the long black laboratory table where the original NEIIS data storage module sat. The module was oval-shaped and had protruding channels as thick as his fingers running the length of it with evenly spaced nodules. The outer casing was constructed of the same bronze-colored metallic alloy the NEIIS used in most of their construction. When they put it under a microscope, they'd seen a field of wafer-like shapes on the spines. Dash walked over to the data module and stared at it for a moment.

Merissa came over to his side and he glanced over at her, his gaze lingering on her long, silky hair. He wanted to run his fingers through it but suspected it wouldn't end well for him if he tried. She'd never given any hint of whether or not she was attracted to him.

"What are you thinking?" Merissa asked.

About how your lips would feel pressed against mine, he thought longingly but then inwardly shrugged it off. *Focus, Dash!*

"I'm trying to think of a way we can get more information off this thing," Dash said, gesturing toward the module.

Merissa brushed a rebellious strand of hair from her cheek. "I thought you made a copy of the data when you first brought the console online."

Dash nodded. "We did, but we're still meshing two completely separate technologies. I don't care what the tech guys say; it's not the same as using NEIIS technology for what it was designed to do. I suspect there's more information on that thing, but I'm not sure how to get to it."

"Can't you just plug it in somewhere and see what happens?" Merissa asked.

Dash frowned and then smiled. "Yeah, we could, I guess. I didn't even consider it before because we made a copy of the data and we had the output from the original console. But what if the console were damaged in such a way that we're just not aware of the extent of it? Plugging the module in someplace else . . . I think you might be on to something," he said.

Dash spun around and hastened over to the nearest workstation where he performed a quick search for any other NEIIS consoles that would be capable of housing the storage device. The others came over and joined him.

"What's he doing?" Selena asked.

"I sparked a brilliant thought in him," Merissa replied.

Dash glanced at her and nodded. "You most certainly did, but I'm not sure this is going to work."

"Why not?" Merissa asked.

Dash pinched the top part of his nose and felt some of the pressure recede from above his eyes. He needed to get outside for a while instead of being stuck looking at screens all day. "Plugging the module into another console isn't going to do it. We need to bring it to the archives."

"At the heart of the city?" Merissa asked.

"That's the one, but they're not going to let us," Dash said.

"Why wouldn't they?" Jim asked.

"Because the NEIIS archive is the most complete data repository we've found to date. They're still cataloging it, and if we show up asking to stick our data module into it, we'll likely get denied because the tech guys will say it's too much of a risk," Dash said.

Jim frowned and glanced at the others.

Merissa seemed to consider what Dash had said for a moment and then smiled. "Maybe you just need the right people to ask them," she said, her eyes alight with mischievous delight.

"Miss Sabine, are you suggesting that you could get the cooperation of two lonely tech guys in charge of the NEIIS data archives so we can get some more information off this data storage module?" Dash asked, gesturing toward the device in question.

Merissa smiled sweetly. "It couldn't hurt to ask, but perhaps you should let Selena and I take the lead on this."

Dash frowned. He didn't like where this was heading. "No deal. Jim and I have to be with you. Besides I'm the only one authorized to take the module from the lab." Dash felt his cheeks becoming a bit warm and wondered if Merissa had noticed. She hadn't.

"Well, at least let us go in first and see if they're open to the idea," Merissa suggested.

"I don't get it," Jim began. "Why can't we all just go ask them for help?"

Dash gave him a sidelong glance and was surprised to see that Jim really didn't understand. "Have you worked with any tech guys here? Sometimes they can be a bit territorial. They think they're the only ones qualified to touch anything and the rest of us just break things that they then have to fix. But what our two esteemed colleagues are suggesting," Dash said and placed one hand on each of the ladies' shoulders, "is that those tech tyrants might be more willing to help them than they would be to help you or me, implying that they might be a sucker for a pretty face. That about sum it up?"

Selena snorted and Merissa glanced at his hand on her shoulder. He quickly withdrew it and her lips curved ever so slightly upward.

"I've been known to do the same thing in reverse," Dash said.

Merissa arched one eyebrow. "I'm sure you've tried, but I'm not sure how successful you've been."

Dash smiled boldly. "*You're* still here, aren't you?"

Jim snorted after a moment and Selena just shook her head. They'd been working closely together for the past few days and had gotten used to his humor.

Merissa eyed him for a moment, her face impassive. "Perhaps I was just bored," she said dryly.

"Me, too. So, you guys ready?" Dash asked.

Merissa shook her head slightly and smiled. "Ready when you are," she said and began to walk away, then stopped and turned back around. "When we get there, try not to hover so close. You'll scare the fish away."

Jim grinned as Dash left to retrieve a case for safe storage of the memory module.

11

"WHAT ARE we going to do if they refuse to help us?" Jim asked.

"We'll have to improvise," Dash said and finished securing the memory module into the storage case.

A small holoscreen appeared above the case where the NEIIS data module had been, with a blank text box that required his attention. In the upper right corner was a five-minute timer that had begun counting down. Dash quickly updated the log to show that he was removing the memory module from the lab. Then, a secondary input screen appeared that required further information. Connor must have updated the security protocols. Dash thought about just entering something general, like "field study" or some such, but he knew Dr. Bishop would see right through that. She believed in him and he didn't want to disappoint her, so he quickly entered some text about bringing the memory module to the NEIIS archive for analysis. He'd see how they reacted to the truth when they received the log update.

Once the update log finished saving, Dash closed the session. It was likely that Dr. Bishop wouldn't notice the update until she returned to the lab, and he didn't know when that was going to happen. She'd been with Connor outside the Research Institute for the past couple of days, meeting with some colonial government official from Sierra. Dash had no idea what that was all about.

Dash and Jim quickly caught up to Merissa and Selena as they left the Research Institute behind, squinting in the bright sunlight. He glanced upward, noting the crystal-clear blue skies with only a few wisps of clouds, and felt some of the tension drain from around his eyes. The others were doing the same.

"It's really nice today. We should get some R&R. Would you guys want to hike out to the lake after we're done at the archives? Maybe go for a swim?" Dash asked.

The day was warm but not overly hot. The others seemed noncommittal about it.

"It's in the safe zone and not off limits," Dash said.

Selena nodded enthusiastically. "Yes, we all need some time out of the lab. I don't know how you guys do it day after day."

Dash looked at Merissa, who shrugged.

"We'll see. Maybe," Merissa said.

"I'll do whatever everyone else wants to," Jim said.

Since the NEIIS hadn't built any stairs, the different levels of the city were connected via a series of ramps, and they quickly reached the subterranean level where the NEIIS archives had been found. Temporary light fixtures automatically turned on, sensing their approach. As they walked, Dash moved next to Merissa.

"So, have you thought about what you're going to say?" Dash asked.

"Do you mean how I'm going to bat my eyelashes at them?" Merissa replied.

"Something like that," Dash said.

Merissa glanced at him, her gaze narrowing playfully and seeming to bore right through him. She leaned toward him. "Well, first I open my eyes really wide and look at them as if they were the most important thing in the entire world. Then, I speak in a really high, airy tone like this and pretend I really need their help," she said and paused, pushing out her chest. Her firm breasts swelled against her shirt and the breath caught in Dash's throat. "Then, I might arch my back like this and maybe swing my hips a little bit—you know, use all my assets," she said in a sultry tone.

Dash found that his mouth was hanging open and he'd taken a step backward. "I . . . I think that could work," he said, sounding awkward.

Merissa lapsed back into her normal persona and laughed at him. "I'm not going to do any of that, you idiot. Do you really think I would do something like that?"

Dash stammered for a moment.

"Choose your words wisely," Merissa warned.

Dash blew out a breath and covered his mouth with his hand for a moment. "I knew you had a sense of humor buried in there somewhere."

"I'm not sure what surprised you more: that I could act like 'that girl,'" she said, using her fingers to make air quotes, "or that I would for a moment entertain the thought of trying to manipulate someone to get something for *you*."

"I thought it was for all of us," Dash replied innocently.

Surprisingly, Merissa smiled back at him. "I can see you coming a mile away, Mr. Dewitt. My plan is to just walk in there and ask them directly. You know, be completely honest. Tell them what we're trying to do. I was just joking before."

Dash nodded. "No, I knew that. I was . . . I thought that's what you meant. I wouldn't think you would . . ."

The edges of her full lips lifted as she watched him stammer away like an idiot.

"Right," Merissa said. "I'm glad we cleared that up. Why is this so important to you?"

"I'm tired of being cooped up. Aren't you?" Dash asked.

"A little bit, I guess. But this whole 'unravel the mystery of the NEIIS' thing seems like it means more to you than most people," Merissa replied.

"All of us almost died a year ago. I was at Sierra during the Vemus attack. I'd volunteered with the colonial militia and we basically ran support for the CDF. It was pretty scary. The fighting was . . ." Dash shook his head. He didn't need to relive that. "When we had to flee the city, I kept thinking about everything I hadn't done yet. After that I was determined to do something important," Dash said.

"And you think unraveling the mystery that surrounds the NEIIS is *that* important something?" Merissa asked.

"Yeah, and . . . we're here. This is our home and I want to see every bit of it," Dash replied.

"I didn't know you were with the militia. Selena and I were here at Sanctuary, hiding during the attack until the end when anyone who could hold a weapon was on the wall. I've heard about what happened at Sierra. It sounded really bad when the city fell," Merissa said.

Dash didn't like to think about it. He'd seen a lot of people die and that was one of the reasons he'd pushed to come to Sanctuary in the first place.

They walked on in silence, but every now and then he thought Merissa was watching him. She seemed to be more at ease since he'd shared that with her. He hadn't planned to talk about his time in the militia but found that it felt good to share something personal with her.

They came to a huge circular building, easily the size of a cathedral. The NEIIS archive had a large round door that had been partially withdrawn into the thick wall. Inside was a well-lit interior with amber lights along the smooth walls. The NEIIS hadn't been big on fixtures inside this building and the spartan interior of the archives was a stark contrast to some of the other sites that had been discovered. The archives were workplaces, but Dash always had the impression that they were also unfinished. Like most things the NEIIS had created, there was just the feeling that they had left in a hurry, and he had no idea why. Discovering other NEIIS sites was the only way to figure it out.

They walked inside and headed to where the tech guys worked. Dash knew they rotated shifts and preferred to do most of their work remotely, but something must have happened for these two guys to be brought in from Sierra. Dash wondered if they were being punished somehow.

Merissa quickened her pace to walk ahead, but Dash decided at the last second to match it and stay by her side. She glanced at him questioningly and he just nodded for her to continue.

Two young men were working on opposite sides of a holoscreen. They'd been chatting quietly until they heard Dash and the others approach. They seemed surprised that anyone would voluntarily come down there.

"Hello. Is there something we can help you with?" one of them asked.

"Yes, we were hoping you could help us out with something," Merissa said and introduced the others.

The one who had spoken introduced himself first. "I'm Brad Kelly and this is Travis Cook. What is it you need down here?" Brad asked.

Dash cleared his throat and held up the storage case. "We have this NEIIS memory module that we'd like to plug into the same system as the archive to retrieve the data on it."

Brad frowned and glanced at his partner. "Okay, I think that can be done, but I'm not sure why you'd want to."

"We have the original NEIIS console in our lab at the Research Institute, but there's a lot of system degradation on it and we're only able to get partial information out of it. We think that if we were to load it up in the archive system, it would automatically do some cross-referencing for us and give us some more information to go on," Dash said.

"So would you guys be able to help us out?" Merissa asked.

Dash watched as Brad blew out a long breath and ran his fingers through his curly blonde hair.

"Why don't you show us the module and then we can decide if we'll be able to help you?" Brad said.

Travis coughed loudly. "Brad, you know we can't do this. The risk to the archive is too great."

Brad glanced at the other tech guy and then looked back at Merissa, who smiled sweetly. Dash was rather impressed.

"What? I just want to take a look at the thing. We might be able to help. You see, Travis, it's people like you who give the rest of us tech guys a bad reputation," Brad said and gestured toward the case Dash was holding.

Dash set the case down on the desk and opened it, carefully lifting out the oval NEIIS data module for the others to see. There were parts where the bronze color shined, but mostly it was obvious it had been exposed to the elements for a long time. Brad and Travis peered at the data module intensely.

"You weren't kidding. This thing has seen better days," Brad remarked.

Travis leaned in and took a closer look. "Are you sure this still works?" he asked doubtfully.

Dash nodded. "It does. We've tested it in our lab."

Travis looked unconvinced and Dash struggled for a moment to keep his irritation with the technical engineer in check.

"How about you let us test it out?" Travis suggested.

Dash resisted the urge to snatch the NEIIS module off the workstation desk. "It's pretty fragile. What is it you think you need to test?" Dash asked.

"We just don't want to burn it out," Brad replied.

Dash used his implants to access his PDA and brought up the test report they'd done at the Research Institute. He then sent it to the nearby holoscreen. "Here, take a look. This is what we've done and the results of the power testing we did. It shouldn't bother the system here."

Brad and Travis turned toward the holoscreen and quickly scanned the report. Brad glanced at Dash and then at the others. "I've seen this testing suite before. You're using the new protocols set up by Noah Barker, a former captain in the CDF."

"Yes, we are. They *are* relatively new," Dash replied.

Brad nodded. "You got that right. We didn't think they were in use anywhere outside the Sierra development group Mr. Barker is heading up. How did you guys get them?"

"He's close friends with Dr. Bishop and Connor Gates," Dash replied.

Brad's eyes widened and he glanced at Travis, who looked just as bewildered for a moment. "I didn't know you worked for Dr. Bishop or that you knew Connor Gates. Of course, we'll help you out. Anything that we can do, we will."

Travis nearly choked, looking as if he'd swallowed a lemon that was struggling to come back up.

Brad glared at Travis. "You can walk away at any time if you want, but I'm going to help these people." Without waiting for

Travis to reply, Brad stood up. "Follow me," he said to Dash and the others.

Dash retrieved the NEIIS data module and followed Brad. The others quickly joined them and eventually Travis followed, muttering to himself about breaking protocol and taking unnecessary risks with the NEIIS archives. Dash was just glad to have their help but for a slight warning in his mind about the implications of doing this work without the knowledge of Dr. Bishop or Connor. If he disclosed that bit of information to Brad and Travis now, they might not help, or at least the help would be delayed until they had official approval from Dr. Bishop. Neither of these appealed to Dash so he kept his mouth firmly shut.

Dash watched as Merissa walked next to Brad and noted the dwindling space between them as they continued on.

"Where are we going?" Merissa asked.

"Down to the lower level where the archive's data storage facility is. There are a few slots we can stick your data module into and see what happens once we bring it online," Brad said.

Merissa smiled at him. "We really appreciate your help."

"It's the least we can do. And don't mind Travis; he's just a bit tightly wound," Brad said.

Dash walked a short distance behind them and watched while they continued talking, finding that he couldn't tear his eyes away from the two of them. His jaw ached from clenching his teeth. He frowned and was surprised to find himself feeling the beginnings of jealousy. It was stupid and immature, and yet it was there inside him like a coiled viper gathering its fury for an attack. He gave himself a mental shake and told himself to stop being an idiot.

Travis caught up to Dash and walked next to him. "So where did you guys find this data module?"

"We found it at a new site about a hundred and twenty kilometers from Sanctuary," Dash replied.

Travis frowned. "And you just took the module out of the console?"

"No, we brought the entire console back to the Research Institute. We had help from the CDF," Dash replied.

Travis's eyes widened. "You have CDF support for field missions here?" he asked.

Dash kept watching Brad and Merissa talking, but since Travis was asking him questions, he couldn't listen to their conversation. "They happened to be in the area. Is it much farther?" Dash asked and didn't bother waiting for Travis to answer. "Hey, Brad, how much farther is it?"

Brad glanced back at them. "Not that much," he said and went back to speaking with Merissa.

Travis continued on ahead of him and Jim came to Dash's side. "What's the matter?" Jim asked.

Dash shook his head. "Nothing," he grumbled.

This is what he'd asked her to do and she was probably just being friendly, so why was it making him so damn crazy? He heard Merissa laugh at something Brad said and almost sneered.

They exited the long corridor and entered an open space with a high cathedral ceiling. Along the walls were multiple NEIIS consoles, all with active glowing mesh screens. Interspersed among the consoles was colonial field equipment that Dash assumed was interconnected with their systems here and probably remotely connected to the ones in Sierra.

"You're so funny," Merissa was saying. "How long are you and Travis going to be at Sanctuary?"

Not that long, Dash hoped. *Please say not that long. Please say you're going home right now.*

"We're only here for a few days," Brad replied.

Yes!

"Oh, that's too bad," Merissa said.

"Yeah, that is too bad," Dash said under his breath in a tone he thought was too soft to hear, but Merissa gave him a sidelong glance. Dash ignored her and looked at Brad. "So, where should I put this thing?"

Brad glanced at the other consoles for a moment. "Travis, why don't you get number fifteen ready while we go get the data module loaded," Brad said and gestured for Dash to follow him.

Brad led him to an open bay that was perfectly sized for the oval-shaped NEIIS data module Dash was carrying. Brad pulled out a tablet computer and entered a few commands. There was a slight humming sound and the open bay began to glow a deep orange.

"Alright, you can put it in there now," Brad said.

Dash slid the data module into the bay and gave it a gentle push to nudge it firmly into place. There was an audible click as the data module locked in.

Brad gave it a quick once-over and then nodded in approval. The others had gathered at the main console in the middle of the large chamber. "Alright, Travis, I want you to power on number fifteen for me," Brad shouted.

Dash glanced back at the others. "Shouldn't we be over there with them?"

Brad shook his head. "No, we need to be here in case something goes wrong with this thing."

Dash had no idea what that meant and didn't get a chance to ask. The open bay doors closed and Dash watched as the spindly ridges on the data module began to glow.

"Looks good from over here," Travis called out.

Brad peered inside the closed bay and then nodded as if he'd arrived at some kind of decision. He glanced at Dash. "Looks good here. Let's go over to the others," he said.

They quickly crossed the room and joined the others around a large mesh screen that Dash assumed was the NEIIS control console for the entire data archive. There was a flashing symbol that looked like a triangle with multiple cross-sections through the middle of it. Travis swiped his finger on it and all the glowing consoles appeared to dim at once.

Dash glanced around, his eyes going wide. "Is it supposed to do that?" he asked.

Brad frowned and shook his head. "This doesn't look good. We need to turn it off, now!"

Travis swiped his hand across the triangle symbol again, but it didn't do anything. He tried another time with the same result—nothing happened. He tried tapping some of the other symbols on the mesh screen, but there was no response. He turned to Brad in alarm. There was a high-pitched whining sound coming from bay fifteen where the data module was. Dash glanced over and saw that the light coming from that bay was much brighter than anywhere else. NEIIS symbols flashed across all the mesh screens of the consoles in the room in rapid succession.

"Shut it down! We need to pull the power!" Travis said.

Brad already had his tablet out and was furiously tapping commands into it.

"What are you waiting for? Shut the damn power down!" Travis shouted.

Brad's eyes widened in shock. "I did shut the power down. It's off. There must be a redundant power source coming in from somewhere."

Dash looked around. All the consoles were still active, so where the hell were they getting power from? The data on the main NEIIS console changed and showed the map they'd been studying for the past few days—only this time it was much more detailed and had more symbols surrounding a site far to the north. It was flashing as if the site had just come online and they were communicating with it from here. All the NEIIS consoles flashed and locked onto the same symbol. Dash had no idea what it meant.

Travis ran from the room, shouting that he was going to try something to shut it down. Dash used his implants to record the data they were seeing and stored it on his PDA. The mesh consoles flashed again and more NEIIS symbols began to scroll across, going from right to left. The mesh screens became full of NEIIS symbols, some of which Dash recognized as system commands. He glanced at Brad, who was still trying to control the NEIIS system from his tablet, his brow furrowed in concentration. Then the consoles all powered off at once. The power had either finally been cut or the redundant system had simply run out of power and they were plunged momentarily into darkness but for the light on Brad's tablet.

"Is everyone alright?" Dash asked.

The others said yes except for Brad, who was walking over to bay fifteen. He pried open the doors and yanked out the module. There was a hissing sound coming from the bay and Dash saw dark scorch marks along the spindly lines of the module. He raced over and Brad glanced at him. Wisps of smoke came from the data module and then there was a slight spark and Brad dropped it to the floor, cursing. He shook his hand. "Damn! That thing burned me."

Merissa had walked over to them. "Here, let me take a look," she said. She had a small flashlight in her hand.

Brad held out his fingers and Merissa shined the light on them. They were hardly red at all. "I'm fine. It just caught me by surprise," Brad said.

Just then the lights turned back on and the NEIIS screens all flickered out. Dash squatted down and held his hand near the data module to see if it was still radiating heat. It was warm to the touch. He opened the storage case and snatched the module up, dropping it inside. He didn't think it would ever work again, but he had a data recording of what had transpired and they'd seen what was on that map. There was definitely more to it. Coming to the archives had paid off.

Travis came back into the room and glared at Brad. "I knew this was a bad idea. We almost lost everything," Travis said and looked at Dash. "What the heck is that thing? We've never had something like this happen where we lost control of the entire system."

Brad was still shaking his hand. "Ease off, Travis. They couldn't have known. It must've activated some kind of latent protocol or something."

Travis shook his head. "Latent protocol," he muttered. "I hope you're ready for some more pain because *you're* filing this report."

Brad rolled his eyes. "Fine. I'll just tell them what happened. Now we gotta run a bunch of system checks to see if we can get this thing back online." Brad glanced at Dash and the others. "Look, I know this isn't your fault, so don't worry about it, okay? We've got a ton of work to do so is it alright if you show yourselves out?"

For a moment, Dash regarded the first decent technical engineer he'd ever met. "Are you sure you don't need any help? We'd be happy to stay and maybe help with that report you need to file," Dash offered.

Brad shook his head and waved them away. "Don't worry about it. Travis is just being dramatic," he said and leaned in. "He'll complain about this for months."

"I heard that," Travis called out from the main console.

Brad grinned. "I better go help him out. Good luck."

Dash thanked him and together they left the NEIIS archives

behind. Once they were out of earshot of the tech experts, they all began talking at once.

"Well, I'd say that was a resounding success. There was much more information on this thing than I thought," Dash said.

Merissa shook her head. "Yeah, but it almost broke the archives. Everything happened so fast and now the module is useless."

"Yes, it did, but I recorded it, and all we have to do is get back to the Research Institute and take a look at what we've got. You saw that new site marked on the map. I think what we were seeing is that it activated the site somehow, or at least opened a communications channel or whatever the NEIIS equivalent is," Dash said.

Merissa's brows furrowed for a moment.

"I think we found something. I mean really found something this time," Dash said, his voice going high with excitement.

Jim nodded and Selena looked excited as well. After a moment's consideration, Merissa smiled.

"Let's hurry back to the laboratory and see what we've got," Dash said.

Jim frowned. "I take it this afternoon's hike is out?"

The others glanced at Dash. "We can still go if you guys want to, but . . ."

"Yeah, we know. I want to see what we found, too," Merissa said.

"Couldn't have said it better myself. Let's get back there," Dash said.

12

THE CDF HELLCAT blazed a trail through the air as it flew over what the colonial cartographers referred to as the Great Plains area of the supercontinent of New Earth. Lieutenant Vince Maddox sat in the cockpit and watched the live video feed of the surrounding area on the large heads-up display that stretched from his left, where he sat in the copilot's seat, all the way to the right, where Lieutenant Mitchell sat piloting the attack craft. The crisp display showed New Earth's landscape in stunning clarity, from the rolling green hills to the forests that were just tiny, puffy specks far off in the distance. A large herd of landrunners galloped below, numbering in the hundreds. Maddox watched the landrunners race along, moving at speeds in excess of eighty kilometers per hour. He knew they could sustain those speeds for hours, which had something to do with the efficiency of their gait when running. Landrunners had four long, thick legs and muscular bodies covered in thick, coarse, dark brown hair. At an all-out run, they moved swiftly, almost graceful in their cadence. Had he been standing on the ground, he would have felt the vibrations of such a large herd pounding by. It wasn't until the landrunners slowed down that their long legs became a liability as they almost clumsily plodded along.

He watched them with the dispassionate eye of a hunter who knew their weaknesses. A well-placed shot could disable a landrunner easily enough. He ought to know; he'd been practicing a lot recently. Landrunners had heavily armored skulls, but toward the rear of their muscular bodies were their flexible, stubby tail, which paradoxically both aided their energy-efficient runner's gait and was also the creatures' Achilles heel. Even from a civilian hunting rifle, a shot in the soft tail section would bring down the large creature, screaming and thrashing in pain. Then other creatures of New Earth would show their true colors as they pounced on the opportunity for an easy meal.

The colonists lived in a dream world, safely tucked away in the encampments, rebuilding their lost cities. They had no idea what kind of world New Earth really was. Humanity's new home wasn't for the faint of heart. Some of the creatures had evolved to become highly efficient killing machines.

The tactical display came to prominence over the video feed and highlighted an area west of their position. Mitchell adjusted their heading. "More ryklars," he said.

Maddox magnified the view and his trained eye saw the backs of the spotted predators as they crept along, almost completely blending in with the ground.

"Another large pack of them," Maddox confirmed.

Ryklars were some of the most dangerous predators they'd encountered on this planet. Maddox had started hunting them while on a remote mission. They'd set up a base camp, and after he'd stood his watch, he'd taken his AR-71 and slipped out of the camp. He hadn't gone looking for ryklars, but he'd stumbled into one of the smaller packs that numbered no more than eight of the creatures. When he'd killed the first one, the remaining seven had pursued him relentlessly. Maddox had been forced to run but had luckily managed to take the rest of them out during his retreat. In that moment of glorious retribution, he'd felt alive, finally having found his place. When he hunted and killed the ryklars, he could forget the faces that haunted him.

A master alarm came to prominence on the heads-up display and the Hellcat dipped down as if they'd encountered severe turbulence.

"It's that damn stabilizer again," Lieutenant Mitchell said.

There was a graphical display of one of the flight stabilizers that required attention.

Captain Fletcher came to the cockpit. "What's happening?"

"It's the rear flight stabilizer again, sir. We'll need to set her down for repairs," Lieutenant Maddox said.

"Very well," Captain Fletcher said. "Send our status back to Central Command, along with our ETA for repairs."

"Yes, sir," Lieutenant Mitchell said.

Captain Fletcher left the cockpit and Maddox glanced at Lieutenant Mitchell. "I'll take over and set her down," Maddox said.

Lieutenant Mitchell switched the flight controls over to Maddox's workstation and then proceeded to send an update to Central Command. With one of the rear stabilizers broken, it felt like the Hellcat was dragging its ass to the side as they flew. It was incredibly sluggish and seemed to fight Maddox for control. He guided the Hellcat well away from the large pack of ryklars they'd observed and found a suitable spot in the open plains. They could defend this position if they needed to. He extended the landing gear and hovered in the air for a moment, checking to make sure the area was clear. The Hellcat bobbed up and down in the air and Maddox's stomach became queasy. He finally set the ship down and the landing gear bit into the ground a little bit harder than he'd anticipated.

Lieutenant Mitchell winced. "Geez, Vince, you really stuck the landing," he groused.

"If you'd repaired it right the first time, it wouldn't have been so rough a landing," Maddox replied.

They'd been doing patch repair jobs for months. The Hellcat was in need of some downtime with a real mechanic crew to do a complete overhaul; however, with resources so constricted there was little chance of that happening. Regardless, Maddox didn't want to return to Sierra anytime soon. Perhaps never. It seemed that the colonial government didn't know what to do with the Colonial Defense Force anymore. Maddox had been a soldier for four years and in the beginning, he'd loved it. He loved the people he served with. They became his brothers and sisters, his family. But the Vemus had killed a lot of them. They were gone. Though the war was over, it seemed that the colonists had forgotten the sacrifice of the CDF. Seeing the general—former General Connor Gates—was like a slap in the face, and the sting of it hadn't left him even though it had been days ago. Among most soldiers in the CDF, General Gates was a legend, and the fact that he'd abandoned them hadn't sat well with anyone Maddox knew.

"You could help with the repairs this time," Lieutenant Mitchell said while shutting down the Hellcat's flight systems.

"I could, but isn't that your job? I'll send Lasky to help you. How's that sound?" Maddox asked.

"That kid doesn't lack enthusiasm, but I don't know if he'd be more of a hindrance when poking around the flight systems," Lieutenant Mitchell replied.

Corporal Lasky was their newest squad member and very eager to prove himself.

"We both know this bird needs a complete overhaul. Just do

the best you can so we can finish this patrol. We'll also need an updated ETA for the repairs as soon as possible," Maddox said.

He left the cockpit as Lieutenant Mitchell went to see about making the repairs. The rear flight stabilizer was part of a multisystem control suite that controlled the thrust coming from the Hellcat's engines. The stabilizer was breaking but hadn't completely broken yet. Maddox suspected that if Mitchell couldn't repair it, he might attempt to bypass that system entirely, which would impact the Hellcat's flight capabilities. They would still be able to fly, but their speed, maneuverability, and capacity for smooth flight would be impacted.

Maddox grabbed his AR-71 and walked down the landing ramp. The other members of the squad had already exited the aircraft and were establishing a perimeter. Maddox spotted Captain Fletcher off to the side and walked over to him, but Captain Fletcher had his hand on his ear and Maddox's internal heads-up display showed that the captain had an active comlink. Maddox came to a stop a short distance away and waited for Captain Fletcher to finish.

"Once we effect repairs, we'll be on our way," Captain Fletcher said over comms. "You *are* aware that this will cut the patrol short?"

After another minute or so, the captain finished the call. He glanced at Maddox and jutted his chin up in greeting.

"Are we being recalled, Captain?" Maddox asked.

Captain Fletcher sighed and nodded. "They want us to return to Sierra at once."

Maddox frowned. "We weren't due to return for another week. I thought this patrol had a much higher priority."

Captain Fletcher regarded him for a moment. "They said they'll send another team to finish our patrol next week," he said, sounding irritated.

Maddox's eyes widened. That wasn't good. "But Captain, we just found another large pack of ryklars in the area—"

"Those are our orders, Lieutenant," Captain Fletcher said.

Maddox forced his face to remain impassive, but his shoulders became rigid. "Understood, sir. But does this have to do with what happened the other day?"

Captain Fletcher drew in a patient breath. "Walk with me for a moment, Vince," he said, and they started heading away from the others.

A few days earlier they'd rescued Connor Gates and a couple of runaways from Sanctuary, and based on Gates's reaction to their rescue, he'd suspected there would be some type of fallout. Apparently, Gates didn't approve of their methods. Perhaps they should've let the ryklars claim the punks from Sanctuary for their foolishness.

"How are you doing?" Captain Fletcher asked.

Maddox frowned. "Permission to speak freely, Captain."

Captain Fletcher nodded.

"I'm getting tired of being jerked around like this. First, they send us a thousand kilometers away from the nearest settlement doing field reconnaissance for ryklar activity and reporting on herd creatures' migratory patterns," Maddox said, quoting from the mission briefing. "We're doing the work of drones, and if they'd put just a bit more of their resources into building a few more satellites, they wouldn't need us to do any of this. We'd be better tasked with actively deterring the ryklars from encroaching upon our territories."

Captain Fletcher nodded. "Is that why you've been taking those nightly excursions?"

Maddox's jaw tightened. He thought he'd been careful. Apparently, he'd been wrong about that.

"I know you've been going off hunting after your watch is done. Does killing ryklars help?" Captain Fletcher asked.

Maddox swallowed and nodded. "Yes," he replied, his voice sounding rough and gravelly. "If those pukes back at Sierra don't recognize the need for a more active role in convincing the ryklars that returning to this region of the continent is detrimental to their health, we may as well let the ryklars in all the encampments."

"So you propose we kill enough ryklars that they stop coming near the settlements. Does that about sum it up?" Captain Fletcher asked.

Maddox considered his answer for a moment before responding. "Honestly, sir, yes, that would be my approach. It's a tough decision, but it's one that has to be made. It's either the ryklars or us. I choose us, sir."

Captain Fletcher seemed to consider this for a moment and then nodded. "One thing I've always liked about you is that you've been forthright with me. To a certain extent, I agree with your assessment of the ryklar situation. The longer we stay here, the more our population grows and the more we're going to clash. There's no easy solution to that problem. However, I'm not sure the colonial government will agree."

"Well, if enough of them start dying from ryklar attacks, they'll have no choice but to take action," Maddox replied.

"You'd like to think so, but look how long it took them to come around to the threat posed by the Vemus. Remember Governor Parish?" Captain Fletcher asked.

Maddox's lips curled into a snarl. "I remember him," he said with a sneer. Governor Parish was one of the reasons so many soldiers had died on Titan Station.

"Left to their own devices, they might deny it until it's too late to do anything about it," Captain Fletcher said.

Maddox's eyes widened. "Sir, what exactly are you saying?"

Captain Fletcher sighed. "Just . . . sometimes I think about ways to get the colonial government's attention."

Maddox glanced around to be sure they weren't being overheard. The other soldiers were still watching the perimeter and Lieutenant Mitchell and Corporal Lasky were working at the rear of the Hellcat.

Captain Fletcher arched an eyebrow. "This surprises you?"

"Yes, it does, Captain. I didn't know you thought that way. I've thought about it a lot and so have Flint and Spencer, who've said the same," Maddox replied.

"I thought as much. Didn't the three of you serve together before?" Captain Fletcher asked.

"That's right, sir. We were stationed at Lunar Base," Maddox said and then frowned. "Sir, I'd like to ask you a question."

"I thought we were still speaking freely, Lieutenant," Captain Fletcher replied.

"Why are we really being recalled?" Maddox asked.

"The official reason is that our equipment needs to be serviced, particularly the Hellcat, and apparently we're overdue for psych evaluations," Captain Fletcher said.

Maddox clenched his teeth for a moment and then took a firm hold of his anger. "Psych evaluations. That has to be because of our run-in with Connor Gates."

Captain Fletcher shrugged. "Perhaps, but it doesn't really matter now. We're on their radar and we will comply with our orders."

Maddox recognized the finality of that tone. "Understood, sir."

"I knew you would, but I should caution you against any further nighttime activities outside camp. That sort of behavior wouldn't hold up in the psych evaluation," Captain Fletcher said.

Maddox blew out a harsh breath. "This is exactly what I'm

talking about, sir. Why does the fact that I enjoy hunting ryklars mean I would get pulled from active duty? Or at least have further psych evaluations and all that other useless crap they try and push on us? I love being part of the squad, sir, and the fact that we get to work so far from Sierra is one of the things that draws many of us to this squad. To you, sir," Maddox said.

"I know you've had a rough time of it, especially of late. I've overlooked a lot and maybe even too much. I just figured that giving you a little bit of leeway would help with what you're going through. And it's not just you—the other guys as well, and even me. But I'm not sure it was the right thing to do," Captain Fletcher admitted.

Maddox felt his stomach clench. "I won't let you down, sir. Not now. Not ever. This is my squad and you're my commanding officer. Just because some of our leaders have forgotten us doesn't mean they all have," Maddox said.

"I've always been able to count on you. That won't change, no matter what happens," Captain Fletcher said.

They didn't speak for a while as they watched the landrunners in the distance, galloping across the Great Plains. Maddox was almost jealous of their freedom.

Lieutenant Mitchell called them over and informed them that the repairs were complete, or as much as they could repair the stabilizers in the field. It would have to do until they could return to Sierra. Captain Fletcher recalled the squad and they began to board the Hellcat.

Maddox glanced longingly at the forest in the distance. He knew there were ryklars not far away and he had an itch to go hunting. He slammed his palm on the loading ramp doors and they withdrew into the ship.

The intercom system came on. "Captain Fletcher, can you please come to the cockpit?" Lieutenant Mitchell said.

Captain Fletcher glanced at Maddox and waved him toward the cockpit. Maddox hastened toward the front of the Hellcat, following closely behind Captain Fletcher.

"What is it, Lieutenant?" Captain Fletcher asked.

"It's this, sir. When I brought the ship systems online, we detected an NEIIS broadcast signal," Lieutenant Mitchell said.

Captain Fletcher frowned for a moment. "Were we scanning for those signals?"

"Actually, no, sir. I was running a systems check and it does a preliminary signal sweep. It happens so fast that it usually doesn't detect anything. It's just dumb luck that we happened to detect the signal when we did," Lieutenant Mitchell said.

"Is it still broadcasting?" Maddox asked.

Lieutenant Mitchell brought up the communications interface on the heads-up display, which was now quiet. "Not anymore, but here's a recording of it."

They couldn't understand the NEIIS signal, and what they saw was just a graphical representation of a signal actually being detected. It didn't match any known colonial broadcast frequencies, which was how they knew it was likely from the NEIIS.

"Do we know where it originated?" Captain Fletcher asked.

Lieutenant Mitchell frowned uncertainly. "I'm sorry, sir, but I'm not sure how to trace it."

"Give me a minute and I'll have it up, sir," Maddox said and went to the copilot's seat. First, he brought up the communications interface and the signal Lieutenant Mitchell had detected, then did a quick analysis and breakdown of the properties of the signal. The computer systems showed the signal source estimate based on the highest probability relative to their current position. "Sir, it's north of here along this heading. Best guess is that it's within five hundred kilometers—six hundred at the most."

Captain Fletcher peered at the information on the heads-up display.

"Captain, I think we should check out the signal. With the increased ryklar activity in this and other areas, this might be what's triggering the change in the creatures' behavior," Maddox said.

Captain Fletcher was silent for a few moments while he considered. Lieutenant Mitchell shifted in his seat, waiting.

"Agreed, Lieutenant," Captain Fletcher finally said. "Set a course and let's go find that signal."

"Roger that, sir," Lieutenant Mitchell replied.

"Captain, shall I send an update back to Command Central in Sierra?" Maddox asked.

"That won't be necessary, Lieutenant. Update the log and I'll forward it later on," Captain Fletcher said and left the cockpit.

Maddox didn't say anything. He knew Captain Fletcher hadn't quite disobeyed orders but loosely interpreted them. This was an intelligence-gathering mission and they had credible evidence to pursue this new lead; however, Maddox knew they should send an update back to Command Central sooner rather than later. Captain Fletcher must have had his reasons to delay sending a response. Tracking a possible cause of all the ryklar activity was much more important than the recall of their CDF team. That would be the official version, but he did wonder how CDF Command would react when they didn't return to Sierra as ordered. What else had Command Central said to Captain Fletcher that had made him so vocal about the current state of the CDF and the colonial government?

13

DASH and the others raced back to the Research Institute, their conversation flying almost as fast as their bodies. Dash couldn't wait to finish putting the proposal together. There was no way they wouldn't get approval to investigate these new sites now. This was a major find that might be even more important than the NEIIS site here at Sanctuary. Dash loved that the others were just as eager as he was about the potential of what they'd discovered. Going to the archives had been a gamble and it had paid off, but he did wonder about the strange effect of the NEIIS data module on the archive.

"I just don't understand how a data module could impact the archive systems like it did," Merissa said.

Dash had heard her say it more than once and he agreed with her. He knew she wasn't going to let it go, nor should she. None of them should.

"I don't understand it either," Dash agreed. "It's something to add to the list."

The Research Institute was just up ahead.

"Any idea how Dr. Bishop will react to this?" Merissa asked.

"She won't overreact, which is how—" Dash stopped himself. "Never mind. Dr. Bishop will find it just as intriguing as we all do. She certainly won't discount it as happenstance. She's a scientist. She'll want to study it and understand why it happened, but it shouldn't impede our ability to go investigate these new sites. The fact that they were active—appeared to be active," Dash hurried to say before Merissa could interject, "should raise the priority of this request and we should be able to go right away."

They headed inside the Research Institute and went straight back to the lab to work, immediately setting about documenting the new discovery. Dash uploaded the data he recorded from the archives while Jim took the damaged NEIIS data module and returned it to its slot on the laboratory table. They'd spent the better part of the last few hours finalizing their proposal when they received word that Dr. Bishop was on her way back to the lab for an update. This news spawned a flurry of activity, as well as a few minor arguments about how the data should be presented. Dash was hard-pressed to keep his excitement under control. He knew Dr. Bishop would appreciate the initiative they'd taken in extracting new data from the NEIIS data module and he didn't think she'd be too upset that it was rendered useless in the process. The data was what was important, not the artifact.

Dr. Bishop entered the lab with Connor and Dr. Malone. Dash glanced at Connor, trying to get a sense of the man's mood. Judging by the intensity of his gaze, Dash assumed that Connor must have a lot on his mind. He wondered if it had anything to do with the visiting colonial government representative.

"I received your update," Dr. Bishop said. "You took the data module to the archives for analysis and you have the results here as part of your proposal. Is that right?"

"Yes, that's correct. If you're up for it, we'd like to go through our proposal right now," Dash said.

Dr. Bishop glanced at all of them and smiled. "I'd very much like to hear it. You've obviously discovered something because . . . well, look at you. You're positively bursting at the seams, chomping at the bit. There's nothing I like to see more. Isn't that right, Connor? Ian?"

Dr. Malone cleared his throat. "I'll go grab us some coffee."

"Thank you, Ian," Lenora said.

Connor looked at Dash. "I've heard that an incident occurred at the archives today. Did that have anything to do with the NEIIS data module?"

News has traveled fast, Dash thought. "Yes, it did, and we'll talk about that when we get to that part of our presentation—if that's alright with you."

Connor nodded.

Dash and the others had decided to each present a portion of their proposal. This had been a team effort and Dash thought it was only fair they each got to share in the limelight. Merissa and Selena were okay with this, but Jim was a little nervous about the whole thing and Dash offered to help him with his part.

Dr. Malone returned with two cups of coffee and hot tea for Dr. Bishop.

For the next half hour, they went through their entire presentation. They started at the beginning with their hypothesis and worked their way through the various research they'd compiled in support of their theories. Each section was broken down by the conclusions they'd arrived at. Dash kept watching for Dr. Bishop's and the others' reactions as they presented their findings. Even though Dr. Bishop supported them in this endeavor, she did ask good questions, most of which they were able to answer. Finally, they came to the final part of their presentation, which Dash would be presenting. He began with his hunch about how the archives might be the best place to extract more data from the NEIIS data module. Then he went into the events that had transpired at the archives. He glanced at Connor during that part of his presentation and took a certain amount of satisfaction in knowing that he hadn't had to sneak in there to get what he wanted. They had done everything by the book—from logging how they took the data module from the Research Institute to leveraging the NEIIS technology at the archives with the help of the technical engineers working there. Dash showed them the updated map and a short video representation of the NEIIS sites coming online.

"As you can see, these look like active connections, or at least they did while the data module was active in the archive system. Unfortunately, there must've been some kind of latent protocol that became active once the connection was established. Brad and Travis were keen to reclaim control of the archive systems, which required a hard shutdown of the entire system. The other unfortunate event was that the NEIIS data module experienced a catastrophic failure and is no longer operable," Dash said and waited for their reactions.

Dr. Bishop glanced at Connor, who gave her a nod, and she looked back at Dash. "This is very good work. It was a risk taking the data module to the archives, but I don't see how we would've gotten this extra data without it. I like the fact that you enlisted the help of the technical engineers at the archives."

"Dr. Bishop," Dash said, "I have one more thing to add. The technical engineers were under the impression that we were doing this with your knowledge. Otherwise, I don't think they would've helped us."

Dr. Bishop frowned and her gaze narrowed thoughtfully. "I see. And you're worried that I'll be upset?"

Dash glanced at Merissa and the others for a moment. "To be completely transparent with you—yes. The technical engineers made an assumption and we didn't correct them."

"I appreciate your honesty," Dr. Bishop said and glanced at the others. "All of you, that is. In this case, I have no issue with it. Would I have liked to have known ahead of time? Yes. In the future, you will contact me beforehand or at least correct people's assumptions. Regardless, you're right in your own assumption that I would have made the request anyway. It was a good plan and we got some valuable data from it."

Dash smiled. "Thank you for understanding. Can we move forward with our proposal? Can we go investigate the new sites? They were active, or at least had the appearance of being online. Given the state of NEIIS technology, I'm not sure how long that will last. Time is of the essence."

Dr. Bishop sighed regretfully. "The timing of this is just terrible."

Dash's stomach clenched as if he'd been struck. They weren't going to get approval.

"All field missions have been canceled for the next few weeks," Dr. Bishop continued.

Dash felt his insides go numb and he stared at Dr. Bishop for a few moments. "But we may never get this opportunity again," he said quickly.

Dr. Bishop glanced at Connor, and Dash noticed just a hint of frustration there. "What you discovered is of vital importance to furthering our understanding of the NEIIS, but other things are going on that make a field mission of this magnitude riskier than it otherwise would be."

Dash felt the heat rise to his chest and he shook his head, trying to tell himself not to get angry and to slow his racing thoughts before he spoke. "I'm really trying to understand. I want to do things the right way. But I'm having trouble with waiting weeks or possibly months before we can go and see these new sites for ourselves. What is so bad that prevents us from going in the first place? Why can't we just go check it out? At the very least, do a flyover and take some pictures. If it's not safe, we'll come back home."

Connor placed his coffee cup on the table. "There've been reports of increased ryklar activity north of every colonial settlement. They don't know why and there are Colonial Defense Force patrols currently investigating. The decision to limit field missions comes from the colonial government, and even if it didn't, we couldn't devote resources to this because we need to bolster our own defenses if the ryklars are heading for Sanctuary," Connor said.

"Are there ryklars heading here?" Dash asked pointedly.

Connor regarded him for a moment. "Not yet, but the locations of these new sites you've discovered are currently beyond our capabilities of detecting ryklars."

Dash glanced at Merissa, Selena, and Jim. They looked almost as frustrated as he felt. They were so close he could taste it.

"What would it take for us to be able to go?" Dash asked.

Connor shook his head. "Did you not hear what I just said? You don't have clearance to go. Any of you. And it's not just you. It's all of us," Connor said and pressed his lips together for a moment. "Let me put it to you this way. It would take more than one of our ships to go, and if we ran into trouble, there would be no support at all. The change in ryklar behavior means there's something else going on, something we don't have a handle on yet, which creates an elevated state of risk for any field mission."

Dash glanced at Dr. Bishop, looking for some kind of support, but there wasn't any. He turned to Dr. Malone and saw the same resolute posture.

"What if we accept the risk?" Dash said. "A C-cat has the range to make the trip. We could stock it up and take all the precautions we need, leverage the use of reconnaissance drones and rifles. We'd be extra careful and better prepared than we were before."

"Do you own any C-cats?" Connor asked.

Dash clenched his teeth and didn't reply.

"You can accept the risk, but it doesn't mean you'll get the resources you need to even make the field mission. Missions like this require multiple days of provisioning and coordination with Field Ops. And I can tell you right now that Field Ops is overwhelmed. These are the facts, and I can't change them. In a few months' time, we'll have more resources. We'll have a better feel for what's going on with the ryklars and able to continue on with the discovery you've made. You just need to be patient," Connor said.

Dash's eyebrows pushed forward. "I'm tired of being patient. I'm tired of having all these restrictions," he said and swung his gaze to Dr. Bishop. "How long are we expected to let Field Ops and the colonial government dictate what we get to do? All of us worked hard to put this presentation together. Our research is ready for peer review. I've looked at the approved peer-reviewed papers in the past and there have been forward operating research bases established for a quarter of the work we just did. It's not fair to us. There's always going to be some crisis impacting the colony. Dr. Bishop, please. There are vehicles we can use that are associated with the Research Institute. Please let us use them to investigate these sites."

Dash could feel Connor's hard gaze on him, but he refused to look at him, keeping his eyes on Dr. Bishop. He could tell that at least on some level she agreed with him. He knew it.

"It's not gonna happen," Connor said.

Dash sneered. "I wasn't talking to you," he snapped. He knew he was crossing a line and didn't care. He'd had enough. Dash's lips formed a thin, frustrated line as he looked back at Dr. Bishop.

Dr. Bishop drew in a steady breath. "Dash, please, I need you to be patient. We need to let the CDF assess the threat. Then we can talk about going to the sites and doing the Field Ops mission the right way."

Dash's throat became thick. He'd never lashed out at Dr. Bishop, but he wouldn't trust himself to look at Connor. He shook his head and tried to think of something else to say, something that would change their minds, but he couldn't think of anything. Instead, he walked toward the door, shoved it open, and left the lab. Once he was outside, he blew out a breath that sounded more like a howl. He clenched his hands into fists and kept walking. When the others left the lab, Jim called out to him to wait, so Dash stopped. He didn't say anything and together they walked out of the Research Institute. A few glances confirmed their angry expressions and told him that they were just as upset as he was. He was glad he wasn't alone in this. They'd done all that work. This was supposed to be the right way and they'd still been denied. They walked in a brooding silence and were almost to the boundaries of Sanctuary before Merissa spoke.

"Alright, let's just stop right here and talk about this," Merissa said.

Dash stopped and turned around. His mouth formed an angry line and he felt the pressure building in his forehead. "You heard them. The answer is no, and I'm willing to bet they're already taking steps to stop us from going on our own," Dash said.

The others seemed to consider this for a moment, but it was Merissa who spoke first. "So what?" she said and glanced at the others. "Are you just going to give up now?"

Of all the responses she could've given, this wasn't one Dash had anticipated. He was beginning to wonder if he would ever be able to anticipate what Merissa would say at any given time. "What can we do?" Dash asked.

Merissa's dark eyebrows raised and her gaze had a hint of a challenge. "That sounds to me like you're giving up. Are you?"

"I'm not giving up, but I'm not sure what we can do. Anything I think of would have lasting repercussions for all of us. I don't want to be responsible for that," Dash replied.

"They're backing us into a corner. We've been heading this way for some time. Honestly, I didn't even realize it until we started working together, but now I can't ignore it anymore," Merissa said.

Selena frowned, her face becoming worried. "I don't think we should be talking about this. We just need to settle down and digest what they said, and make a new request tomorrow. Maybe they'll learn something more by then and realize that the ryklars aren't the threat they thought they were. The field mission ban would get lifted then. I guess what I'm saying is that maybe we should just wait a few days or even weeks if we need to. Is that so bad?"

"If it was just going to be a day or two, that would be fine, but that's not what they're saying. It's never a day or two. They're worried about something. I suspect maybe they aren't telling us everything, or they're just being alarmist," Dash said.

Jim cleared his throat. "What if they're right? What if it's so dangerous out there that maybe we *shouldn't* go to the sites we discovered?"

Dash glanced around. There was a Field Ops station at the entrance to Sanctuary. Everything looked blissfully normal. "If we were really under a serious threat, there'd be CDF troops here. They'd be handing out weapons and we'd be preparing to defend ourselves. We're not doing any of that, so that leads me to believe that they're not sure what's going on out there." He glanced at Merissa. "I'm surprised you're so upset by this."

Merissa ran her fingers through her hair and pushed it behind her ear. Dash tried not to notice the contours of the smooth skin of her neck.

"The fact that they wouldn't even consider any of our suggestions really irritated me. You were right. The Research Institute has vehicles that are capable of reaching those areas. We could do an assessment just as you said, and if it was too dangerous, we could leave. I think they're just preoccupied with saying no. And if every request is met with the same response, we continue to ask their permission. We are part of the Research Institute. We have clearance to do local field missions. But this restriction on requiring Field Ops representation for every long-range survey mission is from a time when we first arrived on New Earth. It made sense then because we knew so little about this place. It seems that the colonial government has a propensity for knee-jerk reactions that involve a clampdown on all activity. Well, I'm sorry. I'm done living like that. I want to go out there and see what we've discovered. We've earned it. We can do it the right way, with or without their approval," Merissa said.

Selena shook her head. "I don't believe this. You're starting to sound like him," she said, nodding toward Dash.

Dash smiled. "You say it like it's a bad thing."

"Just dangerous. If we do what you're hinting at, which is to take matters into our own hands, then it will be dangerous. What if we encounter the ryklars again?" Selena said.

"I think we're getting ahead of ourselves here. I don't want to drag you guys out there. I would go in a heartbeat, but this time I'd want to be better prepared. I don't want to get caught like we did before, so we have to do this right. Would you guys even consider going?" Dash asked.

Selena shook her head. "You see, I knew this was going to

happen. Why don't we just wait a day or two and see what they say?"

"We can, but why don't we prepare to go on our own anyway? I mean if we're going to wait a few days, we might as well be doing something constructive," Dash said with a smile.

"I didn't say I would go," Selena said.

Dash didn't want to push her too far. If Selena got mad enough, she could report what they were talking about and that might land them in even more trouble. Connor would likely have Field Ops lock him up for a few days.

"Selena," Merissa said calmly, "I think waiting a day and seeing if they change their minds is a good suggestion. At the same time, why don't we plan to go anyway? We're just making a plan and we'd have to make a plan for a field mission like this anyway. There are supplies we would need and other things we'd have to take with us. Why don't we do both—hope for the best but be prepared for the worst?"

Selena looked away from them.

Dash cleared his throat. "I'm fine with waiting a day. It's likely we couldn't bring something together with the time we have left today anyway. Plus, they would be watching for it. So, that's two of us in favor of going and one of us on the fence about going at all, which is fine. Jim, what do you think?"

Jim looked at Selena for a moment. "I think waiting a day is the smart thing to do. We should probably calm down, but like you said, we have to plan this mission anyway. That would have been the next step if we had gotten approval. So let's gather some supplies and identify what vehicle we'd want to take. We're certainly not going to trek out there in an ATV, I'll tell you that much. So it's going to have to be a C-cat."

Selena's eyes widened in alarm.

"Hold on a minute," Dash said quickly. "We started this

together and I'd love it if we all finished it together, but I don't want you to feel compelled to go. I just hope you don't prevent the rest of us from going."

Selena looked at Dash for a moment and didn't say anything.

"Why don't we split up for a little while and meet up later on?" Merissa suggested.

They agreed to go their separate ways for a few hours. Merissa and Selena walked off and Jim stayed with Dash.

"Well, that was unexpected," Dash said.

"What? The fact that Merissa agrees with you?" Jim said.

Dash nodded. "Yeah, and the fact that she wants to go. I mean *really* wants to go."

"I sometimes think you underestimate how contagious your enthusiasm for all this stuff is. I mean, I can appreciate the research and the work we did, but I wouldn't be half as excited if it weren't for you. Maybe she likes you after all," Jim said.

Dash felt a growing excitement in his chest. "Maybe . . . she's hard to read, that one. But you know what really bothers me? The fact that I think Dr. Bishop agrees with me. I almost thought she was going to say yes."

Jim shook his head. "That was never going to happen—at least not in the lab. Who knows what she'll be saying once we're out of earshot? Anyway, let's start planning this new camping trip."

14

MADDOX SAT in the copilot's seat of the Hellcat as it sped north, closing in on the NEIIS signal they'd detected earlier. The tactical display showed they were less than eighty kilometers from their target—too far away to see anything, but he had hoped there would be *some* signs of NEIIS buildings. There were none, which meant that this was likely a small NEIIS site.

Lieutenant Mitchell continued to periodically scan for NEIIS frequencies and was unable to detect anything. After the most recent attempt, Mitchell blew out a frustrated breath.

"I wouldn't worry about it too much, Lieutenant," Maddox said.

"I just don't understand why it would suddenly stop broadcasting," Mitchell replied.

"Most NEIIS equipment we find is at least a hundred years old. Frankly, it's a miracle any of it still works, but we have a heading and there's likely something there," Maddox said.

Lieutenant Mitchell harrumphed and continued to tweak the communications interface that had detected the signal in the first place. Maddox left him to it. Try as he might, he couldn't take his mind off the fact that the CDF required him to submit to a psych evaluation. And not just him, but the rest of the squad had to as well. So what if they'd killed a few ryklars to protect their fellow colonists. That didn't mean he was unhinged or unfit for duty. He tried to stop thinking about it, but it kept popping into his mind whether he wanted it to or not.

The Hellcat flew over a sparsely forested area. Spring hadn't come into full bloom yet so most of the trees hadn't sprouted leaves. Maddox spotted dark shapes in the forest and Lieutenant Mitchell flew them in closer. Maddox sent a clone of their heads-up display to the troop area where Captain Fletcher was seated and opened a comlink to him.

"Captain, we're approaching the coordinates for the signal and it looks like there are some old NEIIS buildings on site," Maddox reported.

"Do a quick flyby of the area to be sure we don't have any unwelcome guests, then come join us for the away team. Lieutenant Mitchell, once the away team is off the Hellcat, I want you to immediately take off and be our eyes in the sky. Specialist Stackhouse will stay on board as your gunner. Fletcher out," the captain said and closed the comlink.

Maddox climbed out of his chair. "Looks like you get to stay here. Have fun, Lieutenant, and don't let Stackhouse shoot any of us in the back," he said, only half-joking. Specialist Seth Stackhouse had been cleared to use the Hellcat's weapon systems and the main gunnery chair, but he lacked a certain finesse to pull off any tight-quarter shots that a better gunner would have been able to achieve. Regardless, it wasn't his call to make, and chances were that Captain Fletcher would much rather have a more capable shooter like Sergeant Flint on the ground with them. Carl Flint was the best shot in their entire platoon. Maddox headed to the rear of the Hellcat and grabbed his equipment, then joined the others and they proceeded to do a check of each other's gear before reaching the landing zone.

A few minutes later, Lieutenant Mitchell announced that they were approaching the target. Maddox glanced at the heads-up display nearby and saw a small grouping of NEIIS buildings. Surrounding the central disk-shaped buildings were two bronze monoliths. Some of the buildings looked half buried, which explained why the signal had been temporary. It was likely that whatever had sparked the signal to send in the first place had fried the aged NEIIS computer systems.

Captain Fletcher slammed his palm on the door controls and the landing ramp folded away from the ship. The first four members of the CDF mobile infantry ran down the ramp with their guns held ready. They scanned the area, looking for any threats, and then waved the rest of them forward. Maddox clutched his AR-71 assault rifle and trotted down the ramp. The Hellcat's engines kicked into high gear and the ship immediately took off again. It hovered in the air for a moment and then slowly flew away, doing a quick patrol of the area.

"Alright, let's do this by the numbers. We'll check out each of the buildings and clear them before we proceed. I want to hear you all call it out," Captain Fletcher said.

They repeated their orders and fanned out. Breaking up into teams of four, they approached the nearest building. The NEIIS preferred a rounded architecture that Maddox had seen before. He had no idea what kind of creatures would create this type of building and it didn't matter to him. He only cared about whether there was anything dangerous inside.

Maddox took point for the first team and approached the door. The door controls were easily visible and the panel glowed at his approach. Apparently, this place still had power. The panel showed NEIIS symbols and the internal translator appeared on his helmet's heads-up display. A suggested NEIIS sequence appeared for opening the door and Maddox pressed those buttons in the order advised. The door started to open and then froze in place, showing only several inches of gap. Maddox waved the others forward and together they pulled the door the rest of the way open.

The interior of the NEIIS building was dark but for the light coming in through the doorway. There was a short corridor ahead that opened up into a small atrium. Maddox took point and led the way inside. They quickly reached the atrium and saw that several consoles looked to have been recently activated. One of them still had sparks coming from the bottom and the other two had scorch marks. The signal they'd detected earlier had probably triggered an overload.

"You're up, Chief Spencer," Maddox said.

Chief Spencer detached himself from the group and brought out his tablet. He approached the most intact console and glanced at the control panel on the bottom. Maddox watched as the chief opened the panel and started rooting around inside.

Chief Spencer looked at him after a few moments. "This is going to take me a few minutes, sir."

Maddox nodded. "Carry on then," he said and opened a comlink to Captain Fletcher, apprising him of the situation.

The small atrium wasn't more than fourteen meters across. His helmet's heads-up display enhanced his vision so the otherwise darkened areas appeared as clear as day. He switched the visual spectrum to infrared and glanced around the room. Other than the CDF soldiers, the only heat signatures he detected were from the NEIIS consoles in the room. There was still power here and the source appeared to be located under the floor.

"What's your status, Chief?" Captain Fletcher said as he entered the room.

Chief Spencer was elbows-deep into the NEIIS control console and he glanced up at Captain Fletcher. "Just need another minute, sir. Almost there."

Captain Fletcher nodded and then walked over to Maddox.

"Sir," Maddox acknowledged.

"We may have to cut this short. I sent an update back to Command Central and received an instant reply reiterating our previous orders," Captain Fletcher said.

"They didn't have any reaction to the signal we detected?" Maddox asked.

Captain Fletcher was about to reply when Chief Spencer called out to them.

"Captain, I'm ready to power this thing up," Chief Spencer said.

Captain Fletcher headed back toward the NEIIS console and Maddox followed. "Go ahead, Chief," Captain Fletcher said.

Chief Spencer activated the NEIIS console and the mesh interface immediately started to glow. Just then, Maddox heard something move in the far corner of the atrium. He swung his gaze toward the noise and held his weapon ready. There was nothing there, but he kept his AR-71 trained on the spot where he thought he'd heard the noise.

"Is there a problem, Lieutenant?" Captain Fletcher asked.

Maddox did a quick sweep of the different visual spectrums with his helmet and couldn't see anything. Maybe the noise had come from outside. He could hear several CDF soldiers speaking outside.

"Nothing, sir. I thought I heard something, but it's nothing," Maddox replied.

Captain Fletcher nodded and then walked to the other side of the NEIIS console to get a better look at the mesh screen. The glow coming from the screen became brighter and an NEIIS map appeared. Maddox heard someone gasp and glanced over.

Corporal Lasky was looking at the far corner of the atrium where Maddox had heard the noise before, his eyes wide with terror.

Ryklar!

"Contact!" Maddox shouted and brought up his assault rifle.

He fired his weapon where the ryklar was hiding. There was a snarl and then a roar as several ryklars launched themselves from the walls above. A ryklar slammed into Captain Fletcher, knocking him onto his back. Maddox aimed his weapon and an incendiary round burned through the creature's head. Another ryklar charged forward, attempting to reach Captain Fletcher. Maddox switched his AR-71 to full auto and began spraying the area, making wide sweeps. He heard the others doing the same and the far side of the atrium blazed under the barrage of superheated slugs. Several ryklars were caught in the crossfire and fell. Another ryklar dropped from overhead and slammed its claws into Captain Fletcher's chest. Maddox heard Fletcher cry out in pain and charged forward, throwing his body at the creature. The ryklar rolled away and Maddox was instantly on his feet again. He was about to fire his weapon when Corporal Lasky took it out. The room was silent but for several dying ryklars, and Maddox made quick work of them.

"We need a medic in here!" Chief Spencer shouted.

Maddox turned around and saw Chief Spencer kneeling at Captain Fletcher's side. There was a river of blood flowing from the captain's chest, and Maddox saw that the ryklar's claws had pierced his body armor. Maddox knew the smart-mesh undershirt must have sensed the injury and constricted around the area in an attempt to stifle the bleeding, which was the only reason Captain Fletcher was still alive.

Captain Fletcher groaned in pain and tried to get up, but Maddox held him down. "Just lie still, Captain. You've been wounded. Corporal Gibbs is on his way," Maddox said.

Captain Fletcher winced in pain and Maddox did a quick check to see if there were other wounds. He found more on the captain's side below his armpit.

"Make a space!" Corporal Gibbs shouted and Chief Spencer immediately moved out of the way.

They pulled off Captain Fletcher's outer layer of armor and found two more wounds they couldn't see before.

God damn ryklars, Maddox thought.

Maddox opened a comlink to the rest of the squad. "Do a sweep of the area using the sonic wave detectors. The ryklars set up an ambush. If any are detected, take them out. Maddox out."

He watched as Corporal Gibbs assessed the wounds. He applied medipaste to the one on the side and brought out a handheld scanner to assess the deep wound on Fletcher's chest. The captain groaned in pain and Corporal Gibbs administered painkillers.

"There, that's it. Just relax," Corporal Gibbs said.

Captain Fletcher closed his eyes and became still.

"How is he?" Maddox asked.

"He's got several deep lacerations. Medipaste can stop the bleeding, but I need to give him a full dose of medical nanites to repair the internal damage. They'll take care of the broken ribs, too. Then we'll have to wait and see," Corporal Gibbs said.

Maddox opened a comlink to Lieutenant Mitchell and ordered him to bring the Hellcat back to their position. He left Corporal Gibbs with Captain Fletcher, telling him he'd send a stretcher once the Hellcat arrived.

Maddox headed outside and Sergeant Flint ran over to him.

"Sir, no ryklars in the other buildings or in the immediate area. What the hell happened, sir?"

"It was the damnedest thing I've ever seen. The ryklars waited for us to get inside and lower our guard. I didn't detect them with infrared," Maddox said, and noticed Corporal Lasky standing off to the side. "How did you know they were there, Corporal?"

"I did a sweep of the visual spectrum and then switched to sonic wave detection. That's when I saw all of them. There were so many. I'm so sorry, Lieutenant. I froze . . ." Corporal Lasky said.

"You've got nothing to be sorry about, Corporal. If it weren't for you, we'd all be dead," Maddox said.

It was the truth and Maddox itched to shoot something, but he knew better than that. If there was any failure to be found, it had been with him. Corporal Lasky was always trying to make himself useful to the squad. He'd followed standard protocol when the rest of them hadn't.

The Hellcat landed nearby and a stretcher was brought out for Captain Fletcher. The rest of the soldiers gathered outside the main building and looked at Maddox. He was second-in-command and now had to decide what to do.

"Corporal Gibbs has informed me that Captain Fletcher is in stable condition. He's given the captain a treatment of medical nanites that will repair his internal injuries, but it was a close thing. We got caught with our pants down and that shouldn't have happened," Maddox said and looked at the rest of the CDF squad with flinty eyes. "Our orders are to investigate the NEIIS signal that led us here. The console was able to show us a map, and according to Chief Spencer, there was another location identified. However, we'll need to make camp here since it's so late in the day and Captain Fletcher needs time to recover from his wounds. Then we'll continue on in the morning. I want a mobile camp set up within the next fifteen minutes. Sergeant Flint, I want two sets of guards on duty at all times. Standard deterrent measures are to be set up at once. We don't need any more ryklars ambushing our position."

"Yes, Lieutenant," Sergeant Flint said.

As the soldiers started setting up camp, Maddox caught Corporal Lasky looking at him strangely from time to time. Maddox went to the Hellcat and opened the comms systems. He recorded a video log of what had happened and what their current status was. He then set a timer to delay sending the update for another six hours. He wanted to be sure that by the time Central Command received the update they wouldn't order Maddox to return right away. They might try, but Maddox intended to be well on their way to the main NEIIS site they'd seen on the map. To give his report more gravitas, he included that Corporal Gibbs had recommended not moving Captain Fletcher for the next twelve hours even though no such recommendation had been made, but Maddox didn't much care. He wasn't returning to Sierra anytime soon. He wanted payback. He wanted to hunt ryklars.

15

CIVILIAN-CLASS AERIAL TRANSPORT VEHICLES, or C-cats as they were commonly referenced, weren't that difficult to steal, and Dash hadn't been too concerned with acquiring some type of transport for their long-range field survey expedition. He'd found it amusing that Connor had tried to lock him out of all vehicle systems at Sanctuary. He'd expected it and hadn't been too surprised when Jim confirmed it. But Dash wasn't foolish enough to use his own credentials to access a transport vehicle because he knew that would send an alert to Field Operations and Security, who would then inform Connor that an attempt had been made. Such action would bring the former CDF general down on him quicker than a landrunner in full stride across the Great Plains. What *had* surprised him was that he and his companions were all on a Field Ops and Security watch list. This was also a shock to both Merissa and Selena, finding themselves in the same boat as Dash. He'd had a good laugh about it and welcomed them to the dark side. Merissa seemed to take this in stride, but Selena still appeared bothered by the whole thing.

They'd waited a whole day before setting off on their own. Nothing had changed and Field Ops still had the travel ban in place. Dash had expected as much and had already started stockpiling the supplies they'd need. But the method he'd used to gather their supplies had impressed his small group of rebels, and he was actually surprised none of *them* had thought to use drones as a means of transporting equipment to a predetermined location they could later pick up. No one closely monitored drone activity in the immediate vicinity of Sanctuary, so when he temporarily appropriated a small army of them, no one was the wiser. To anyone monitoring them, the drones had just taken a more circuitous route on their final predefined patrol.

Together, the four of them left various supplies on the rooftop of the Research Institute. The drones would then pick up their supplies and whisk them a few kilometers outside Sanctuary. Dash had the drones working throughout the night, so when it came time to leave, they had relatively little to bring with them in their "borrowed," newly minted Field Ops C-cat. Apparently, there had been a delivery of five C-cats from the fabrication units at Sierra. They hadn't even been registered with Sanctuary's computer systems yet, which allowed any one of them to use the vehicles without tripping alarms. The C-cat they'd borrowed was an airbus model that was capable of transporting up to twenty people comfortably, chosen so they'd have plenty of room for their supplies.

Jim was in the pilot's seat, flying them toward their first destination. They'd elected to travel to one of the NEIIS locations farther east than they'd originally planned. Hoping there would be less of a chance of encountering any ryklars at the more remote locations, they were traveling about six hundred and fifty kilometers north of Sanctuary's location. Since they'd left later in the morning, they wouldn't reach their destination until well past the middle of the day. They were flying "low and slow" as Jim liked to say, making his voice sound deeper than it normally was, so it was likely they hadn't been missed yet.

"How long do you think it'll take them to realize we've flown the coop?" Jim asked.

Dash had been glancing behind them, trying not to glare. They had an extra passenger he hadn't anticipated would be joining them.

Jim had to repeat his question and then snap his fingers to get Dash's attention.

"What?" Dash asked in a slightly annoyed tone, but Jim just looked at him. "I don't know. Probably pretty soon. We've been gone for three hours and I know Connor's keeping tabs on us."

Dash glanced behind them again and almost scowled at the sleeping form of one Brad Kelly. Merissa had decided they could use the help of one of the technical engineers working at the archives, and she and Selena had "happened" to run into the one technical engineer who was intrigued by the work they were doing. Dash hadn't wanted anyone else joining them, at least until Merissa kindly pointed out that they could use the help of an expert in NEIIS technology. Dash had to admit (if only to himself) that bringing a tech expert with them was actually a good idea, but why did it have to be Brad? And why did Merissa have to look at him like she'd just been served her favorite dessert?

Brad wasn't the stereotypical technical engineer. He had perfect blonde hair, blue eyes, and a chiseled chin, with a charming dimple in his cheek thrown in for good measure. Dash actually entertained a cheerful vision of Brad being horribly scarred by a tragic hiking accident but then immediately dismissed the thought as being beneath him. It wasn't Brad's fault he was good looking, and if he was being honest, Brad wasn't a bad guy. He was just the competition.

"You've got to get over it already. He's here, and if you keep acting like an idiot, she's gonna notice—if she hasn't already," Jim advised.

Dash glanced at his friend. When there weren't any pretty girls around, Dash actually appreciated Jim's generally useful advice. But even in this case, Dash had to admit that Jim was right. Perhaps he was overreacting just a bit. Brad was here. Still, Dash didn't have to like how Merissa seemed to go all doe-eyed when the guy simply laughed. Did the C-cat have an ejection seat?

A message appeared on the heads-up display that indicated a general broadcast had been sent from Sanctuary. The message required their acknowledgment and Dash frowned. "If we acknowledge that message, can they trace it to us?" he asked.

Jim shook his head. "They shouldn't be able to. It's just a broadcast. Maybe we should ask—"

"Don't you dare," Dash said.

Jim shrugged.

"Hey, we've got a message," Merissa said as she made her way toward them at the front of the C-cat. "Aren't you going to acknowledge it and see what it says?"

"We're not sure if it can be traced," Dash said.

Merissa peered at the message. "Let's just ask Brad," she said and called back to him.

Dash rolled his eyes and Merissa frowned at him, confused.

The technical engineer woke from his slumber and rubbed his hands over his face in an attempt to wake up. Then he joined them at the front. After hearing their concerns, he cocked his head to the side and thought for a moment.

"I can check the message header to look for any latent protocols used for tracking. They'd likely appear just beneath it," Brad said.

Dash climbed out of the front seat so Brad could sit there and use the C-cat's computer systems. Brad brought up a command window and checked the initial message. After examining the raw code that Dash had no hope of understanding, he closed it up.

"It's just a standard message without any tracers. It should be safe to download," Brad said and stood up.

Merissa glanced at Dash for a moment and then brought up the message. It was from Dr. Bishop. The short message was a simple request for them to check in, along with an advisory that requested they return their borrowed C-cat.

Dash reread the message, looking for some kind of hidden meaning in it. Then he closed it and cleared the screen.

Merissa's brows drew up in concern. "Aren't you going to reply to her?"

"Not right now," Dash said.

Merissa closed her eyes and sighed heavily. "What's the harm in sending a reply?"

"The only thing I can send back now is that we received her message. I'd much rather have an update to send back after we reach our destination," Dash said.

Merissa pursed her lips together as she thought about it. "Alright, I see your point, but we should send some kind of reply back later then. Agreed?"

Dash nodded. "Sounds good to me. We're almost there so let's start getting ready."

Jim had managed to acquire some Field Ops equipment for their journey. In particular, he'd found lightly armored shirts that were made of smart-mesh material. The tan-colored shirts were comfortable and extremely durable. Depending on the weather, they could change their composition to protect against the cold or become more breathable in warmer climates. They wouldn't help much if they found themselves in extreme weather conditions, but there was little risk of that where they were heading.

Dash already had his equipment ready, but he checked his backpack anyway. They'd brought extra CAR-74 standard issue hunting rifles, as well as sonic blasters. They had plenty of ammunition, but Dash honestly hoped they wouldn't need any of it.

"A hunting knife?" Merissa asked when she glanced into Dash's open pack.

The blade was forty-six centimeters in length and made from a carbon metallic alloy that was light and strong.

"It was a gift and sometimes it's useful to have out in the field," Dash replied.

Seeing the knife, Brad's eyes lit up. "Oh, hey, that's a Bowie knife! I love these things. Do you mind if I take a look?"

Dash grabbed the polished wooden handle that was made of synthetic cherry wood with two decorative inlays for the pins. The sheath was made of soft synthetic leather that he had water-molded to the knife. He handed it to Brad, who looked at the sheath appreciatively and gave Dash an approving nod. Brad grasped the handle and pulled out the blade, making a low whistling sound. "Now that's a knife," Brad said.

Merissa glanced from the Bowie knife to Dash. "Who gave it to you?"

Brad handed back the knife and Dash put it in his pack. "Connor."

Merissa's eyes widened in surprise. "I thought the two of you didn't get along so well."

Dash shrugged and secured his backpack. "It was a few months after I arrived and we'd just done a local field mission. Hunting rifles and sonic blasters are all good to have, but sometimes an old-fashioned knife is just as useful. And as far as Connor and I not getting along—well, that's a more recent development."

Merissa nodded knowingly.

"We're reaching the coordinates," Jim called out from the front of the C-cat.

Dash and the others went to the front and saw a small NEIIS outpost on the heads-up display. "Look at it! It's just sitting there right in the open," Dash said.

Jim slowed their approach and hovered in the air.

"It looks remarkably well-preserved," Merissa said. She placed her hand on Dash's shoulder as she leaned forward to peer at the heads-up display. Her head came so close that he could smell the flowery scent of her hair.

"Don't mind me," Dash said, grinning, which caught Merissa by surprise and she quickly backed away, muttering a hasty apology.

Dash brought the scanners online and cycled through the different visual spectrums. The infrared didn't show any heat signatures from inside the NEIIS building, but that didn't mean there wasn't a power supply inside, and since the outpost appeared intact it was safe to assume there were no ryklars waiting inside. Dash kept that thought to himself.

The NEIIS building was on top of a hill out in the open, and they didn't see any ryklars or any other animals in the area. He switched to the sonic wave detector and had the sensor pivot back and forth. The C-cat's computer systems filtered out any noises detected by the sensors, then analyzed the new data, comparing it to all known ryklar sounds in the onboard database. Also, the computer system could detect the beating hearts of any ryklars in the area. The whole process only took milliseconds. Dash had reviewed how it worked before leaving.

"Looks clear to me. Let's set her down just outside the building," Dash said.

Jim circled the NEIIS outpost one more time and then extended the landing gear. The C-cat touched down softly and Jim cut the engines. Dash glanced at the others and saw the brimming excitement in their eyes. Even Selena, who had finally agreed to come along with them only at the last minute, was eager to see what was inside the outpost.

As Dash opened the rear doors of the C-cat and waited for the ramp to extend, a soft breeze of cool, fresh air entered the enclosed space. The air this far north was noticeably drier, but the temperature was comfortable.

Inside the C-cat, they were all armed with hunting rifles except Selena, who preferred the sonic blaster. Dash went down the ramp first and took a quick glance around. The area was quiet, and the only sound was the breeze blowing over the grass-covered hills. The others exited the C-cat and looked around, then headed toward the NEIIS outpost.

"Any theories on why they built these outposts?" Jim asked.

"Nothing concrete," Dash replied. "Perhaps they were future sites for cities, but it's hard to know for sure."

The NEIIS had seemed to alternate between curvature and angles in their buildings. In this case, the outpost was octagonal in shape rather than the rounded architecture they'd encountered near Sanctuary, and Dr. Bishop had hypothesized that those differences reflected two separate populations of NEIIS who possibly were parts of different cultures. But the feature common to both types of architecture was the bronze metallic alloy of which this outpost was constructed. It was extremely durable to have lasted this long, and upon closer inspection, there was a deep, almost golden hue that remained untarnished by the weather or the sun.

They found the main doors on the northern side of the building. The control panel activated when Dash touched it and the main door opened easily. Lighted panels inside the outpost came on as the door opened, revealing several NEIIS consoles.

Dash led the way and saw that there were NEIIS living quarters on one side and a standard work area at the far end. He glanced inside the living quarters and noted the lack of furniture, particularly a bed. How had the NEIIS slept? Judging by the height of the shelves and what passed for chairs, he believed the NEIIS weren't very tall. If he had to guess based on the few pieces of furniture in the room, they might have averaged a little over one and a half meters—or perhaps they just preferred smaller furniture. No one could be sure because they hadn't found any NEIIS skeletal remains.

"Not a lot in the way of comfort, is there?" Merissa said.

"It doesn't look that way, or maybe they took the furniture with them when they left," Dash said.

Merissa stepped inside the living quarters and looked at a control panel just inside the door. She peered at it for a moment and then wiped away the dust before pressing one of the buttons. A table extended from the wall. "Or the furniture could just be hidden away. The NEIIS seem to be a pragmatic bunch," Merissa said.

Dash's eyes widened in surprise and he took a closer look at the control panel for the room. There was a grouping of triangular buttons with a small, pale mesh screen above it. He walked over to the table and pressed his hand on the smooth surface. The table didn't give at all.

"What is it?" Merissa asked.

"The table is pretty strong," Dash replied and glanced around the room. "I keep wondering what the NEIIS were doing here. Why build these in the first place? Though there are living quarters, I don't get the feeling that this was anyone's home."

Merissa looked around. "Reminds me of one of our FORBs."

Dash nodded. "Exactly, but why were they here? What were they studying . . ."

"And why did they leave?" Merissa said.

"Yeah," Dash said. "I keep hoping we'll find some kind of indication of what happened to them."

"Did you ever consider that perhaps the NEIIS weren't from this world?" Merissa asked.

"It's not a very popular theory. Based on what we know about them, we don't think they were space-faring," Dash said.

"As far as we know," Merissa said, sounding unconvinced. She smiled when he looked at her. "Come on, you know we haven't come anywhere near to learning all we can about the NEIIS."

"You'll get no argument from me. So are you proposing that the NEIIS came to this planet and played in their proverbial sandbox for a few hundred or maybe even a thousand years, then just decided to leave?" Dash asked.

Merissa shrugged.

Brad called out to them from the outer room. "These consoles look to be in working order."

"Let's go see what our tech guy's found," Dash said.

They left the living quarters and walked over to the consoles as Jim and Selena came in through the main doorway.

"I have two recon drones on a tight-knit patrol of the area just as a precaution," Jim said.

Dash nodded. They'd agreed beforehand that they would take every precaution regarding their safety. Even though they hadn't detected anything on the C-cat scanners, using the recon drones was just good sense.

Brad glanced at Dash. "When you were at the other outpost, what exactly did you do?"

"I opened the control panel on the bottom to clear out some of the debris. It was in pretty bad shape, much worse than this one. Then I powered it on. It went through some kind of automated startup sequence and then highlighted a particular symbol. I selected the symbol and that's when we noticed the map with the highlighted locations. We didn't have much time because the ryklars attacked," Dash replied.

Brad pressed his lips together and his brows pulled in tight while he thought. After a few moments, he shrugged. "Alright, I'll just power it on now," Brad said.

They gathered around the NEIIS console and watched as Brad glided his fingers across the pale mesh screen. The console immediately activated, as if it had been in standby mode all these years, then went through some kind of startup sequence with different flashing symbols. Then, NEIIS symbols began scrolling from right to left across the screen. Dash recognized the triangle with a few slashes across the middle and pressed his fingers on that one. The other symbols disappeared and a map came to prominence on the console.

"It looks the same as before," Dash said. He brought out his PDA and engaged the holo-display to show the map they'd seen from the other outpost.

"They're identical," Merissa said.

Several of the NEIIS sites were flashing. Then, the entire map refreshed and another city appeared far to the north. The NEIIS reference had a subset of symbols circling around the new location.

Dash peered at the symbols and brought up the translator on his PDA.

"Why do you think those sites are highlighted?" Jim asked.

"I think those are the active sites, meaning that it's able to establish some kind of connection," Dash said and frowned for a moment. Then he looked at Brad. "Can you scan for any NEIIS signals or anything to indicate that they were using a network of some kind?"

Brad nodded and brought out his tablet. He entered a few

commands and then held it up as if he was trying to get a radio signal. He slowly turned, stopping at various points and making a circle. "There's definitely a broadcast being sent and received. I think you're right."

Merissa glanced at Dash's PDA. "It's another city reference, almost like Sanctuary, but not quite . . ."

Selena cleared her throat. "If there *is* something broadcasting, shouldn't we turn it off?"

Dash frowned, not understanding why she was so worried.

Selena shook her head in exasperation. "This outpost is checking in with the other sites. That's fine, but what if it's also signaling the ryklars? We know they do that, too. How would we know if turning this thing on sends a signal to the ryklars? You know, enacting the protection protocol they were following for some of the other sites that have been discovered," she said, looking at all of them.

Dash pursed his lips in thought. He hadn't considered that. "She might have a point. Let's copy the data from this map and shut down the console, unless you know how to stop the broadcast," he said, looking at Brad.

Brad glanced at the console and tapped one of the symbols in the upper left corner. The map disappeared. Then he looked at his own tablet. "It's still broadcasting a signal. Let me just see if I can do something in the control panel."

Brad squatted down and opened the panel at the base of the console. He reached inside and after a few moments the mesh console went dark. Standing back up, he checked his tablet and nodded. "The broadcast has stopped."

Dash did a quick check of the recon drones and they hadn't detected anything. For the first time since leaving Sanctuary, he was glad Brad had been with them.

"Alright, so we've confirmed that there are active sites out there. I think we should go check out the central one that's about fifteen hundred kilometers north of here. What do the rest of you think?" Dash asked.

Jim glanced out the door and then looked back at them. "I'm not sure we should make the trip today. It would be nightfall before we reached it and I don't want to explore an NEIIS city in the dark."

Dash nodded. "We could camp here tonight and explore this outpost, maybe see if we can get more information off the console as long as it doesn't broadcast our position," he said, looking at Selena. "Good call on that, by the way."

Selena smiled and then nodded.

"I think camping here's a good idea," Merissa said. "There's a control panel in the living quarters, and who knows? Maybe the NEIIS have other things hidden away. It's worth taking a look."

"Alright, then it's decided. We'll stay here and explore the area a bit. I'll draft a reply to send to Dr. Bishop to let them know what we've discovered, but I'm not going to send them our current location—at least not yet. Jim, since we're staying here, we should utilize all the recon drones. How far can they patrol?" Dash asked.

"They have a ten-kilometer range. I can task a couple to go a bit farther out and daisy-chain them, but I think we should keep a majority in closer. I'll go set those up," Jim said.

"I'll give you a hand," Brad offered.

Merissa caught Dash's eye after Jim and Brad left. "See, I told you he'd be helpful."

Dash smiled. "I'm sorry I ever doubted you."

Merissa chuckled.

They went back to the C-cat and unloaded the equipment they needed to make camp and cook some food, then spent the next few hours exploring the outpost and the surrounding area. It was remarkably intact and the systems still worked.

The sun dipped below the horizon and a starry night showed above while New Earth's rings shone like bright celestial pathways arching over the horizon. Despite their tranquil surroundings, Dash found that he kept checking the recon drones just to be sure nothing was trying to sneak up on them undetected. Not wanting to be caught off guard this time, he made sure the alarms were in place in case anything larger than a small dog was detected. Things were going pretty well for their first night away from Sanctuary. They were learning a lot about the NEIIS, given the pristine condition the outpost was in. This was an excellent start to what he hoped was going to be an unforgettable journey.

16

CONNOR WALKED outside the Field Ops landing ground. This was the last place to search and he suspected he should've gone there first. If nothing else, Dash had proven that he was quite clever when he focused his extremely active brain on a task.

A comlink request appeared on his internal heads-up display showing Lenora's identification. He allowed it to come through.

"You still trying to figure out which vehicle they stole?" Lenora asked.

"Yes, because that'll give us some indication of how far they can travel in a day. Still think we need to wait for them to check in?" Connor replied.

There was a long pause before Lenora answered. She'd been snippy with him for the past few days.

"Yes, I do. I know Dash; he'll check in," Lenora said.

Connor continued walking across the airfield and came to a small hangar. "I hope you're right."

"You'll see," Lenora answered.

"In the meantime, I'm going to keep looking for whatever vehicle they stole," Connor said.

Lenora closed the comlink and Connor headed toward the hangar. In the past twenty-four hours he'd studied the NEIIS map Dash had discovered so often that he knew it like the back of his hand. However, he couldn't just go charging off, even if they did find the vehicle Dash and the others had taken. Lenora might be right and the best thing they could do was wait. Connor thought they'd taken every precaution to prevent what Dash and the others had successfully pulled off. Even Captain Ramsey had been surprised and a bit amused.

As Connor reached the hangar, the large doors opened and Captain Ramsey poked his head out. Upon seeing Connor, he chuckled.

"I finally figured it out," Captain Ramsey said and pulled the hangar bay doors open so Connor could see inside. "Thanks to our good friend Bernard Duncan, we received a shipment of C-cats to help with our vehicle shortages," Captain Ramsey said and led Connor inside, bringing him to an empty space between two of the Airbus model C-cats designed for large capacity. "I have to admit, the kid is smart. He must've figured out that we locked him out of the vehicle control systems for anything currently registered with Sanctuary. But since these vehicles just arrived, we haven't registered them yet."

Connor's eyes widened in surprise. "Well, Lenora wouldn't keep the kid around if he wasn't smart. What's the range of these things?"

Captain Ramsey grinned tiredly. "You're gonna love this. These C-cats have newer fuel cells, which increases their range considerably. And since they're not hauling any weapon systems like a Hellcat does, the range is pretty far. They could make the trip from here to Sierra almost three or four times before having to recharge. This gives them a range of five thousand kilometers, easy."

Connor blew out a long, frustrated breath and rubbed his chin. With that kind of range, Dash and his team could be anywhere. "Well, shit," he said.

"You got that right, and you can bet those little shits disabled the transponder on that C-cat. We have no idea where they are. On top of that, there is a ten-minute window where we had a couple of monitoring stations go offline," Captain Ramsey said.

"Let me guess, this was one of them along with a few others seemingly at random so as not to draw attention," Connor replied.

Ramsey nodded. "You've got that right."

They left the hangar behind and Captain Ramsey locked it up, not that it would do much good now.

"I'll send some of my guys here to get these C-cats fully registered in case anyone else gets any bright ideas," Captain Ramsey said.

"It's a start. The other thing I can't figure out is why none of the security feeds show them bringing any equipment. I know Dash wouldn't leave without everything he thought he needed—things like weapons, provisions for at least a week or possibly more, and other gear used for accessing NEIIS systems. I can go on and on, but I know he definitely didn't do this on his own. I've run enough operations to appreciate the level of capable execution at work here," Connor said.

Captain Ramsey arched an eyebrow. "Careful now, that almost sounds like a compliment."

Connor chuckled. "I suppose it is. I just wish it was under different circumstances."

During their walk back to the Field Ops Command Center, Captain Ramsey received an alert for a CDF briefing being sent from Sierra at the top of the hour.

"Must be important if they're letting us know ahead of time about the briefing," Captain Ramsey said.

"They wouldn't send a heads up if it wasn't serious. This isn't gonna be good," Connor replied.

They quickened their pace, and when they reached the Field Ops Command Center, Connor sent Lenora a text message asking her to join them. Captain Ramsey sent a Field Ops agent to register the new C-cats in their hangar.

Connor saw Bernard Duncan leave the conference room with Lenora following. She looked at him and gave him a tight smile.

"I guess I didn't need to send that message," Connor said.

"I was already here, talking to Bernard," Lenora replied in an even tone.

Connor nodded a greeting to Bernard.

"I feel somewhat responsible for what happened," Bernard said. "I should've transferred the registration for those new C-cats as soon as they arrived."

Connor shook his head. "This is hardly your fault."

"But it does reveal an underlying problem we'll have to deal with," Lenora said.

Here we go, Connor thought to himself.

Bernard's bushy brows pulled together tightly. "I'm not sure I understand what you mean," he said.

Connor glanced around the busy command center and then looked at the time. "We have about fifteen minutes before the CDF sends its official update about the ryklars. Why don't we go to the conference room for a few minutes to talk?" he suggested.

They went to the conference room and Captain Ramsey joined them.

"Alright, tell me what I'm missing," Bernard said.

"There's been a growing frustration from the people at the Research Institute regarding limitations on field missions, myself included. Waiting for Field Ops to be available for escort duty has put a severe bottleneck on the work we're doing," Lenora said.

Connor snorted bitterly. "There's a difference between being frustrated with how things are and just doing whatever you want, which is exactly what Dash has done. And not only that, he's convinced others to join his foolhardy crusade."

Lenora glared at him. "Sometimes clipping its wings isn't the way to teach an eagle to soar. Dash didn't make the others go with him. He didn't even have to convince them; they chose to go. They tried to follow the rules we laid out for them first, and when that didn't work, they took matters into their own hands. If there's failure and blame to be had, it's in this room."

"So we're to blame for Dash's actions? We made him steal equipment so he could go off and make a 'discovery?'" Connor said.

"Yes, we did," Lenora said.

Connor glanced at Captain Ramsey and then at Bernard for a moment. "This is ridiculous. We have rules—"

"Don't you dare lecture me about the damn rules," Lenora snarled. "I'm not one of your followers. It's not like Dash, Jim, Merissa, and Selena took the C-cat for some joyride or as an act of latent adolescent rebellion. They took the C-cat so they could explore and further their research. This is not the act of misguided youth. This is the result of you trying to control everything and everyone around you."

Connor's mouth opened wide with surprise. "I'm not trying to control everything."

"Yes, you are, whether you realize it or not," Lenora snapped.

Bernard blew out a breath. "Perhaps we need to take a moment here," he said and paused before continuing. "Just so I understand, these young scientists made a discovery and took one of the new

C-cats to try and find an undiscovered NEIIS site to prove that the map they'd found was accurate?"

"That's part of it," Connor said. "Also, we have the travel ban that's currently in place and other limitations due to the Field Ops staff shortages you're already aware of."

Lenora crossed her arms in front of her. "Dash tried to find a viable alternative, but you wouldn't hear of it, and he did the only thing he felt he could do. He did exactly what I would've done in his place."

Connor felt the heat rise in his face. She was blaming him for Dash's actions. "Then you'd both be wrong. The travel ban isn't an optional thing. It wasn't put in place because we think it's a good idea; it was put in place to save lives. The CDF didn't send a heads-up about their upcoming briefing because everything's okay. There's more going on here than the discovery of another NEIIS city."

Lenora shook her head. "If it were just that, we wouldn't be arguing. Ever since we discovered he was gone you've been chomping at the bit to go after him. You might have convinced yourself that it's to save him, but what's really going on is that he defied you. How dare he go against the great Connor Gates? Do you want to know what really irritates you about him?" Lenora said, and waited a moment. "He's *just like you*. You and he are so much alike I'm surprised you don't see it yourself. Put yourself in his shoes. What would you have done?"

Connor looked away, his shoulders tight.

Captain Ramsey cleared his throat. "When I was his age, I was getting into trouble back on Earth. I know they're good kids, but they should've waited. I'm concerned that other people are going to follow his example. And I don't mean just other kids."

Connor clenched his teeth. Lenora was furious with him. In all the time he'd known her, he'd seen different levels of Lenora's anger, but this cold fury was by far the most dangerous, and he didn't trust himself to reply to her because he could feel his own anger rising. This wasn't his fault.

Bernard cleared his throat. "The broadcast is about to begin."

"We can watch it in here," Captain Ramsey said and activated the holoscreen.

The CDF logo showed before the broadcast began. Then, an image of Colonel Sean Quinn standing at a podium and looking into the camera filled the screen.

"I'm Colonel Sean Quinn, commanding officer of the CDF mobile infantry that is tasked with defending the colony. The purpose of this briefing is to apprise you of the current situation facing us. In addition to this briefing, a packet with the supporting documentation has been sent to all cities and forward operating research bases. We have compiled a list of satellite images that shows a massive migration of ryklars moving south. Tens of thousands of ryklars are heading in our direction. We're not sure what triggered the migration; we just know they're coming. We don't know how far south they'll actually come, but I've ordered the mobilization of CDF soldiers and recalled soldiers who are on leave. I've also ordered the immediate evacuation of all forward operating research bases. Any field research teams away from colonial settlements are to be recalled to their home locations immediately. The CDF will focus its efforts on defending major population centers. These will include Sierra, Haven, Delphi, and Sanctuary. At this time we will not be evacuating any colonists to the bunkers that were used in our war with the Vemus. The colonial government and CDF are meeting with scientific advisors and are formulating multiple plans on how to deal with this new threat. We will send you updates as decisions are made. That's all for now."

The video feed returned to the CDF logo and Captain Ramsey turned off the holoscreen.

Connor looked at Lenora, but her face wasn't giving anything away as she took in the briefing, so he looked at Captain Ramsey. "We're going to need to study that information the CDF sent. We need to know where the ryklars are in relation to the NEIIS map. Those kids don't know what's coming to them. We need to send another broadcast," Connor said and looked at Lenora. "It's got to come from you. He'll listen to you. We need to warn him of the danger. Everything else can wait."

"Can we track their signal?" Bernard asked.

"We won't get their precise location, but we can get in the vicinity if he replies. It would be enough to start with," Connor replied.

"You're going after him?" Bernard asked.

"Of course. Most research teams are already at Sanctuary due to the travel ban," Connor said and looked at Captain Ramsey. "I'm going to need some help with this one. This just became a rescue mission. Officially I don't have a position . . ."

"I'll be going with you," Captain Ramsey said. "Just give me a list of what you think we need and I'll get it."

"I'm going too," Lenora said.

Bernard glanced at both of them. "Could you use an extra pair of hands?"

Connor regarded Bernard for a moment. While Bernard was a good man, he wasn't someone Connor would want to take into the field. "You'll be needed here to help organize things. I'm sure the CDF is going to send a few platoons to secure this area."

Bernard chuckled. "Is that your way of telling me I'm no good in the field?" he asked and then held up his hands. "Never mind, don't answer that."

"Do you think you guys could give Lenora and me a few minutes alone?" Connor asked.

Captain Ramsey and Bernard quickly left the conference room.

"Lenora, I'm sorry."

She stood up but still had her arms crossed in front of her chest. When she looked at him, her eyes were tight with worry. "They're good kids, Connor. They deserve better."

Connor knew Lenora was fiercely loyal to anyone she cared about. Noah Barker was like family to her and somehow Dash DeWitt had become the same.

"We'll get to them in time. I can't imagine they would just blindly go to any location again after that first encounter with ryklars," Connor said. Lenora didn't reply. "I know you think this is my fault and I don't want to argue about that right now. I just want to keep everyone safe."

Lenora sighed heavily. "That's just it. You can't. Most people accept that fact, but you don't."

Connor's brows drew together as he tried to think of something to say.

"I'm going to send another message to Dash and the others," Lenora said and left the conference room.

Connor watched her leave, hating the tension between them, but he couldn't dwell on what she'd said for long. If Sean had mobilized the CDF infantry, it meant they considered the ryklar migration a serious threat to the colony. He had to make this right with Lenora, and if that meant finding some sort of compromise with Dash, that's exactly what he needed to do. But first he had to find him and convince him and the others of the danger they were all in.

17

DASH HAD BEEN on remote field research expeditions before that required overnight trips away from Sanctuary. There hadn't been many of them and they had all been memorable and exciting for the young archaeologist, but none of those trips compared with the night they'd spent at the NEIIS outpost.

They'd worked long into the night. Dash had divided his time between working with Brad, gleaning information off the console, and exploring the nuances of the NEIIS living quarters with Merissa. They'd all taken turns exploring the outpost and doing a field survey of the surrounding area. Dash had painstakingly cataloged all their findings and observations. They'd discovered various storage bins containing items the NEIIS had used and, like the outpost, they were well-preserved. Some of the things they found looked like tools and spare parts for the outpost. They definitely found a spare control panel and what passed for an NEIIS PDA. They tagged the items and stored them on the C-cat.

The NEIIS PDA was rudimentary when compared with what the colonists were using, but this had been developed by an alien species. It was the shape of a large brick and the outer casing was comprised of hardened plastic. The internal components were smaller versions of what the NEIIS used to construct their consoles. For some strange reason, the NEIIS hadn't developed glass—or at least none had been found in the buildings of other known NEIIS sites. The NEIIS PDA had a small, pale mesh screen that doubled as an interface for the system. He hadn't been able to get it to power up because the internal power supply had long since been used up. Brad thought he could adapt one of their own power supplies to the PDA and promised to work on it during their trip out to the central NEIIS city they'd identified on the map.

They'd brought several space heaters into the outpost and camped out in the small atrium where the consoles were located. They preferred to stick together, and none of them felt comfortable spending the night in one of the NEIIS living quarters. Dash didn't mind and was actually happy for the company. They'd talked for a long time after the work was done and the recon drones they had patrolling the area hadn't detected anything, much to their relief.

The next morning they packed everything back up into the C-cat and Dash finished a report to send back to Dr. Bishop. He'd decided to include a lengthy summary of everything they'd found so far and had included the location of the outpost. He was standing outside the NEIIS outpost, working with the holo-interface of his PDA. The morning air was crisp and the sun had just started to come up over the horizon in pinks and reds. Merissa walked out the door of the outpost and stretched her arms overhead. Upon seeing him she walked over.

"When are you going to send the report back to Dr. Bishop?" Merissa asked.

"I was just finishing it up now. I'm sending everything we've put together so far," Dash replied. "Do you want to take a look at it? Maybe you'll have something to add."

Merissa leaned in so she could see what he had on his holo-interface. Dash watched as her eyes scanned the screen. Then she looked at him, her eyes wide with surprise. "You're telling them where we're going. I didn't think we were going to do that."

"I've been thinking about it all night and I didn't think anyone would have any real objections. Since the NEIIS site is so far away I thought it would be a good idea to let them know where we are. By the time they get this and read through all the information, we'll already be there, so I thought what the heck. Do you think the others will mind?" Dash asked.

Merissa shook her head. "Not at all, especially since you've tucked it in at the end, which means they'll have to read the entire thing before getting that nugget of information."

"Unless Connor starts with the end, which he might do," Dash replied.

"Do you think Lenora will show Connor the message?"

"Without a doubt. They generally don't hide anything from each other; they just disagree in public," Dash said with a grin.

They helped the others finish packing up their camp and Dash took one last look around. They'd recalled the recon drones earlier and stowed them aboard the C-cat. Dash used the control panel to close up the NEIIS outpost and was the last to climb aboard. He glanced toward the front and saw that Brad and Jim were in the front seats. Brad had the NEIIS PDA and was tinkering with it while Jim was in the pilot's seat.

"Are you tired of flying us around yet?" Dash asked.

Jim glanced back at him. "No, I don't mind. I figured you guys could use the time to plan our next stop."

Jim engaged the C-cat's engines and they headed off.

Their Airbus transport had several rows of seats that could be moved, folded down, and reconfigured so they could all face each other if they wanted. There was an open seat between Merissa and Selena, and Dash sat there. Setting his PDA on a small table, he enlarged the holodisplay so they could take a closer look at the map. He then enlarged the portion of the map that showed the central NEIIS city they were heading to.

"If this is any indication of scale, this new site could be a lot bigger than what they found at Sanctuary," Merissa said.

Dash nodded. "I think it will be. Sanctuary was built more recently in comparison to the other NEIIS sites that have been discovered."

"If that's the case, the city could have been built using the older construction style and might reveal more about them," Selena said.

"Have you given any thought to whether we might actually find a living NEIIS in the city?" Merissa asked.

Dash's thoughts came to a screeching halt and his mouth hung open. He shook his head.

Merissa's beautiful face held a bemused expression. "Are you serious? You never considered that we might actually find someone living in the city?"

"No," Dash said quickly. "The *Galileo* seed ship had about twenty years to study this planet before we even got here and there was no detection of a living intelligent species on New Earth. Plus, we've been here for eight years and certainly haven't been quiet about it. If there were any NEIIS here, why wouldn't they have contacted us?"

Merissa shrugged and pursed her lips. "I don't know. I was just raising the question."

"You make a good point," Selena said. "We don't know where they went. What if they developed some kind of stasis technology and are simply weathering some kind of catastrophe?"

Dash leaned back in his chair. "Stasis technology isn't the easiest thing to develop. We've had the concept for hundreds of years, but it was only within the last fifty years before the *Ark* left that we perfected it. Even though the NEIIS cities are impressive and they did develop some technology, we just don't have any evidence to support them having stasis technology."

"Yeah, but they genetically modified certain species on this planet so they definitely were capable of some advanced technology," Merissa said.

Dash smiled. "It would be amazing if we found someone alive, but I just don't think we will."

Selena started making a note on her own PDA. "You might be right, but it's not outside the realm of possibility."

They spent the next hour going over what they should do first once they reached the city. Safety was always a primary concern, so ruling out any ryklar presence was at the top of their list. They settled on doing several flybys and noting key locations before they even landed anywhere. Yesterday, they'd flown low and slow to reach the outpost, but since they were already hundreds of kilometers away from Sanctuary, they flew high and fast. They would make the fifteen-hundred-kilometer journey in a matter of a few hours.

Selena decided to move to another seat because she wanted to refresh her knowledge of first-contact protocols. She'd really latched onto the idea that there was some chance they would encounter an actual NEIIS at the city.

Dash kept studying the map, noting some of the highlighted locations they wouldn't be stopping at and marking them for a future expedition. At some point during their journey, Merissa had dozed off in her chair, a fact he only became aware of when her head leaned on his shoulder. He glanced over in surprise and found that he didn't mind so much. He settled his head back and closed his eyes.

Dash woke up to Jim calling his name. His eyes snapped open and he rubbed his face for a moment, waking up. He glanced next to him and saw that Merissa was waking up as well.

"You guys looked so cute sleeping together," Selena grinned.

She was sitting across from them. Dash and Merissa shared a quick, uncomfortable glance.

"In his dreams," Merissa said.

Dash pursed his lips in thought. "Wouldn't be a bad dream," he said, and Merissa narrowed her gaze at him. He glanced up at Jim at the front of the C-cat. "What did you say?"

"You should bring up the HUD back there. The NEIIS city is huge. I can see a bunch of tall monoliths from here," Jim replied.

Dash brought up the heads-up display in the back and they caught their first glimpse of the biggest NEIIS city they'd ever seen. The sheer size of it made Sanctuary look like a lone frontier town.

"Millions of them must've lived here," Dash said in hushed tones. "You were right—this place is built in the old NEIIS style," he said, looking at Merissa.

"I thought that was your theory—one of the more brilliant ones," Merissa said.

Dash feigned surprise. "I think that's the nicest thing you've ever said to me."

He turned back to the holodisplay and magnified the view. Though the NEIIS city was huge, even at this distance there was evidence of the surrounding forests reclaiming the city. There was little chance that anyone lived there anymore. Dash brought up the scanner interface and began looking for any power signatures.

"We have an incoming message from Sanctuary," Jim said, sounding surprised.

Dash brought up the communications interface and acknowledged the message. It was a video message from Dr. Bishop and he started it.

"Thank you for sending an update. It sounds like you've made quite the discovery. I look forward to hearing all about it," Dr. Bishop said and glanced at someone off-screen for a moment. "The Colonial Defense Force has issued a major alert about increased ryklar activity—"

The message was cut off and Dash frowned. There was a bright flash on the heads-up display at the front of the C-cat and then all power was cut off. The heads-up displays all winked out at once and automated seatbelts sprang into action, locking the passengers in place. Seemingly of its own volition, the C-cat began to drop from the higher altitudes as the engines sputtered to silence.

Brad, who had been sleeping in the front seat, was startled awake.

"What the hell happened?" Dash shouted.

He watched as Jim tried to get the engines to restart. "I don't know. Something took out the main power and the auxiliary failed as well."

"Try the manual override," Dash said.

"What do you think I've been trying?" Jim snapped.

The C-cat's nose dipped and Dash was pressed against his seatbelt. He glanced out the window to see the ground barreling toward them.

"I can't get power restored. We're going to crash. Brace for impact!" Jim said.

Dash snatched his PDA from his pocket and brought up the power schematics for the C-cat. "Here, hold this," he said and handed the PDA to Merissa.

Dash unstrapped his seatbelt and Merissa's eyes widened in alarm.

"What are you doing? You'll be killed, you idiot!" Merissa shouted.

As Dash stood, the C-cat banked hard to the side. He grabbed onto the nearest seat back and held on tight, then climbed over the seat, moving toward the rear of the vehicle. He was still accessing his PDA through his neural implants. There was a power relay control unit at the back of the Airbus. Something had shorted out the power, but there was an override for the emergency thrusters. The C-cat banked hard to the side again and Dash slammed against the window. The air expelled from his lungs and he reached for the nearest seatback to pull himself down.

There was a high-pitched whine as the C-cat continued to plummet toward the ground. Dash heard the others scream and he lunged toward the back, grabbing onto the arms of the seats and pulling himself toward the floor. The C-cat began to tumble over and over, spinning through the air, but he managed to reach the back and grabbed onto a handle. He lunged toward the emergency control panel and pulled the lever to open it. Inside was a large switch that had been jarred loose. He grabbed the switch and pushed it back into place, then turned it to emergency. The C-cat's emergency thrusters kicked in automatically, compensating for the spin they were in. Dash was tossed about in the rear of the ship. His head knocked into the ceiling and then he was slammed down to the floor. He heard Merissa calling out his name and glanced out the window. The last thing he heard was Jim shouting for them all to hold on.

18

DASH WOKE up to Merissa shouting his name and shaking his shoulders. He groaned as he felt a sharp pain lance across his middle. He might've cracked a few ribs.

"I'm awake . . . please stop shouting," Dash said.

He opened his eyes and saw Merissa leaning over him.

"God, you're beautiful."

Merissa's eyebrows raised in surprise and Dash heard Selena start to laugh.

Did I say that out loud?

He tried to sit up.

"Lie still, you idiot," Merissa scolded and Dash lay back down.

He rubbed his side gingerly. "I think I bruised my ribs."

Merissa pulled his hand away from his ribcage, then lifted up his shirt and rubbed a numbing agent on his skin. "What were you thinking? You could've died."

The numbing agent was cool and went to work right away. "We were crashing," Dash snorted weakly. "I was trying to not crash."

Merissa's fingers lingered on his chest for a few moments longer than necessary.

"I think you got the problem spot," Dash said.

Merissa scowled, stood up, and walked away, muttering under her breath.

Dash sat up. "Was it something I said?" he said to Selena.

Selena just shook her head. Now that the numbing agent was working, Dash was able to climb to his feet. He'd been lying on the floor, which was a good sign because that meant the C-cat must have landed right-side up. His head was throbbing and he had a few scratches, but other than that he felt fine.

"We can't just stay in here," Jim said and walked toward the back. He saw Dash and smiled. "That was some quick thinking. You saved our asses back there. How'd you know about the emergency thrusters?"

"I didn't. I had to pull up the C-cat's schematics on my PDA and highlight the emergency systems. I figured that was our best bet," Dash said. He took a quick glance around, noting the fractured windows. "Do you know how we lost power?"

Brad joined them and Jim shook his head. "The only thing I saw was a bright flash and then everything just turned off. I have no idea what happened."

"Where are we?" Dash asked.

"We were on our final approach vector to the city. We can't be more than four or five kilometers away," Jim answered.

Dash nodded. "We should try and restore power."

"Thank you! That's what I've been telling them," Selena said.

Dash frowned and looked at Jim.

"I'm not sure we can turn the power back on," Jim said.

"Well, going off on foot is out of the question. You heard Dr. Bishop's message. The CDF sent out a major warning about ryklar activity," Selena said.

Dash closed his eyes for a moment, trying to remember Dr. Bishop's message. "The message was cut off—" he began.

"Not you, too. Are you going to say we have to set off on foot now?" Selena asked.

Dash shook his head. "Let's assess the damage first and then decide on a way forward. One thing at a time."

Selena seemed to consider this for a moment and then nodded.

All their equipment was scattered about the C-cat. It took Dash a few minutes just to find the case that held the recon drones.

"I'll get these set up and deployed. Then I'll help with the assessment. Hopefully we can get power restored," Dash said

Jim's ominous expression didn't give Dash much hope and he secretly prayed Jim was wrong. Dash opened the top hatch and activated three of the recon drones. He selected the option for standard short-range patrol, which would keep them within a half-kilometer of the C-cat. He pulled one more drone from the case and configured it for a longer-range patrol for general reconnaissance. This would enable the drone to have more of a bird's-eye view of their position.

Jim and Brad had already gone outside. Dash grabbed his hunting rifle from where it had been secured and headed for the side door. He saw Merissa and Selena speaking in hushed tones, and they stopped talking as he approached.

"I just wanted to thank you for taking care of me," Dash said and smiled.

He was trying to sound as sincere as possible and Merissa regarded him for a moment.

"I'm glad you're alright," Merissa said.

Point one for civility, Dash thought.

"I'm going to go outside and see what kind of damage we

sustained. Do you guys want to come?" Dash asked.

Selena's face became pale.

"It's fine. Just stay here for a few minutes. The drones will report in if there are any ryklars in the area," Dash said quickly.

Merissa smiled gratefully and then tried to comfort Selena.

Dash went outside and found Jim and Brad speaking near the front of the C-cat. Dash rounded the corner of the ship and saw that there were large scorch marks along one side, with more on the roof.

Jim looked over at him in alarm and Brad looked equally as troubled.

"I think someone took a shot at us," Jim said.

Dash leaned in for a closer look at the scorched corner panel of the C-cat and then glanced at the roof. "What was up there?"

"That was our antenna. It's been sheared off. We have no communications capability," Brad said.

Dash heard Merissa and Selena exit the C-cat, talking loudly.

"We can't even call for help?" Dash asked in a hushed tone.

"Not anymore, or at least not with the C-cat. There might be an emergency beacon we can activate," Brad said.

Merissa and Selena were getting closer.

Dash looked at Jim. "Can we get the power turned back on?"

Jim's eyes widened and he looked uncertain. "I don't even know what hit us."

Dash was about to reply, but Merissa and Selena had rounded the corner and saw the scorch marks. Selena's brows drew up an alarm and Merissa looked at him for an explanation.

"We're going to die out here," Selena said in a shrill voice.

Dash brought his hands up in front of his chest in a placating gesture. "Calm down. We don't know anything yet. I know it looks bad, but let's try to work the problem and not freak out."

"Not freak out! Between yesterday's excursion and today we're almost two thousand kilometers away from Sanctuary, our ship has crashed, and there's an alert about ryklars. When would be the appropriate time to freak out?" Selena said.

"First, it was a partial message. We don't even know if ryklars are in *this* area. I just checked and nothing has been detected by the drones. Second, we're still trying to figure out if we can fix this thing, and if we can't, we'll have to come up with another plan. I need you to calm down. We need your help," Dash said.

Merissa wrapped her arm around Selena's shoulder. "What do you need me to do?"

Dash pointed to the roof of the C-cat. "Our antenna got damaged in the crash. I need you guys to find the emergency beacon. Just find it; don't activate it yet. We might be able to salvage the C-cat and be on our way. I just want to know that it can be used and is available. I also need someone to monitor the drone feeds while I help Jim and Brad try to fix the C-cat."

Selena swallowed hard and drew in a shaky breath. "I can do that."

Dash smiled. "Thank you," he said.

Selena turned around and Merissa mouthed the words *thank you,* smiling at him.

Once they left, Dash turned back toward Jim. "So you think some kind of weapon hit us? I wonder what it could have been," he said.

"It would have to be some kind of energy weapon," Brad said.

"How do you know that?" Jim asked.

"Because if it was something like a rail-gun, there would be a lot more damage. It looks like whatever got us only fried the electrical components," Brad said and then frowned in thought.

"What is it?" Dash asked.

"Right before we lost power, we were receiving that message from Sanctuary. At the same time, there was a massive spike in signal strength, but I'm not sure what it was. Then there was the bright flash," Brad said.

Dash looked at Jim. "What happened when you tried to restore the power?"

"I got no response," Jim said.

"Well, the main battery is in the front, but the auxiliary is in the back. The front is obviously damaged, so we should try getting auxiliary power back on," Dash said.

"We can't fly two thousand kilometers on auxiliary power. Not even close," Jim said.

"I know, but maybe we can get the communication system up and running," Dash said.

"We still don't have an antenna," Brad said.

"I take it there're no spares?" Dash asked.

Brad frowned. "I doubt it."

"Maybe we could put something together. All we have to do is send a message to Sanctuary with our current location," Dash said.

"Yeah, but we're really exposed here," Jim said and glanced around them.

Dash's brows pulled together. "I don't have all the answers. Yes, we're exposed here, but let's see if we can at least call for help, and if we can't, we should head to the city. At least there we can find some kind of shelter we can use."

Jim sighed. "What if there are ryklars in the city?"

Both of them were looking at Dash. "We have to go there anyway. If the ryklars discover we're here, the C-cat is only going to provide minimal protection and not for very long. This isn't an armored vehicle. I'm still wondering what the hell shot us down."

"Maybe there were some latent city defenses or something," Brad said.

"We'll have to figure it out later. First, let's see if we can get the auxiliary power on. If we can, let's see if this thing can still fly. If not, we gotta make other plans," Dash said.

They got to work. So much for a smooth trip.

In the next thirty minutes, they learned that the C-cat would not be flying again anytime soon. Interestingly enough, Selena hadn't freaked out like Dash expected when they told her the news.

Dash stood by the rear hatch of the C-cat where the brains of the vehicle were stowed. Brad was at the auxiliary power access panel, trying to bypass it so they could get the communication systems up and running.

"Alright, give it another shot," Brad said.

Dash pressed the power button near the wallscreen and waited. "I've got power," he said.

"Good. Activate the emergency beacon," Brad said, coming toward the back of the C-cat.

Dash brought up the communication systems on the C-cat's interface and activated the emergency beacon. The beacon could operate without the main antenna, but the range was much smaller. They knew the beacon would attempt to beam a signal to the communication satellites in orbit, but they had no way of knowing whether satellite coverage would extend to their current location.

"The emergency beacon is active, for all the good it's going to do," Dash said.

"You don't think the beacon will reach anyone?" Merissa asked.

"Without the main antenna, it might take them longer to receive the message," Dash answered.

"But you already told them where we were heading," Selena said.

He still had the communication systems up and frowned when

he saw the status. "Aw, hell," Dash said, looking at Merissa and the others in alarm. "My update to Dr. Bishop never got sent."

Merissa glanced at the wallscreen and then looked at Dash. "You never sent it?"

Typical. She *would* think he'd done something wrong.

"I *did* send it. When we were at the outpost, I finalized the message and clicked the transmit option, then closed down my PDA," Dash answered quickly. He didn't much care for the accusatory tone Merissa had just used.

"Why didn't it go through then?" Selena asked.

Dash just stood there while he tried to formulate a reply. He didn't know why the damn thing hadn't been sent. It should've worked.

"Mind if I take a quick look?" Brad asked.

Dash stepped to the side so Brad could see.

Brad checked the communications system for a few seconds and then glanced back at them. "It's not his fault. The comms systems in C-cats is an older cobra model so the transmission takes longer to achieve because of the low-grade antenna."

Dash frowned, trying to remember the status he'd received when he'd sent the update. "But I saw it go through," he said.

Brad nodded knowingly. "Yeah, it says it goes through, but it's just in a holding place until it can fully transmit. The data gets broken up into chunks so it's possible that only part of it was sent."

Merissa shook her head. "That's just great."

Dash narrowed his gaze. "You're acting like I should've known this."

"Yes, I am."

"Well, you didn't know either," Dash replied.

Brad cleared his throat. "Guys, most people don't know this. And most people don't know about the lower-grade antennas on

C-cats. We're over two thousand kilometers from Sanctuary. You can make the connection, but it'll take time."

Merissa swung her gaze to Brad. "And how long is the auxiliary power supposed to last?"

Dash's annoyance with Merissa was almost instantly gone now that she had turned her wrath toward Brad, and she had asked a good question.

Brad had opened his mouth to answer when the wallscreen winked out. The system was down again.

Merissa sneered. "Evidently not that long."

Brad shook his head and went back to the auxiliary power supply. Jim and Selena went with him.

Once they were out of earshot, Dash looked at Merissa. "Snapping at everyone isn't going to help all that much."

Merissa's cheeks reddened. "What are we going to do? We're so far from Sanctuary, and we might not even be able to call for help."

Dash knew she was scared. Hell, he was scared. "We might have to leave the C-cat and head into the city. It could be our best bet."

Merissa's eyes widened. "Leave the safety of the vehicle again? That didn't work out so good the last time we did it."

"Do you have a better idea? Because I'm open to ideas," Dash said and then sighed. "Right now, the only thing I can think of is to head to the NEIIS city and find a way to transmit the emergency beacon broadcast from there. I saw several monoliths from the video feed. I think if we get to the top of one, the higher elevation will perhaps help the signal further its range. I don't know, but it's the best thing I can think of," Dash said.

"Didn't you send Dr. Bishop a message last night?" Merissa asked.

"I did, and they should be able to find the outpost. If they go there . . ." Dash said and let his voice trail off. He was making too many assumptions and he hated doing that.

Jim glanced back at them from the middle of the C-cat. "The auxiliary power supply is damaged. We can't fix it without replacing it entirely and there are no extras onboard."

Merissa glanced at him and he shrugged. With the C-cat not having any power, they didn't have a choice now.

"There's only a few hours of daylight left. I think we should camp here for the night and head out to the city in the morning," Dash said.

Selena's eyes widened. "You want to spend the night out here?"

Jim nodded and Selena looked at him. "We don't have a choice."

"We could make it to the city, but we'd have to scramble to find somewhere to camp inside and we don't know what could be waiting for us there. I think it will be safer to stay here, gather our supplies and the emergency beacon, and then head for the NEIIS city in the morning. Perhaps there we can find a way to call for help," Dash said.

No one else protested the decision to leave the safety of the C-cat anymore. Jim and Selena went back into the transport to gather the supplies they'd need to take with them. Merissa walked over to Dash.

"You said earlier that satellite coverage is limited at our current location. What good is going to the city gonna do?" she asked.

"The transmission would be stronger the higher up we are so it would increase our odds of the message going out. Also, there might be NEIIS technology we can use to boost the signal. We know they used ultrahigh-frequency waves so there might be something there we can adapt," Dash replied.

"I wonder if we can figure out when the satellites will be

passing overhead," Merissa said and went to speak with Brad about it.

Dash activated the rest of the recon drones so if anything dangerous did wander nearby they'd have ample notice of it. Somewhere in the back of his mind, he felt like Connor was judging him, as if Dash should've known something like this could happen. But he pushed those thoughts out of his mind and focused on all of them reaching the city safely.

19

CONNOR SAT in the passenger area of a former CDF troop-carrier transport ship that had been adapted to mainly doing supply runs between Sanctuary and Sierra. The main body could hold large supply caches, as well as a Polaris ATV. Given the heightened ryklar activity being reported, he wasn't taking any chances with this mission, so they'd brought the ATV with them, as well as additional supplies for a search and rescue mission. They had just left the second previously-undiscovered NEIIS site and there was no sign of Dash or the others ever having been there. Even though he knew Lenora wanted to find their wayward students, Connor could tell she also wanted to do a proper field evaluation of the new sites.

"That's two down," Lenora said.

Connor nodded. "We continue east for the next one, which is farther from any colonial settlement and the last one within the triangulation area we identified based on Dash's initial message. I guess he figured if he went farther east there would be less of a chance of running into ryklars."

"He did say they would send us a follow-up message. I'm not sure why we haven't gotten it yet," Lenora said, sounding worried.

Connor glanced at her. She looked tired and anxious. "He could've changed his mind."

Lenora shook her head. "No, he wouldn't have changed his mind or else he wouldn't have said it initially."

Then something must've gone wrong, but Connor didn't want to voice that without sufficient evidence.

Captain Ramsey walked out of the cockpit and headed toward them. "We just sent an update back to Sanctuary. There's been no further contact with Dash or any of the others, but we did learn that they brought a fifth person with them—Brad Kelly, who's one of the tech engineers working in the archives," Captain Ramsey said.

"Why would a tech engineer go with them?" Connor asked.

"He helped them before. Maybe they asked him for help again," Lenora said.

Connor thought about it for a moment and then snorted. "Right. It's as simple as that and has nothing to do with the two pretty young girls with them."

Lenora looked unconvinced.

"Don't give me that. These guys are young and I'm just saying it's a motivating factor. It worked for me. I wouldn't be here if it wasn't for you," Connor said.

Lenora rolled her eyes and smiled. "I'm sure you say that to all the girls."

"Some of them like a man in uniform," Connor replied.

Captain Ramsey cleared his throat. "As entertaining as this is, it doesn't help us all that much."

Connor drew in a breath. "Dash is already an expert with NEIIS technology, so why bring someone like Brad Kelly?"

Lenora shook her head. "Assuming it was his idea, it couldn't hurt to bring a backup. Also, a technical engineer like Brad has skills that go beyond NEIIS technology. Perhaps Brad was just intrigued by what happened at the archives and they knew they were going far from Sanctuary without support so they brought him along."

A comlink opened from the cockpit. "Captain, we received a strange transmission burst, but it's not from any colonial frequencies in our database," Sergeant Regina Hale said.

"Do you know the source of the signal? Is it coming from site three?" Captain Ramsey asked.

"That's a negative, sir. I'm not able to pinpoint the exact location, but our best guess is that it's from a good deal farther to the north," Sergeant Hale said.

Captain Ramsey glanced at Connor.

"We should maintain course and heading and monitor for more signal bursts," Connor said.

"Did you hear that, Sergeant?" Captain Ramsey asked.

"Yes, Captain. Maintaining course and heading," Sergeant Hale said.

The comlink closed.

"You sure we shouldn't investigate that signal?" Captain Ramsey asked.

"If we have no other leads after we visit the third site, we can look into it," Connor said and paused in thought. "We could forward the information about the signal burst to Sierra, just to keep them in the loop."

Lenora glanced at Captain Ramsey for a moment. "Do you think this has to do with the CDF alert for ryklar activity?"

"I'm not sure, to be honest. It just seems like a lot of things are happening all at once and I can't help but think it's all related somehow—the signal bursts along with the increased ryklar migration, these NEIIS sites and the fact that the NEIIS data module had such an effect on the archive's computer systems," Captain Ramsey said and shrugged.

"I've been thinking the same thing," Connor said, sliding his fingertips across his chin. "Sometimes I wonder if we haven't accidentally tripped the signal bursts we've been seeing—you know, like a latent NEIIS automated protection protocol."

Lenora frowned. "How would we even have done that? The first time that happened was when we were exploring actual ruins. Then Dash brought up that console from the outpost, which only showed them a map before it got fried, and nothing was triggered from that other than some kind of check-in protocol. We checked to see if the ryklar protection protocol had been initiated and there was no indication of that."

"I just think they're all related, but I'm not sure how. If the NEIIS have one way to trigger ryklars into taking action, then why not another?" Connor said.

There was a long silence while the others considered what Connor had said.

"Geez, Connor, that's a cheerful thought," Captain Ramsey said.

"It's just a thought, and I hope I'm wrong," Connor said.

"Maybe we should get some help from the CDF to investigate it," Captain Ramsey said.

Connor cocked his head to the side. "I'd prefer to have more concrete evidence. We wouldn't even know where to send them."

A loud snore sounded from a row of seats behind them.

Lenora glanced back and grinned. "So that's why no one likes to camp with Ian."

"I thought you knew," Connor said, grinning, and for a moment things were just as they'd always been. But all too soon, the tension crept back between them, shattering their brief moment of playful familiarity. Lenora seemed to notice it as well.

A message appeared on the nearby wallscreen. They were about to land at the third NEIIS site. It'd taken them nearly all day to investigate the first two sites and daylight was running out.

The troop-carrier transport landed and Connor retrieved his modified CAR-74 hunting rifle. Lenora grabbed her own hunting rifle while Connor activated three of the recon drones they brought with them. He knew Sergeant Hale would've run initial scans of the area, and if she'd found anything, they would've been notified immediately.

Ian Malone finally woke up and was gathering his own equipment. They were joined by Sergeant Hale and Corporal Julia Bennett, both armed with standard Field Ops equipment. Connor lowered the loading ramp and a cool breeze blew in. The sun was starting to dip on the horizon.

Connor moved to go down the loading ramp first and Captain Ramsey called out to him.

"Why don't you let my team go first?" Captain Ramsey said.

Connor glanced at Sergeant Hale and Corporal Bennett and nodded. "Sorry. Old habits."

The Field Ops team, including Captain Ramsey, headed for the NEIIS outpost first. They quickly opened the door and gestured for the rest to follow.

Connor took a quick glance, scanning the surrounding area, and then headed inside the NEIIS outpost.

"This site is remarkably well-preserved," Lenora said while looking at the almost pristine interior of the NEIIS outpost. "They were here," she said and gestured toward the NEIIS console.

Connor walked over to the console and squatted down. "Looks like those control panels have been opened recently."

Lenora came over to him and activated the console. Connor stood and watched as the startup sequence showed the familiar NEIIS symbols. Lenora then brought up the map. They waited a minute for the map to finish initializing and then the output on the mesh screen changed.

Captain Ramsey tasked Sergeant Hale and Corporal Bennett to do a quick patrol around the outpost and then joined Connor, Lenora, and Ian at the console.

"This map is more detailed than the one we have," Ian observed.

There were several more sites identified on the map, each with a series of NEIIS symbols.

"How do we figure out which one they went to?" Connor asked.

Lenora glanced at him, slightly amused. "I'm surprised you haven't figured it out already, given what you know about Dash."

Connor frowned and peered at the map. There were multiple sites far to the north. They'd have to run it through their own software in order to bring it to scale, but there was one particular site that was clearly distinguishable from the others. He glanced at Lenora.

"Oh, yes," Lenora confirmed. "It's that one way to the north, farther than any field survey expedition has gone before."

Connor blew out a breath and sighed. "It would have to be."

"Why would he go all the way there?" Captain Ramsey asked.

"Because that's the major find. It must be a city that's even larger than Sanctuary. My guess is they'd want to go there, do a survey of the area for a few days, and then report their findings. They're not equipped for an expedition that could take months, but the discovery would be crucial for requesting a FORB for that location. They've only taken two weeks of provisions, at best," Lenora said.

Connor glanced out the open door where the New Earth sky and clouds were awash in a deep red as the sun continued to set. "Even if we left now, it would be the middle of the night by the time we got there," Connor said.

"I'd rather not try to search for this city in the middle of the night, if it's all the same to you," Captain Ramsey said.

Connor had no doubt that they could reach the city, but searching for Dash and the others might be a problem given the limitations of the troop-carrier systems.

"We could camp here and get an early start," Ian said.

"I agree," Lenora said. "We'll leave before sunrise. That way it will be full daylight by the time we reach the city."

Connor smiled. "I guess it's settled then. Plus, it gives us a chance to explore this outpost a little bit. Hopefully, we'll receive an update from Dash by then."

He'd started to walk out of the NEIIS outpost when Lenora asked where he was going.

"I'm sending an update to Sanctuary just so they know what we've discovered so far," Connor said.

20

Colonel Sean Quinn stood in his office at the Colonial Defense Force base at Sierra, located on the outskirts of the city's rebuilding efforts. This main administration building was also home to the centralized command center of all CDF activities and had been his station for the past year since General Nathan Hayes had made Sean his second-in-command.

Sean's office was large in comparison to his previous post and could function quite easily as a mobile command center on its own. He'd insisted on this setup for his office because it saved him from having to go to the actual command center to see the current status of any activity. He glanced to the right at the multitude of wallscreens that were active with live feeds from CDF Command Central, placing his hands on his hips while he took in the information being displayed.

There was a quick knock at his door and Sean glanced over as Captain Juan Diaz walked in.

Diaz looked at all the wallscreens and nodded in appreciation. "You get all the cool toys," he said and grinned.

"You could have cool toys, too, if you'd just take that promotion Nathan and I have been trying to give you for the past year," Sean replied.

Diaz made a show of peering at the wallscreens and then looked back at Sean. "Then I'd get my own mobile command center in my office? No thanks. I told you I'm only good at my current rank."

Sean shook his head. "That's crap, and you know it. Connor let you get away with it, but I think I'm just gonna give you the same work I would give a CDF major. How's that sound, Captain?"

Diaz straightened and saluted. "Outstanding, sir."

Sean snorted and turned back toward the wallscreens, frowning.

Diaz cleared his throat. "We have a call with General Hayes in five minutes, sir."

Sean nodded. "We'll take it in here."

Diaz came over to his side. "You'd think that with all the drills we did in preparation for the Vemus invasion, the colonists wouldn't be so slow to respond in the face of an imminent threat."

"The colonists are doing just fine. We've only told them there was the *possibility* of an imminent threat from the ryklars. What frustrates me is the fact that we've been caught so unprepared," Sean said.

"What do you mean, sir?" Diaz asked.

"The CDF was designed in response to a threat coming from space—the Vemus. The fact that the ryklars have all but disappeared for the past few years has lulled us into a false sense of security, but that doesn't change the fact that we're ill-equipped for the current situation," Sean said.

"We could just send every Hellcat we have, armed to the teeth, which would ruin any ryklar's day. We also have heavy weapons at Lunar Base that could be brought down here to further drive the point home to those beasts that they should leave us alone," Diaz said.

Sean arched an eyebrow toward the captain. "Where do we send them? Why have the ryklars begun moving south en force? We're still estimating, but we put their numbers at almost a million."

Captain Diaz's eyes widened. "A million!" he said in a tone of disbelief. "The last report I saw was that it was a few hundred thousand. In that case, we can skip the Hellcats and just move in with heavy weapons."

Sean shook his head. "Dropping bombs may not be the best answer to this threat. The fact of the matter is, we have more insight into this star system than we do the planet surface. Granted, the Vemus did wipe out our satellite network, which we're addressing, but it does represent a significant oversight on our part."

A comlink alert highlighted in yellow came to prominence on the central wallscreen. Sean acknowledged it and General Nathan Hayes' face appeared while all the other wallscreens dimmed. The general was at the command center at Lunar Base and had been there for the past several weeks to inspect the rebuilding efforts, as well as to tour the shipyards being rebuilt. It would still be months before they were able to start building actual warships, but at least they'd made some headway just in case there was a remnant Vemus force that hadn't yet arrived. No deep space probe or observation platform had detected any sign of a Vemus presence, but General Hayes was taking a page from Connor's book. He wanted to be prepared and rule out any external threats to the New Earth star system.

Sean and Captain Diaz stood at attention and snapped a salute.

"As you were," General Hayes said. "What's the status of the ryklar situation? Is this an animal migration, or is something else prompting this sudden movement in their population?"

"We're not sure yet, General. I have multiple CDF teams doing remote reconnaissance, but without eyes in the sky it's taking a lot longer than we'd anticipated," Sean replied.

"That's not likely to change—the eyes in the sky, I mean. Even if we started building satellites, it would take weeks to get what we need. So break it down for me and give me your best guess," General Hayes said.

"I've ordered the recall of all colonists to the population centers here at Sierra, New Haven, and Delphi. All Field Ops missions have been recalled and canceled. However, we still have a small number of colonists outside the population centers. These colonists are mostly made up of scientists and support personnel at the FORBs. I've mobilized the infantry in preparation to defend the main population centers, along with a contingency force that will be sent to Sanctuary this afternoon," Sean replied.

General Hayes nodded. "Have you heard anything from Connor?"

Sean shook his head. "He's currently out in the field, and this update just came in less than an hour ago. One of Sanctuary's field survey expeditions has lost contact and they've gone to investigate. They did detect a powerful NEIIS signal broadcast, but it cut off almost immediately. We've had a few other CDF teams report similar broadcasts, but we're not sure what they mean. I've tasked CDF Intelligence with analysis of the signal data. We do know it's not the latent NEIIS protection protocol that triggered the ryklar attack when we were first establishing the colony."

"What are our options for city defense?" General Hayes asked.

"Our infantry is well armed, but our best guess is that the ryklar population heading our way is at least a million. This number updates almost hourly, and there's some overlap between the reconnaissance missions. Our computer systems are disseminating the data and putting forth that number as its best estimate. The problem is that the ryklars don't move in one massive force. They're pretty widespread, and we only occupy a tiny portion of this continent so visibility beyond our immediate area is quite limited. We can hold them off for a time, but the vehemence of the ryklar engagement depends on what's triggering their mass migration, meaning that if this activity is some other NEIIS protection-type protocol, the ryklars may throw themselves at our population centers almost without regard to themselves," Sean said.

"And we don't understand why they're suddenly migrating in the first place," General Hayes said, his gaze sliding to Captain Diaz. "What's your take on this, Captain?"

"I say we unleash holy hell on them, General. We have heavy weapons and we should use them," Captain Diaz said.

"I don't disagree with you, Captain," General Hayes said and looked back at Sean. "What do you think about using heavy weapons on the rykars, Colonel?"

"It's an option but not one I want to commit to at this time," Sean said. "I have a couple of reasons for this. One, there would be an uproar from the colonists about wiping out an entire species, not to mention creating a significant environmental impact on our home. Secondly, heavy weapons on the planetary surface would take a toll that would require years to recover from. If it comes down to it, I have no issue with protecting the colony, even at the expense of the ryklars, but simply pointing our heaviest weapons at them doesn't necessarily make the problem go away. We don't know how many ryklars there actually are. This supercontinent could be home to quite a few of them, many more than our weapons could even take out. We need to understand what's triggered the migration, as well as defend the population centers."

General Hayes considered this for a moment. "Alright, Colonel, we'll do it your way. It sounds like we're still in the information-gathering stage, but if there's a significant risk to the colony, you're authorized to bring the option of using heavy weapons against the ryklars to the governor for approval."

"Understood, General. I'll keep you apprised of the situation," Sean said.

"Very well. Carry on," General Hayes said.

As the comlink closed, the wallscreens returned to their normal display of CDF alerts and activities.

"What do you need from me, sir?" Captain Diaz said.

Sean brought up a map that highlighted the colonial cities, as well as the evacuated forward operating research bases. "This large swath to the north is our blind spot."

Captain Diaz peered at the map and then pointed to an area far to the right. "Sanctuary, in addition to being the farthest east, is located pretty far north itself."

"Yeah, but the ryklar activity being reported is to the west," Sean replied.

"Even so, perhaps we can spare a few Hellcats to do a proper survey of the area near Sanctuary," Captain Diaz said.

"Since Connor's been living there, they've already done a pretty extensive survey given the capabilities of their equipment," Sean replied.

Captain Diaz nodded. "Yes, but it *is* a blind spot, and we've got better equipment."

Sean sighed. "Fine. Take a platoon and do a bit of your own reconnaissance using Sanctuary as your base of operations."

"Right away, Colonel," Captain Diaz said and left.

Sean gazed at the map for a few moments more. Prior to the ryklar alert, he'd received a message from Connor highlighting their lack of insight into the area they were living in and pointing out that it was going to cause problems in the long run. The colony was focused on rebuilding what they'd lost and perhaps they should have devoted more resources to further study of their new home. A majority of the supercontinent remained largely unexplored.

There was a soft knock at the door and Corporal Hudson stuck his head in. "The Colonial Defense Committee is waiting for you, Colonel."

"I'll be right there," Sean replied and gathered the materials he needed for his next meeting. One thing he could always count on since taking this post was the seemingly endless number of meetings.

21

LIEUTENANT MADDOX STOOD in their temporary encampment at the largest NEIIS city he'd ever laid eyes on. Bronze-colored monoliths reached to the sky, dotting the horizon. He'd used the monoliths as tactical references for the drones they had patrolling the city.

The city had very little structural damage, aside from some overgrown plant life making an effort to reclaim what the NEIIS had left behind. Maddox had no idea how old the city was and didn't much care. He was more interested in what they'd found here. Their ryklar hunt had led them to the origin of the initial signal burst. They'd cleared the area of ryklars and established sonic emitters, configured to send out a signal to keep the creatures away, but there were still ryklars in the vast city and there were limitations to what their twenty-four-man team could accomplish.

The CDF encampment was located amongst a central complex of NEIIS buildings. The ryklars had initially tried to ambush them there, but the CDF team had unleashed the fury of their weapons.

They'd burned the corpses, but sometimes the ryklars returned despite the sonic emitters. They always approached from different attack vectors, probing the encampment's defenses. Maddox had deployed a full complement of twelve recon drones that were patrolling the immediate area.

The NEIIS city was easily eight kilometers across, but despite its vastness, there were no inhabitants. Like everything else they found on New Earth, the NEIIS had simply vanished. He didn't like the emptiness of the city. It was almost like they were camped at a vast graveyard, but where were the ghosts? The NEIIS civilization had created cities that Maddox guessed had spanned the supercontinent, so where the hell did they all go? What happened to them?

Maddox turned to the Hellcat and started walking toward it as the ground crunched under his feet. He walked up the ramp and headed back toward where Captain Fletcher was resting. Corporal Gibbs' back blocked his view of the captain, but the corporal turned at his approach, his face pale and his eyes wide in shock.

"I don't know what happened, sir. Captain Fletcher is dead," Corporal Gibbs said in a hushed tone.

Maddox rushed to Captain Fletcher's side and looked down at him. There was no steady rise and fall of his chest, and the bio-signs on the monitor were all flat-lined. Maddox narrowed his gaze. "What do you mean you don't know what happened? How did he die, Corporal?"

Corporal Gibbs glanced down at the captain for a moment, bewildered. "I was coming back here to check on his wounds. The medipaste had made steady progress with healing his lacerations. Then I received an alert that the medical nanites were failing. By the time I got back here he was already dead, sir."

Maddox used his implants to access the onboard medical computer interface and view the alert for himself. Gibbs was right;

the nanites were failing to repair the internal damage. Maddox also noted that several systems failure messages hadn't sent alerts. He slammed his fist on the side bulkhead and snarled.

Corporal Gibbs flinched. "Sir, I . . . I didn't know—" he began, but Maddox cut him off.

"This isn't your fault, Corporal. This is equipment failure . . . goddamn equipment failure," Maddox said in a bitter tone.

Corporal Gibbs swallowed and looked down at Captain Fletcher's body. "Sir, he shouldn't have died. If I'd been here, I could've saved him."

Maddox clenched his teeth. Captain Fletcher was dead. He looked around at the rough state of their equipment on the Hellcat. Much of it was merely patched together, used well past its intended lifecycle.

He heard someone run up the loading ramp and then gasp.

"The captain . . . Is he dead?" Corporal Lasky asked.

Maddox glared at the corporal, whose mouth was agape. "Yes. Go summon the rest of the platoon. Now!" Maddox barked.

Corporal Lasky tore his eyes away from Captain Fletcher's body and immediately ran back down the loading ramp. Maddox could hear Lasky shouting for the CDF soldiers to return to the Hellcat.

Maddox felt his rage boil up to the surface as he placed his hand on Captain Fletcher's shoulder. "I promise to make this right, sir," he said softly and removed his hand. He looked at Corporal Gibbs. "I want you to come outside with me while I address the men," Maddox said.

Corporal Gibbs turned his wide-eyed gaze toward Maddox, then reluctantly headed for the loading ramp. Maddox followed him down. The CDF soldiers were gathering outside the Hellcat, forming a circle.

Sergeant Flint was among the last to arrive, but Maddox had

expected as much since he was the farthest away. Maddox held his AR-71 in his hands with practiced familiarity as the rest of the squad waited to be addressed.

Maddox looked around grimly. "Captain Fletcher has died," he said and gave them a moment to take the information in. More than a few people glanced at Corporal Gibbs as if to confirm the news from the medic. "His death had nothing to do with Corporal Gibbs. The captain's death is directly related to equipment failure on board the Hellcat, equipment we trust our lives to and that we're being called on to utilize long after it should have been dumped for salvage."

Sergeant Flint raised his hand and Maddox jutted his chin up, signaling his second-in-command to speak. "What sort of equipment failure caused Captain Fletcher's death, sir?" he asked.

"The comms system failed to send alert messages until it was too late," Maddox replied.

Sergeant Flint frowned in thought and didn't say anything.

Maddox swept his gaze toward the rest of the platoon. "I guess this really shouldn't be a surprise—the equipment failure, I mean. The CDF hasn't been getting the support it needs and now it's cost Captain Fletcher his life."

There were several head–bobs of agreement among the soldiers.

"What's our next move, sir?" Chief Spencer asked.

Sergeant Flint turned toward Spencer. "We report Captain Fletcher's death to COMCENT and return to Sierra as we were ordered, Chief."

Several squad members glanced at Sergeant Flint, looking as if the thought of returning to Sierra didn't appeal to them in the slightest.

"On the surface, that seems like the correct thing to do," Maddox said, claiming their attention once more. "We can return to Sierra with Captain Fletcher's body, where his death will undoubtedly be determined a tragic accident, but will it fix the problem?" He paused, letting the question percolate in their minds for a moment.

"What problem is that, sir?" Chief Spencer asked.

"The problem is that the whole colony has been negligent in their support of the CDF. We put our lives on the line for them, and once the immediate danger passed, they cast us aside like vermin. Even from within our own ranks this negligence has spread. Captain Fletcher informed me that we've been recalled to Sierra so we can undergo psych evaluations. These orders came after we rescued former CDF General Connor Gates, the very same man who turned his back on the entire Colonial Defense Force. And for what? Because we killed a few ryklars? I, for one, won't lose any sleep over that and neither did Captain Fletcher. He didn't disclose this information to the rest of you because he thought it was unfair, and I agreed with him. The CDF has lost its way. The colony has lost its way. We have an opportunity here should we choose to exploit it."

Sergeant Flint's brows pulled together tightly. "Sir, our orders are clear. Captain Fletcher should have—"

"Captain Fletcher made a decision to investigate the NEIIS signal broadcast," Maddox said firmly. "He was in stable condition, and if the CDF had proper support from the colony, he'd still be alive. So don't talk to me about what Captain Fletcher should have done, Sergeant. Instead, bring your attention to what the colony should've done," Maddox said and glared at the sergeant until he looked away. Maddox swung his gaze toward the other soldiers and saw the same angry glint in many of their gazes. "Specialist Stackhouse, why don't you share with the rest of the men what you told me less than an hour ago?"

Specialist Stackhouse blinked his brown eyes rapidly in

surprise at being called out. He was of average height and build and carried a few pieces of specialized technical equipment.

"Yes, Lieutenant," Specialist Stackhouse said and began to address the men. "We've found a control interface room that appears to be the source of the NEIIS signal burst. One of the protocols appears to be related to the ryklars." Maddox waited a few moments. "So it's no accident the ryklars have increased their activity. I say we use that. I say we use the NEIIS technology to make the colony realize how much they need the CDF."

"Are you saying we can control the ryklars?" Sergeant Flint asked.

Specialist Stackhouse shook his head. "No, we can't. At least not yet, I think. I'm not an expert in the NEIIS language. I just know enough that I'm able to translate some of the symbols using the known-symbols database. This indicates that what I'm seeing has to do with ryklars."

Maddox held his arms up, his palms facing upward. "So, you see, we can't just leave. We can gather intelligence here that the CDF needs."

"But Lieutenant, you mentioned using the NEIIS technology to make the colony appreciate the CDF. How do you propose to do that?" Corporal Gibbs asked.

Maddox had expected the question to come from Sergeant Flint, so he added Gibbs and Flint to a very short list of people who would need watching. "You saw the latest alerts. There's a massive ryklar migration heading south, right for colonial settlements. If we can work out how to control the ryklars here and now, we can be heroes."

Maddox glanced around at the platoon and saw several soldiers' eyes brighten at the mention of being heroes but not as many as he'd thought he would. Many of them had a hardened glint in their eyes. They were angry, just like he was. He almost felt as if he were looking in the mirror. But he saw that not all of them felt that way. Sergeant Flint gave him a wary look.

"I can tell that some of you don't care about being heroes. We've already saved the colony once. If Captain Fletcher were still alive, he'd be urging us to stay here and learn all we can. What's there to rush back to Sierra for? Psych evaluations? Screw that!" Maddox said and brought his gaze to Sergeant Flint. "My orders are that we stay here and continue our investigation into this site. Top priority is given to the investigation of the NEIIS control interface room. Fall out."

The CDF soldiers began to disperse and Maddox waved Sergeant Flint over.

"What's on your mind, Sergeant?" Maddox asked.

"Permission to speak freely, Lieutenant?" Sergeant Flint asked.

"Granted," Maddox replied.

"Sir, I know you and Captain Fletcher were close. Losing him in this way has gotta be tough. And I just want you to know I understand your frustration with CDF Command and the colonial government. But I'm concerned that with everything that's been happening . . . I think your anger might be affecting your judgment," Sergeant Flint said.

Maddox drew in a breath and sighed. "I know that couldn't have been easy for you to say. You're second-in-command now and it's your responsibility to raise those concerns with me. I *am* angry . . . I'm furious. You're right about that, but my judgment has never been clearer. I'll always do what I think is best for our platoon and the CDF. I'll follow our orders, but when we're out in the field, we have a little bit of latitude in how we carry them out. Is that understood?"

Sergeant Flint met his gaze. "Yes, Lieutenant."

Maddox didn't believe him. He knew it in his gut; Flint was going to be a problem.

Corporal Lasky approached and waited a short distance from them. Maddox waved him over.

"What is it, Corporal?" Maddox asked.

"Sir, one of the long-range recon drones has detected a small group of colonists walking toward the city," Corporal Lasky said.

"Colonists!" Sergeant Flint said. "How'd they get out here?"

Maddox glanced at Sergeant Flint. "Sergeant, I'd like you to oversee Specialist Stackhouse's work with the NEIIS console. Make sure he has what he needs and keep them on task."

Sergeant Flint paused for barely a second. "At once, Lieutenant," he said and stalked off.

Maddox turned his gaze back to Corporal Lasky. "Corporal, I need you to do something for me."

"Anything. I'm your man, Lieutenant," Corporal Lasky said.

"I like to think that I can count on you. The news of Captain Fletcher's death is going to affect certain members of the platoon in different ways. I want you to keep an eye on a couple of them for me. I just want to know if they start acting strangely. That sort of thing. Can you do that for me?" Maddox asked.

Corporal Lasky's eyes narrowed with grim determination. "Absolutely, Lieutenant. Do you have anyone in mind?"

"A few people, but before we get to that, where exactly are these colonists you saw?" Maddox asked.

Corporal Lasky shared the drone's video feed with him and Maddox's eyes widened as he recognized them. This was the very same group they'd rescued the week before. He pulled up the name of one of the young archaeological students from the report they'd filed—Dash DeWitt, an expert in NEIIS technology and an expert in engineering.

"I'll take it from here," Maddox said.

Corporal Lasky saluted him and left.

Maddox studied the video feed. Perhaps he'd be able to get

Specialist Stackhouse a little bit of extra help, but he'd need to use people he could trust for what he had in mind. The colonists were still over an hour away, more than enough time to herd them in the right direction. Hearing a group of men resupplying at the arms locker on the other side of the Hellcat, he began to form a plan in his mind and circled around toward them. A squad of six infantrymen was gathered around the supply cache. They stopped what they were doing when they saw him approach and saluted him.

Maddox strode over to the squad commander. He was a bear of a man, despite the smooth features of his young face. "Corporal Winston, I need you and your men for a field mission," he said and glanced at the rest of the squad. "How would you boys like to join me on a little excursion?"

Corporal Winston grinned. "Ready, willing, and able, sir. Just point the way and we're there."

Maddox had started his military career as an infantryman. They were a no-nonsense bunch and he knew they had no love for ryklars.

22

CONNOR WOKE up on the cold, hard ground of the NEIIS outpost. The padding they'd used for bedding wasn't nearly as comfortable as his own bed that he shared with Lenora. His back was stiff and he stretched his arms overhead, a slight groan escaping his lips.

Lenora woke up at the same time and looked at him from within her sleeping bag. "What are you smiling at?" she asked.

Connor hadn't realized he'd been smiling. "I was just thinking I've gotten used to sleeping in a bed. I think our home at Sanctuary is the longest I've ever spent in one place."

Lenora's eyes softened and she reached her hand out from her sleeping bag to give his a gentle squeeze. Her hand was warm compared to the chilly air.

Yesterday, they'd spent a few hours studying the outpost and the two consoles. It hadn't taken them long to find the updated map and it was a safe bet they knew exactly where Dash and the others had gone, whereas they'd only had a vague notion before. Connor regularly checked their comms system looking for some kind of update from Dash, but there was none.

They packed up their camp within the hour. Connor found Lenora standing just outside the outpost, frowning at her PDA.

"Still no word from Dash?" Connor asked.

Lenora shook her head. "I really expected he'd have contacted us by now."

Captain Ramsey came over. "There hasn't been any distress beacon detected at those coordinates. You don't think they disabled their C-cat's communication systems, do you?"

Lenora shook her head immediately and glanced at Connor.

"It wouldn't make much sense now," Connor said finally. "He'd have no reason to at this point and I don't think he would have anyway. He sent the initial update because he wanted us to know where they'd gone."

Captain Ramsey nodded. "So I guess we'll keep going then, unless you have any objections."

"I really wish we had some kind of update from them by now. The fact that we don't could mean they're in trouble, or at the very least that they have a damaged comms system," Connor said.

"Well, let's stop wasting time and get going already," Lenora said and hastened aboard the ship.

Captain Ramsey arched an eyebrow at Connor.

"She's worried about them," Connor said.

Captain Ramsey nodded. Sergeant Hale called for them to get aboard and Connor noted the urgent tone of her voice. They hurriedly climbed in and Sergeant Hale immediately lifted off even before the loading ramp had completely closed. Connor followed Captain Ramsey to the cockpit.

"What's with the hasty departure, Sergeant?" Captain Ramsey asked.

"Sir, there are ryklars in the area," Sergeant Hale replied.

"Can you put it on screen?" Connor asked.

Corporal Bennett brought up the recent scan on the heads-up

display and Connor's eyes widened.

Connor pressed his lips together. "There are hundreds of them heading right for us."

"They're still half a kilometer outside the drone's patrol area," Captain Ramsey said.

The scan showed the ryklars closing in on the outpost, but they were moving at what could be considered a leisurely pace for a ryklar.

"Sergeant, we need best speed to our target coordinates. Is that understood?" Connor said.

"Yes, sir. Best speed," Sergeant Hale replied.

Connor closed his eyes for a moment and looked at Captain Ramsey. "Sorry. Old habits."

Captain Ramsey shook his head. "You don't need to apologize to me and we can't get caught up with who's in command. I know you're retired, but you haven't been retired that long. And besides, the future mayor of Sanctuary would be our boss anyway."

Connor snorted. Captain Ramsey was a practical man, which was one of the reasons Connor got along with him so well. "We'll see about the mayor part, but thanks."

If the ryklars were this far south and east, there was a good chance they were also at the city Dash and the others had gone to. Whatever assumptions they'd previously had went right out the window.

Connor returned to the passenger area and sat next to Lenora, quickly filling her and Ian in about the ryklars.

"So many of them," Ian said.

Connor looked at Lenora, who had gone rigid at the news. "Dash and the others are a resourceful bunch. They won't get caught out in the open again. We'll get to them in time."

Lenora nodded and moved to check her PDA again. Captain Ramsey joined them and they started planning their next move.

23

DASH and the others hiked through the wilderness on their way toward the NEIIS city. He'd had the drones scout ahead and had spotted a path that looked to have been a road many years ago. One of them was always on drone-monitoring duty as they walked so their progress was a little bit slower than he would have liked, but that was the price they paid for safety. No matter how they sliced it, they were exposed, and if they encountered a large group of ryklars, they'd be in trouble. There were other creatures to be watchful for on New Earth that ranged in size from berwolves to the snake-like hybrids that lived in the thick treetop canopies. They heard the long calls of a furry squirrel-type creature that had long fins on their backs. Those animals kept to the trees, running among the high branches and occasionally stopping to peer at the colonists.

They spoke in hushed tones and kept their passage as quiet as possible until they emerged from the forest. As they caught their first close-up look at the NEIIS city, their meager comms system detected another NEIIS broadcast.

"The signal is definitely being broadcast from the city," Brad said.

Dash brought out the NEIIS version of a personal digital assistant. Brad had managed to use a small battery to power the device, but he was adamant that he wasn't sure how long it was going to last. Dash swiped his fingertips across the small mesh screen and the PDA came online. The NEIIS had a symbol the colonists had come to associate with the ryklars. Colonial linguists referred to the symbol as "protectors," but Dash didn't think the meaning was entirely accurate. Perhaps in some circumstances the ryklars could be seen as such, but they were much more than protectors.

"I think this PDA is detecting the signal. It definitely has something to do with the ryklars, but I'm not sure what these other symbols mean and I can't work on it while we walk," Dash said.

"I'd rather not stop here. Are you sure the signal has nothing to do with that attack protocol?" Merissa asked.

Dash shook his head. "It's the protection protocol, but I know what you mean. And no, it's much more complex." He placed the NEIIS PDA carefully back in his pack and glanced at Selena. She'd calmed down since they'd left their C-cat behind.

They quickened their pace, eager to reach the NEIIS city. Dash brought out his own PDA and captured an image of the city. It was built in the old architectural style, with rounded buildings—some with long, finger-like spires on top. The outer material was a form of molded concrete that was still smooth, showing little signs of wear. Tall monoliths towered above the cityscape, the largest of them centrally located and appearing to form a circle. Once they were closer, Dash would send a drone on ahead to confirm.

"Isn't it odd that the NEIIS didn't use any kind of vehicles?" Jim said. "We couldn't build a city like this without machinery. Surely they must have used the same. Why wouldn't we have found anything like that yet?"

Dash gestured toward the city with a wide smile. "Look at it. According to my PDA, it's almost eight kilometers wide. This is the biggest NEIIS find ever. If we hadn't been so preoccupied with preparing for an invasion, we would've explored a place like this already. But we're here now, and we're about to get a lot of questions about the NEIIS answered."

"Someone's a little excited," Merissa teased.

"You think?" Jim said with a grin. "We better get moving or he'll run off without us."

"Very funny," Dash said, quickening his pace.

They closed in on the city. There was no distinct boundary between the thinning forest and the actual city because one gradually gave way to the other. A main thoroughfare stretched out in front of them and they began to walk down it. Dash stopped and squatted down, gliding his fingers across the pavement. The streets had once been smooth but now were cracked, with some sunken sections of old pavement looking more like small craters. The clear dividing lines between the sheets of intact pavement must have been a sight to behold. Dash wasn't sure what material they were constructed from.

"Hold up," Jim said, peering down at his PDA. "There are other drone signals here."

Dash sent out a broadcast on the drone communications network and received a reply. "It's using CDF protocols," he said.

Brad glanced at him in surprise. "How'd you know?"

"Connor Gates showed me once," Dash said and felt a slight satisfaction at knowing something Brad didn't.

"Good," Selena said. "That means we're not alone here." She cupped her hands around her mouth and started to shout, but Merissa quickly stopped her.

A CDF drone flew overhead and hovered above their position. Dash glanced up at it and waved. The drone slowly flew away from them, going down the street toward the central part of the city, and then stopped twenty yards away.

"I think we should follow it," Dash said.

The others agreed, and once they started following the drone, it kept a steady pace. A few minutes later a small CDF squad met them.

"You guys are a bit far from home, aren't you?" a soldier asked.

He had dark hair and Dash could see the muscles bulging under his uniform. There were five others with them and they looked familiar.

The soldier who had just spoken smiled with what might have looked like a friendly smile except for his eyes. There was something off about the way the man was looking at them.

"We didn't expect to see anyone else here," Dash said.

The soldiers were well armed and seemed to be watching the area around them as much as they were watching Dash and the others.

"We're so glad you found us," Selena said.

The CDF soldier nodded and looked back at Dash. "You're Dash DeWitt, right?" the soldier asked.

Dash's eyes widened and he wasn't the only one. He nodded quickly. "Who are you?"

The CDF soldier frowned and his gaze narrowed for a split second. "You don't remember me? The ryklar attack last week. We're the squad that rescued you."

Dash smiled uncertainly. "I thought you looked familiar. I just didn't expect to see any of you here." He nodded in greeting to the other soldiers. "I'm sorry, but I don't remember your name."

The soldier waved off his apology. "I'm Lieutenant Maddox.

And I'm actually glad you're here. There's something we could use your help with."

Dash glanced at the other soldiers, who kept a steady watch on them.

"We're so glad *you're* here," Selena said excitedly. "Something happened to our C-cat and we've had to hike here."

Lieutenant Maddox's eyes widened at this. "What happened to your C-cat? And what were you doing way out here?"

"We found a map at that first NEIIS outpost where you helped us with the ryklars," Dash said and Lieutenant Maddox nodded. "The map contained previously undiscovered NEIIS sites, but we had some trouble with the equipment we recovered. We took a C-cat and found another outpost about fifteen hundred kilometers south of here, and that one was much more intact. We accessed the consoles there, which pointed us here," Dash said with a shrug. "That's the long and short of it."

"And you were able to decipher the information on the NEIIS console?" Lieutenant Maddox asked.

Dash glanced at the others. "It was a team effort."

Lieutenant Maddox nodded appreciatively. "Very impressive, but what happened with your C-cat and why didn't you call for help?"

"Our C-cat was damaged by some kind of energy-beam weapon," Dash said, and Lieutenant Maddox nodded for him to continue. "At least, we *think* it was an energy weapon. Something took out our comms antenna, which caused the failure with the C-cat's main power supply. We tried to fix our communication system, but the range wasn't enough to reach any colonial settlement. We thought our best chance to call for help was to come here, climb one of those monoliths, and hopefully send word back to Sanctuary. Our updates are overdue by now."

"You're right about satellite communications being spotty in this area—yet another thing the colonial government failed to address in their rebuilding efforts," Lieutenant Maddox said and shook his head. Then he arched an eyebrow, his gaze intent. "So, your updates are overdue. That means someone knows you're out here this time."

Dash didn't know why, but he felt like there was something off about the lieutenant, as if he was moments away from lashing out. "That's right. They know we're out here and they have our coordinates," he said and hoped the others wouldn't overreact to him bending the truth.

Selena was about to speak, but Merissa cut her off. "Excuse me, sir," Merissa said, giving Selena a pointed look, "were there any ryklars in the city when you got here?"

Lieutenant Maddox moistened his lips and glanced at the area beyond them. "You better believe there were. We had to clear some out, but we have measures in place to keep us safe—in the encampment, at least, but they're still out there," he said and glanced at the weapons they carried. "Too many for those rifles. You're lucky one of our drones alerted us to your approach."

"But you do have a way to leave here?" Merissa asked.

"Of course," Lieutenant Maddox answered.

"If you don't mind me asking, what brings the CDF to an unknown NEIIS city? How did you guys find this place?" Dash asked.

"We should start heading back to base camp and I'll tell you about it on the way," Lieutenant Maddox said.

Two soldiers walked ahead of them and the rest brought up the rear. Dash glanced behind at them and noticed that they were watching him and the others almost as much as the surrounding area. What did they expect?

"You were saying, sir?" Dash prompted.

Lieutenant Maddox glanced at him. "You'll have to forgive me, but we've experienced a tragedy just before you arrived. Captain Fletcher, our commanding officer, died of ryklar wounds."

"Oh, I'm so sorry," Dash said and the others echoed the same. "I didn't really know him, but he seemed like a good man."

Lieutenant Maddox narrowed his gaze. "You hardly recognized us. Would you have remembered him if you'd seen him?"

Dash's cheeks reddened in embarrassment. Lieutenant Maddox's angry glare was unyielding, and for moment Dash thought he was going to strike. Then it was gone.

"I'm sorry," Lieutenant Maddox said quickly. "Captain Fletcher . . . He and I had served together for a long time. He was a good man and shouldn't have died."

Dash swallowed uneasily and nodded.

Lieutenant Maddox blew out a breath. "As for how we found this place," he began and turned to address the others as well, "we detected a strong NEIIS signal from this location and tracked it here. We believe it has something to do with ryklar activity. That's why all of you being here is actually a blessing. My specialist, while good with CDF technology, is somewhat lacking when it comes to understanding NEIIS systems."

"You've got the right bunch for that," Brad said, speaking up for the first time. "I'm Brad Kelly with the Colonial Research and Development Group, and my latest assignment was with the archives at Sanctuary. I specialize in NEIIS technology and Dash here understands it very well."

Lieutenant Maddox smiled widely, showing a strong set of pearly chompers that made his smile almost as menacing as it was friendly. Having seen that flash of anger from the man, Dash really didn't want to piss this guy off.

"Two experts in our midst," Lieutenant Maddox said. "You hear that, Corporal Winston?"

Corporal Winston's heavy footfalls sounded ahead of them. He was easily twice the size of Dash.

"Outstanding, sir. Shall I radio ahead and inform Specialist Stackhouse that he has help coming?" Corporal Winston asked.

"That would be a negative, Corporal," Lieutenant Maddox said and looked at Dash. "I wouldn't want to spoil the surprise."

Dash found himself nodding as Lieutenant Maddox quickened his pace to speak with one of the other soldiers, who then ran off.

Jim walked next to Dash and gave him a tap on the arm. He leaned in. "I don't know why, but that guy scares the hell out of me," he said quietly.

"Me, too," Dash agreed.

Merissa was the only one close enough to hear them, and when Dash looked at her, she gave a small nod. At least he wasn't the only one put off by the arrival of their help. He watched as Brad and Selena walked ahead to speak with Lieutenant Maddox.

24

THE SPEED of the Field Ops troop-carrier was greater than any C-cat could ever hope to achieve. Connor used his implants to access the ship's systems and noted that they were closing in on the NEIIS city so he decided to stretch his legs and walk to the cockpit. Lenora and Ian were poring over some initial scan data of the NEIIS city. Captain Ramsey followed Connor.

Connor opened the door and saw the NEIIS city in the distance on the heads-up display. "Have you been able to detect the C-cat?"

"Negative, sir," Sergeant Hale replied.

They'd taken the most direct path from the NEIIS outpost, believing that Dash and the others would do the same. Suddenly, the troop-carrier dropped sharply to the side and a klaxon alarm blared. Captain Ramsey stumbled into him and both of them slammed into the wall.

"Main engines unresponsive!" Sergeant Hale cried.

Connor pushed himself off the wall and Captain Ramsey

grabbed onto Corporal Bennett's chair for support. They were losing altitude fast.

"Emergency thrusters are online," Corporal Bennett said.

"What the hell happened?" Captain Ramsey said.

"Something hit us, sir," Sergeant Hale said.

The breath caught in Connor's throat as they plummeted toward the ground. He saw a flash of something zip by the heads-up display.

"Go strap yourselves in. We're going down," Sergeant Hale said.

Connor stumbled out of the cockpit toward the nearest chair and fastened the strap. The cabin was awash in flashing red lights. Connor looked at Lenora and saw that she was strapped into her seat. The troop-carrier suddenly dipped again and then the emergency thrusters fired. The floor of the transport gave a sudden jolt upward and Connor's stomach tightened.

"Hold on!"

The Field Ops troop-carrier skidded onto the ground in a somewhat controlled manner, but the force of the landing jostled Connor's teeth. He bit into the side of his cheek, and the copper taste of blood filled his mouth. The entire ship seemed to shudder and then a harsh metallic clang of twisting metal could be heard as the ship came to a halt. Master alarms continued to blare. The straps had dug into his shoulders and Connor pressed the button to release them. He saw Lenora doing the same and turned toward Captain Ramsey. The Field Ops captain had a shallow cut on his forehead and there was a trickle of blood down the side of his face. He asked the captain if he was okay but Captain Ramsey waved him off.

Connor checked on Sergeant Hale and Corporal Bennett in the cockpit, and they were fine. Sergeant Hale killed the alarms, but there was a long list of failed systems on the heads-up display.

"What's the status?" Connor asked.

Captain Ramsey stood in the doorway, wiping his forehead with his sleeve and smearing blood.

"Something hit our engines. The logs show that an impact registered just before we went offline. I'll need to go check," Sergeant Hale said. She stood up and did another quick check of the troop-carrier's error messages.

"Make sure you're armed, Sergeant. Corporal Bennett, you should go with her," Connor said.

The two Field Ops agents hesitated for a moment.

"There could be ryklars in the area."

"I'll go with them," Captain Ramsey said.

Connor headed back to the cabin and saw Lenora helping Ian stand up. He had a red gash on the side of his head.

"Are you alright?" Connor asked.

"I'm fine," Lenora said. "Ian hurt his head."

Connor looked at Ian for a moment. "He does have a wooden head. I'm sure he'll be fine."

Ian grinned and then winced as Lenora pressed a bandage onto the side of his head.

"Hold this here," Lenora scolded Ian.

"I'm fine, by the way," Connor said.

Lenora glanced at him. "Hardly surprising. What happened?"

So much for sympathy, Connor thought. "They think something hit us."

"Who would fire a weapon at us way out here?" Lenora asked.

Connor retrieved his weapon and the others did the same. The ship still had power and the doors still worked. They walked outside and saw the Field Ops team toward the back of the ship. The rear engines were a mass of twisted metal in a gaping hole.

Sergeant Hale was peering inside the troop-carrier's new hole and stepped back, shaking her head. "Looks like whatever hit us is gone. I can't find any sign of it," she said.

Captain Ramsey glanced at Connor. "What do you think?"

Connor walked around and looked at where the main engine pod had been. "That area isn't where we were hit. That's where whatever hit us exited."

Sergeant Hale frowned in confusion. "How can you tell, sir?"

Connor pointed. "This is the point of entry, Sergeant. Whatever hit us tore through the hull and went out where you're standing. That's why the hull is bending out toward you."

Sergeant Hale and the others glanced back at the hull in surprise.

"Don't worry about it, Sergeant. He does that stuff to me all the time," Captain Ramsey consoled her.

Connor shrugged. "I've seen more than my share of weapon impacts, but I'm not sure what would cause this," he said and glanced at the area behind them. "We'd have to find pieces of the engine to figure that out."

"Sir," Corporal Bennett said, "just before the crash, I thought I saw another ship on the ground. It might've been a C-cat. I think it was small enough, but I can't be sure. Everything happened so fast."

Connor walked over to them. "How far back do you think it is?"

Corporal Bennett closed her eyes and her brows knitted tightly. Then she shook her head. "Maybe five or six kilometers back. I'm not sure where because we veered off course."

"It's alright. I understand, Corporal," Connor said.

"Do you think we should go back and find the C-cat?" Lenora asked.

Connor drew in a breath and took another look at the

damaged troop-carrier. "No, if they had a problem with their ship, they would've headed to the city on foot."

"You think they'd leave their ship?" Captain Ramsey asked.

Connor nodded. "We're a day behind them, and this," he said, gesturing toward the ruined hull, "wasn't an accident."

"But they could be hurt. Can't you send a recon drone at the very least?" Lenora asked.

Connor did a quick calculation of how many drones they'd brought with them. Someone or something had knocked them out of the sky. They'd known just where to hit them. The question was why.

"Okay, we'll send a couple of drones southwest of our position and have them do a few sweeps while we head toward the city, but I don't think they're back there. I think that whatever got our ship must have done the same to them and that's the reason we haven't heard from them. If they're alive, they would've headed toward the city. It's the closest shelter and has the highest vantage point," Connor said.

Captain Ramsey nodded knowingly.

"I'm glad you understand, Captain. How about filling the rest of us in," Ian said.

"Communications this far away from any colonial settlement is spotty at best," Lenora said, chiming in. "They probably have only one or two chances a day to beam a transmission to the comms satellite," she said and looked at Connor. "I told you I pay attention."

"I never doubted you for a minute," Connor said.

"But who would shoot down our ship?" Ian said.

Connor scratched the back of his head. "I think whoever did this was just trying to disable our ship."

"That doesn't answer the question of who," Ian replied.

Connor glanced at Lenora. "Is there anything in the NEIIS archives that indicates they had city defenses?"

Lenora pursed her lips in thought.

Ian's eyes widened and he looked toward the city. "You think we tripped some kind of NEIIS automated defense?"

That wasn't Connor's first thought, but he wasn't sure about sharing his real thoughts with the others. He shrugged instead.

"I can't remember. I'd have to do a search in the archives to know for sure," Lenora said.

"Even if it was some kind of latent defense, they'd have to know just where to hit us or have one hell of a lucky shot," Captain Ramsey said.

Connor looked away from them.

Lenora cleared her throat. "Come on, out with it already."

He should've known better. Connor turned back toward them. "Vemus attack force," he said.

Lenora's eyes widened and then she frowned. Sergeant Hale and Corporal Bennett stopped what they were doing at the mention of the Vemus.

"The Vemus are gone," Captain Ramsey said.

Connor's jaw tightened for a moment. This was why he hadn't wanted to mention it to them. "It's just a possibility. I know the CDF did a massive sweep of the debris field, but who's to say that one of their drop-ships wasn't knocked off course and they've been out here all this time? We're thousands of kilometers away from the nearest colonial settlement. With no command structure, who's to say how a Vemus soldier would react? Our troop-carrier's design would be known to them and that would explain how they'd know just where to hit us to bring down our ship."

Connor watched as the others considered what he'd said, but his attention was focused on Lenora. Her eyes drew downward in sympathy. "Connor," she said softly.

Connor clenched his teeth and looked away. "I know you're going to say I'm being paranoid, but I'm not. If anyone else has a better explanation, feel free to share it."

Lenora walked over to him. "I wasn't going to say any of that."

She reached out and put her hand on his arm, rubbing it gently. Connor looked at her and nodded.

Ian snorted and then sighed. "I hate to say this, but I think I liked it better when we just had ryklars to contend with. This changes things."

"You're right, it does," Captain Ramsey said. "It means those kids are in even more trouble than we thought. I don't know how to deal with the Vemus."

Connor pressed his lips together and his shoulders became tight. They weren't equipped to deal with the Vemus. "We need to get to the city. We also need to send our drones out to start sweeping the area and learn as much as we can so we can alert the CDF. Gather what supplies you need and let's get a move on."

The others headed back into the transport to gather supplies and Lenora lingered behind with him.

"I'm sorry for how I've been acting," Lenora said.

Connor sighed heavily. "I'm sorry, too. Let's go get them."

Lenora bit her lip. "If the Vemus are here . . ."

Connor wanted to hold her in his arms but there wasn't time. "Dash is smart. They brought drones with them and he knows how to use them. He may not have been in the military, but he can think on his feet. There's a good chance they're still alive."

Lenora drew in a breath and her face set with determination. That was the woman he knew. She'd never cowered from anything. They joined the others in the troop-carrier. Connor hoped he was wrong about the Vemus but kept trying to think of what they would do if they did encounter them. If a drop-ship had landed way out here, there could be a small force of them in the area; however, if it was multiple drop-ships, they were all in real trouble.

25

DASH WISHED he could've enjoyed his first walk through the newly discovered city. The type of the buildings changed in style for a purpose he could only guess at as they walked further into the city. Near the outskirts, the buildings were dome-shaped, with several spires along the edges, like a crown. After walking a kilometer, the building style changed, becoming square with the rooftops appearing to be on a pedestal because there was a large overhang. The smooth walls looked to be made of concrete, but even after all the time the city had been abandoned, there were no cracks on any of the exterior walls that Dash could see. He glanced at the rooftops again, puzzling over the two-meter extension past the walls. Even if one could climb the walls, the wider rooftops would make it extremely difficult to reach the top. He would have liked to spend some time exploring these buildings, assuming the rooftops were only accessible from the inside.

Dash stumbled into Merissa and muttered a hasty apology.

"What do you keep looking at?" Merissa asked.

"The rooftops," Dash said and gestured ahead of them. The

buildings in this part of the city were almost uniform in size, easily ten meters tall.

Merissa looked where he gestured. "What's so special about them?"

"I was trying to think of why they'd build roofs like that. Early dwellings serve a practical purpose—shelter and what not—but eventually dwellings evolve to become more aesthetic. I can't decide which the NEIIS constructed these buildings for," Dash said.

Merissa pursed her lips, pensive. "Perhaps the NEIIS just liked the pattern."

"Maybe, but I keep thinking that each of these buildings is like a small fortress," Dash said.

Merissa glanced toward the other side of the street. "We're pretty far into the city. Why would they need something like that here? Wouldn't they defend their cities at the edge?"

Dash shrugged. "I don't know," he admitted.

As they reached the CDF encampment, all semblance of friendliness seemed to leave their escorts. They became colder toward them, as if now that they were within the encampment the soldiers could treat them however they wanted.

"Time to leave," Lieutenant Maddox said to them after they'd been at the camp for only a few minutes. "There is an NEIIS Command Center not far from here."

Selena was sitting down and looked as if the mere thought of getting up again was too much to consider. Dash thought they should stick together and one glance at Merissa told him she felt the same. Merissa went over and coaxed Selena back to her feet.

As they were escorted to the NEIIS Command Center, they saw other CDF soldiers who seemed to regard them as unwanted guests. Dash felt as if he were intruding upon something rather than participating in a coincidental meeting.

Jim and Merissa stayed close to him. A few times during their walk from the encampment, Merissa tried to get Selena to stay near them, but she and Brad kept talking and going on as if there was nothing wrong. Dash kept thinking about his first encounter with the squad and how they'd rescued the research team from the ryklars. He'd been appreciative at the time, but the more he thought about it, the more he remembered how Connor hadn't approved of the CDF soldiers' methods for dealing with the ryklars. Somehow Connor had known something wasn't right with these men.

"How long do you think it will be before anyone comes looking for us?" Jim asked quietly.

"They're probably on their way here, so not too long," Dash replied.

"How do you know?" Merissa asked.

"Because I told them I would send an update and it didn't go through. I'm pretty sure they've found the NEIIS outpost by now. It wouldn't take much for them to figure out where we'd go from there," Dash answered.

Merissa blew out a breath and glanced worriedly ahead at the soldiers. "Let's hope so. I don't like this one bit."

Dash nodded and noticed Lieutenant Maddox glancing back at them. His gaze had the intensity of a berwolf that'd found its prey.

Lieutenant Maddox strode over to them. "We're almost there."

Dash met his gaze and his stomach clenched. "What is it you need me to do?"

Lieutenant Maddox seemed to consider this for a moment, letting the silence hang in the air. "It's better if I show you when we get there."

"Have you been able to reach Sierra?" Merissa asked.

Lieutenant Maddox swung his gaze toward her. "I have my

team working on it. Our communications window is limited. Not to worry though, we'll get you sorted."

Access to their communication systems would have been nice, but Dash didn't want to push his luck. The CDF soldier might not have said anything, but Dash didn't think he'd been fooled by their compliance. He had no idea what to do but go along with what the CDF lieutenant wanted from them.

It took them about fifteen minutes to reach the NEIIS Command Center, the name of which didn't do the huge complex justice. Dash glanced overhead and saw large monoliths circling the massive campus. This was the area of the city they'd spotted on their approach. There were several large structures ahead and Lieutenant Maddox led them toward the central one. Dash noted the squarish architecture and defensibility of the buildings, and he wondered if this was the NEIIS version of a military installation. He supposed it could have been a government complex as well, but he couldn't be sure. The central building was forty meters tall, which wasn't that much larger than what they'd seen elsewhere in the city. He knew the NEIIS could create large structures, but no other sites had monoliths like those that surrounded the central building. They were easily a hundred meters tall.

"Lieutenant Maddox," Dash called. "Is the command center you found subterranean?"

Some of their escorts seem surprised by Dash's question, but Lieutenant Maddox appeared to file the information away.

"That's correct. I see you know how they construct their buildings," Lieutenant Maddox said.

"It follows what they've done at Sanctuary," Dash said.

They went through the main entranceway, which opened into a large atrium with a pathway leading down to lower levels. The way down was dimly lit by temporary lighting the CDF had deployed. The floor was smooth, and though they were now belowground, the air was relatively dry. Dash's implants adjusted to the dim lighting. The pathway curved around in a large circle until they reached the bottom.

"Were you able to isolate where the signal was broadcast from?" Dash asked.

Lieutenant Maddox didn't even turn around. "Not important. The main consoles are this way."

They entered a darkened corridor and Dash wondered why the CDF hadn't turned on the lights. The NEIIS didn't work in the dark, but the soldiers were using their own supplies to light the way. They finally reached the NEIIS Command Center where ten consoles were stationed around a large, pyramid-like structure that was upside down. Dash knew from the reports that the pyramids were kept in place using a series of magnets. Two glowing amber lines ran along the base of the pyramids. Just below them were several CDF soldiers clustered around a large mesh screen.

Lieutenant Maddox strode forward. "What's your status, Specialist Stackhouse?"

"I haven't made much progress, sir," Specialist Stackhouse said.

Dash looked at the young CDF soldier, who couldn't have been more than a year older than he was.

"I was afraid you'd say that, so I brought you some help," Lieutenant Maddox said and introduced them. Dash and Brad walked toward the console while the others stayed nearby.

Specialist Stackhouse looked relieved to have help. "I keep finding these references to ryklars, but I'm not sure what they mean."

Dash peered at the screen as he accessed his own translator on his PDA, but the output only appeared on his internal heads-up display. The CDF soldier was using the bare minimum when it came to NEIIS translation. No wonder he was having so much trouble. He shared a look with Brad, who seemed to arrive at the same conclusion.

"Can you decipher it?" Lieutenant Maddox asked.

Dash reread the screen and had started to touch the console when a strong hand grabbed his arm. One of their CDF escorts had silently moved next to him and prevented him from accessing the console.

"I'm afraid we can't have you touching the console just yet," Lieutenant Maddox said.

Dash jerked his arm away from the soldier. "I can decipher it and it does have to do with ryklars, but to get to the true meaning, I need to access the console. What we're looking at is something akin to submenu options."

Lieutenant Maddox narrowed his gaze suspiciously. "What kind of menu options?"

"Something called a purge protocol," Dash said.

Lieutenant Maddox looked at Brad. "Do you agree with him?"

Brad nodded.

Lieutenant Maddox glanced back at Dash and then at Stackhouse. "Alright, Specialist, give up the console for a moment."

Specialist Stackhouse stepped away from the NEIIS console and Dash immediately took his place.

"What do you mean by a purge protocol?" Lieutenant Maddox asked.

Dash frowned, trying to think of a way he could explain it.

"I can help with that," Brad said. "You know how when you access the CDF systems for the Hellcat, as an example. It's just a hierarchy for the system options for whatever it is you're trying to do. Almost half of our struggle with NEIIS computer systems is learning their hierarchy. What your specialist stumbled onto is definitely ryklar related, but what Dash is doing right now is backtracking toward the root menu in order to gain context."

Dash navigated through the interface, doing precisely as Brad had just described. "We'd always suspected the NEIIS had control over the ryklars, but I'd never suspected it was this granular."

"Does this have to do with the ryklar migration?" Lieutenant Maddox asked.

Dash nodded. "It most certainly does. That's what I'm just getting to. These options over here have to do with that," he said and gestured to a series of NEIIS symbols. He was stretching the limits of his own internal translator, but when it finished translating the NEIIS symbols, he snatched his hands away from the console. His eyes widened and his jaw hung. He glanced over at Brad and saw the same shocked expression on his face.

"What is it? What have you discovered?" Lieutenant Maddox asked.

Dash's mouth went dry and he looked at Maddox. The CDF soldier must have suspected something like this. "The ryklars were their foot soldiers."

"Are you saying the ryklars were NEIIS military?" Lieutenant Maddox asked.

Dash swallowed nervously and nodded.

"Is this happening because of what we did at the outpost, or when we loaded that data module in Sanctuary?" Merissa asked.

Dash felt the color drain from his face and he looked at Brad.

"Latent protocols were engaged . . ." Brad muttered.

Dash swiped his fingers across the NEIIS console. There had to be a way to stop this.

"I need you to stop what you're doing," Lieutenant Maddox said, and something in the soldier's tone made Dash turn around.

The other CDF soldiers had closed in and were waiting for a command from Lieutenant Maddox.

"Sir, we can stop the ryklar migration right here and now. I know it. I just need a little bit of time with the console," Dash said.

Lieutenant Maddox shook his head. "You need to step away from the console."

Dash edged toward the console. "I just need a few—" He was cut off as one of the soldiers grabbed him and pulled him away.

"Hey! Hey, let him go," Jim said.

Dash struggled against the soldier but it was no use. He wasn't getting free. Selena gasped and Merissa had started toward him when several CDF soldiers aimed their weapons at them. Dash glanced at Brad, who'd been momentarily forgotten by Lieutenant Maddox, and jerked his head slightly toward the console.

Brad started toward the console but Lieutenant Maddox noticed the movement. He used the butt of his weapon and struck Brad in the back of the head. Brad collapsed. Dash lunged forward, slipping from the soldier's grasp. He charged toward Maddox, but the lieutenant smoothly stepped to the side and Dash felt as if a battering ram had struck him in the chest. The air fled his lungs and Dash collapsed to his knees. He looked up just in time to see Maddox's fist sailing toward his face, and he heard a loud smack, immediately followed by a bright red flash as pain exploded from his nose. Dash went down, suddenly having no control of his limbs. He heard the sounds of people struggling and then a gunshot, followed by screams.

"Enough!" Lieutenant Maddox shouted.

Dash lay on his side and pushed himself to his feet. Maddox pointed his weapon directly at him and Dash held his hands up. His eyes kept tearing up and his nose throbbed in pain.

"Now that we've covered that, I expect complete cooperation from the lot of you," Lieutenant Maddox said.

Dash's head ached and he glared at the soldier.

"You've no right to do this to us," Selena shrieked.

Merissa tried to quiet her down, but Lieutenant Maddox strode over toward the fear-stricken girl. Selena's eyes widened in terror and she attempted to back away, but a soldier came behind her and held her in place.

"Stop this now," Merissa said.

Lieutenant Maddox used the barrel of his assault rifle to lift Selena's trembling chin. "You were saying about who has the right?"

Tears streamed down Selena's face and her lips trembled.

"Leave them alone," Dash said. He had to do something. He glanced around at the soldiers. They were all armed and didn't look the slightest bit concerned by Dash and the others. "Please," he said as calmly as he could.

Lieutenant Maddox kept the barrel of his gun pressed against Selena's cheek, despite her turning away. She cried out.

Dash heard Jim struggling and knew his friend was moments from being struck down.

"You said you needed our help," Dash said. "Tell me what you need me to do and I'll do it. Just leave them alone."

Lieutenant Maddox pulled the barrel of his gun away from Selena's face and she sagged toward the floor, only to be held up by the soldier.

Merissa cursed at Maddox through gritted teeth and the big CDF commander stepped toward her with a hard glare.

"I said I'll help you!" Dash shouted. "Leave them alone."

Lieutenant Maddox grabbed a fistful of Merissa's hair and jerked her head back. Another soldier held her arms behind her and grinned. "What did you say to me?" Lieutenant Maddox asked through clenched teeth.

Merissa glared at him. "You're a monster."

Lieutenant Maddox sneered. "*I am* a monster," he said as if relishing the thought. "Perhaps I'll have my men take you to the ryklars and then we can talk about who the real monster is."

Lieutenant Maddox gestured for his soldiers to take her away. Merissa struggled against them, but it was hopeless. Dash shouted for them to stop, but it fell on deaf ears. He took a few steps toward Merissa and a soldier pointed his weapon at Dash.

"Your man, the soldier you had working here, damaged the console. Without me, you'll never control the ryklars. That's what you want, isn't it?" Dash said.

Lieutenant Maddox looked at him.

"Bring her back and I'll do whatever you say," Dash said.

Lieutenant Maddox walked over to him until his face was inches from Dash's. "I know you will."

"But only if you don't hurt my friends," Dash said. He kept his voice firm, despite the shudder that swept through his body.

Lieutenant Maddox's hand snapped forward, grabbing him by the throat. "You don't get to give orders here."

Dash heard Merissa's screams coming from the corridor. He glared at the lieutenant angrily, but there was nothing he could do. Lieutenant Maddox waited for him to come to that conclusion.

"There, I see it now. You'll do exactly as I say and I'll let you live. Try anything stupid and . . . Let's just say there are other ways to motivate you. Do you understand?" Lieutenant Maddox asked. He spoke quietly but the words were harsh.

Dash's stomach clenched and he nodded. He glanced toward the corridor and Lieutenant Maddox followed his gaze. Dash looked back at the lieutenant but didn't dare say anything.

The lieutenant watched him for a long moment.

"Bring her back in," Lieutenant Maddox shouted and looked at Dash. "Now, you're going to educate my specialist on how to control the ryklars. You remember how we dealt with the ryklars?"

Dash nodded.

Lieutenant Maddox's fist lashed out and Dash spun almost completely around from the blow. "You'll answer me when I speak to you, boy."

Dash tasted blood in his mouth and a powerful ache wracked his skull. "Yes, I remember."

"Good. I'll have no problem doing the same to you and your friends—make no mistake," Lieutenant Maddox said.

Dash felt something cold slide down his back and he shivered. This man wouldn't hesitate to kill any of them.

26

SINCE GENERAL HAYES was still at Lunar Base, it fell to Sean to go to the governor's office in Sierra. Sean's path didn't usually cross with that of his mother in any official capacity, unless it was a social occasion. However, since he was the ranking CDF officer in command of the colonial army, he was required to keep the colonial government apprised of the ryklar threat. Colonial government officials hated that term, but Sean didn't know how else to refer to it. The ryklars were, in fact, a threat to the colony.

He sat in a spacious conference room across from his mother, Governor Ashley Quinn. The long, oval-shaped table had chairs crafted from a New Earth hardwood similar to that of an ash tree back on Earth. The sturdy hardwood could be bent and shaped, but whereas ash was light brown in color, the New Earth variety was a deep red, similar to mahogany. His father had enjoyed woodworking. He said it helped him focus, especially when dealing with difficult problems. And there was no shortage of those, Sean mused. He glanced at the advisors who sat at the table and wondered if any of them knew Tobias had actually crafted each one of the decorative chairs upon which they sat. His gaze came to rest on his mother. Sean knew she didn't want to be the governor of the colony. She'd stepped in because his father had died during the Vemus war. She was serving out his father's emergency term of governorship, which only had another thirty days left before elections were held.

"Please continue, Colonel," his mother said.

Here in this room, among these people, they were not mother and son; they were governor and colonel. Sean sensed some of the nervousness from the colonial advisors. The last time Sean had been left in command of the defense of Sierra he'd orchestrated the destruction of the city to save the colony from the Vemus. Sean had strong-armed the colonial government based on the fact that they were about to die and he had an army at his command. Sean still had soldiers at his command, but he was answerable to the civilian government now. However, there were still too many in the room who remembered Sean's behavior from a year ago. While the decision had been a tough one to make, destroying Sierra with the Vemus inside had purchased enough time for Connor to take out the Vemus Alpha ship.

"The ryklar deterrents do work but only for a short time. We've dropped several frequency generators in the direct path of the ryklars. They do, in fact, change direction for a short time, but then the NEIIS signal burst occurs and the ryklars change directions once again. We're actively trying to locate and suppress the NEIIS signals," Sean said.

"It sounds to me like we're in a shouting match with the NEIIS and we're losing. Does that about sum it up?" his mother said.

Sean smiled and nodded. "I'm sure some of the scientists would have a much lengthier explanation, but yes, that does sum it up nicely." He glanced at the colonial advisors. "We do have a military response prepared for when the ryklars reach our settlements."

Several of the colonial advisors stiffened at this. Sean had already been witness to a heated debate about the future of the ryklars on this planet.

His mother nodded. "A military response will be considered when we exhaust all other options, Colonel. Have you been able to discover the source of the NEIIS signals being broadcast?"

Sean shook his head. "The signals, while powerful, are short-lived. Our search grid is extremely large, looking for any signal source we're able to identify. They also appear to broadcast at random from multiple locations, which are different from those that previously sent a broadcast. We have our analysts working on it, but I'm afraid I don't have anything concrete for you at this moment."

"Governor Quinn," Dr. Burke said with a raised hand.

Sean recognized the man as one of the scientific advisors. He watched as his mother looked over at Dr. Burke and gestured for him to speak. One thing Sean had noticed was that his mother ran a tight ship, whether it was colonial advisors or the doctors who had reported to her when she was chief of medicine. She'd been firm but fair and had the respect of her peers.

"I must warn against the annihilation of an apex predator on this planet. It could have unforeseen consequences that may be hard to quantify. The elimination of the ryklars would more than likely allow another predator to take its place, but it could also contribute to a significant surge in a number of other species the ryklars hunt," Dr. Burke said.

Sean knew this was the scientist's way of saying he wasn't sure what was going to happen if the CDF executed their plans to put a significant dent in the ryklar population.

"Annihilation of the ryklars isn't our plan," Sean replied.

Dr. Burke's lips curled. "I'm well aware of the CDF's plan for the ryklars."

Sean nodded. "Good. Then you'll acknowledge that it's the only real plan on the table. We've only been successful in delaying the ryklars from reaching our population centers and we can only keep that going for so long." He'd been about to say something about delaying the inevitable, but he'd learned that sometimes with civilians he had to hold back certain strong language. Sean returned his gaze toward his mother. "Governor, the call is yours to make. I'm merely presenting you with the option, and I don't like the option any more than anyone else in this room. The ryklars are extremely dangerous. Some of our own projections show a significant risk of the ryklars being able to overwhelm some of our defenses if they attack in force. We need to be proactive in our approach to dealing with this threat."

His mother narrowed her gaze. "I thought we were already being proactive, Colonel. That's why I approved the mobilization of the Colonial Defense Force. However, I'm also aware that there's a time constraint before a decision must be made and we haven't reached it yet. We have a significant portion of colonial resources devoted to this effort and we should be able to come up with a solution that will hopefully not include the wholesale slaughter of an indigenous species."

"Of course, Madam Governor. We'll continue to gather intelligence and present everything we learn to your office," Sean said.

His mother ended the meeting shortly thereafter and asked him to stay behind. The rest of the advisors left the room, his mother's assistant being the last one to go.

Sean raised his eyebrows. "I think we'll have a whole five minutes before someone knocks on that door."

His mother smiled tiredly. He'd been witness to the effects of this job on his father and was seeing the same in his mother. The past year hadn't been easy for anyone.

"In thirty days, it'll be someone else's problem," Sean offered.

"That really doesn't help, son."

"We're doing everything we can. I promise you we are, but we might not have much of a choice."

Ashley walked over to the windows and gazed at the commotion of a city being rebuilt. She sighed. "I thought after the Vemus were gone we wouldn't have a need for you to use those weapons again. I don't understand how this all started, but I guess that's not important. I've read your report multiple times. Conventionally, you don't have enough firepower if the ryklars come at us in force."

Sean's chin drew down stubbornly. "That's based on not knowing just how many ryklars there are."

His mother smiled. "You just reminded me of Connor. I wasn't making a slight against the CDF's capabilities. I was saying we may need to resort to more large-scale weapons."

Sean sighed. "I'm not sure we can defend population centers and keep our consciences clear."

His mother waved the comment away. "I wouldn't worry about that. No one is really saying we should all die for the ryklars. They just want us to exhaust all our options. Have you spoken to Connor? I'd be curious to know what he has to say about all this."

"A large-scale ryklar attack could be almost as bad as when the Vemus attacked us. They're not your garden-variety creatures and have been engineered for killing. Heavy weapons may be our only viable option," Sean said.

His mother leveled her gaze at him. "I don't want to destroy large portions of our home as part of our 'only option.' I'm well aware of what the ryklars are capable of; after all, I was the one who treated *your* injuries."

Sean snorted. How could he forget? "I sent Diaz to Sanctuary, but Connor has been out of communication for the past twenty-four hours."

"Chasing one of Lenora's gifted students," his mother said and frowned. "Are you worried about him?"

"No, not really," Sean said and meant it. He'd worked closely with Connor Gates since the colony was first founded. He had no doubts about Connor's skills and said as much.

"Everyone can use some help every now and then—even Connor," his mother said.

"That's why I sent Diaz to Sanctuary," Sean said.

There was a soft knock at the door and Sean smiled. "It appears that our five minutes is just about up. I'll send you another status report in a few hours if we learn anything new."

Sean gave his mother a brief hug and left the room.

27

Winter was only just starting to lose its grasp this far north of the colonial settlements. There was a chill in the air and Connor saw moist vapors escaping his lips as he breathed. They'd left the Field Ops troop-carrier behind over an hour before. Lenora shifted the straps of her backpack again. The emergency beacon they'd brought was sticking out on one side.

"Want me to carry it?" Connor offered.

"No, I've got it," Lenora replied. "Besides, you already have the secondary beacon."

She was right, of course, but the secondary beacon was much smaller. Since his backpack was stuffed with survival gear, as well as ammunition, Lenora had offered to carry the bulky emergency beacon.

Lenora pulled her survival knife and sheath from the belt on her hip and handed it to him. "There, already better."

Connor took the knife and attached it to his belt on the opposite side of his own, then checked the status of the drones they had patrolling the area around them.

"Still quiet out there?" Lenora asked.

Connor nodded. "So far, so good." Unless the ryklars were concealing their body heat.

Captain Ramsey and Sergeant Hale walked a short distance ahead of them while Ian and Corporal Bennett brought up the rear.

"Does it bother you?" Lenora asked and gestured toward Captain Ramsey.

"He's good at his job. I wouldn't do anything different," Connor replied.

Lenora arched an eyebrow, her gaze challenging him to dodge the question again.

"I don't need to be in charge of everything," Connor said.

Lenora grinned.

Connor looked away, taking in the area around them. "I do miss it sometimes . . . a lot of the time. The CDF and Field Ops. Before Bernard showed up with Ashley's proposal, I'd offered to train a volunteer group to assist Field Ops."

"I know." Lenora smiled wittingly. "You are who you are, Connor. I never asked you to become something you're not."

"I thought you didn't want me involved with the CDF and Field Ops anymore."

"Leading the CDF would require you to be away from me, and I selfishly want you all to myself. I want you near me, but I never expected you to be completely removed from it," Lenora replied.

Connor didn't know what to say. He'd left the military, but there was always the allure of a life that was familiar to him. The more he thought about it, the more the ingrained patterns of who he used to be yearned for that life. But the fact that he could identify those patterns within himself meant that he had moved on, and if he went back to his old life, he suspected it wouldn't be enough for him anymore. It wouldn't be like it was before. So many of the old familiar faces were gone now. They'd paid the ultimate price in their fight against the Vemus, but he still thought about them, even dreamed about them, and Lenora was all too aware of the nightmares he sometimes had.

"We can talk about it after we get back," Connor said finally.

"You should make Dash a member of this new group to support Field Ops," Lenora said.

Connor's brows knitted together and his mouth formed a thin line.

"You can't honestly believe nothing is going to change once we get back home."

Connor sighed and didn't reply.

"I actually agree with many of the things Dash said about field missions," Lenora said, continuing, "and with you as well, but you need to remember that you're working with people outside the military. The way we've done things until now isn't working anymore and I think they'll be more instances like these where Dash or someone just like him will take it upon themselves to lead their own field expeditions. The best we can do is to train them on how to do it as safely as possible. Our methods need to evolve just as we do."

Lenora was right about one thing. Maintaining the status quo definitely wasn't going to work for them anymore.

"We'll see about that—" Connor began but stopped when Lenora quickened her pace. The forest had thinned and they had a clear view of the bronze-colored buildings of the NEIIS city in the distance. Connor caught up with her.

"I knew we should've surveyed more of the continent. We stayed relatively close to the settlements for support, but that will need to change as well," Lenora said.

The seed ship *Galileo* had arrived well before the *Ark*, but it had based its analysis purely on maximum survivability for the new colony. The *Galileo's* equipment might have, in fact, seen the NEIIS cities but didn't note them as anything other than a habitat unsuitable for the colony.

Connor saw Captain Ramsey and Sergeant Hale come to a stop. Sergeant Hale had her weapon up as she peered into the area to their right. Connor brought his own weapon up and immediately accessed the drone feeds. He saw the gray spotted backs of twenty ryklars closing in on them less than half a kilometer away. The ryklars staggered their approach but moved on a path directly toward their location, which meant they already knew Connor and the others were there.

"Ryklars," Connor said. "We need to move. We're too exposed here."

He urged Lenora on.

"He's right," Captain Ramsey said. "The city is our best bet."

They quickened their pace, trying to move as quietly as possible. Connor positioned himself to keep pace with Corporal Bennett at the rear and kept the drone feed on his internal heads-up display. The ryklars hadn't changed direction yet, but he knew it was only a matter of time.

Finally, they left the forest behind and made their way through the thick grassland that surrounded the NEIIS city. One of the drone feeds showed where the forests had begun to overtake the city, but it hadn't happened yet where they were.

A flurry of activity showed on the drone feed. The ryklars had figured out that they'd been detected and were coming for them.

"Run!" Connor shouted.

The others sprinted ahead toward the safety and cover of the NEIIS city. Connor glanced behind him as he ran and saw multiple heads bobbing as the ryklars propelled themselves toward them, using their arms to get the greatest amount of speed possible. He'd seen them take down a landrunner before and knew the ryklars would soon be upon them. Connor stopped and brought up his modified CAR-74 hunting rifle. He picked the lead ryklar, and as its head popped up, he squeezed the trigger. A high-velocity dart left the barrel and slammed into the creature's head, causing it to miss its stride and tumble to the ground. Several other ryklars barely swerved out of the way. Connor spun around and ran. He heard the cadence of clawed feet pounding the ground and the ryklars' harsh breathing as they closed in on him.

A hundred meters ahead, the others had reached the city. Captain Ramsey stopped, brought up his own rifle, and started firing toward the ryklars. Connor's thighs burned as he ran. A ryklar screeched in pain as one of Captain Ramsey's shots found its mark. As Connor reached the city, Captain Ramsey turned and ran next to him. The others were ahead of them, running on uneven pavement.

"We need to find cover!" Connor shouted.

Sergeant Hale went toward the nearest building, which had a square bottom and a rounded rooftop with a large overhang. Lenora was at the door controls, trying to open it.

"It's dead. I can't get it open," Lenora said.

The door was sealed shut and they didn't have time to try and pry it open.

Connor slowed and turned around. A group of ryklars was racing down the street toward them. He brought up his rifle and began firing on them. It would take multiple shots for the others to bring down a ryklar, but a well-placed shot from his rifle would bring them down permanently.

"More ryklars are on the way," Sergeant Hale said.

Connor clenched his teeth. They couldn't stay there. They moved deeper into the city, pausing to fire a few shots at the ryklars to slow them down. Connor glanced at the rooftops and saw more ryklars running up there, following along in an attempt to cut them off. These were much closer and he could see the thick protrusions from the creatures' cheekbones. Those protrusions ended in red tissue, giving it the look of fresh blood from their latest kill. They needed to get off the street.

Connor saw a narrow gap between two buildings that was wide enough for them to fit in single-file and shouted for the others to go there. Quickly responding to his shout, they left the main street and ran down the alleyway, taking the first turn they came to. Connor heard the harsh breaths of the ryklars running on the rooftops nearby, stopping periodically to sniff the air. At least the alley was a bottleneck if it came to a fight, but Connor knew they couldn't stay there very long. More ryklars would come. They were relentless once they were on the hunt.

Connor and the others kept running and the alleyway opened to another street. He peered around the corner.

"That way will take us further into the city," Lenora said and gestured to the right.

They had no choice; they had to keep moving. Connor led them out from the alleyway. They stuck close to the buildings on one side of the street, which provided some cover. No sooner were they away from the alleyway than several ryklars burst from it in an all-out run. More jumped down from the rooftop, their powerful legs absorbing the impact of the impressive leap.

"There are more behind us!" Captain Ramsey shouted.

Connor glanced behind them and cursed. They were trapped. A quick check of his ammunition told him he was half-empty. "Our only chance is to hold them off as long as we can and try to find another alleyway. Conserve your ammunition as much as possible and kill as many as you can."

They divided their efforts, each facing the group of ryklars closing in on them from opposite sides. Connor aimed his rifle and fired. Several of the ryklars paired up near the walls, with one lifting the other in a grand leap to propel themselves along the walls in an attempt to reach them. Connor aimed for their legs, causing them to lose their footing and fall.

"Ian, do you still have the sonic blaster I gave you?" Connor asked.

Ian's eyes were wide and he pulled the sonic blaster from the holster.

"I modified it like before. Wait until they get in close," Connor said.

Ian nodded.

"Hold your fire," Connor said.

The others stopped shooting their weapons and clustered together, the wall of a building at their backs.

Ryklars approached cautiously.

"I hope you have something clever up that sleeve of yours," Captain Ramsey said.

Connor brought up his modified sonic blaster. He'd changed the configuration of the weapon before they'd left the troop-carrier. The weapon would now emit a powerful sonic blast that could break rock apart.

"Be ready to fire your weapons after," Connor said, and Captain Ramsey glanced at the sonic blaster in Connor's hand.

The ryklars closed in, their predatory instincts overriding caution. Connor held his breath and sensed Lenora just behind him. The nearest ryklar was within three meters of them, poised to leap as he squeezed the trigger. The modified sonic blaster let out a powerful wave, catching the ryklars by surprise. Those closest to him were blown apart, drenching the street with their grisly remains. Connor strode forward and fired again. More ryklars instantly died. He heard Ian firing his weapon as well. The remaining ryklars, sensing the danger, quickly scrambled backward. The sonic blaster's power supply fizzled out and it went dead.

The remaining ryklars continued to back away. Connor heard the distinct sounds of a CDF-issued AR-71 assault rifle being fired and saw CDF soldiers closing in on their position. An alert appeared on Connor's internal heads-up display for a ryklar-signal broadcast and he watched as the red ends of the protrusions lining the ryklars' jaws became a dark gray, matching the rest of their skin.

Connor and the others crouched, keeping their weapons ready in case the ryklars decided to make one last-ditch effort to kill them. The CDF soldiers moved into position, cutting the ryklars off from them. The few remaining ryklars fled. There were seven CDF soldiers and Connor recognized the squad designation.

"Boy, are we glad to see you," Captain Ramsey said.

A tall soldier joined the others and Connor caught the intense gaze of Lieutenant Maddox. The CDF lieutenant looked just as surprised to see him.

"It seems that we keep running into each other in the oddest places," Lieutenant Maddox said and looked over at one of the soldiers. "Hudson, put one of our drones on them and make sure they don't circle around."

"We have several of our own drones in the air," Captain Ramsey said.

"I think we can both agree that the drones in our arsenal are better suited for this task," Lieutenant Maddox said and looked at Connor. "Gates," he acknowledged, about as charming as he'd been before.

"Lieutenant, thank you for the assist. Where's Captain Fletcher?"

Lieutenant Maddox's gaze hardened for a moment. "He's not available."

"Excuse me, sir. We should go back to the encampment," Private Hudson said.

Lieutenant Maddox nodded and turned back to Connor and the others. "The ryklars probe our defenses every few hours. We should get you back to the encampment."

"Have you seen any other colonists?" Captain Ramsey asked.

Lieutenant Maddox smiled and Connor noted that there was something cold and lifeless in it.

"Yes, we have. They arrived this morning," Maddox said and turned back toward Connor. "It appears young Dash DeWitt has gone on another field expedition."

"Are they alright?" Connor asked.

"No worse for wear. They're actually helping us with something we found in the city," Lieutenant Maddox said.

The CDF soldiers started guiding them away.

"What brings your squad way out here?" Connor asked.

"Does it really matter? We're here and we saved your ass—again," Lieutenant Maddox said.

"There's no cause for that," Captain Ramsey said. "You know you're addressing a former general in the CDF, right, soldier?"

Lieutenant Maddox's gaze narrowed. "I know who I'm addressing."

Connor leveled his gaze at the man. The lieutenant's eyes blazed with anger. "I don't know what your problem is with me and I don't care. I want to speak with Captain Fletcher right now."

Lieutenant Maddox clutched his weapon and stomped toward Connor. "Do you think for a second I give a damn about what you want?"

The other soldiers raised their weapons several inches but hadn't actually pointed their weapons at them.

"What do you think you're doing?" Captain Ramsey snapped.

Lieutenant Maddox swung his gaze toward Ramsey. "Field Ops

has no authority here, Captain. This is a CDF operation, so stuff it."

Connor made no move to raise his weapon, though he wanted to. "And CDF soldiers have no authority over civilians. Your assistance is required. Now where is Captain Fletcher?"

Lieutenant Maddox glared at him.

"Lieutenant," Private Hudson said. "I have a comlink from Corporal Lasky. He said it's urgent, sir."

"Let's keep moving and I'll take you to Captain Fletcher," Lieutenant Maddox said, turning away.

As they continued walking through the city, Lenora moved next to Connor. "What's his problem?"

Connor shook his head. "I wish I knew."

Connor used his implants to scan for comms traffic, so when another comlink signal came to Lieutenant Maddox, he was able to detect it. Though he was officially retired from the CDF, he still retained access to their communications systems. He'd helped design them and hadn't brought it to anyone's attention that he still had access.

"Sir, I've been keeping an eye on Flint as you said. He's been speaking quite a bit with Rex and Shea. I haven't been able to get close enough to actually hear what they're saying. They quiet down whenever anyone gets near them," Corporal Lasky said.

"Understood. What else do you have for me?" Lieutenant Maddox asked.

Connor was able to access the Hellcat's computer systems using the comlink. Lenora walked over to the other side of the street to look at a faded emblem on an NEIIS building. He was about to call out when Captain Ramsey followed her.

"The colonists are helping Stackhouse translate the information on the NEIIS console, but they seem to be stalling," Corporal Lasky continued.

Connor continued to listen while he brought up the latest logs filed by Captain Fletcher. They were from two days ago.

"Sounds like they're getting too comfortable. Get Riggs over there to keep them on track," Lieutenant Maddox said.

"What should I do about Flint, sir?" Corporal Lasky asked.

Connor didn't like where this conversation was heading. The latest log entry was from Maddox and hadn't been sent to COMCENT. Connor accessed the log and started reading.

"I'll deal with him when I get back. Tell Riggs he's authorized to subdue Flint if necessary," Lieutenant Maddox said.

Connor's eyes widened at what he'd heard. Maddox was out of control. He continued reading the lieutenant's log entry.

Captain Fletcher is dead!

Connor's eyes darted toward Lieutenant Maddox's back.

Ian walked next to Connor and glanced at him. "You look like you've just seen a ghost," he said quietly.

Connor ignored him. Captain Fletcher being dead meant that Maddox was in command. He accessed the Hellcat's communication systems and brought them online. He had to get word back to COMCENT so Sean could send another team to them—a team that wasn't led by someone like Maddox. The comms array was re-aligning to beam a transmission.

"Sir, someone is accessing the Hellcat's comms systems," Corporal Lasky said.

"Find out who it is!" Lieutenant Maddox said.

"Sir, it's not any of us. Someone from outside the squad is accessing our systems."

Lieutenant Maddox swung around toward Connor, bringing up his weapon. Connor grabbed Ian by his shirt and shoved him to the side just as Maddox fired.

Ian stumbled ahead of him. "Why is he shooting at us?"

Connor pushed Ian down an alleyway and heard Maddox shouting. A drone flew overhead and Connor shot it down.

"Keep running," Connor said.

Ian finally got his feet under him and ran. "What about the others?"

Connor didn't know. Maddox shot at him because he'd accessed the Hellcat's systems and found what the lieutenant had been hiding. If the others didn't fight, Maddox would just take them prisoner, and he said as much to Ian.

"When has Lenora ever not put up a fight?" Ian said.

Connor was thinking along those same lines. He needed to regroup and figure out what the hell was going on with this rogue CDF squad, but first they needed to find someplace to hide. In the distance, he heard several ryklars howling.

28

DASH AND BRAD had spent the last hour working with Specialist Stackhouse, and the young CDF soldier appeared to be just as disturbed by Lieutenant Maddox as the rest of them were. Dash wondered why Stackhouse continued to follow orders from a man like that. Lucky for them, deciphering the NEIIS language on the console wasn't a simple matter. He and Brad had an unspoken agreement to stall the CDF specialist and keep him from learning as much as he needed to control the NEIIS purge protocol. At the same time, Dash was trying to understand what the purge protocol actually was and how to stop it. Why would the NEIIS need something like that? The purge protocol was a system-wide broadcast that seemed to control the ryklars—all the ryklars— within range of the signal and cause them to converge on population centers, killing anyone caught in the open. The purge protocol wasn't meant for humans specifically, but other NEIIS. What sort of species would even construct something like this? The ryklars, in addition to being genetically enhanced, were being used as weapons of war between NEIIS factions. Had this led to their demise? If it had, they still should've been able to find some sort of remains. Regardless of what had happened to the NEIIS, the ryklars obeying the purge protocol was his problem to deal with.

"Let me get this straight," Specialist Stackhouse said. "We can control the purge protocol from the consoles here, but how do we change the specifics of what the protocol actually does?"

Dash looked at the CDF soldier. They were back to this again, and since both Dash and Brad had dodged the question earlier, he knew it wouldn't work this time. "The protocol can be accessed from here, but we're not sure if it's limited to just this location. As far as the specific commands go, we're not sure how to change them. This is the most intact NEIIS computer system we've found to date."

There was a rough clearing of a throat from behind them and Dash turned to see another CDF soldier glaring at them. The soldier had a broad chest and long, thick arms. He looked as if he could crush boulders.

"Sounds like crap to me," Sergeant Riggs said.

Sergeant Riggs had joined them a short while ago. He'd just chime in every now and then as if he could sense when Dash was lying to Stackhouse. Corporal Lasky called over to Riggs and Stackhouse, saying he needed to speak with them. They left Dash and Brad at the NEIIS console, but not before Riggs gave them a warning look.

Brad looked at him once the soldiers left. "I don't know how much longer we can keep stalling them."

Dash glanced down to the floor and saw Specialist Stackhouse's pack. "I know," Dash replied quietly and peered into the pack. Stackhouse had his PDA in there. Dash used his implants to access his own PDA and connect it to Stackhouse's. He waited a moment and then Stackhouse's PDA powered off. "We need to escape and shut this thing down—" He stopped speaking when Riggs glanced over in their direction. Once the CDF soldier looked away, Dash bent over as if adjusting his boot and snatched the PDA from the pack.

Brad frowned and glanced over at the CDF soldiers who seemed to be in a heated discussion. "What are you doing?" he asked quietly.

Dash ejected the portable power supply, took one of the tiny spare wires from the pack, and wrapped it around the PDA. He took a quick look at the soldiers. Riggs seemed to be arguing with Lasky. The soldier was speaking in hushed tones but jabbing his finger like it was a knife. It was now or never. Dash bent over again and opened the control panel. He dumped the PDA inside and connected the wire to the NEIIS power line. Brad grunted as Dash hastily stood up and closed the panel the best he could.

"We're getting out of here," Dash said.

Brad's eyes widened and he glanced at the control panel. "How did you—"

Dash shook his head. "It's not important. I've accidentally broken enough NEIIS equipment to know how to make it fail on purpose."

"Yeah, but an overload of this console isn't going to stop them."

There were other consoles in the room, but Dash couldn't access any of those. "Yeah, but it could give us a chance to escape. There might be the equivalent of a computing core around here that we can find and stop them for good."

Brad pressed his lips together, his Adam's apple rolling in his throat. Riggs and Stackhouse rejoined them. Dash glanced at Merissa and the others, who were sitting on the ground with a soldier standing guard.

"What were you guys talking about?" Riggs said, his eyes narrowing suspiciously. "I hope you're not thinking of doing something foolish because that would be a big mistake. We need to move this along. Lieutenant Maddox has authorized me to get you to work a little bit faster."

Brad shook his head. "We weren't doing anything. My friend here simply needs to go to the bathroom and was too afraid to ask."

Riggs glanced at Dash and immediately he brought his hands to his crotch. "Yeah . . . yes, I need to hit the head in a bad way."

Riggs seemed amused. "Maybe I should just make you stay here until you have an accident," he said and cocked his head to the side. "Perhaps the smell will make you work faster."

Dash swallowed nervously. He didn't need to act afraid because Riggs looked as if he was completely serious, but now that there was mention of it, Dash did have to go to the bathroom. *Oh, not now!*

"Come on, Sergeant," Specialist Stackhouse said. "We've been working here for hours. Let him go to the bathroom. They smell ripe enough as it is."

Riggs glared at Dash for a moment and then jerked his head to the side. "This one has to hit the head." He called out to the other soldiers nearby.

Dash walked toward the others and glanced back at Brad, who nodded at him. It would be suspicious if they both suddenly had to leave. Brad was electing to stay behind so they could get away. Dash started walking toward the others, trying to think of something he could do so Brad could get away, too, but his mind was blank.

As he got closer to the others, he heard Merissa ask the soldier about going to the bathroom as well. The soldier flatly refused and then gave Dash a challenging stare, but Dash kept his eyes ahead of him. He used his implants to access his PDA and sent the overload signal to the NEIIS console. There was a bright flash and the small explosion snatched the soldier's attention. Dash used the distraction to run to the side, tucking in his shoulder and then slamming into the soldier. The guard was knocked off his feet and Dash rolled away. Merissa and the others shot to their feet.

"Come on, we have to go," Dash said.

He glanced behind him and saw that Brad and the others were on the ground near the console. Brad wasn't moving. Dash herded the others out of the room and they started running.

"We can't leave Brad behind," Merissa said.

"I know," Dash said.

He heard shouting from behind them and they quickened their pace, turning down another corridor.

"What are we going to do?" Jim asked.

"We need to get out of here and find some way to call for help," Dash said.

"Dr. Bishop and the others are on their way here. We have to warn them!" Jim said.

Dash was about to reply when he heard the sound of a CDF weapon being fired. Jim cried out and tumbled to the ground. Dash reached down and tried to help Jim back to his feet, but his leg was bleeding. He'd been shot. The end of the corridor was just ahead and it split two ways. Merissa grabbed Jim's other arm and helped him up. They reached the end of the corridor as more shots were fired in their direction. They ducked their heads and Dash scrambled to the right while Merissa, Jim, and Selena went to the left.

Dash glanced at the others across the corridor. There were multiple CDF weapons being fired and deadly darts were piercing the wall. He couldn't get across. Jim cried out in pain and slumped to the floor.

Merissa took off her belt and tied it around Jim's thigh, making a tourniquet. She looked over at Dash. "He's bleeding, bad."

Dash looked at Jim's bleeding leg helplessly. There was no way they were going to be able to run away. Maybe he could . . . He faced them, poised to run across the open corridor to them, but suddenly there was shouting from down the corridor away from them. The CDF soldiers would be there in moments.

"Don't!" Merissa said. "Run!"

Dash's eyes became saucers. "I can't leave you behind."

Merissa's eyes softened. "Go get help. They need us alive. You go get help."

Dash glanced behind him and heard the CDF soldiers getting closer, shouting for them to give up. It was hopeless. They would never get away, but Dash could get help.

"Go, you idiot. Run!" Merissa said. She stood up and raised her hands. "Don't shoot! I'm coming out," she shouted, then stepped out into the corridor. She was stalling the CDF soldiers to buy him some time.

Dash took one last glance at her and then ran. He hated himself for leaving them behind. Why couldn't he fight? Why couldn't he protect them? Gritting his teeth in fury, Dash fled.

29

CONNOR CHECKED his weapon and gritted his teeth. He was running low on ammunition and didn't have any more spares to use. He glanced at Ian, who was looking behind them. The ammunition meter showed that Ian was near empty. Not good.

"Do you think they're following us?" Ian asked.

"They are, but not more than four of them," Connor replied.

They reached the end of the alleyway and Connor checked the street. He didn't expect to run into CDF soldiers, but there were still ryklars in the city. The streets were clear. Connor kept close to the buildings and the overhang provided some cover.

"How do you know there are only four of them following us?" Ian asked.

"There were seven soldiers with Maddox and he has to guard the others. Standard CDF protocol for small teams is three to four men," Connor replied.

"Why did they start shooting at us? It doesn't make any sense," Ian said.

Connor accessed the drones they still had in the air. He had one of them set to whisper mode, spying the area behind them.

"Maddox was hiding the fact that Captain Fletcher is dead. He was attacked by ryklars," Connor said.

"That doesn't explain why he's trying to kill us now," Ian said, his voice becoming louder.

Connor gestured for him to be a little quieter. "I don't know why Maddox is trying to kill us, but my guess is that they found something here in the city. The last time we met this squad, I reported that some of them were showing signs of severe issues."

"Why didn't they listen to you?"

"They did. Captain Fletcher's squad was recalled, but they didn't obey. The report I saw on the Hellcat said they were investigating the NEIIS signal. They didn't wait for the go-ahead, but given that communication is somewhat spotty this far out from Sierra, they haven't actually disobeyed direct orders," Connor said.

Ian snorted. "How convenient for them."

Connor shrugged.

Ian pressed his lips together in thought and gave Connor a sidelong glance. "But wouldn't they . . ."

Connor shook his head. "There's no reason for them to obey any order I give. I'm not in the CDF anymore."

"Yeah, but the whole squad can't be okay with this madness. Some of them have to realize Maddox is clearly off his rocker," Ian said.

Connor came to a stop. Across the street was another alleyway, and the drone video feed showed that the four CDF soldiers following them were getting closer. They needed to get off the street. Connor tried to access their comlinks so he could listen in, but he was denied. Maddox had worked fast to block Connor's backdoor. They crossed the street and peered down the alleyway. It wasn't long and branched off into two directions ten meters in.

"The soldiers following us are fine with it," Connor said. Soldiers serving in the same squad became family. They'd squabble and disagree, but when it came down to it, they'd support one another.

They reached the end of the alleyway, and a short distance off to the right Connor saw there was another alley that went back out to the street. He glanced at Ian, who looked as if he could barely keep up.

"Why don't you stay here? I'm going to see if I can lure them in," Connor said.

Ian's eyes widened. "We should stick together."

"They're going to find us, so I'm going to get their attention and lure them into a trap. Then we can shoot them," Connor said.

Ian's mouth opened in shock. "I don't know if I can. Can't we just try and reason with them?"

Connor shook his head and almost clenched his teeth. He didn't have time for this. "It's them or us, Ian."

"I know," Ian said, taking a deep breath. "I just don't know if I can ..."

Connor glanced behind him because he didn't want Ian to see how angry he was. When Ian started speaking again, Connor stopped him. "It's alright. Just wait here. Can you do that?" Connor said.

Ian was clearly anxious about staying, but he nodded.

Connor left him and went back the way they'd come. Ian was just scared, but the soldiers were getting closer and Connor doubted they would hesitate to shoot. He slowly approached the street and waited in the shadows. As the soldiers approached, he had one of his drones fly low, sending it right over them.

"Is that one of ours?" a soldier named Parker asked.

Connor heard the crunch of their boots on the street as they headed toward the alleyway where he waited.

"Negative, they must have brought it with them. That means the bastard knows we're coming."

"Wait a minute. We're hunting General Gates! You sure we should even be doing this?" a soldier named Foster asked.

Corporal Stewart looked at him. "Gates abandoned the CDF. He hung all of us out to dry."

Foster shook his head. "He saved us."

"Shall I open a comlink to Maddox and tell him you have serious issues with pursuing Gates?" Stewart asked.

Connor watched the four soldiers from a second drone he had hidden away on a nearby rooftop.

"No, sir," Foster muttered.

Connor sent the first drone a command and it looped around, gaining speed.

"Hey, what's that drone doing?" Parker asked.

Connor edged closer to the alleyway entrance and heard the whine of the drone's repulsor engines as it raced toward the soldiers.

"Doesn't matter. Take it out," Corporal Stewart ordered.

As the four soldiers fired their weapons at the drone, tearing it apart, Connor broke from cover and came to the edge of the street where he fired at Corporal Stewart. Connor took out another soldier before the rest of them dove for cover.

"They're dead!" Parker said and spun around. "The shot came from that alleyway."

Connor backed down the alleyway and rounded the corner, then raised his hunting rifle, looked through the scope, and waited. One of the soldiers stuck his head into the alleyway and Connor fired another round, which ricocheted off his helmet. The soldier swore.

"We're coming for you, Gates!" Parker shouted.

"What's keeping you?" Connor shouted back but didn't wait for an answer. Instead, he ran toward Ian. "Come on," he said quietly.

The soldiers were still shouting as Connor and Ian ran toward the street, circling around behind them. It was too risky to fly his remaining drone overhead to get a view of exactly where the soldiers were, so he peeked around the corner and saw them on either side of the alleyway he'd last been in. They were forty meters away. The soldier closest to him was Foster, the least likely of the two to want to shoot on sight, but Connor couldn't take that chance and raised his rifle. The movement caught Foster's attention and he opened fire. Connor squeezed off a shot and Foster went down, screaming. Connor traded rifles with Ian.

"Where are you going?" Foster shouted at Parker.

"I'm going to get help," Parker answered, his voice coming from a distance.

Connor peeked around the corner and watched as Parker ran away and ducked out of sight into another alleyway. Connor brought his rifle up and stepped out from where he was hiding, keeping his sights on Foster.

"Looks like he left you behind," Connor said.

Ian was at his side and had Connor's empty rifle pointed at Foster. The soldier's leg was bleeding. Foster glanced at his AR-71 laying nearby, but Connor quickly closed in on him and retrieved the CDF assault rifle.

"You were empty," Foster said, looking at Connor's weapon and then wincing in pain.

Connor checked the AR-71, which was fully loaded. "Not anymore," he said as he looked at Foster's wounded leg. "The way I see it, I can either let you bleed out, or you can help us. Which is it going to be?"

Foster winced in pain and shook his head. "I didn't want to be here . . ."

"Maybe we should—" Ian began, but Connor cut him off.

Connor squatted down and looked at the soldier. "What happened here?"

Foster let go of his leg and the blood began to pool on the street. The soldier had no other weapons and his face was becoming pale. Connor put his rifle down and pressed his hands on the wound, trying to staunch the bleeding.

"Stay with me. Tell me what happened," Connor said.

Foster looked at him, his eyes becoming distant. "Maddox . . . Captain Fletcher died. Maddox blames the government."

Foster's eyes closed, but when Connor shook him, he opened his eyes again and spoke in a low, faltering voice. "He hates you . . . ever since we saw you . . . he's been so angry."

"What did he find here?" Connor asked.

Foster didn't answer and Connor shook him again but got no further response.

"He's dead," Ian said.

Connor pulled his bloodied hands away from the wound. His shot had hit the major artery in Foster's leg and he'd bled out. Connor snatched the soldier's helmet off and checked his pockets for anything useful.

"What are you doing?" Ian asked, not hiding the disgust in his voice.

Connor didn't answer him and kept searching the dead soldier. When he finished that, he got up, went to Corporal Stewart's body, and started searching it for anything they could use. Ian came up behind him and grabbed his shoulder, but Connor shot to his feet and shoved Ian away, glaring.

Ian's eyes widened in shock.

"They have Lenora and the others," Connor said through clenched teeth.

Ian was clearly conflicted but looked away as Connor finished searching the body. He accessed the soldier's PDA and retrieved the comlink access codes.

"What are you going to do?" Ian asked.

Connor stood up with the AR-71 in his hands. "I'm going to get them back."

"There have to be over twenty soldiers back there. Shouldn't we go for help?"

Connor shook his head. "No time. Maddox is crazy enough to kill all his prisoners. I need to stop him."

Ian's jaw tightened. "How?"

"I'm going to hunt him down, along with the rest of his squad," Connor said. It'd been a long time since he'd felt rage like this and he greeted it like an old friend. He couldn't let Maddox hurt Lenora or any of the others, and Maddox was just crazy enough to use Lenora against him. "Once he learns what happened here, he's gonna hurt them. He's gonna hurt *her*. If you don't want to come, fine, but I'm going."

Ian glanced at the dead soldiers for a moment. "I'm with you. Just tell me what you need me to do."

Connor was about to reply when he picked up a comlink signal from Parker. Connor waved Ian over so he could listen.

"Sir, Stewart, Dixon, and Foster are down. I barely got away," Parker said.

"How did he get you?" Maddox asked harshly.

"Sir, he surprised us. He used a drone and . . ." Parker said.

Connor heard someone speaking in the background.

"You idiot! You're broadcasting," Maddox said. "Only direct comlink from now on."

The comlink went off. Connor had been hoping Maddox wouldn't catch on so quickly, but no such luck. He was smart.

"Were you able to hear what they were saying in the background?" Ian asked.

"I think some of them have escaped, but I'm not sure who. Let's head toward the encampment and see what else we can learn. Parker went that way," Connor said, pointing.

Ian walked next to him and Connor could tell there was more he wanted to say. "Go on, say what you need to say," Connor said.

"I've just never seen this side of you. I sometimes forget you were a soldier," Ian said.

Throughout his career, Connor had noticed that people reacted differently to killing. Some people immediately despised it while others embraced it, but for Connor it was something to be endured. Ian would never kill another human. He just didn't have it in him.

"I know we need to get the others back, but we should also try and call for help. Do you still have the secondary beacon in your pack?" Ian asked.

Connor handed his backpack to Ian. "Our best bet would be to climb to the highest point and activate it."

"Or we could just attach it to the drone and send it up," Ian said.

Connor frowned. He didn't like losing his only remaining drone, but Ian was right; they needed to call for help. Working quickly, they recalled the drone and attached the secondary emergency beacon, then sent it off. Hopefully someone back home would be monitoring for it.

30

MADDOX MARCHED his prisoners directly to the NEIIS Command Center. He had no need to go back to the encampment and sent orders for his men who weren't in the field to meet him at the center.

He glanced at the Field Ops captain, a man named Ramsey who had finally learned to keep his mouth shut. The man's eye was swollen almost completely closed and his cheek was already turning purple. Dr. Bishop glared at him whenever he looked over at her, but she still served his purpose—for the moment.

He walked into the command center and saw that one of the prisoners was bleeding. Gibbs was at his side, treating the wound. Maddox sent Dr. Bishop and the others to join the original prisoners.

As Sergeant Riggs joined him, Maddox noticed that he had a long scratch on his cheek and his hands were black. Maddox glanced at the consoles and saw one was destroyed. Dash was missing.

"Sir," Sergeant Riggs said. "They rigged the console to overload and tried to escape during the confusion. We ran them down, but one managed to get away."

Maddox motioned for Specialist Stackhouse to join them. "Do you know the NEIIS interface enough to control the ryklars?"

"We're getting there, sir, but the overload injured the other person who knows the NEIIS language better," Specialist Stackhouse said.

Maddox swung his gaze toward the prisoners and saw that Brad had multiple injuries, but he was conscious. Striding over to Brad, Maddox grabbed his hair and yanked him to his feet, dragging the injured man toward one of the working consoles and shoving him to the ground. The other prisoners looked on in horror but could do nothing because the soldiers were closely guarding them.

Maddox pulled out his sidearm and pointed the barrel at Brad's head. "Feel like cooperating now?"

Brad's eyes were wide with fear.

In order to drive home his point, Maddox moved the barrel of the gun away from Brad's head and fired.

Brad jumped. "I'll help. I'll help," he said quickly.

Maddox turned toward Specialist Stackhouse. "Get to work," he said and looked at Sergeant Riggs. "If the prisoner so much as sneezes funny, shoot him."

Maddox watched as Brad struggled to regain his footing. "Specialist, I just need to feed that console a special set of coordinates and then engage the signal."

"Understood, Lieutenant," Specialist Stackhouse said.

"Sir," Sergeant Riggs said, "what about the prisoner that escaped?"

Maddox glanced at Dr. Bishop. "Shoot on sight. I'll be sending out patrols."

Dr. Bishop returned his gaze with wry amusement and then

laughed. The sound of it made his lip curl and he stomped toward her. "Does any of this seem funny to you?"

Dr. Bishop smirked. "That's your plan? This purge protocol?"

Maddox glanced at the other prisoners. "I see you've wasted no time being brought up to speed. Yes, this is my plan. Part of it anyway. Once Brad shows my specialist the precise commands we need, I'm going to send out a signal that will draw every ryklar across the entire damn continent and point them directly at Sierra."

"The CDF will stop them," Dr. Bishop said.

Maddox nodded. "Possibly, but not before several thousand of them break through their ranks and wreak havoc on the colony."

Dr. Bishop's eyes widened. "Why would you do this? Kill all those innocent people? Do you hate the colony that much?"

"The colony is weak. They've lost their way. They've already forgotten the sacrifice of my fellow soldiers." He watched Dr. Bishop look at the other soldiers. "They agree with me."

"Then they're just as stupid as you are," Dr. Bishop said.

Maddox stepped forward and backhanded the woman. Dr. Bishop went to the ground. He heard her spit and then laugh again as she pushed herself up.

"What's the matter? Did I strike a nerve?" Dr. Bishop said and wiped a trickle of blood from her lip.

Maddox sneered and pointed his weapon toward the other prisoners.

"You don't need to do this," Dr. Bishop said quickly. "Leave them out of this."

Maddox aimed his weapon at one of the Field Ops agents he'd chosen at random and pulled the trigger. The Field Ops agent dropped dead. Captain Ramsey screamed and lunged toward him, but his soldiers held him back. Maddox turned back to Dr. Bishop.

Dr. Bishop's face clouded with fury as she took in the sight of the dead Field Ops agent. Then she turned back to him with fire in her eyes. She wasn't lacking in spirit.

"You bastard," Dr. Bishop hissed and lunged at him.

Maddox grabbed her wrist and twisted her around so her back was pressed against him. He smiled coldly. "And then some," he whispered harshly into her ear, then shoved her away.

Corporal Lasky came over to him. "Excuse me, sir, but Spencer's team is overdue."

Maddox frowned. Chief Spencer had been on patrol. "Do we have their last known location, and are there any ryklars in the area?"

"We know where they were," Corporal Lasky said, frowning. "You need to take a look at this, sir," he said and held out his PDA.

Maddox took the PDA and peered at the image. Chief Spencer's team was lined up, dead on the street. He heard Dr. Bishop gasp and then she smiled.

"It doesn't look like ryklars killed those men. That makes five or six of your men Connor has already taken out," Dr. Bishop said.

Maddox ignored her. "Men, we have some hunting to do. It appears that one Connor Gates believes he can get the better of us. We're going to prove him wrong."

"You actually think you can hunt down Connor Gates?" Dr. Bishop said derisively and turned toward the other soldiers. "All of you think you stand a chance against Connor? Did you forget who he is? Do you remember what he's done? None of you would be here if it weren't for him. He *created* the Colonial Defense Force. Don't any of you remember what he did before he came to the colony?"

Maddox snorted. "He's one man."

"He's the one man who created your training based on his experiences in the special forces of the NA Alliance military. You don't stand a chance. If you give up this foolish plan, you might yet get to live," Dr. Bishop said, her gaze taking in all of them.

Maddox raised his gun and pointed it at Dr. Bishop.

Dr. Bishop sneered. "You think killing me is going to stop Connor? All of you are going to die if you do this. You have no idea what he's capable of."

Maddox pressed the barrel of the gun to Dr. Bishop's forehead. "And you have no idea what *I* am capable of, doctor."

Dr. Bishop would not be cowed and she stared back at him in defiance.

"Bind her hands. She's coming with us," Maddox said.

The other prisoners started to protest and Maddox swung his gaze toward them. "I don't need any of you alive," he said coldly.

The CDF soldiers aimed their weapons at the prisoners and they went silent.

Maddox gestured for Sergeant Riggs. "I'm going to leave you in charge. Once Stackhouse has what he needs, execute the prisoners."

Sergeant Riggs looked over at the captives.

"Do you have a problem with your orders, Sergeant?" Maddox asked.

Sergeant Riggs looked at him. "No, sir."

"Very well," Maddox said.

He thought about returning to their camp first, believing Connor might be heading there, but he suspected Connor would anticipate that. They would be better off leaving from here. He felt a surge of excitement far beyond anything he'd felt when hunting ryklars.

31

Dash ran down the street, staying close to the buildings in an effort to keep out of sight. He'd learned the hard way that the CDF soldiers had drones patrolling overhead looking for him, and he'd almost been spotted once. He was confident he'd managed to slip away from them, but he kept moving just to be sure. He didn't know how many soldiers were following him, but Merissa had delayed them enough to give him a head start. He'd decided to stay within a few kilometers of the NEIIS Command Center, and he thought one of the monoliths would be an ideal place to call for help. The problem was he had no way to actually make that call. Someone else had been carrying the long-range communications equipment from the C-cat. He couldn't remember who and it didn't matter since he didn't have it. He had to come up with a new plan.

Running around the corner of a building that looked to have collapsed long ago, he glanced down the street and saw that several dilapidated buildings seemed to have been struck from above. The area nearby was more of the same, but he couldn't take the time to wonder why this part of the city wasn't as pristine as the rest of what they'd seen. Dash stepped off the street and leaned against the wall, catching his breath. He needed a few moments to think. The others were depending on him to get help. And if that lunatic Maddox figured out what he actually had, there would be no stopping what he'd set into motion.

Dash glanced at the clear skies overhead. Connor and Dr. Bishop should have made it there by now, and he was starting to think that whatever had taken out the engines on the C-cat had done something to prevent the others from arriving.

A high-pitched whine from a drone's repulsor engines became louder as it flew nearby and Dash held his breath. Connor had told him about CDF drone capabilities, which went well beyond what they were using at Sanctuary. CDF drones had better detection capabilities and could fly faster than the drones he normally used, but at least they weren't armed.

He'd found a small niche to hide in that kept him off the main street. The NEIIS buildings outside the complex were much smaller and closer together, reminding him of residential apartments. If he hadn't been running for his life, as well as the lives of his friends, he would have enjoyed his tour through the alien city. There was so much he wanted to explore further, especially as it appeared the NEIIS easily had achieved the technological equivalent of twenty-first century Earth.

The CDF drone was coming closer. It was flying slowly, and Dash clenched his teeth. The drone must have been able to detect him or at least somehow suspect that he was nearby. He tried to hold his breath and not make a sound. The drone hovered along, flying at a snail's pace less than ten meters away from him. Without warning, something chimed from his backpack and he quickly swung the pack off his shoulder, fumbling to silence whatever the hell had decided now would be a good time to go off.

The drone flew right over him and stopped. Dash glared at it, knowing he'd just shown up on someone's video feed. He stepped away from the wall and darted out into the street.

"Stop!" a voice shouted from the drone as it followed him.

Dash came to a halt and turned around.

"We won't hurt you if you just stop," the voice said.

Not going to happen, Dash thought. "I'll take my chances," he called out over his shoulder and started running again.

He heard the voice shout something else but he couldn't hear it. *We won't hurt you . . . yeah, right.* Dash turned down the first corner he found and heard the drone following him. Whatever was in his backpack continued to chime. He tried fumbling with the straps as he ran, managing to pull the flap open and peer inside. The glowing mesh screen of an NEIIS PDA stared back at him. He remembered that Brad had been able to use some of the small NEIIS power cells and it must have turned on when he'd leaned against the wall at just the right angle. The PDA was receiving a broadcast signal from the NEIIS complex, but he couldn't take the time to study it right then so he just silenced the alert. The drone flew overhead, following him but remaining stubbornly out of reach. He came to another street and it stretched far away from him. There was no way he could outrun the drone.

A short distance in the opposite direction he saw what looked like the main thoroughfare and he ran toward it. The drone stayed well behind him and seemed to slow down. He reached the end of the small street he was on and cautiously peered around the corner. Three CDF soldiers were heading right for him and they noticed each other at the same time.

"Don't run," the soldier in the middle said. The two soldiers on either side of him raised their weapons slightly but didn't quite point them at Dash.

He looked behind him at the drone hovering in the air. There was nowhere for him to go. The three CDF soldiers walked toward him.

"You've got nowhere to go," one of them said, echoing his own thoughts.

Dash raised his hands into the air, but he knew he couldn't allow himself to be caught. His friends were depending on him. "I can't go with you," he said and stepped back into the small street he'd been on.

"Dash, I'm Sergeant Flint, and I promise we will not hurt you."

Dash could still see them as he backed farther down the street. "Tell that to Jim. You shot him in the leg, so you'll have to forgive me if I don't trust you."

"That wasn't us, but if you run, I *will* order my men to stop you," Sergeant Flint replied.

Dash took another step back, getting ready to turn and run. "What happened to not hurting me?"

Sergeant Flint smiled. "I think you'll survive a stunner dart, but I'd rather not have to carry you."

Dash gritted his teeth and watched as the three soldiers continued to close in on him. There was a loud pop and the drone crashed to the ground behind him. Dash spun toward it in shock.

"Drop your weapons. We have you surrounded," said a familiar voice.

Dash raised his hands and turned back to the soldiers, who looked just as surprised as he was.

"I know you can hear me. Don't try anything stupid. Do anything other than drop your weapons and I'll drop all of you," Connor said.

Dash heard another pop and he flinched. He wasn't the only one.

"Do as he says," Sergeant Flint said and then spoke over his shoulder. "I'm dropping my weapon."

Sergeant Flint let his weapon fall to the ground and the other two soldiers did the same.

"Put your hands on your heads and step back out onto the street," Connor said.

Dash could hear Connor's voice, but he hadn't actually seen him yet. Until Connor arrived, he'd thought his luck had finally run out. Dash waited for the other soldiers to comply with Connor's orders and then followed them out onto the street.

With his mouth set in a thin, grim line, Connor barely glanced at Dash. He was focusing all his attention on Sergeant Flint and the others.

"The only reason you're still alive is because you didn't kill *him*," Connor said and gestured with his rifle toward Dash.

Standing next to Connor, Dr. Malone looked haggard, but he smiled at Dash tiredly. Connor also looked at Dash. "We heard some prisoners escaped. Is there anyone else with you?"

Dash's throat became thick and he shook his head. He hadn't realized how scared he'd been until the danger had passed.

"Are you alright?" Dr. Malone asked.

"I'm fine, but the others are still at the complex," Dash said and explained where the others were being kept.

He watched as Connor listened but kept his attention on the CDF soldiers.

Sergeant Flint still had his hands up. "What are you going to do with us, General?"

Connor regarded the soldier for a moment. "As the rest of your squad likes to point out, I'm no longer with the CDF. Are you trying to say you're different?"

"We *are* different. This is Dax and Shea. We served on Titan Station under Colonel Douglass," Sergeant Flint said and paused for a moment. Dash didn't know who Colonel Douglass was, but Connor seemed to. Every colonist knew of Titan Station. It had been their first line of defense against the Vemus. Titan Station had been destroyed and there'd been very few survivors. Sergeant Flint continued. "We didn't know Maddox was going to take prisoners or do any of this. Captain Fletcher wanted to investigate the NEIIS signal and then he died . . ." Sergeant Flint's voice trailed off.

"Maddox is crazy. Why didn't you stop him?" Dash asked.

"We couldn't. The rest of the men—most—are loyal to him," Sergeant Flint said.

"And you're not?" Connor said, looking unconvinced.

Sergeant Flint's gaze hardened. "Captain Fletcher was a good man who deserved better than what happened to him. He died because we're using equipment long overdue to be serviced, and we're not the only ones. It feels like after the threat of the Vemus passed, the colony didn't need us anymore. At first, Maddox wanted to continue to investigate the NEIIS signal, but then he started taking prisoners." Flint paused and looked at Dash. "He shouldn't have done that to any of you."

"I'm curious, Sergeant," Connor began. "What would you have done with Dash if we hadn't come along?"

"You wouldn't believe me if I told you," Sergeant Flint answered.

Connor didn't reply but merely waited for the soldier to answer his question.

"He knows the NEIIS system," Sergeant Flint said, jutting his chin toward Dash. "Maddox discovered that the NEIIS have a way to control the ryklars. Something in their systems is causing the ryklars to head for the colony. We all have family there and would do anything to protect the colony. When the other squad came back with the prisoners, I knew the best chance to stop Maddox was to capture him," he said and gestured toward Dash. "I figured you knew how to stop what he was trying to do."

Connor arched an eyebrow and glanced at Dash. "You need to fill me in, but make it quick because everyone who came with us has been captured. Ian and I barely escaped."

Dash nodded and explained to Connor about the purge protocol. He brought out the NEIIS PDA and reconnected the power cell.

"Can you control the NEIIS systems with that?" Connor asked.

Dash didn't know. He tried to navigate the interface and then shook his head. "It's just receiving the signal."

Connor frowned in thought. "What do you need to stop it?"

"I would need to access the NEIIS system to override the purge protocol. That would stop the broadcast signals from going out, but we'd also need time for the cancellation to make its way to all the NEIIS cities across the continent," Dash said.

"We noticed the signals seemed to appear at random," Connor said.

Dash's eyes widened and he shook his head. "It could be because the automated signals are being activated on old systems and they're simply burning out . . ."

"Which means we might not be able to cancel the last commands sent to the ryklars," Connor said.

"We have to try. You didn't see the data cache here. There are cities spread throughout the continent. The NEIIS were more widespread than we ever thought possible," Dash said.

"We still have a problem," Dr. Malone said.

Connor nodded and looked at Sergeant Flint and the others.

32

CONNOR DIDN'T HAVE a choice but to trust Sergeant Flint. Their plan wouldn't work otherwise.

"But what about the others at the NEIIS Command Center?" Dash asked.

Connor knew Dash was worried about his friends. "We need to alert the CDF and stop the NEIIS broadcast signal. We have an emergency beacon deployed with our last drone, but I don't think it's gonna be enough."

"I have a suggestion about how we can accomplish both, General. But you're not gonna like it," Sergeant Flint said. He glanced purposefully at Dash.

Connor followed his gaze and could guess what the sergeant was suggesting. Dash's eyebrows dropped with concern. "I don't understand," he said.

"We need to split up. It's the only way," Connor said.

Ian started to protest and Dash looked at Connor as if he'd lost his mind.

Connor looked at Ian. "Give them back their weapons," he said and nodded toward the CDF soldiers.

"I hope you know what you're doing," Ian said.

Sergeant Flint and the others took their weapons back and looked to Connor.

"This is crazy. How do you know we can trust them?" Dash said.

Much to Sergeant Flint's credit, he didn't try to voice any reasons for them to be trusted, and Connor knew that a lesser man would have. He turned toward Dash.

"I need you to go back and stop the NEIIS broadcast and contact the CDF. Sergeant Flint will help you with that," Connor said.

Dash frowned in confusion. "Wait, what are you going to do? And why would Sergeant Flint need me to contact the CDF?"

"Don't worry about me. Can you do this? Can you do what I need you to do?" Connor asked.

They hadn't always seen eye to eye, but Connor could tell that this experience had changed Dash. There was genuine concern in the young man's eyes and he nodded.

"I'm going after Maddox," Connor said.

"Sir, he has ten men with him, at least," Sergeant Flint said.

"Understood, Sergeant," Connor replied.

"You're going to take them all on by yourself?" Dash asked.

Connor shook his head. "No, course not. Ian is coming with me." He glanced at Sergeant Flint. "That should be enough to convince the others of the plan."

"What plan?" Dash asked.

"The plan for you to contact the CDF and stop the NEIIS broadcast," Connor said.

"But why can't we . . ." Dash began.

Connor shook his head. "We can't stop Maddox in a standup

fight. It would waste valuable time and leave the others at risk. Sergeant Flint will get you where you need to go."

Connor watched as Dash bit his lower lip in thought. "I'm so sorry I caused all this."

"This isn't your fault," Connor said and waited for Dash to look at him. "You need to focus on what needs to get done. Then we'll take it from there."

Sergeant Flint cleared his throat. "Sir, I really wish you'd consider taking Rex or Shea with you. They could help you."

Connor shook his head. "I could use their help, but you know as well as I that Maddox will want to see your squad in its entirety if our ruse is going to work."

Sergeant Flint nodded and leaned in so only Connor could hear. "I'll make sure he stays safe," he said with a nod toward Dash.

Connor nodded and then gestured for Dash to come closer. "Have you got your PDA?"

Dash handed his PDA to Connor, who accessed the PDA's interface and uploaded his secure credentials to it. "Make sure you use this when you communicate with the CDF."

Dash took his PDA back and stuffed it in his backpack. "I won't let you down."

"I know you won't. Good luck," Connor said.

33

MADDOX and his CDF team made their way through the NEIIS city. They were thirty minutes away from the command center and the team moved through the streets with practiced efficiency, leaving no corner unsecured as they went. Maddox had them heading northwest of their base. This was where Connor would be; he knew it in his gut.

"Sir," Lieutenant Mitchell said. "Nunez and Lambert are overdue."

Maddox had sent the two soldiers to scout an area half a kilometer away. He heard Dr. Bishop snort and mutter under her breath, but he suspected he knew the gist of it. He looked over at her and she returned his gaze with a challenge.

"What's the matter, Lieutenant? More of your men go missing?" Dr. Bishop asked.

Her cheek was still red from where he'd slapped her before and Maddox knew hitting her again wouldn't do any good, but how he yearned to. He was about to put her in her place when a comlink broadcast appeared on his internal heads-up display. It was an image of two CDF soldiers, their bodies lying in the middle of the street and their uniforms stained with blood, but he saw their names printed clearly on their chests. Nunez and Lambert.

"When are all of you going to realize you're hopelessly outclassed? If you surrender now, you at least get to keep your lives," Dr. Bishop said.

Maddox stomped over to her and grabbed her by the throat. Dr. Bishop kicked him in the shins, but he just squeezed his hand and she went down to her knees. "I think we've heard enough from you," he sneered. Dr. Bishop's face became red as she tried to break free from his grasp. "It's hopeless. When are *you* going to realize *that*?" He pulled her closer to him and turned her head so her ear was in front of his mouth. "I'd kill you right now, snap your neck, but I want to see the look on his face when you die right in front of him." He held her for a few moments longer, then shoved her to the ground.

The other soldiers grinned as they watched her struggle to her feet, coughing as she gasped for breath. She eventually regained her footing and lifted her gaze toward Maddox, baring her teeth. Her throat was red from where his hands had been but he recognized the cold fury in her eyes. He'd seen it many times when he'd look in the mirror. He watched as her eyes slipped toward the knife on his belt. Maddox made a show of looking down at it and grinned when she looked away from him.

"Sir, I have a comlink from Sergeant Flint," Lieutenant Mitchell said. "He's caught the escaped prisoner and is bringing him back to the command center."

"Excellent. Tell Flint and his team that drinks are on me," Maddox said and looked toward Dr. Bishop. For once her smug look had been replaced with one of concern. "We've caught your student. Dash is now on his way back to the command center."

Dr. Bishop didn't reply.

"Still think Connor is going to stop us?" Maddox asked.

Again, she remained silent, but he'd expected as much. Maddox marched over to her and she flinched. He smirked, loving the fact that he was finally breaking her resolve. "I asked you a question."

Dr. Bishop looked away from him and he leaned in. She kicked her foot out, striking his knee, and Maddox toppled to the ground, feeling a sharp stab to his side as the woman kicked him in the ribs. As Maddox rolled away and sprang back up, Dr. Bishop turned to run. Growling, he brought up his rifle, intending to shoot her in the back, but two of his soldiers grabbed her to prevent her from getting away. Maddox stormed over toward her.

"Sir, you need to look at this," Lieutenant Mitchell said and Maddox swung his gaze toward him. "It's the Hellcat, sir."

Maddox used his implants to access the Hellcat's systems and found that he was locked out. His eyes widened and he looked at Lieutenant Mitchell in alarm.

"Someone has set off a distress beacon, sir," Lieutenant Mitchell said.

"I'm locked out. Can you stop it?" Maddox asked.

A distress beacon from the Hellcat would be detected by COMCENT.

Lieutenant Mitchell frowned and then shook his head. "I can't."

Maddox gritted his teeth and swore. He scanned the comlink channels of all his men, but there were none near the encampment.

"Shouldn't we send someone back to camp, sir?" Lieutenant Mitchell asked.

Maddox looked at Dr. Bishop for a moment and the pieces finally started to click into place. "That's what he'd like us to do," he said with a wide smile and glanced at his squad. "Split us up and keep grinding our numbers down. No, I don't think we'll oblige Gates this time."

Maddox saw the men give an approving nod. They were ready for this. "We head back to camp. All of us. It's time to end this."

34

Dash followed Sergeant Flint away from the encampment. When they'd left Connor, he wondered if Flint would betray them and he imagined Flint holding him hostage, but none of that happened. They'd gone right for the Hellcat and Flint had him use Connor's credentials to activate the emergency beacon. Connor's credentials would ensure that the beacon would reach the people who could facilitate a quick response. Now that the first part of their plan was taken care of, it was time to rescue the others and stop the purge protocol.

Sergeant Flint stopped and waited for Dash to catch up to him. "Do you remember who was guarding you at the command center?"

Dash frowned, trying to recall all the details. "I didn't get a good look at the others. I was mostly working with Specialist Stackhouse."

"I wouldn't worry about Stackhouse," Sergeant Flint said.

Dash had to agree. He hadn't gotten the sense that Stackhouse was particularly dangerous, but he *was* following orders. "There was a real mean one with a big chip on his shoulder, but I can't remember his name."

"Can you describe him?" Sergeant Flint asked.

Dash looked away for a moment. He could hear the soldier's voice in his head, but he couldn't remember his name.

Sergeant Flint looked over at Shea. "Do you know who's guarding the prisoners?"

Shea thought about it for a minute. "Lambert was there for sure. Maybe O'Brien and Riggs."

"Riggs!" Dash cried. "He's the one Maddox had watching Brad and me at the console."

Sergeant Flint nodded and shared a look with the other soldiers.

Dash watched the exchange. "That doesn't look good."

"It's not. Riggs has always been an ass," Sergeant Flint said and sighed. "He's the one we have to take out first."

"Great. How are we going to do that?" Dash asked.

Sergeant Flint glanced at the assault rifle Dash was carrying. "I'm going to need you to give up that rifle."

Dash glanced down at the rifle and then handed it over to Flint.

"The easiest way for us to get into position is if they think you're our prisoner," Sergeant Flint said.

Dash sucked in a deep breath and felt his stomach clench. If they went in with their guns blazing, some of his friends would undoubtedly die. He knew that, but it didn't change how scared he was.

"We'll protect you, I promise," Sergeant Flint said.

Dash glanced at the other soldiers and saw the same determination in each of their eyes. "I don't get it. Weren't these guys your friends?"

Sergeant Flint pressed his lips together. "Some of them. We

serve together, but the CDF is supposed to protect the colony.
What Maddox is doing . . . isn't right and anyone who follows him
is just as wrong. They need to be stopped."

Dash almost couldn't imagine how difficult a decision like this
would be, but the line had been drawn—and crossed—it seemed.
"I'm sorry," he said, not knowing what else to say and feeling like
even that wasn't appropriate.

Sergeant Flint nodded.

"Is there anything you can give me so I'm not in there
unarmed?" Dash asked.

Sergeant Flint regarded him for a moment and then pulled out
his sidearm pistol. It was small and sleek. "This is only good at
short range. Do you know how to shoot one of these?"

"I've never used one before. I've only used rifles and the sonic
blasters," Dash said.

"Same principles apply," Flint said and showed him how to
arm the pistol. "Just hide it. Chances are good they won't search
you for weapons because they'll think you're in our custody, but if
they do, they'll realize something is up if they find the pistol. I'm
willing to take that risk. Are you?" Sergeant Flint asked.

Dash's eyes slid to the pistol and he remembered something
Dr. Bishop had told him more than once: Better to have something
and not need it than to need something and not have it. He took
the pistol.

They made their way to the NEIIS Command Center and
Dash heard shouting from inside. He quickened his step and felt a
firm hand grip his shoulder, slowing him down. Sergeant Flint
took the lead and they went inside. Dash saw Merissa and the
others with three soldiers standing guard. He quickly looked away,
relieved she was still alive and the others looked unharmed. He
wanted to tell them he'd brought help but couldn't.

He recognized Captain Ramsey from Field Ops. One of

Ramsey's eyes was a swollen, red mess, but he glanced over at Dash with his good eye. One of the three soldiers looked over at them with mild surprise, and Dash remembered that his name was Lasky.

Dash saw that Jim was on his knees and Sergeant Riggs was standing over him with his weapon pointed at his head. Dash clamped his mouth shut and kept his eyes to the ground.

"What's going on here?" Sergeant Flint asked.

Riggs looked at Dash and narrowed his gaze. "It seems you've caught our runaway," he said and stormed over.

Dash saw that Riggs had multiple wounds on his face, and even with the application of medipaste, he could tell they were burns from when the console had exploded.

Sergeant Flint blocked Riggs from getting to Dash. "I asked you a question."

Dash didn't know how CDF ranks worked, but he hazarded a guess that Sergeant Flint was the ranking soldier there.

Riggs tore his eyes away from Dash. "Lieutenant Maddox said I should motivate that one over there to translate the NEIIS console," he said and gestured toward Brad.

Dash met Brad's terrified gaze and swallowed hard.

Sergeant Flint grinned heartily, grabbed Dash by the scruff of his neck, and shoved him to the ground next to Jim. "This one's been nothing but trouble. If we're going to motivate them to cooperate, I'd say we use this one," Flint said and gestured for Jim to back away. "You go join the others. You'll get your turn."

Jim turned toward Dash.

"Just go," Dash said softly. His neck ached from where Flint had grabbed him, but he knew that Flint had to make it look convincing to the other soldiers.

"You heard him!" Riggs shouted, and Jim hurried away.

Dash watched as Jim went back to the others, Rex and Shea

following close behind. It seemed natural that they would pose as escorts, but Dash knew they were moving into position.

Riggs stomped over and stopped. "Mind if I borrow this one?"

Flint nodded and looked toward the console where Brad and Specialist Stackhouse watched. Brad appeared to be drained of all color and Specialist Stackhouse didn't look much better. Riggs grabbed a clump of Dash's hair and dragged him toward the console. White-hot pain seemed to scald his head and he struggled to move so Riggs wouldn't tear a piece of scalp off his head.

"There's no need to do this," Brad said. "I already told you we're ready to upload the command."

Riggs raised his AR-71 and there was a slight popping sound. Brad cried out and fell backward, clutching his leg. Dash tried to go to him, but Riggs held onto him and pressed the barrel of his AR-71 against Dash's forehead. The breath caught in his throat as he looked up into the soldier's murderous gaze. Dash turned his gaze toward Brad. There was a crimson stain forming over his thigh.

"Sir," Specialist Stackhouse said and glanced down at Brad regretfully. "He's right. We're ready to go here. We've augmented the purge protocol per the lieutenant's instructions."

Riggs kept his eyes on Dash. "I don't trust them—"

A sensor alarm echoed through the corridors of the NEIIS Command Center. Dash looked at Flint, but the CDF Sergeant looked just as surprised as he was.

"Those are the northern perimeter alarms. There are ryklars near the encampment," Corporal Lasky said.

Dash watched as Riggs looked away from him. "Send the update, Specialist."

Dash reached his hand ever so slowly toward the pistol he had hidden at the small of his back, but Riggs swung his gaze toward

Dash suspiciously. Dash froze for a moment before glancing toward Brad and Specialist Stackhouse. The specialist was staring at the NEIIS console, frowning.

"What's the problem?" Riggs said.

Specialist Stackhouse looked perplexed. "The command . . ." he said and looked over at them in alarm. "It's not working."

Dash snatched the pistol from its hiding place and rolled to the side, extending his arm. Riggs turned toward him, snarling. Dash squeezed the trigger multiple times and one of his shots took Riggs in the arm, but it was someone else who shot him in the chest. Riggs looked confused for a moment, as if he wasn't quite sure what had happened, and then he slumped to the floor. Dash looked over and saw that Sergeant Flint had shot him.

Flint turned to the remaining soldiers. "Stand down. That's an order."

Dex and Shea kept their weapons trained on the soldiers. Corporal Lasky closed his eyes for a long moment and then dropped his weapon. Dash watched as the remaining two soldiers looked at Flint with hatred in their eyes, and Dash thought they were going to take their chances.

"You heard Sergeant Flint. It's over," Shea said.

The two soldiers dropped their weapons and then raised their hands.

"Bind their hands," Flint said and looked around. "Where's Gibbs?"

Corporal Lasky cleared his throat. "He's with Lieutenant Maddox, sir."

Dash heard Brad groan and hastened over to him, and pressed his hands onto the wound to stop the bleeding. As he looked around for something to use as a tourniquet, he noticed that Merissa was across from him.

"I'll help him. They need you at the console," she said, giving him a slight smile.

Dash reached out to give her shoulder a gentle squeeze, and Selena replaced him at Brad's side as Flint called him over to the console.

Dash approached Specialist Stackhouse, who was looking at Riggs's body and then at Dash. "I'm sorry," he said.

Flint looked at Stackhouse. "Go with the others," he said and then turned to Dash. "The ryklars are here. Can you use this console to send them away?"

Dash looked at the console, thinking. "They're following the instructions of the purge protocol."

"What does that mean?" Sergeant Flint asked.

"It means that the ryklars will sweep through this city, killing anyone on the streets as they must have done as they made their way across the continent," Dash said. He navigated through the NEIIS interface, looking for what he'd found before.

"Can it be stopped or should we evacuate?" Sergeant Flint asked.

Dash's eyes darted to where Brad lay on the floor. "I'll stay here. Take them back to the Hellcat."

Flint shook his head. "Not a chance. We'll make sure this gets done first."

Dash spent the next few minutes going through the NEIIS interface and figured out what Brad had done to stall the soldiers. It wasn't difficult, and Dash assumed Brad had used that method expressly so Dash could figure out what he'd done. Dash glanced at Stackhouse. The CDF specialist must have known they were stalling and had gone along with it, but he'd also inputted the update to the purge protocol that would send the ryklars to Sierra. How could he have followed those orders? Stackhouse looked away from him.

Dash found the symbols he thought would cancel the purge protocol and activated them, hopefully executing the commands that would send one final NEIIS broadcast. "It's done," Dash said. "It should be picked up by any working NEIIS transmitter."

Captain Ramsey walked over. "I'm assuming you're here because you met up with Connor. Do you know where he is now?"

Sergeant Flint glanced at the CDF soldiers they were holding prisoner and Captain Ramsey followed his gaze.

Dash leaned down and picked up the AR-71 Riggs had dropped. "Let's go help him."

The NEIIS consoles all went dark at the same time, and the only light in the command center came from the temporary lighting the CDF brought with them.

"What happened?" Sergeant Flint asked.

Dash went over to the nearest console but it was dead. "I'm not sure," he said and glanced over at his backpack where a glowing light came from the NEIIS PDA. He went over and pulled out the PDA, but as he read the information on the screen, his stomach sank to his feet. "We have a problem. The last signal broadcast contains Maddox's update and not the cancellation."

"We need to fix this, now," Flint said.

Dash pressed his lips together, his eyes darting to the dead consoles, and then his eyes fell on Brad, who appeared to be only slightly conscious. Dash raced to his side, took hold of his shoulder, and shook him. "I need you to wake up," Dash said and called out Brad's name loudly. Brad's eyes opened and he looked at Dash. "The power here has gone offline. I need to get it back on so we can cancel the purge protocol. How'd you do it back at Sanctuary?"

Brad's eyes squeezed shut in pain and then he started to speak softly. Dash leaned in so he could hear. Thousands of lives depended on him.

35

CONNOR HAD JUST LEFT the area where the Hellcat sat nestled a half-kilometer from the central building. One of the bronze monoliths glowed toward the tip, signifying another imminent broadcast. He'd left Ian tucked into a nook where he could lay down suppressing fire. An old special forces adage came to his mind: *slow is smooth; smooth is fast; fast is deadly.* He had weapons and ammunition aplenty, and he'd even set up a few surprises on the path Maddox would likely take back to camp. Maddox believed Connor's only weapon was an AR-71, but they had other uses, particularly the power cores. He'd also taken out two more soldiers who hadn't given him a choice and sent their images to Maddox, knowing it would goad him into coming for Connor. Now Maddox was down to eight men instead of ten. Better, but not good enough. He didn't know these men and couldn't guess whether the odds swinging out of favor for Maddox would cause them to surrender or switch sides. This unit was sick at heart, and Connor wondered how many other CDF units were in the same state.

Connor heard Ian whistle, meaning Maddox was closing in on them. Connor hadn't been able to make it to his own hiding spot so he hastened back toward the Hellcat, then ducked behind a storage crate.

"You know coming here is suicide, right?" Lenora said.

Connor closed his eyes and silently pleaded with Lenora to keep her mouth shut for once. He had no more drones to use, but he was patched into the Hellcat's systems. Sergeant Flint had given him access when they'd sent the emergency broadcast to COMCENT.

Using the Hellcat systems, he saw the CDF soldiers cautiously approaching the camp. The soldiers split up, each going to different sides as they entered, and Connor waited. He couldn't see Lenora or Maddox yet, so he watched as the soldiers made a sweep of the camp, knowing Maddox wouldn't enter until the soldiers gave the all clear. Both groups of soldiers were within range of the traps he'd set. Connor detonated the power cores from the AR-71s he'd collected and the blast took out four CDF soldiers. The explosion tossed their bodies into the air and they didn't rise from their falling place.

Connor left his position behind the storage crate and circled around, staying out of sight.

"I know you're out there! Come out now or I'll kill her!" Maddox shouted.

Connor sucked in a deep breath. He had the video feed from the Hellcat systems on his own internal heads-up display. Maddox still had three soldiers with him and was holding Lenora close to him with his sidearm pistol pointed directly at her head. Connor gritted his teeth. Maddox had gagged her. Even if he could take them by surprise, he didn't have a clear shot at Maddox with Lenora right in front of him.

"You don't even realize you've lost. The ryklars will converge on Sierra," Maddox said.

"About that," Connor replied, his voice coming from the Hellcat's external speaker system so Maddox couldn't pinpoint his position, "I think you'll find the purge protocol has been canceled."

Maddox laughed. "I've just received confirmation that the signal has already been sent."

The glowing tip of the bronze monolith suddenly became dark, and Connor craned his neck around the storage crate, seeing that Maddox and the others were looking up at it. He darted from cover, shooting the closest soldier. Lenora kicked out with her leg, knocking Maddox back and giving Connor an opportunity to knock him off his feet. As Connor became tangled with the CDF soldier, he heard shots being fired but focused on freeing himself from Maddox. He rolled to his feet and glanced at the assault rifle nearby. Maddox lunged for the rifle, but Connor tackled him, and Maddox squirmed forward and grabbed his pistol instead. Connor seized his wrist and then drove his elbow into Maddox's ear. Maddox growled but somehow got to his feet.

They both struggled against each other, but Maddox had the pistol in his hand. Connor kicked at his leg while twisting Maddox's wrist, forcing him to drop the gun. Maddox quickly recovered and hammered a blow into Connor's face. Connor was momentarily stunned and Maddox kicked him in the stomach, but Connor grabbed Maddox's leg and delivered a crushing blow to his throat, catching the soldier by surprise. Maddox fell backward, stunned and gasping for a mouthful of air, but he saw the pistol on the ground nearby and managed to lunge for it. Connor dove to the side to avoid being shot and felt something searing his side. As he rolled to his feet, Connor pulled his knife from its sheath and threw it at Maddox. The soldier flinched as the knife bit into his arm. The pistol dropped from Maddox's grasp and spun away.

"Come on, you don't need the gun. You hate me, right?" Connor said, stomping toward him. "I'm standing right here."

Maddox sneered and charged, putting all his momentum into a single crushing blow. Connor stepped aside at the last moment and kicked at Maddox's knee, causing the big soldier to drop. Maddox spun, catching Connor by surprise, lifting him into the air, and slamming his body to the ground. He punched Connor in his wounded side. Each blow sent waves of pain coursing through him. Maddox picked up Connor's knife, and Connor grabbed his wrist to prevent himself from being stabbed. Connor gritted his teeth, straining against Maddox, but the knife kept inching closer. As if in slow motion, Connor watched as Lenora stepped behind Maddox and shot him in the back. Connor shoved the soldier off him and Maddox lay on his back, gasping.

Connor pushed himself up to a sitting position breathing hard. He looked at Lenora who had the pistol aimed at Maddox.

"Sierra is still going to fall," Maddox said, his voice becoming weak.

Connor gritted his teeth and glared. "Not today."

Maddox coughed weakly and a crimson wreath ringed his mouth. Even after the soldier had taken his last breath, his lifeless stare was still full of hate.

The pistol thudded to the ground and Lenora helped Connor to his feet. He pulled her into a firm embrace, almost afraid to let her go. He didn't want to think about how close he'd come to losing her forever. She hugged him tighter and he winced.

"You're hurt," Lenora said and started checking him for injuries.

Pain lanced across Connor's side. "Ouch!" he gasped. "I think you found it."

Lenora looked behind her and waved over the only remaining soldier, then looked back at Connor. "It's alright. He helped with the other soldiers."

Connor looked at the soldier warily as he approached.

"My name is Gibbs, sir. I'm a medic."

"That's nice. Give your kit to her and step away," Connor said.

Gibbs handed his medical kit to Lenora and did as Connor ordered. The central monolith began to glow once again and he opened a comlink to the others. Lenora tore his shirt open near his wound and Connor swore.

"A little gentler."

"Stop being such a baby," Lenora replied. She applied medipaste to the wound and it immediately became numb. "Dash escaped."

Connor nodded and filled her in on what had happened. He saw the bruising on her cheek and glared at Maddox's dead body.

"He's gone," Lenora said. "He can't hurt anyone else."

A comlink opened to Connor. It was from Dash.

"We have a problem," Dash said.

"Were you able to stop the purge protocol?" Connor asked.

"Yes. It's being sent out now, but there are ryklars in the area," Dash said.

As if in response to Dash's statement, Connor heard several screeches outside the camp. They sounded close.

"How close are they?" Connor asked.

Dash sounded as if he was running. "Getting pretty close," he said. "Can you open the Hellcat? We'll be there in a minute."

Connor glanced around and then yelled for Ian to come down. "We've got to go."

They headed to the Hellcat and Connor opened the loading ramp. Ian was already on his way.

"Go do the preflight checks," Connor said to Lenora. "It's almost the same as the troop-carriers you've flown. We need to be ready to go quickly."

Lenora ran toward the cockpit and Connor looked at Gibbs. "Grab a rifle and cover the area outside the ramp. The others are on their way here."

Connor went over to Ian. "Thanks for your help back there."

"You'd do the same for me," Ian said. "Why are the ryklars still coming? Didn't Dash send a command telling them to stop the purge?"

"It's not as simple as an on-and-off button," Connor replied and glanced up at the monolith. "Even if they received the new update, it may take them some time to process it. They won't suddenly stop, but when enough time passes, the ryklars should revert back to their natural behavior when not under the NEIIS influence."

"We really need to figure this out," Ian said.

Connor agreed there was a lot that needed to change.

The others joined them on the Hellcat and Connor put Gibbs' medical training to good use on the wounded. Sergeant Flint secured the prisoners away from the others while Connor closed the loading ramp on the ryklars' threatening screeches.

Sergeant Flint handed Connor his weapon. "It doesn't seem right that we hold onto our weapons, sir. We disgraced ourselves and surrender to whatever the colonial government has in store for us."

The CDF soldiers who had helped Connor turned in their weapons and joined the other prisoners. Connor took a long look at the men, and after a few moments, Captain Ramsey came over to his side.

"What do you think will happen to them?" Captain Ramsey asked.

Connor looked at him and saw that he had a bandage covering one of his eyes. "To be honest, I have no idea," he said.

They finished securing the loading ramp and began the long flight home.

36

ON THEIR WAY back to Sanctuary, they were met by several Hellcats that escorted them to the CDF main base at Sierra. There was very little talking throughout the flight, but Corporal Gibbs was able to stabilize Brad's wounded leg and it was apparent that he would make a full recovery. Afterward, Gibbs joined the other CDF soldiers in the cargo hold.

Connor glanced around at the others and realized the wounds they'd have to deal with were the ones they couldn't see. Most of them were still in shock. Even he was still coming to grips with what had happened. Maddox hadn't been just a solitary figure who had completely snapped. The CDF lieutenant had been able to convince his team to follow him and represented a deep-seated sickness that Connor couldn't allow to take root.

Connor returned to the cockpit and sat in the copilot's seat next to Lenora.

"Want me to take over?" Connor offered.

Lenora set the controls on autopilot and nearly tackled him in his seat. She clung to him, and he held her tightly. She was the strongest person he'd ever met, but this experience had taken its toll on her, as it would on anyone. Connor tried to think of something to say that would comfort her, but it all sounded foolish in his mind, and Lenora remained quiet in his lap. Once they reached Sierra, they'd have to relive the whole thing for the debriefings that were surely coming.

A few hours later they were approaching Sierra. Connor hadn't been there in months, and he noted the defenses that had been put in place in preparation for the ryklar attack. According to Diaz, who flew one of the Hellcats escorting them back, there were still ryklars in the area, but they'd stopped their advance.

Connor landed their ship and a squad of CDF soldiers took the prisoners into custody. Connor looked at Sergeant Flint as he was led away and gave him a nod, promising himself to do what he could for them. Nearby soldiers stood at attention and saluted. Connor had to fight years of training to keep from returning the salute, but then he realized they weren't saluting him and almost grinned. Colonel Sean Quinn was walking toward him.

"I'd salute you, General, but then you'd only remind me that you're retired," Sean said and saluted anyway, then extended his hand and Connor shook it. Sean looked at the others for a moment before his gaze returned to Connor. "I should have known you were somehow involved in all this."

"It's quite a story, but we could all use some food and rest," Connor replied.

"I think that could be arranged," Sean said.

They were given temporary quarters on base where they were allowed to clean up, and Connor noted that they were being kept under observation. They weren't in any trouble, but he knew they'd be debriefed before they were allowed to go home. There was a knock at the door and Connor opened it.

Dash stood outside. "They're ready for us, but I wanted to ask you something first."

Connor and Lenora joined Dash outside and together they headed to where they'd be meeting with the others. "Sure thing," Connor said. "Was this for me, or would you rather speak to Lenora?"

"For you, actually," Dash said. "I'm not sure what to say in this debriefing they want from us."

"Just tell them the truth as you see it. That's all there is to it," Connor said.

He watched as Dash looked away worriedly. "I feel like this is all my fault—not the sneaking away part, but we triggered this purge protocol."

"It was an accident. It could have happened to any of us," Connor said.

"But it didn't; it happened to me. I was the one who was there, and I was the one who pushed for this," Dash said.

"You were also the one who stopped it. And you're also the one who's always telling me you're ready for the risks that come with fieldwork. So now you know this is what can happen, but I do think we'll get a little more support than we did before," Connor said.

"You have nothing to worry about, Dash," Lenora said.

Connor noticed that Dash had matured a little bit beyond the shocking nature of this experience. He still saw the same youthful vigor, but there had been a dose of caution and forethought instilled in him, which was a good thing.

They were debriefed over the next few hours. Each of them was brought into a separate room with both CDF and colonial government representatives while they gave their accounts of what had transpired. The representatives were sensitive to the fact that they'd been through a terrible ordeal.

Afterward, they were given some time to rest, and Connor and Lenora had decided it would be best if they gave Dash and the others the option to return to Sanctuary if they wanted. Sean had quickly arranged transport for them, but Connor and Lenora chose to remain in Sierra for a few days.

Connor learned from one of the soldiers in Captain Fletcher's squad that they'd used an armored drone to take out the troop-carrier Connor and the others had flown in on their way to the city. The energy weapon that had taken out the C-cat Dash had used remained a mystery. Recent evidence supported the theory that the NEIIS were no strangers to war and conflict. Given what they'd been able to do with the ryklars, this wasn't surprising, but city defenses *were* a surprise and meant that as they explored these new cities, they'd have to be aware that there could still be automated defenses online.

Connor and Lenora were brought to the seat of the colonial government and spent the next several hours going over all the events. Connor had been too many of these sessions throughout his career, and it was almost strange for him to be on the other side for once. He noticed that both General Nathan Hayes and Governor Ashley Quinn glanced at him with wry amusement outside the subject they were addressing.

"I know I've said this before, but we owe you—all of you—a debt of gratitude," Ashley said.

"We did have help," Connor said. "There were several soldiers who, upon learning what Lieutenant Maddox truly intended, were working to stop him when we arrived."

Ashley nodded and turned toward Nathan. "This latest development concerning the Colonial Defense Force is quite alarming. Each soldier's actions will go before the consideration of our courts. We'll need a full investigation and perhaps rethink our priorities. I certainly don't want the CDF to believe the colony doesn't appreciate them, but this latest development doesn't put us in the best position given the imminent threat the ryklars pose."

"I have a couple of suggestions regarding priorities," Connor said.

Ashley arched an eyebrow and smiled. "Now my curiosity is piqued. Go on."

Despite how tired he was, Connor smiled. Ashley had always been like a sister to him. He'd rather be at an informal dinner with her and Lenora discussing these things, but it was what it was. "We obviously need to take care of our soldiers, but I think we need a place for them to recharge—a place they can go that will help them rejoin the colony, and a place where they can contribute but not necessarily be on the front lines so to speak. We train them for combat, rescue, and salvage, but we don't address how they can best move on from the CDF."

Nathan frowned and glanced at Ashley.

"Do you have someplace in mind?" Ashley said.

Connor glanced at Lenora and she gave him an encouraging nod. "I do, actually—at least initially for the more difficult cases. I suggest sending them to me at Sanctuary. It's far enough away from the main colonial centers and people seem to like the simplicity of the place. Captain Fletcher was a good man. His men trusted him, but even he thought his men needed something more. While putting them on duty in remote locations got them away from some of the pressures they'd have had to deal with in the population centers, it may not have been what was best for them. General Hayes has allowed me to review the service records of Lieutenant Maddox and the others of the squad. There were some warning signs that he was on the verge of the breakdown that led him to do what he did. We're stretched thin, and not just the CDF but all facets of our colony. We're trying to get back to where we were before the Vemus attack, but we need to slow things down a bit. But getting back to my suggestion that we allow soldiers to come to Sanctuary and spend some time, it would be a good thing for them."

"Is this your first request as the interim mayor of Sanctuary?" Ashley asked.

Even though Connor hadn't officially accepted the job yet, he said, "If it has to be."

"Why don't you work with General Hayes and a few psychologists, then present me with a proposal," Ashley said and glanced at the others. "Now, we need to address the ryklars and how best to deal with them." Connor watched as she gave a sidelong glance at Sean. "I do have a proposal for a military solution that involves cutting down the ryklar population significantly."

There were several grim looks from those in attendance.

"Considering the current events, some might think this an appropriate response," Ashley began. "However, I don't agree, and while the option is certainly there, I think we can afford to explore other options that include disabling all communication systems that the NEIIS currently have in place across the entire continent."

Connor cleared his throat and Ashley nodded for him to speak. "I know someone who would be an ideal candidate to be involved in that effort . . ." He went on to describe what he and Lenora had come up with that didn't involve the wholesale slaughter of an indigenous species. Though there was a need for population control, what they had in mind would allow the ryklars to occupy a portion of the continent.

The fact that the NEIIS had used ryklars as some kind of military weapon gave a strong indication of who they actually were, and Connor was glad they hadn't found any remains of the intelligent species that used to occupy New Earth. He still wanted to understand what had happened to them, but those questions wouldn't be answered there. It would take time to unravel that particular mystery.

37

Dash had returned to Sanctuary shortly after providing his testimony to the colonial officials. The NEIIS city they'd found had been nicknamed The Capital, but he was sure the name wouldn't stick. Most of New Earth's supercontinent remained largely unexplored, and to believe that they'd discovered an NEIIS capital city was a bit presumptuous, to say the least. He thought Dr. Bishop felt the same, but she was preoccupied with something she and Connor were doing with the colonial government. Dash, along with Jim and Selena, had been sent back to Sanctuary. They were supposed to take some time off and rest, which he'd done for a few days, but a week later he started having nightmares. He'd wake up sweaty and gasping, believing he was still in the NEIIS city being hunted by ryklars or CDF soldiers—sometimes both at the same time—but there was also one time when the ryklars had been wearing CDF uniforms.

One of Sanctuary's newest residents was a counselor named Dr. Tran who had relocated there to be part of a recovery program for CDF soldiers. Dash had spoken to him about the nightmares, which Dr. Tran didn't find surprising. He assured Dash that they would fade in time and offered to meet with him on a weekly basis to talk about it. Dash wasn't sure if he wanted to do that. He'd already talked about what happened and wasn't sure talking about it more would help. Instead, he began planning another expedition to better explore the NEIIS city. The CDF had sent a team to recover equipment and retrieve the bodies of the colonists who had died there.

"So you're really going back there?" Jim said for the second time. They had just finished eating lunch.

"Yeah," Dash said, nodding. "There's a lot of work to be done there and I'm going to establish a research base. After that, Dr. Bishop will be coming with the rest of the team. We'll all be rotating through there for the next six months at least."

"Better you than me," Jim said.

"I guess this means you don't want one of the coveted spots on the away team?" Dash asked. He knew what the answer would be but still hoped Jim would change his mind.

Jim shook his head. "Selena isn't ready for that. She's said she wants to stay near Sanctuary for a while."

Dash wasn't surprised by this. "Maybe next time."

Jim smiled. "Yeah, maybe," he said and stood up. "I need to get back to Field Ops."

Dash nodded. "By the way, congratulations on your appointment."

"Thanks. I'm officially part of Field Ops since Captain Ramsey pushed my application through," Jim said and looked at Dash with a bit of regret in his eyes.

Dash shook his head. "Hey, don't worry about it. You've got things happening here, but if you get bored or need a break, I'll be just a comlink away."

Jim left him to go back to Field Ops Headquarters and Dash

returned to the Research Institute. He walked through the hallways toward Dr. Bishop's lab and thought about when he, Jim, Selena, and Merissa had been working on the NEIIS console they'd retrieved from the outpost. He thought about opening a comlink to Merissa, who'd stayed behind at Sierra to visit family and friends she had living there. He supposed it was no coincidence she'd stayed there because that was where Brad lived.

He opened the door to the dark lab and the automatic lighting turned on. Dash stood in the doorway, his eyes scanning the mostly empty lab, but pieces of the NEIIS console were still cataloged on the long tables. He looked over at the wallscreens and thought about the presentation they'd worked on. The lab seemed so barren now where once it had been a place he hadn't minded spending time.

He realized he was frowning and sighed, allowing the lab door to close as he took a step back out into the hall and rubbed his hand over his face. A few moments later, he heard the soft footsteps of someone walking toward him. He turned toward the sound and saw Merissa, her lips lifted into a smile, and he felt like he'd been punched in the stomach.

"I heard you were recruiting a new team and was wondering if you had any openings," Merissa said.

Dash made a show of looking behind her and grinned. "I don't know. It's pretty competitive and there's this whole lengthy application process. They'd have to be resourceful and intelligent. Do you know someone who might be a good candidate? They'd have to have done field work before—"

"And keep the team leader from doing anything foolish? Yeah, I might know someone," Merissa said and smiled.

Dash nodded and then looked at her with mock severity. "The team is already full. You see, the co-leader of the team just arrived. You might have heard of her . . ."

The rest of what he was going to say fled his mind as Merissa reached up and pulled him down into a kiss. The soft contour of her lips on his was sweeter than anything he could have imagined, and for once the NEIIS were the furthest thing from his thoughts.

38

TEMPORARY HOUSING HAD BEEN BUILT near Field Ops Headquarters at Sanctuary. They were simple, one-room units that would house both current and former CDF soldiers for a time. Connor stood outside and rubbed his chin in thought.

"Well, what do you think, Mayor Gates?" Lenora said.

She still found it amusing to call him mayor, though it was only a temporary position.

"It'll do for now. Most of these might never have any residents," Connor said. There were a hundred units, and some were able to accommodate more than a single occupant. Connor glanced at Lenora. "This could be short-lived if no one volunteers."

Lenora cocked her head to the side and nodded. "At least you tried. Did you see the last colonial bulletin that was sent out recently?" she asked.

"The one about the travel ban being lifted?"

Lenora smiled and shook her head. "Figures that's all you saw in it. There was also that last bit about the call for procreation."

Connor frowned and then arched an eyebrow. "What about it?"

They hadn't discussed starting a family with both of them so immersed in their work.

"Well, we're not getting any younger," Lenora replied.

The sound of several troop-carriers drew steadily closer to Sanctuary.

"We have plenty of time with prolonging treatments and such, so there's no rush," Connor said.

Lenora narrowed her gaze as the troop-carriers' thrusters became louder and they made their final approach to the landing field nearby. Connor didn't look over at them. Instead, he kept his gaze on Lenora. She was serious.

"I didn't know this was so important to you, but do you really think this is the best time?" Connor said.

"Come now, it's important to you, too," Lenora said and sauntered ahead of him in the direction of the landing field.

Connor felt a flush of adrenaline tingling through his body and then he caught up to her. He snatched her from behind and swung her around. Lenora giggled and told him to put her down.

"It would be fun trying, no matter how busy we'll be," Lenora said.

Connor kept smiling. Thoughts of a family had always come with a pang of regret for having left his own family behind on Earth. Circumstances had been more complicated than that, but those regrets would always be there. He couldn't change what he'd done and he was slowly coming to accept that, but what surprised him were moments like these when he looked into Lenora's eyes and knew he could take that next step with her.

Lenora glanced away from him toward the landing field. "Look at them all," she said.

When Connor finally looked over and saw the large group of

soldiers leaving the troop-carriers, he began to wonder if they had enough housing units.

"Looks like help has arrived," Connor said. "This is for Sanctuary as much as it is for them."

Lenora didn't say anything but just watched.

"We'll talk more about your other request later," Connor said.

Lenora laughed. "You say that as if you have a choice in the matter," she said and glanced at the approaching group. "Look sharp, Mayor Gates."

Connor snorted. She was right, of course, as he'd learned over the years that she usually was. He'd never really deny Lenora anything she wanted, but what surprised him was how much he wanted it, too.

THANK YOU FOR READING SANCTUARY - FIRST COLONY - BOOK FOUR.

If you loved this book, please consider leaving a review. Comments and reviews allow readers to discover authors, so if you want others to enjoy *Sanctuary* as you have, please leave a short note.

The First Colony series continues with the 5th book.

FIRST COLONY - DISCOVERY

ABOUT THE AUTHOR

Ken Lozito is the author of multiple science fiction and fantasy series. I've been reading both genres for a long time. Books were my way to escape everyday life of a teenager to my current ripe old(?) age. What started out as a love of stories has turned into a full-blown passion for writing them. My ultimate intent for writing stories is to provide fun escapism for readers. I write stories that I would like to read and I hope you enjoy them as well.

If you have questions or comments about any of my works I would love to hear from you, even if its only to drop by to say hello at
KenLozito.com

Thanks again for reading *First Colony - Sanctuary*.

Don't be shy about emails, I love getting them, and try to respond to everyone.

ALSO BY KEN LOZITO

FIRST COLONY SERIES

GENESIS

NEMESIS

LEGACY

SANCTUARY

DISCOVERY

EMERGENCE

VIGILANCE

FRACTURE

HARBINGER

ASCENSION SERIES

STAR SHROUD

STAR DIVIDE

STAR ALLIANCE

INFINITY'S EDGE

RISING FORCE

ASCENSION

SAFANARION ORDER SERIES

ROAD TO SHANDARA

ECHOES OF A GLORIED PAST

AMIDST THE RISING SHADOWS

Heir of Shandara

Broken Crown Series

Haven of Shadows

If you would like to be notified when my next book is released visit
KENLOZITO.COM

Printed in Great Britain
by Amazon